Half-Light

Half-Light

Neil M. Gunn

Compiled by
Dairmid Gunn

Whittles Publishing

Published by
Whittles Publishing Ltd.,
Dunbeath,
Caithness, KW6 6EG,
Scotland, UK

www.whittlespublishing.com

Introduction © 2011 Dairmid Gunn

ISBN 978-184995-045-9

Printed by
Short Run Press Ltd

Contents

Introduction

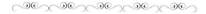

Neil Gunn (1891–1973) was one of Scotland's most distinguished and highly regarded novelists of the 20th century. While he is best known for his novels, he is also recognised as a perceptive and meditative essayist and accomplished writer of short stories. Most of his short stories, and the majority in this collection, *Half-Light*, were written in the early years of his creative life. Some were written before the appearance of his first novel, *The Grey Coast* (1926); these reflect his apprenticeship in the art of writing and were part of the process of finding a structure within which to accommodate his ideas on life and living. Land and sea feature prominently and are more than a simple backdrop to the stories; they have a persona of their own and provide insights into man's search for harmony and self realisation in his or her passage through life. This search exudes a humility and understanding that pervade most of the stories. The themes explored find their way directly or indirectly into many of Gunn's novels; the stories themselves are attractive in their own right and have a freshness and immediacy that give a clarity and concision to the subject matter. *Half-Light* by its diversity of topic and theme makes for compulsive reading and provides an invitation to enjoy Gunn's other creative work in the genres of novels and essays.

In 1929 Gunn's first collection of short stories appeared under the title *Hidden Doors*. Some of these stories were to appear in 1954 in a second collection entitled *The White Hour*. *Half-Light* includes stories from both collections; it also includes stories that have only been published in magazines, and two essays from *Highland Pack* (1949); the essays, almost poetry in prose, emphasise the importance Gunn attaches to the quiet rhythm and healing properties of life on land and sea.

Neil Gunn, the son of a successful fishing boat skipper, was born in the small coastal village of Dunbeath in Caithness, in which crofting and fishing were the principal means of livelihood. After an idyllic childhood in a landscape of moor, hill and sea, during which Gunn was exposed to the dying art of story-telling in the community, he was sent to pursue his secondary education at the hands of a tutor engaged by an elder sister married to a doctor in the rural county of Kirkcudbrightshire in the south west of Scotland. He received a sound grounding in literature and a sufficient grasp of mathematics to enter the Civil Service. Four years later in 1911 he began his career in the Customs and Excise Service, which was to take him back to the Highlands. During the First World War he combined his professional duties with War work for the Admiralty. It was during these years that he developed a lifelong friendship with the Irish novelist to-be, Maurice Walsh, a fellow customs and excise officer. After marriage to a Highland girl from Dingwall, the county town of Ross and Cromarty, and after a short time in industrial England, he returned to the North, and Caithness. He was shocked to find his home county in a state of serious economic and social decline. The sadness and bitterness of this was one of the factors that stimulated his interest in writing. His rich imagination and his fascination by the fundamental aspects of living and being, however, ensured that the scope of his writing was wide enough to accommodate universal themes.

A settled and happy existence in Inverness and the skilful management of his work there provided the ideal conditions for some serious writing in his spare time. In 1937 after the award of the prestigious James Tait Black Memorial prize for his novel *Highland River* he decided to become a full-time writer. The powerful formative influences of a northern childhood, a unique education at the hands of a private tutor, time spent in both London and Edinburgh, the friendship with Maurice Walsh and the very close relationship with his immediate younger brother John, a mathematician and physicist and veteran of the First World War, all gave him ideas to ponder and themes to explore. Essential themes were: childhood and a sense of wonder; love in its deepest and most subtle sense; death as part of the cycle of existence and the place of land and sea in the development of man himself in his search for greater self understanding.

The theme of childhood is charmingly and perceptively described in such novels as *Morning Tide* (1931), *Highland River* (1937), *The Silver Darlings* (1941), *Young Art and Old Hector* (1942), and *The Green Isle of the Great Deep* (1944). Yet despite the lengthy and loving coverage the novels give to childhood, the short stories *Paper Boats* (1931), *Dance of the Atoms* (1939) and *Whistle for a Bridge* (1933) have something to add. They depart from the distant childhood memories of the author and deal with the attitudes and sensitivities of contemporary children. The beginnings of the transition from childhood to adulthood are delicately explored through experience and experiment.

In the domain of the relationships between men and women Gunn is often accused of dwelling on the psychology of love at the expense of the physiology of these relationships. Gunn's interest lay in the exploration of the sensibility, tenderness and delicacy of feeling of people in love. It is an attempt to explain the inexplicable and can only be understood—and partially at that—through experience. *Love's Dialectic* (1941), *Blaeberries* (1928), *The Black Woollen Gloves* (1928) and *The Poster* (1936) look at love in its different manifestations, from introspection, physical attraction and imagination to the freshness of early love.

Love and death as stages in life's journey are explored in *The Chariot* (1943) and *The White Hour* (1950). Although the acceptance of death differs in the two stories, the approach and final passing act as a spring board for the onset of love in young witnesses. The ebb tide is followed by the flood tide, and the inevitability of death finds its balance in the exuberance and abandonment of early love.

The presence of land and sea are at the heart of most of Gunn's stories. Man's relationship with these elements is a bond that outgrows geographical and temporal limits and becomes a search for a greater harmony and reconciliation. *Such Stuff as Dreams* (1925), *Down to the Sea* (1933) and *Henry Drake goes Home* (1941) deal most perceptively and sympathetically with this longing to return to roots on land and sea. The sadness of death is tempered by a feeling of fulfilment and homecoming.

Land and sea are not always associated with death and primeval longing. In *Hill Fever* (1934) a man on honeymoon is so at one with the hill landscape surrounding him that he resents the intrusion of friends subtly invited by a wife who does not share his feelings. In *The Moor* (1929) a young woman living with a mentally deranged mother in a remote cottage becomes the focus of attention and desire for a twenty year old man who sees her as the personification of the moor in all its remoteness and splendour.

The theme of the lure of homecoming and subsequent death is explored in an unusual way in *Half-Light* (1929); a man with academic success behind him decides to abandon the possibility of a prestigious career to return to the village of his youth as a teacher. His surroundings assert themselves, and he identifies himself more and more with his ancestral heritage. Memories of what had been dominate his thoughts, and his death by drowning during a daily swim can be seen in terms of a reunion with his native element. It poses questions as his life had held the promise of future success. In this respect the story of a returning man of academic potential differs radically from those in the novels *The Lost Glen* (1932) and *The Drinking Well* (1946), which concern men who have failed in their career aspirations. The lure of the landscape also dominates *Hidden Doors* (1929) but the main protagonist and the setting are different. An Englishman who is drawn to the landscape of the Highlands is convinced that its sights and sounds open doors for him psychologically. His ideas of the supernatural and powerful influence of the pibroch are obsessive and destructive and factors leading to his death on the moors. In both short stories there are hints of the thinking and background developed by Gunn in his final novel *The Other Landscape* (1954).

The influence of nature is very marked in *The Tree* (1936), a story in which an irritable old widower is wrestling with his conscience over the need to fell a tree greatly prized by him; this had been desired by his deceased wife in the interests of letting more light into the garden she loved. Tensions develop between the gardener and the widower over the issue but all is resolved by nature in the form of a storm. *Snow in March* (1938) concerns a single middle-aged cultivated lady, who is temporarily running the farm left to her by a recently deceased brother. Her rescue of a lamb from a dying ewe in a snow storm brings her into friendly contact with her shepherd; the combination of maternal instincts through the reviving of the lamb and the romantic presence of a handsome young man stir up latent longings within her, which are destined not to be realised. Contrasted in this moving and gentle story are the fullness of country life and the possible aridity of intellect divorced from reality.

To explore this theme of the wholesome influence of rural living two essays from the collection *Highland Pack* (1949) have been included in this collection. Like *Snow in March* they were written during the most fruitful period of Gunn's writing career, the years he lived in a farmhouse on the hills near Dingwall. They were written at a time when the country as a whole was still suffering from the aftermath of the Second World War and needed a reminder that happiness could still be achieved in the ordinary round of human activity.

Other stories in this collection do not fall into the categories described above but each contains a serious element: the transmutation of imagination into action, *Visioning* (1925); the power of maternal instincts, *Gentlemen* (1924); the absence of creative inspiration, *The Mirror* (1929); the importance of hope, *The Telegram*, the strange phenomenon of coincidence, *Pure Chance* (1945) and the occasional conflict between duty and sympathetic understanding, *The Tax-Gatherer* (1943).

Most of the stories in this collection are set in the Highlands, that part of Scotland so loved by Gunn and from which he drew much of his creative inspiration. This does not mean that there is anything parochial in his work as his exploration of important aspects of living reflect a depth of understanding that can only captivate and enchant the perceptive reader. He is in communion with the land and sea, and the people he describes; there is no judgement in his writing – only a profound sympathy and acceptance.

Dairmid Gunn

The Black Woollen Gloves

The look in his eyes fascinated her. He sat at the opposite side of the reading-room table and a little to her left, so that, with the *Times Educational Supplement* before her, she could covertly watch him. He was reading the *Literary Supplement*—or, rather, had been reading. Whatever the article it had stilled him to absorbed reflection. With the iris gone black in the indifferent lighting, his eyes glowed under dark hair that came over his brows without any parting. His thin pale face had the delicate finish of egg-shell porcelain, dulled a little in grey strength. The pale student, emaciated a trifle, underfed possibly, but burning with inner fires. Her young woman's heart continued its beating.

At last he pushed the *Supplement* away like an empty plate, got up, and walked out of the door. Then the little incident happened that made an instant appeal to her. As he shoved open a leaf of the swing door and passed out some part of his mind must have registered a suspension of rhythm and, just as he was taking the third step down, made him look back—to find the door gaping open. He balanced a moment, then returned and touched the glass panel when immediately it flapped windily into position.

She continued to gaze through the vacant panel. Now why had he done that? Lest they suffer from a draught—where a draught of fresh air would be a godsend? … But she did not really question herself. It was enough that she *knew*. His act revealed him to her in a swift intimate way. She got up and went round the table to the *Supplement*.

On Herman Melville. Her brows puckered. She sat down and got lost. Then spreading a vague arm outward in order to lay bare the page, she felt something hairy touch her wrist. Her eyes leapt—and steadied on a pair of black woollen gloves.

Without any process of making up her mind, she picked up the gloves, went hurriedly out through the swing door, down the stairs, and on to the cobbled street. He was gone. A policeman, passing to headquarters next door, looked at her officially. She was new to the town and her scholastic appointment was a respectable one; in fact, her first really responsible Higher Grade post, for she was just twenty-four. She turned from the policeman and began mounting the stone stairs. At the top the swing door welcomed her—open. She looked at it, touched the glass panel, when immediately it flapped windily into position. A small smile, another moment's hesitation, and she turned and went down the stairs again and out on to the street, carrying the gloves with her.

On the pavement edge opposite the Town Hall, she paused, and for a minute or two surreptitiously watched the faces of passers-by. Then experiencing the woman's discomfort of standing alone in a public place, she went down the narrow street to the great swing bridge over the river. An old man with a grey beard walked up and down in front of his cardboard row of chalk pictures, rubbing his chilled hands. The air was cold and gusty and blew wisps of white hair about his bared head. She clutched the woollen gloves. The tide was in and the water was broad and dark, with the riverside lamps casting golden spears into its trembling sides. She turned back and dropped twopence in the old man's cap. "God's blessing on you!" he said. She hurried from the blessing, hunching her furred shoulders towards her head in a snuggle of secrecy.

In her little sitting-room she examined the gloves. Cheap, with the right thumb rather crudely darned; long-fingered, thin. Gloves that sheathed a spare hand, a dreamer's hand. She saw again the deep glow in his eyes as he gazed far beyond the realms of the *Supplement*, while she stared at the frugal gloves. The finger waggled emptily, with here a cut on the tip of a forefinger. Long nails, of course.

Normally her fastidious nature would have withdrawn from even touching a stranger's belongings, particularly when found in a public place. The atmosphere of the reading-room was sometimes so thick that it turned her nostrils into deliberate filters. Her complexion was fresh, alive with a warm blood flush, and her eyes glowed darkly. She tried the right glove on, studied the waggling effect, and was about to laugh when her landlady came in. She concealed the glove and asked for a black worsted thread.

Having neatly darned the rent, she once more studied the waggling effect, then turned to her cupboard of books and fished out *Moby Dick*, the only thing of Melville's she had in her irreducible collection of working classics.

But she could find no certain solution of her riddle there. In fact, the more she attempted to work it out the more bogged she got; which proved tantalisingly interesting, there being so many quite fantastic possibilities. She read the chapter on whiteness right through. It gripped her now in a profound way, her intuitions realising themselves in a sort of "translated" vision, uncannily vivid. Her landlady came in with cocoa.

The cocoa was warm and stimulating. She spilt a solid brown drop of it on the abstraction of whiteness … and as she eyed this monstrous stain on the ideal, her concern slowly caught a glint of humour and daring. So far she had found this Highland town most respectably unexciting. Some far steeple bell started ringing. She looked at her watch. Ten o'clock. She would have a walk. Why not? She took the gloves with her.

He was standing on the bridge, looking at the black water and the golden spears. Except for one or two hurrying figures, they had it to themselves. Her pulses stirred uncomfortably but deliciously. And just before her hesitating feet reached him, he turned. She felt the flush mounting to her face as she smiled. The flush and the arc-lamp glitter in her excited eyes arrested him for one blank moment—before he mumbled incoherently and strode hurriedly off the pavement, leaving her with her hand extended, clutching the woollen gloves.

She got home somehow, but with no memory of the way she took. It had felt like walking under the black water with the golden spears quivering in her side. As she entered her sitting-room the first thing she saw was the brown cocoa stain on the white cloth.

Something had happened to her so unexampled that Melville's "incantation of whiteness" seemed the light side of an incantation of darkness under which she wanted to bury her head. Nor would humour come to her rescue. He had thought her "one of these"! Soliciting him… . Her flesh curdled and cramped. Served her right! Oh, served her right! She ought to have left the gloves where they lay, black gloves, black… . But in a swift seriousness she knew that it did not serve her right. It made life mean and suspicious, ugly, horrid… . He had recoiled from her. From *her*! … She was very wide awake when at last she went to bed, but after an hour she fell through the hypnotism of protest into perfect sleep, and next morning hid away the black gloves and went cheerfully about her business all day.

At tea-time she thought, How upset I was last night! and smiled. But somehow now, with the beginning of night again, the smile lingered and twisted the merest trifle. After all, it was humiliating! ... Within ten minutes she was in almost as disturbed a state as she had been the night before. This was really intolerable! The thought of the black gloves positively gathered a criminal taint. It was manifestly too late now to give them up to the librarian. Where had she found them and when? She could hardly reply that she had kept them for a night! ... Well, burn them, why not? That was it—burn them. But instantly her mind associated the idea with the latest murder mystery in the press where the murderer had attempted to burn the dismembered portions of his lady love. The brown cocoa stain blotted out the last speck of white.

Of course, really it was all very amusing. Only it was irritating.... And so it started all over again.

About the hour when he had left the library the previous evening, she was on the bridge. Chance was interested (and perhaps library habits regular) for she saw him coming. Her warm features stilled to the serenity of ice as she stopped right in front of him and held out the gloves. "You left these, I think, on the reading-room table last night." His hand fumbled and she knew the gloves dropped to the street, but she walked on evenly as though his unexceptional person had been less interesting than a dog. She knew, too, as she went on that he was still standing, lost in a sort of stupor. He had recognised her all right. Her heart began to beat wildly with vindictive pleasure, with conscious victory. Perfectly done! That was that wiped out, thank goodness! She met a fellow teacher and they got laughing and decided on a couple of hours in the picture house.

The following night at the same time she found herself crossing the bridge again. A little stroll before supper.... And there he was—standing as if waiting. Ah! she observed him pull himself together. As she came nearer she saw that his pale face was flushed and excessively uncomfortable. She looked straight at it. The arc-light in his shy eyes made them glitter. Just as she came abreast he paused and began, "E- excuse———" She looked right through him as though he weren't and continued her even pace—under a suddenly crowing sky. Oh, it was sweet! It was perfect! Not often do we deserve so well of fate! She felt inexpressibly happy.

The following night she was a quarter of an hour late. He was waiting. But at the critical moment he turned to the river. Within the week she was keeping him waiting a full hour. And now it seemed the mere sight of her was enough. He no more made any attempt to speak. Until one evening he was not on the bridge … but as she passed by the end pillar she was conscious of a tall figure in shadow. Her heart mounted again.

Then one evening she wasn't going to go out at all. After cocoa, however, she changed her mind. It was so cold for even a dog to wait about. And anyway he couldn't still be waiting. As it chanced they met in front of the chalk pictures, and because her head was a trifle too erect she missed the begging cap and kicked it and the few pennies it contained all about the gutter. With profuse apologies she began hunting assiduously with the white-haired man, who said, being Irish, "God bless you, it doesn't matter at all." She was about his best client.

"Excuse me," said a voice, "there's one under your foot." She jerked her foot away from a spare hand which picked up the copper and dropped it in the cap.

"That's all," said the artist. "Just four of them."

"I'm sorry," she mumbled, "I haven't …" She hadn't her handbag.

A shilling dropped in the cap.

"God bless the two av you together!" said the old man.

For some reason the shilling turned her heart to water. It was too much. It wasn't—he couldn't… . They were walking side by side with the hot discomfort of the old man's blessing in their ears.

"I have wanted—wanted to say—that that first night I—I——" He stopped. She didn't help him any. Her sense of power suddenly held a cruelty exquisitely surprising. "I didn't mean—anything," he concluded.

She made a vague uninterested sound.

"I mean—that first night. I wasn't thinking. I couldn't get over it all night." The sound firmed to "Oh."

"I was such a fool," he stuttered. "I wasn't thinking. I mean I was thinking——"

"About Herman Melville." The words slipped out.

"Yes! Yes! Old Melville. Nineteen years all alone—never did anything. Astonishing! After—after what he had done. Wasn't it?" He was so shy that his voice had a gulping break in it.

"I suppose it is," she conceded coldly.

"Yes, wasn't it? Pretty lonely and—and miserable, after what he had done. Such a waste. Curious that those who might have understood … but I suppose it's always the same. Do you know Melville?"

"A bit."

They were walking up the riverside, having been deflected at the bridge-end by a sudden car. The water was dark, but the farther up they went the more perceptible became its smooth downward sweep. It gathered all the mysterious, lonely attributes of water flowing under dark heaven to an eternal sea. Melville's loneliness was in it, and all the loneliness of those who traffick in imagination. This lean figure by her side was in it. And out of its desperation he was struggling to the exciting warmth and gaiety of walking by her side like a man clutching at—a straw? She smiled secretively to the water and let him talk. At the right moment she asked:

"What, then, did you find in the article?"

"It's what I didn't find!" he answered. "Most English critics never find it, because deep in their minds they mistrust it. It's against their tradition. In spite of themselves they react against it. Carlyle and Melville … they admit their greatness and their immense vitality, but they don't admit the greatness of their prose. They detest it."

"Their style?"

"Yes, their style. But it's more than that. It's the old Scots in them. It's fundamental. And it comes out in their English. It's the most fascinating thing in the world." He went on. His mind seemed to be very clear on some traditional idea both subtle and vital, and an underlying warmth communicated itself. There was something so unique and hopeless in his enthusiasm, so visionary, and yet so fine and profitless, that the protective instinct moved in her. And all the time he was talking his shy spirit was gaining confidence. She watched it. It began to laugh here and there. This was so obviously a new experience for it. Then suddenly they came under the shadow of trees where wooded islands lay in the river spanned by white bridges, and abruptly he stopped talking. She laughed, a little low chuckle, as she turned to a handrail and leant on it, above the water.

"I know," he said, "I've been talking too much."

The small current beneath them ran into the main stream and got lost in grey-black undulations like the sleek movements of some fabulous river-monster.

"I've enjoyed it. They don't teach your views of English—at Edinburgh."

"No," he answered, self-conscious again.

Low trees hung over the water, and tall trees behind stretched bare thin fingers to a grey-black sky where here and there a fugitive star gleamed and died.

"Why?" she gleamed.

"I don't know," he answered.

"I'm surprised," she said.

He stirred. "Why are you surprised?" He did not look at her.

She knew what was troubling him, as though she felt her girl's presence trembling to his heart. Now that they were standing still he did not know what to do with himself. And sensitiveness can so quickly withdraw, become remote.

"Surprised?" she echoed. "Because in your mind you are so sure you know!"

"Finally one can be sure of nothing," he said, "except this—that all the fine things are built on nothing."

"Like Scots prose?"

He smiled.

"Or like our being here now," he added.

They were both leaning against the handrail and she felt it tremble. He did not speak. She saw his bare hands clutching the rail. Her mind's eye saw the gloves.

"Obviously your gloves brought us here," she said.

"No—not my gloves."

"But certainly."

"No."

Something about his aloofness was robbing her of that comforting sense of being complete mistress of the situation.

"Have it your own way!" she argued.

He did not answer.

Irrational excitement set up a small vortex inside her breast. There was something extraordinarily evasive about him now like the wind moving about the tall branches. It wasn't fair to her, and less fair to this young moment. Did he mean that what brought them together was something more than—than—— Oh, nonsense! Yet she could not turn and go. Nor could she remain silent.

"Oh, well!" she said, and stirred.

"You see, the gloves were nothing."

"At least they were yours," she argued, and turned to him. Their pale shadowy faces gazed at each other. The dark world swirled in about them. She held her breath.

"They weren't even that," he said. "I, too, saw them on the table, but—they weren't my gloves."

Paper Boats

The two boys fashioned their paper boats with great care. One boy was fair and sturdy and he made folds and bends with the precision of a carpenter. The other boy was dark and so intent on making as good a boat as his companion that he was excited and every now and then stole glances. Clearly this dark boy, whose name was Hugh, was never intended for a carpenter. His fingers were thinner and more nervous, his ruling thumb less firm than George's. His body, too, was more slender, even if it seemed full of an eager fire. It was as though this fire was more potent than the power in his fingers, and his glances were at once jealous and despairing. In his eagerness he completed his boat and cried exultantly:

"I'm finished first!"

George paid no direct attention because he was making a perfect boat and knew that crowing over time was just weakness. He only made a slight sound in his nose as he cocked his head to one side and examined his work, but not loud enough to distract himself. Deliberately he became slower than ever and surer.

Hugh watched him with increasing vexation. He shouldn't have rushed his own one so much. He saw where certain folds did not meet and began pushing them together. But he succeeded only in crumpling the paper, and no matter how he tried to smooth the crumple he failed, so that the last state was noticeably worse than the first.

At last George finished his boat and holding it out on his palm regarded it with great admiration. "There you are!" he said.

It was so perfectly made that Hugh cried loudly but at the same time carelessly, "Mine's just as good!"

George looked at it—and smiled mockingly. "See that—and that: they should be together. And look at the bulge there! It's crooked. That's no use."

"It's use enough," cried Hugh heatedly. "Wait till you see her in the water."

"All right," said George. "You wait." And they ran to the small mound of sand that was by the cooperage wall near the harbour weather-glass. This glass, in its deep case, still recorded the weather, as it did when there was a harbour master to set it and fishermen to trouble it with anxious eyes. The two boys had the dying creek to themselves. The tide was full in and the fine Saturday morning sun made wheels of light on the water. A gull or two, crying as if they had lost something, heeled over. The boys ballasted their paper boats with sand and stuck a gull's feather upright in the fold amidships. Then they turned towards the stone pier, carrying their craft with eager care.

A breach in the front of the pier allowed them to scramble down over huge slabs to the sea edge.

"You haven't enough sand in yours," said George.

"Haven't I?" challenged Hugh, glancing quickly into his rival's hold. "You wait!"

"You always need plenty of ballast if a boat's going to hold to the wind."

"Do you think I didn't know that?" asked Hugh. "Ho! ho! What wind's in it today? Circumstances alter cases."

George snorted. Hugh felt pleased with himself over his blind hit about the weather and became more excited than ever.

"Even if there's no wind on the shore, a gale can be blowing outside."

"If you think I didn't know that," said Hugh, "you can tell it to your grannie."

"Are you ready?" asked George grimly.

"I am," said Hugh.

"Go!" said George.

And they both pushed their boats upon the sea.

George pushed his carefully, but Hugh in order to gain all possible headway thrust his rather forcibly so that the ballast shifted slightly aft; thus George's boat rode perfectly the water while Hugh's stern was too deep.

When George laughed at this, Hugh felt himself grow hot with anger. He wished ardently that his boat would beat George's out into the open sea. He would have given everything he possessed at that moment, including the world, if only his craft would outpace her opponent. For he knew in his heart that she couldn't do it, just as in his heart he knew that he could never draw a straight line like George, that he couldn't press down a crease with his thumb in the flawless manner. George's thumb made a steady unfaltering hiss all along the paper. The paper lay down before it like a cringing dog.

There was a fitful air of wind from the land, but not enough near the pier to stain the water. Thus the two boats for a time scarcely moved at all. Yet it was noticeable that Hugh's boat kept her head to the sea whereas George's boat on an even keel did not know what to do. She seemed to have no spirit of her own and her dead perfection floated listlessly broadside on.

"Mine's gaining!" cried Hugh. The great rock behind the pier echoed his cry, all the way up to its grassy scalp.

"You wait!" said George.

"She's gaining steadily," cried Hugh, and laughed shrilly. His eyes were on fire. The bow of his boat, cocked up, swung a little from side to side, as if it had just been troubled by a real breath. The stern by being low in the water at once steadied and helped this action. The little craft was oddly alive as though it delighted in its imperfection.

George regarded his own craft with hopeful grimness.

"Wait till she gets the wind proper," he said.

By the time they were four yards from the pier Hugh's boat was leading by no more than a foot. George's had straightened up and was overhauling her. They both rose and fell on the slow glistening undulations. George's boat would have overtaken the other but getting an extra little puff of air turned broadside on again and began moving aimlessly across the harbour mouth.

Although the bow of Hugh's boat swung dangerously, it steadied—on the open sea.

For the first time real hope entered into Hugh. He saw with elation that his boat was going to beat George's. All that she had to do was to keep her head to the open sea. He had not expected this. He had been prepared for defeat. For George was better with his hands. He knew that, even if he would never give in to it; and he would never give in to it because the fire in his mind was irked by straight lines. His mind had steeled itself to defeat—and here was victory.

The open sea! His heart sang.

George was annoyed. His boat had no sense in her at all. But if only she would get the right sort of wind…. There she was, straightening up again.

Hugh laughed derisively. "She's yards behind already," he cried.

"You wait!" said George.

At that moment a large stone fell between the boats with a mighty splash.

The boys stumbled back against a slab, their hearts in their mouths. Up on the grassy scalp of the rock, they saw three young men laughing in the excitement of their sudden game.

Stones began to fall thick and fast.

"Stop it!" yelled George, whose temper was getting the better of him.

"Stop it!" yelled Hugh also.

"Keep back!" shouted one of the young men, and signalled warningly with an arm.

The stones landed very near the boats and frequently between them so that George's boat began to wash inshore again in a helpless way. Once a stone very nearly got it and it shipped sparks of water from the jabble. It looked completely beaten, the most lifeless thing anyone could see.

"Stop it!" yelled George. "Ye great fools!"

But Hugh's boat, helped outward by the wash from the stones and now far enough from the shelter of the pier to catch what wind was going, was making steadily to sea. As though she were escaping them, the young men on the cliff-top made up their minds to get her and ignored George's boat altogether.

Excitement got such a hold of Hugh that he could not speak. As each stone splashed and missed, he drew breath—waiting for the next. He cast an agonising glance at the cliff top. But there was no mercy there. Then a stone, cutting under her, made her jump.

A laugh came down and a voice: "That was near her!"

"Watch this!" shouted a second voice.

"This'll settle her!" said a third.

Hugh began to gather a thrilling confidence. Some of their stones were already falling short. She still had her head to the sea, her feather upright, her passage perilous but steady. Already, indeed, she was beginning to look small, removed from them, as if the great glistening sea had taken her for its own. Pride came into his confidence and the spirit of daring of his forefathers.

Only one thrower now could come within a yard of her. The stones slackened.

George's voice came suddenly from Hugh's back: "They can't reach her. Watch this!"

Hugh wheeled round as George threw. His stone was the length but a yard wide.

"You stop it!" shouted Hugh.

George bent, looking for another suitable stone.

"Stop it, do you hear?"

George straightened himself. "Who'll make me stop it?"

"I will!" said Hugh, a pale flame in his face as he squared up to George.

"Oh, you will!" said George.

"Yes, I will!"

"Oh, I see," said George, opening his mouth and adding "huh!". Then he began looking in cracks of the masonry for a stone. He found one and weighed it on his palm. "Too light," he muttered.

But Hugh knew it was not too light.

A voice yelled from above: "Here, stop that, boys!"

They looked up.

"Go on, now," and a threatening head jerked, "clear out!"

George made a mocking mouth. "I'll see you again about this," he said, as if baffled for the time being, and slouched off trying to whistle.

Like three gods the young men passed beyond the crest of the cliffs, laughing. Hugh, left alone, found himself breathing hard in and out as if he had really had a fight. Then a great tingling delight came upon him. His heart spilled over. He wanted to do swift violent acts with arms and body; acts of defiance and dancing.

His eyes sought his boat eagerly but now could not find her. She had sailed away into the sea. She was out of sight, going away, away…. A tremendous emotion of wonder and triumph overcame him. But then in a moment he saw her. She wasn't really far out, after all. But this, somehow, did not disappoint him; on the contrary it gave him an awesome conception of the size of the sea.

For a long time he played the game of lifting his eyes from the boat and then trying to find her again.

A time came when he could not find her any more. Staring at the glistening undulating sea he found himself listening, holding his breath. All the world grew silent as though a shining finger had been laid on it. Hugh got up and went away, smiling secretly to himself.

Dance of the Atoms

When the siren hooted outside, Charlie dropped the book he had got lost in and sat listening, his face white and taut, as if the high sound had come from another world; but as it hooted again he leapt to his feet and with a shrill cry of "Wait!" was out the door, along the passage, down the stair-rail on his stomach, and racing full speed along the drive. "Wait!" He was impatient and imperative.

Heath, the cairn terrier, had so well beaten him that he was already on his master's knee, glancing excitedly through the windscreen.

"Well, son; forgotten all about me?"

Charlie did not answer, hardly even looked at his father in his concentrated excitement. The driver's seat had already been vacated. Charlie slammed the door and settled himself; then gathered his brows at the little red light on the instrument-board.

"Sorry!" apologised his father, as he switched off the engine.

Charlie waggled the gear lever, switched on and started up, stretched forward right off the seat until he had pressed the clutch out, put the lever in first and, as he slowly accelerated, let the clutch in and the handbrake off. The car moved forward in an imperceptible and perfect start.

"Sound work!" said his father.

Heath barked. Charlie changed up into second, swung smoothly round on to the gravel in front of the house, changed down to first behind a neat zoom of acceleration, negotiated the off corner of the house, two flower-beds, the trellised arch, and the very awkward garden walk behind the house with its special layout of bulb-beds, crazy paving, and flowering shrubs. Having circled the house he arrived in front of the garage, but with the rear of the car towards the door. All in a minute the gear was in neutral, the handbrake on, and Charlie climbing down from the seat and racing towards the garage door.

"Pretty smart son, this of mine," said Charles senior to the cairn, whose ears he fondled. Brown eyes shining with affection, Heath tried to lick his face, and succeeded, after the remarkable fashion of dogs, in looking humanly foolish. "Pouf!" said Charles generously. He was a large man, well groomed, and full of a smiling fleshy complacence.

Charlie was in his seat again and the gear lever in reverse.

"Ladies and gentlemen," said Charles to Heath, "we are now about to witness the last thrilling act——"

A tiny jerk of the car stopped him. "Ho-ho?" he criticised.

"Ho-ho! to you," said Charlie as, head over shoulder, he smoothly backed the car to a standstill in the small garage.

His father laughed. "Did you jerk her intentionally?"

Charlie was tempted to say "Yes", but the boyish quality of fun had not been developed in him, nor could he tell a direct lie. So he merely continued to be excited and intense. He was over eight years old, and when he was stirred his laughter, instead of being helplessly merry, was fiercely shrill.

His father had scarcely turned the key in the garage door when Charlie had him by the hand, and was pulling him with all his might towards the front entrance of their country house, Heath doing his agile best to add jollity to welcome.

In this strenuous fashion they progressed towards the doorstep upon which Charles saw the welcoming figure of his pale, dark-haired, brown-eyed wife. She was smiling.

"Here!" protested Charles, "this young fellow is getting a bit too strong for me" —he kissed his wife— "he's nearly pulled the arm out of me."

Charlie was still tugging.

"I wish——" said Dorothy, and paused, her thoughtful half-worried smile on her son's head.

He chuckled. "You wish he would! Busy?"

"Drowned. Everybody seems to be coming down at once."

"Here?"

"Don't be an ass. Tomorrow afternoon ——"

"Come on!" tugged Charlie.

As he allowed himself to be dragged into the hall, Charles kept talking to Dorothy and making little jokes and throwing tags of laughter about. As lord of the manor, he was obviously not displeased by this flattering welcome. From the straining eagerness of his son, he turned to his wife and winked.

"I know," she said with resigned good-nature. "He's been lost there all morning." She sighed.

As Charlie threw the door of his playroom open he told Heath sharply to get out. Heath's ears went down and again his eyes looked human, but now not at all foolish. Charles shook his head at him sadly. "These engineers, y'know," he explained; "very touchy."

"You don't want to come in, Mother?" said Charlie.

She smiled. "Oh, well, if you'd rather not!" Then she turned to her husband. "Lunch in twenty minutes—remember—and no rushing off to wash after the gong."

He chuckled. "All right."

Charlie had the whole intricate railway circuit running very smoothly. Stations, signal-boxes, loop-lines, up-traffic and down-traffic. The recurring trouble of engines getting derailed at the points had been completely overcome. The new siding, however, which had been well discussed, was not completed.

"Of course, I knew it was a ticklish job," said his father. "It will take time. You see——"

"I was reading—that's why," said Charlie as he uncoupled the Flying Scotsman.

"Reading! Ha-ha! Fairy story, was it?"

Charlie looked up at his father with gleaming eyes. The absurd joke about a fairy story did not even touch his thought. "I don't think I want to be an engine-driver any more," he said.

"Hullo! What's gone wrong?"

"I want", said Charlie—and now his excitement could hardly be repressed—"to be a scientist." The gleaming eyes searched his father's face; but the face nodded solemnly.

Thereupon the book was produced. *Shooting Electrons* was its title, and the fly-leaf bore a greeting from Uncle Ned in the Air Force.

"It tells all about what's inside the atom, and it's for boys," said Charlie. "It's very simple. Do you know about all the different kinds of atoms—and how wireless is made?"

"I'm afraid not," said Charles.

"Oh, it's exciting. You see, if you have a thing in the centre and another thing flying round about it then that's one atom. If there's two things flying round it, then it's a different atom. The things that fly round are the electrons, and the thing in the centre is the nucleus. Now when the electrons are flying round and round they knock into other electrons flying round and round, and then—and then——" His voice grew highpitched; his eyes glittered; the gong reverberated.

"Come on!" said Charles, and together they dashed for the nearest wash-basin.

"Hah-haa?" said Dorothy as they arrived at table breathless. But father and son were full of secret male jubilation. In an excited gesture Charlie splashed his breast with gravy and nearly broke his plate.

"Oh, I wish you could keep calm," said his mother, wiping him.

Over her shoulder Charles winked to his son, and the white face closed its lips tightly.

After lunch, when they were walking together in the garden, Dorothy said, "I'm not too happy about Charlie. I wish he wasn't always so strung up."

"But boys are like that," replied her husband, smiling. He had seen how she had had to control her annoyance at lunch-time, otherwise Charlie would have flown into sharp bits.

"No, they're not," she said. "And you know it. There's something wrong in Charlie—or going wrong. I blame the concentration on mechanical things. And you encourage him in it."

"You think a good fairy tale, perhaps?"

"Please don't chuckle, Charles. I really mean it. I do. I'm serious. I know about the spirit of the age and all that. But at times I am uneasy. I wish he could be warmer, more boyish."

"But he is affectionate. Dash it, you can't have him——"

"He can almost strangle you with affection at times, I know."

Charles looked at her.

"Dorothy, you musn't let your fancy run away with you. Nowadays a boy gets all his fun and excitement out of mechanical things. Even little Charlie there can tell me things in science that I didn't know. All I know really is where money comes from and how it's made." He chuckled again.

This chuckle was the only thing about him that she had never quite got used to. It had an irritating complacency. He was always so reasonable and so sure of himself; everybody else must be wrong.

16

But that was a small thing at the moment. "Don't imagine", she said, trying to meet his humour, "that I'm jealous because he prefers the company of locomotives and you. Anyone who prefers locomotives and you cannot have much wrong with him. I know. You also imagine I'm probably upset a bit because he isn't dependent enough upon me; starved mother instinct. I wish you wouldn't. I'm merely afraid for his health and his balance. All I want you to do is to make him exercise more. If you could make him do—do foolish, boyish things."

She looked up at her husband. He was smiling.

"You merely think I'm old fashioned?" she said.

He let the chuckle out, glancing at her like a great, sly overgrown boy himself.

He was a loyal and generous husband, who never bothered his head with other women. He had his points. But strangely enough it was the irritating obtuse self-sufficiency in him that frequently was his strongest point of all with her. At a difficult moment, like the present, when she could do nothing about it, she found comfort, a sort of obliterating ease, in giving in to it and letting it envelop her.

She had fought against this many times, but always with completely negative results, apart from the fraying of her own nerves. She had come to realise that when you may not alter what is fundamental in a man, the next best thing to do is to find comfort in giving in to it.

When he saw that she was prepared to be assured, he risked saying, "You mustn't blame him for having some of your own nerves!"

She smiled.

He chuckled, delighted. "And he really has brains. You again! He is going to be a pretty hot-stuff scientist, take my word for it. We're going to be proud of him yet." He nodded confidently. "Science is the coming thing. In the business world, too. I mean, it's *the* thing. Everything else derived from it. I don't want to say anything against your literature or music——"

"But for a healthy boy you think they're pretty poor hobbies?"

When he laughed at her wry mouth, Heath got excited and danced across a newly-planted plot.

"Go it, Heath!" he encouraged the dog as he made circles round his pursuing wife.

It's easy to manage things when you're right—and know how.

And he was certainly right about Charlie's getting pleasure out of his playroom activities. At times the pleasure was so intense that he would cry out to himself and at the things in front of him.

In his book *Shooting Electrons* everything was made delightfully clear and was illustrated with drawings that could make one laugh. The molecule of water, for example, is made up of two atoms of hydrogen and one of oxygen. The oxygen atom is shown like a round white face and the two hydrogen atoms are stuck on it like black ears. Oxygen, of course, is what you breathe and hydrogen is the light gas that lifts balloons. But when two atoms of hydrogen and one of oxygen come together, you get water. Here on this page, again, is an illustration of a motor car in a garage. The engine is running and the dotted line shows the door is closed. Through the exhaust pipe are pouring myriads of atoms of carbon. (Charlie knows what decarbonising an engine means, because he once saw the carbon being scraped off the piston tops.) Well, these carbon atoms coming pouring out through the exhaust tried to join up with the oxygen atoms in the cylinders. Each carbon atom would like to join up with two oxygen ones, and when this happens there is formed the gas that makes ginger beer fizzy. (Charlie likes ginger beer.) But as the supply of oxygen atoms is restricted, some carbon atoms have to be pleased with one oxygen atom, and then the two of them form the deadly gas called carbon monoxide. If a fellow stayed in a closed garage with the engine running he would be dead in no time, because the carbon monoxide would kill him.

While his father and mother were at last deeply and happily engrossed in the layout of new bulb beds (companioned by Heath, almost equally happy, for now and then Charles threw a stone away absentmindedly), Charlie sat with the book on his knees and stared before him in a pale trance. The marvellousness of the simple but terrific transformation from ginger beer to death overwhelmed him. So highly strung was his mind that it became receptive to the most delicate suggestions from this new atomic world. In fact, when the writer referred to the ceaseless whirling of atoms as "the dance of the atoms", Charlie visualised the dance itself.

But when the wonder of all this had had its innings, the inevitable next stage followed—the desire to act, to experiment, to prove. A craving to make atoms perform, as he could make locomotives and coaches perform, began to get a feverish grip on him. He had never indeed experienced anything quite like the heat of this desire. By night-time it was consuming him.

Moreover, the writer was never tired of showing how always the most thrilling discoveries were made by scientists in their laboratories by pure chance or accident, and often, in fact, when they were looking for something quite different. Then from a simple discovery the whole world benefited, and the scientist became immortal. But he, Charlie, had no test tubes, no batteries, no laboratory, no nothing. The only illustration in the whole book that was not new to him was that of the motor car in the garage.

The following morning his father set off across the fields with him and Heath. Charlie was very pleased to go, because he thought it would be a good chance of talking about the laboratory. Heath could hardly credit his luck and showed it. Charles himself was in good form, both because he enjoyed the country air after the recent hot spell of city life and because he knew Dorothy would be pleased at his taking Charlie away from his mechanics.

And there was the hidden joke, too, in the idea that Charlie *could* be got away from his mechanics! Actually, no doubt, he could have been made as keen on birds and plants as on atoms. And perhaps this might yet be done. But meanwhile a yellow wagtail hovering in sunlight was a dance of atoms; the scent of wild briar a drift of electrons (or was it?).

"Is it, Dad? Or what do you think?"

"I don't know, son, but drift of electrons sounds good to me."

"I'm tired of these trains now."

"I'm sorry to hear that. They were pretty expensive."

"I should like to have a little, just a little laboratory. Would that be expensive? I could keep the trains and make them go, too, if you like."

"But you're too young for a laboratory. Good gracious me! And besides, when you go to school you'll have a laboratory there—a great big one—with all sorts of—of retorts and things in it. You see, you haven't been to school so far because you had that illness when you were six. But you'll go now very likely after this vacation. And *then* you'll have your laboratory."

"But I don't want to go. And I won't have it anyway. Because little boys' schools don't have laboratories."

"Who told you that?"

"Do they?"

"Well——" Charles was stumped.

"They don't. They don't." His voice was growing shrill. "I asked——"

"Heath!" shouted Charles. "Come here!"

The cairn came flat-eared from the warren.

"They don't!" cried Charlie. "Go away, Heath! Go away!" And he kicked the dog that momentarily grovelled in guilt before their feet.

Charles stopped. "Here, son," he said quietly. "You must never do a thing like that."

Charlie's face drew white and taut.

"Say you're sorry to Heath."

The dark eyebrows gathered stormily above the glittering eyes. The teeth were clenched.

Charles saw how hard he was fighting for control.

"Come on, then," he said, and taking the boy's hand he walked on in silence, Heath at their heels.

His son was a dynamic force. Genius in youth was often eccentric. Charles did not want the boy to fly into bits. It was necessary to dominate him, of course, and he would. On this business of the laboratory, for example, he would not give in to him. And meanwhile Dorothy need not see that the paternal authority had been endangered!

And he got over the difficulty very nicely, as it happened. Immediately lunch was finished, Charlie, silent, rose and left the room.

"What went wrong?" asked Dorothy.

Charles chuckled. "He wants a laboratory!"

"A what?"

"A laboratory of his own!" And now it really did sound a splendid joke. Just the sort of grandiose thing a genius would want. Immense, really! The young rascal!

"Look here, Charles. You're not going to indulge him in this?" There was fear in her voice.

"Oh no. I told him that. All the same, he has the ideas. A laboratory of his own—at eight!"

That afternoon the two Nicholsons called for them to take them along to the opening of the new club house.

There was laughter and loud talk. Charlie was sent for and presented.

"Now see you be a good boy till mother comes back," said Dorothy, giving him a kiss.

"'Bye, son!" called Charles, waving a hand with an intimate friendly smile as he stepped after Dorothy into the Nicholsons' car.

They all waved to him.

"Looks as if he was going to run to brains, Charles," said Tom Nicholson.

"Looks like a little imperious aristocrat, *I* think," said Vera his wife.

Charles chuckled. "He's a bit on his dignity because …" And then he told them the story about the laboratory. Even Dorothy joined in the laughter. Her husband might be right—as usual. They might yet really be proud of him.

Instinctively she touched wood, and smiled away the horrid involuntary picture she sometimes got of his face—white and intense.

When the sound of their car had died in the distance Charlie turned into the hall. At the foot of the stairs he paused, listening to the muffled sound of a loudspeaker and high, mirthful voices in the kitchen premises. Clearly everyone was having the day off.

In the front rooms of the house was the sensation of emptiness in which tall things could happen; towards evening it was touched with an eerie thrill.

His own room was too small now, too locked in. Besides, he could not go and read the atom book. That would be intolerable. He had no particular anger against his father. Nor had he pity for himself. He simply felt lonely like the rooms. The intolerance in him did not hate grown-ups; it ignored them. Yet he was haunted by the something tall in them that thwarted him.

He turned from the stairs and went out again at the front door. Heath yapped a welcome at his feet. "Shut up!" he said, startled. Then, as if strolling nowhere in particular, he went very quietly round the corner of the house.

There was the garage exactly as in the illustration—-and the car was inside. He saw the key sticking in the lock. No footsteps were following him. He was quite alone.

He turned the key and opened the door. Heath, hoping for the best, was in before he could stop him. Charlie pulled the door behind him and, while he stood listening, found himself gazing at Heath's eyes which shone with expectancy in the gloom.

An odd constriction of pain came on Charlie's heart as if a hand had suddenly gripped it.

In that instant his thought had been given a certain terrible direction. His mouth fell open to let the breath pass more silently while he listened.

"Come on," he whispered.

Heath was in through the driving door before it was properly opened. Charlie followed, switched on, and pressed the self-starter. When the engine was turning over regularly he said to Heath: "Wait here."

He withdrew from the garage and quietly turned the key in the lock of the door.

His full mind was not really doing this experiment deliberately. It was all a sort of beginning to see what would happen; a direction towards experiment, terribly hampered by the fact that his father had absolutely forbidden him to touch the car when he himself was not present. If Nanna came out at that moment and caught him she would tell, and if his father turned on him and thrashed him the whole world would crash to nothing.

"Charlie!" Nanna's voice! While his body stood rigid his brain wondered if he would have time to slip in and switch off. "Charlie!" She was coming his way. In a moment she would be at the corner. He broke out of his stance and ran to meet her so that she would not hear the car.

"Where have you been?"

He was now extremely excited and shouted: "Nowhere!" He rushed into the house, hating her. But she went after him, calling him, and finally took him forcibly from the playroom.

"What way is this to behave?" He resisted her. "What you need," she said in a flash of temper, "is a good sound spanking . And if you're not careful you'll get it, though I get the sack. Now you'll drink that."

But he could not drink his blood warm milk. The sight of it revolted him. Because of the roaring noise his own emotion made within him, he was not even hearing properly what she was saying. "I won't drink it!" he shouted. He turned on her and defied her. He was utterly obstreperous. She did her best with him over a considerable time, ignoring him, stopping his wild rushes. When his voice shrilled in hysteria, she smacked him.

For one moment he stared at her, his eyes wide and glittering; then he attacked her, sobbing and screeching madly, loathing the touch of her, hitting her. When her arm closed on him he bit it.

She dropped him like a snake; called him a demon. Her deepest woman-instinct was revolted, even while it recognised that here there was something tragically wrong. It has the bitter taste of defeat for a normally sound kind woman to be hated by a child.

"Go away!" he was screaming at her. "Leave me alone!"

"All right," she said at last, and left the room.

He listened to her tapping heels ostentatiously dying away; then, before she could steal back, he slipped out of the door and into the drawing room. With the help of a chair he unlatched the french window and was soon rushing on tiptoes for the garage. As the door swung open, the fumes drove him back. Holding his breath, he dashed for the engine-switch, turned it off, and dashed back.

But Heath did not follow. "Heath!" he whispered intensely. "Heath! Heath!"

Nothing came from the garage but the slow, upcurling smoke-coloured fumes.

He found Heath stretched out by the engine exhaust pipe, overcome no doubt in a whimpering turn-away from the closed door. He dragged him round the off corner of the garage in among some rhododendron bushes, then slipped back, locked the door, and was caught by Nanna as he was re-entering the french window. He gazed at her, swayed giddily and fell, retching a little.

Alarmed, she picked him up and carried him to his bed asking distractedly if he had been eating anything. He did not answer. "Tell me! Tell Nanna!" she implored, kneeling beside him. Then she got a curious, stale odour off his clothes. She knew tobacco more by its stale morning smell than otherwise. Her eyes widened. "Have you been smoking?"

He turned his head away weakly and, without opening his eyes, said "Yes".

Her mouth closed firmly. No wonder he couldn't eat. She nodded to herself. A light of healthy satisfaction dawned firmly upon her countenance. Telling him how much it served him right, she undressed him relentlessly. She had not thought it was in him!

Late that night his father and mother stood looking down on his pale, sleeping face.

"The young rascal, I'll have to give him a hiding, I suppose," said Charles.

"A real good one," nodded Dorothy with a sweet, remote smile.

"I believe", said Charles, "that you are delighted he smoked. I believe you are."

"Hush," she said. "Don't chuckle." Then she stooped and kissed the frail forehead of her son. "Mother's own darling," she murmured.

Charles groaned discreetly.

As they went downstairs, he had his chuckle out. "You feel that he is human having smoked? What a perverted notion for the mother of a coming scientist!"

"Mother of a son, you great donkey!"

He chuckled again. "I wonder where the devil Heath can have gone?"

"Where do dogs go when they don't come home at night?"

"Hush!" He brought his lips to her ear. "That's a question for the scientists."

Whistle For Bridge

Donald's father was responsible for English in a large secondary school in a Scots industrial town, a slight fair man who at irregular intervals told the barber he would have nothing on his hair. When walking through a field he would sometimes take his son's hand, for he always appeared cool and unhurried and was rather given to staring through pale blue eyes.

This particular summer, Donald, who was nine years old, had quite a lot of freedom, for in the Highland town to which they had come for the vacation, his father had run into an old college acquaintance named Murray, who taught science but whose passion was for what he called analytic psychology. It was, for example, quite a simple affair for Murray to explain specifically why Shelley came to write the singular things he did write. Donald's father thought that what Shelley wrote had also a certain interest in or for itself. "I know," said Murray, "and I'll tell you exactly why you think so." In no time they were having great talks, wandering about or sitting on a wall or a bank. Actually, however, Donald's father mostly listened, and when he did not quite agree said "Um", while his eyes gazed remotely over a meadow.

It was out of such subtle indications of resistance that Murray first got his theory. In acute ways he pursued it, for he was a bright, intelligent analyst, until the truth seemed to lie veiled before him like a hidden vice. His old college friend was a secret poet!

So young Donald left them on a seat by a cemetery and wandered along a path that passed near a farm cottage beside which two men were quarrelling. "You can whistle for it," said one. "By God," said the other, following him, "I'll make you whistle out of the crooked side of your mouth." They disappeared behind the steading.

The path at last climbed up a steep wooded bank and Donald found himself by a slow-winding waterway. It was lovely and quiet here. The banks on each side were golden with broom and whin taller and thicker than ever Donald had seen. There was a scent that came up to him and went away in a mysterious fashion. The scent, although elusive, had yet a thickness in it that might have choked him if it had stayed. He pursued it tentatively in a world that had waked out of a drowsy afternoon and become watchful. The water was clear and still. There was not a human being anywhere. The birds sang in notes loud and challenging. The colour of the scent was yellow. And the thousands of golden flowers, all packed together like swarming bees, dazzled the eyes. Donald listened and became watchful, too, and faintly dazed about the forehead.

He might have hummed to himself and run away back; but he didn't, though he was now excited with the fear of something about to happen to him. And then as he stepped carefully along his heart gave a leap. Through the clear water towards him came a great grey-backed salmon. It swam slowly with a lazy movement of the whole body. It had a white patch on its side and on the top of its head. He saw its eyes, and its mouth kept opening whitely as if it had a half-crown in it. Donald could not move because he was rigid with fear of this beast that was not a beast but an apparition. Its nose touched the stones blindly beneath his feet; its back fin cut the water; it wriggled clumsily, disturbing the water to a faint panic, and set off again.

But Donald could not set off blindly. The bank held him, as curiosity holds fear by cramping it. He saw the moving angle in the water. The nose of the angle touched the other side. There was a disturbance on the surface. But the beast did not start back again. It hung about that off side, quietly engaged on its strange business. What could that business be? What awful secret thing was it doing? If Donald could have tiptoed over a bridge, he would have … Swallowing his heart out of his throat and panting a little, he looked about him. Rising out of the golden broom beside him was a black board with great white letters:

WHISTLE

FOR

BRIDGE

Donald stared at the board.

But in a little while he assured himself that the board could hardly be enchanted because it was too real. It just meant to whistle for the bridge. Yet he was frightened to whistle for it, as any grown person might very well be frightened to create something out of nothing. For already he knew how the bridge would come. It would spring out of the thick bushes beyond the gorse on the other side and curve in a great dark arch over to his side. But the temptation was terrible. It nearly made him sick with excitement. And at first he was safe enough because his lips were so dry that they could make no sound. Then his lips moistened themselves, and he had to become extremely careful, so that, to begin with, he made only the very tiniest whistles. The whistles grew bigger, and at last in a splendid frenzy he whistled all he could. Nothing happened. Not a thing. He whistled again. And again. No arch invaded the sky. He was safe! Until in a flash he knew he was wrong: he had to whistle out of the crooked side of his mouth. The crooked side was for him the right side. Try as he might, the right side would produce nothing but breath. Quite by accident, however, the left side of his mouth gave a low mysterious whistle, and at once the earth responded in a hissing sound.

The sound was well down, but it was coming up—and up—it was coming upon him from behind… .

It was a steamer, with a slim bow cocked up on the water. She had grey coils of rope and black buoys on her deck. A man stood near the little wheel-house, broad-shouldered as a whaler. He saw the white scared face by the board and smiled and pulled a string. At once there was a hollow, shattering whistle that went on as if it were never more to stop. It stopped, and the man, who had the face of all the kind sailors in the world, waved to the boy and, pulling the string again, made an extra playful little cough of a whistle all for his benefit.

As the vessel disappeared round the bend, the man looked back. Then the place was emptier than it had been in the beginning, and the boy started running back to find his father.

One of the two men who had been quarrelling was now with a young woman who, as Donald passed, said in a strange, challenging voice, "He may whistle for it, but he'll get it some day." His father and Murray were no longer by the cemetery. At last he saw them away across a field, and by the time he overtook them they were walking along a road. They were still talking, or at least Murray was, when he came up with them. As he felt his father look at him, warmth came into his face, he did not know why. But his father said nothing.

Murray's talk was full of intricate and difficult words so that one could shelter behind them, though his little hard laugh occasionally was disturbing. They came to a low bridge over water.

"This," said his father to him, "is the Caledonian Canal."

"Boats go right through it," explained Murray, "from Inverness to the West Coast."

Donald recognised the water. "But the bridge——"

"They whistle for it," said Murray, "and the two men turn that handle and the bridge opens."

Revelation caught Donald in a flash of light and he went hot with secret shame.

"What did you think?" asked Murray, eyeing him.

Donald brought to his face the calm, far-eyed expression of his father, and said, "I was just wondering." His father took his hand.

Pure Chance

Have you ever thrown a stone at a weasel in an old drystone dike? The stone knocks smoke off the edges of the hole. With a thrill you think, That's given him the fright of his life!

Then you begin to wonder if you really did hit him, if, after all, the brown marauder was a tiny fraction of a second too late. So you go across and examine the hole and get the faint smell of brimstone. But the hole is empty and clean. More absolutely than if you had hit it, the weasel has vanished.

However, as you are walking away, something makes you turn your head over your shoulder. There is no movement in the dike, but your eye is at once held by the weasel's head. It has come out of another hole. It is perfectly still, watching you.

For a time you stare at it. Then, without moving, you stealthily scan the ground at hand. But there is no suitable stone within reach. Raucous primitive sounds suddenly burst from your mouth in an unaccountable fury.

The weasel is not affected. So profound an insult is this that you hurl yourself forward. The weasel vanishes. The old grey dike remains still as a mask.

My mind has grown expert at drawing pictures of the sort, at creating little allegories of this kind. I find a certain comfort in them. The weasel may appear to bob out by a kind of magic, but actually, of course, its procedure is perfectly understandable and natural. The dike has its myriad of little dark tunnels to which the conscious eye remains blind.

But how subtle the game! For I find that I am thinking like this, slipping from one picture to another, in order to give a certain weasel no time to appear. Not that I remain unconscious of it. Tonight, obviously, I can think of nothing else.

But I am perfectly calm. And I won't admit that this calm is fatalistic. I can argue too well for that. I could wish indeed for the appearance of the most cunning metaphysician so that I could argue him off his feet. Indeed I think of him as I write this. I create him suddenly for my own purpose. I make another picture.

So it goes on.

For I am alone tonight. I left to get certain things ready for the wedding. But I did not let my own people here know that I was coming back to town. The flat is all prepared. It is a modest place. I really had, and have, nothing much to do. This is where Morag and I are going to live.

I liked the sound of the key in the lock and the empty swing of the door as I came in. I had a premonition of extraordinary happiness, of a stillness of happiness—to which, however, I did not listen very long.

There is something in having a place of one's own. Its very emptiness creates the illusion of marvellous things to come. Never before had I understood this properly. Although I am at last a qualified architect in a good firm, never before had the human aspect of house-hunger struck me in this way. I see why a couple hunt with such desperation for a place of their very own.

I'll sleep here tonight, in the spare bed, like a guest. How rare the inexplicable mirth that thrusts its face out of the wild!

Donald MacBain has a curious face. Perhaps I think so because he is fair. Only dark men, I feel, should have his kind of mind. It was when I first heard him play the violin that I looked at him twice. He did not play with force and power.

The strings did not hiss harshly. There was no scrape. The tone came away clear and somehow extraordinarily sweet. Yet it was not lost in the shouts and stamping feet of the merriest reel. The violin looked like a toy in his hands, and he used only the upper part of the bow, as if he were not playing so much as trying a thing over, quietly, to himself.

He had been abroad, and, in India, had won fame, it was said, in some memorable tug-of-war contest.

The first time I ever set eyes on Arduan was from the cockpit of the *Kittiwake*. The four of us had sailed her from the Clyde. By the distance we adventured north you can see we had been lucky with the weather on that, to me, first and ever memorable trip. There were other cruises before the owner got married. But of all the places that we visited, never again did a spot come upon me with the brightness, the charm, of Arduan. A year ago I went there overland, for the second time, for a holiday. I did not stay in the hotel, which is very expensive anyhow, but in the white house with the slated roof, belonging to Mrs. Mackenzie, at the off end of the village.

Long narrow cultivated crofts behind; open fishing boats and the sea in front. Being a west coast sea, there are skerries and islands. Lobster pots and tangle and wettings. All the things I thrive amongst. I can feel the cold, the wet discomfort, the shudder; I can walk down the beach and get the sun on my neck and listen to the low hissing of the brimming sea on a divine morning-now, as I write this.

So they got to know me pretty well, the folk in Arduan. And I liked them so much that I don't think I could even unconsciously intrude, though I was always about with some of them, on the sea, or squatting by the barnacled stone jetty or stirring a pot of paint. My name, Stewart, is a familiar enough one to Highland folk.

There are little gatherings of an evening in one house or another in Arduan. They don't like going to bed. The children play about till all hours. You talk, or listen to a song, and if there is space and young spirits are running high, a boy will race off to Donald MacBain's house for his fiddle. A fast reel sends the spirits through the roof.

I am very fond of some of the old traditional Gaelic songs. They affect me in a way that I cannot analyse. I must make some effort to tell about this. I have never heard it discussed or seen it written about, but what happens is always surprising. A certain song will affect me in the profoundest way. With no knowledge of the Gaelic words, I yet seem to understand their emotional content so overwhelmingly that, as it were, they take on an imagery which has the attributes of fate itself, ultimate expressions of the instincts and emotions, and they deploy before me, vaguely perhaps, but with tremendous power and significance.

The first time this happened strongly I bided my time until I got the schoolmaster, a pleasant, friendly fellow, to give me a translation of the words. When I had finally satisfied myself that they were just the words of an ordinary love song which you may find in any language, I was secretly dismayed, experienced a distinct sensation of being let down!

I did not show anything of this to the schoolmaster, of course, and he agreed that it was a fine song. But he knew better songs, he said. I found, however, that his better songs were for the most part better because of their words. In this way, through experience, I began to realise that I had within me a sort of absolute capacity for appreciating this particular kind of melody. Call it my ancestral illusion if you like—sometimes I could wish it were….

I haul myself back from these dark runways in the ancient dike. I have the usual uncomfortable reaction to them.

Though we travelled up on the same train, I did not see Morag until we were leaving the little country station. She got into the bus, two seats in front of me. The freshness of her fair skin was very attractive, as full of light as my own mind of its holiday. She was gay, too, talking and laughing and really good-looking, not in any "distinguished" way, but just as life looks good. She was full of life, and her brown hair glistened.

Every time the bus stopped so did my thought. The last stop but one she got up. But it was only to say goodbye. Off went the bus again, carrying us to Arduan.

So I knew quite a lot about her—what Mrs. Mackenzie doesn't know about folk isn't worth the asking—when a mixture of us gathered one evening in Sandy Munro's house. Sandy clips his whiskers with his own blunt scissors and is fond of fun as a boy. I have never known a man so naturally at home in a boat. I suspect him of dodging work on the croft in ways too devious for even himself to follow. In bleak moments the care-free thought of him does the heart good.

It must have been pretty late that night when Morag sang. I don't mean late for Arduan. Whether the afterglow or the dawn, the light was in that still, ghostly phase, which I swear no man ever gets used to. I remembered it as I went home, and looked along the shore for Donald MacBain without appearing to look, and heard a wader crying on the edge of the tide. And I thought, beneath the wonder and delight, in a strange, sombre way, "God knows why she sang like that."

I refuse to analyse these irrational words, even now; they go too deep for me. I can't understand them.

If Morag has nothing very exceptional in the way of a singing voice—for I can discount my own prejudice in its favour—she does have the good sense to sing well within its compass. But that's just it; she sings much as Donald MacBain plays the fiddle. He is, in fact, her uncle.

There is that intimacy, that singing of the song to the inner mind, that terrible, dreadful process of evoking the elemental. I shall never lightly ask her to sing, not until I'm ready, with the inner forces secretly gathered—I was going to say "for the contest".

Not that I should write like this if I thought my words were utterly meaningless. But, after all, Donald MacBain did get up when she had finished singing, did get up and walk out into the night without a word.

The drama of that moment is utterly beyond telling. Plainly he could not have been overcome, as I was overcome, for I couldn't move. Besides, it was quite natural to be profoundly affected now and then. One merely kept silent for a little. An eye might glisten here or there, a girl sigh. Then expression came through in softness, in laughter, in a rare chattering friendliness, and a girl did not look back at one—or did. But the thought of separation, of leaving, was the last of all.

Something went with him that absolutely drained the room. His bulk going out seemed terrific. We held our breaths and strained our ears to listen, as though we might overhear him meeting what he had to meet. We broke up after that.

We talk of a "conspiracy of silence". That was not the kind of silence at all. It wasn't a conspiracy; it was a taboo. Anyway, it was the first time in my life that I got a glimmering of the meaning, the queer potency, of that word. As men, we didn't speak of Donald's behaviour next day.

I suspect the girls, in twos or threes, didn't speak of anything else. But I am equally certain they instinctively dropped the subject as men drew near. I cannot tell you quite how I know this, but I know it. In this region of the mind you seem to know things without evidence. That's the appalling thing about it. The weasel's head is suddenly looking at you.

In this same hopelessly unscientific way I became aware, as if told it explicitly, of a certain relationship between Donald and Morag, a curious *rapport*. They were of the same kind. Need I say that in their behaviour they were completely different. Morag's gay, bright ways were in perfect contrast to her uncle's quiet presence. But somewhere, somewhere below all that, they were of a kind, and you apprehended this in a stillness, the stillness that was the silence in which they became conscious of each other and walked away from you.

Not that they ever so walked. My mind is merely at its maddening game of making pictures. Outside pictures, I don't know how we are going to apprehend the truth. I wish someone could tell me about this. Logic is no use. It has no pictures. And without pictures how are we going to grasp, to understand, human relationships? I suppose this has something to do with the function of art. God, it wearies me.

Meg—she helps Mrs. Mackenzie in the house and is distantly related to her—was tentative as a bird with a doubtful morsel.

"You enjoyed the ceilidh last night," I suggested.

"Yes." Her hands were very busy setting the tablecloth dead straight.

"That was a new one to me—Morag's song."

"Yes."

"You knew it?"

"No. At least, I never heard it before."

"What was it all about?"

"What?"

"The song."

"It was a very nice song. Didn't you like it?"

"I did."

I deliberately waited. "There's Mrs. Mackenzie," she said with a fluster, and out she went for some dishes.

Mrs. Mackenzie could stand talking for an hour on end. But she hadn't been to the ceilidh—and clearly Meg had told her nothing about the incident. I didn't say anything about it myself.

"Morag sang very well," I ventured,

"Why wouldn't she? She would always be listening to that uncle of hers when she was a little girl."

A series of pictures followed. The note in Mrs. Mackenzie's voice was not exactly one of condemnation. She didn't slight Donald MacBain. But she did convey the idea that "it was a pity he hadn't made more of it considering all his chances" —meaning more of his life. I glimpsed Meg's face in the passage beyond. It held a brighter innocence than any bird's—and wasn't missing much.

I sensed the change in Donald, for you could hardly observe it. This grew on me. Days of it. And there was Morag. Then I got the fantastic notion that Morag was avoiding her uncle. This worked on me like a diluted acid. I was beginning to understand what avoidance meant. I watched her, without looking.

She was, I must admit, very friendly to me. You don't just run after a girl in Arduan. A small place is all eyes. You do your best in secret or delicate ways, and then nature, thriving on this kind of game, arranges the chance that throws you together naturally. This happens, and can be very exciting.

One day chance did its job perfectly. We were out of sight of houses when we met, among some close-cropped green slopes, with steep sheep-paths to shingly beaches and little caves.

She was really entrancing, something the wind blows on from the sea. At that moment, emotion got me by the throat. I felt reckless, so I laughed, for words were difficult.

However, I managed a few, but she would not come. No, she said, billowing like a sail you can't get hold of. Really, she said, she must go home.

I don't suppose she backed a step from me or billowed much either, for the wind was nothing out of the way. But suddenly I saw she wasn't going to come, and in an instant I felt: this is a test.

The usual kind of jesting followed, the sort of idiotic "Oh well, if you don't want to come!" meant to be meaningful. Suiting the action to the word, I turned my head away—and saw Donald MacBain appearing above the grassy crest below us.

Don't misunderstand me. They hadn't been together—though, of course, it would have been perfectly natural had they been. He was her uncle, a man of forty-seven. She was twenty-three and, as a child, had played at his knee. I had seen Morag coming along the path from Cromag.

She left, and I didn't offer to go with her. I had the feeling she didn't want me to go with her *then*. So I sat down, for there was a tremor in my legs, and waited for Donald MacBain. He was carrying a batten of timber which he had obviously picked up on the shore. My voice was ready, even over-loud with greeting. What was he going to do with that, I cried.

For the first time I felt something deliberately distant in him. He did not answer until he was beside me, then spoke quietly, telling what he hoped to do with the batten. It was his normal manner. But after that first direct glance, he did not look at me. He started walking home.

I tried to make conversation, and that exhausts a fellow. He left me at the proper spot with a nod. I went on in complete turmoil, in a state of frustration that made me laugh. I mean I actually did make laughing sounds, though I did not hear them until I saw old Kirsty Munro looking at me, her head lifted from an old tub. I cried a respectful greeting and passed on, making sounds that might imply I had been attempting to sing. A red heat went over my flesh.

Irritation, anger—I became mentally unsteady. My mind could watch for signs and signals like a sick hawk. Shameful. I avoided Morag; and that I should *have* to do this made me wretched. Why did I *have* to do it? Heaven alone knows. Not that it was obvious, I hoped, for I did not want others to see—except, perhaps, Morag, and I merely wanted her to be uncertain—and wretched, too.

Strange as it may seem, this set up some perverse current of attraction between Donald and me. In sea terms, a sort of dangerous undertow. I felt my body being sucked towards him—but with some dark intent of its own. And I was not afraid, though he could have killed me with one straight punch.

A friendship developed, a deep reticence being its wordless mode, almost uncanny at times, as when his voice went gentle.

I knew what folk on land—say, Morag—would think when they saw us pulling out and then setting sail for the haddock ground. It was not the kind of evening to go sea-fishing, but the smash of the wooden shell on the waves was invigorating. Cleansing and good. Sandy Munro had come out from his cottage and was watching us. "You can almost see him shaking his head," I said.

But trying to hold the boat up over the fishing ground was impossible, though it showed me Donald's enormous strength. When, with half a dozen haddock in the boat, I insisted on taking the oars, Donald shook his head. As he lay back on the pull, I saw the veins in his neck.

"Dry work," he said. "Would you like a drink?" The light smile was deep in his eyes as they steadied on me.

I got the sail ready, while he kept her head to the weather, then smartly—he could move with an extraordinary purposeful swiftness—he shipped the oars and had her underway before she had time to fall off. But he was not making back for Arduan with its "Bar" tucked discreetly away at the back of the expensive hotel.

He acknowledged my surprise with a silent humour, and I knew a sudden relief, a pleasure, in the thought that we were getting away from it. It was an exhilarating bit of sailing. Wonderful what some of these open inshore fishing boats can do, how near they can stand to the wind with a sail as tight as a board.

We made Melnavreckan long before closing time, wet a bit from inlashings and spray, but not enough to notice, and the sea-fight left peace in the flesh and anticipation in the mind.

As a pub it is nearly half human, but we got thrown out in due course, though not before I had bought a bottle of whisky. The place had been rather crowded, and this had eased talk and continued, as it were, the exhilaration of the sea.

Meanwhile the wind had risen. You could hear the roar outside. There was much talk with three men who told us we shouldn't risk it. They became very confidential about this. We went round a corner and had a drink from a bottle. They had "signs". One of the signs was the way the water spouted from an outer skerry. There were those who had ignored that sign. (I gathered they had been drowned, though this was not explicitly stated.)

Dark and enigmatic grew the talk, but warm, warm and friendly, full of strange portents mixed with soft laughter and earnestness. I produced my bottle.

The three good fellows wet their feet (for she had grounded by this time) in helping to set us afloat. I can still see Callum's face in the faint gloom as he kept a hand on her bow. As if only now realising what was happening, he said with gentle incredulity: "Gode, Donnie boy, you're no' going?" They stood there watching us until we passed from sight.

I had not the least fear. On the contrary, I was enjoying an easy recklessness, a fine excitement. Then we were hit, and then we were thrown. I got a crack on the back of the head and had a complete vision of disaster, of everything breaking up, scattered and sinking.

Wild turmoil, a whistling wind, and now Donald's voice crying near my ear: "We stopped too long. Tide has turned against wind. Going to be dirty."

I am bailing. Hanging on and bailing, with the perfected sensation of being hurled into eternity. Take it from me, that sea was eternity. Not the sea itself and only, but something in it—as the spirit is in the flesh. (There is, however, no mortal picture for it.)

The sail was reefed to a peak, and she sat at times so low that you could see the hunger in the grey-green beast as it reared behind with smoking crest, gathering itself for the drowning smash. Beasts beyond beasts, heaving backs of endless herds, racing on their primordial hunt in the twilight of the world. So will the earth itself go under them at the end, under just such a ravening seeking and smothering.

We fought them out. We preserved the mortal tune. But we did not make Arduan. We could not. By grace and Donald's seamanship we made the sheltered side of Shag Island. In the cove there we found some driftwood, and by doctoring damp matches we got one to strike. I had stuck the half-full bottle of whisky in a coil of rope. It was unbroken.

Raw fire, raw whisky, and a cave. You won't get much nearer the core of what you may mean than that. Not the cave-man core. Just the core of all meaning for you at that moment. The social reticences cease to have point. Reticence itself is seen as a force, the force of restraint. There is a loneliness without meaning. The heart knows its only glow of warmth in giving and receiving, in telling and being told. Thus have things happened to man, and made him the strange social beast he is, the beast who tells and is told.

"God knows," answered Donald, the flames red on his face and hands, in that cave with midnight roaring darkly from its mouth. He sat still for a long time. At last he said: "I may as well tell you." Then his head drooped a little, and if I hadn't been able to see his eyeballs, I might have thought he had fallen asleep.

"We are all affected like that, Some more than others. One of these old songs can at times get the better of a person. I have noticed now and then how they get a grip on you." He turned his head and looked at me objectively. A piece of wood hissed intensely.

"It's natural enough," he continued. "That's what they're for." The hiss died down and a jet of black smoke volleyed toward me. He stared into the core of the heat.

"I don't remember its beginnings. It was like something before me, that I guided. Perhaps something I had heard from some old woman, heard once as a child, and forgotten. God knows. Sometimes you seem to get things out of the air. The past is always around somewhere. Anyway, I didn't deliberately make the tune. It grew in my head. I can remember trying bits of it on the fiddle and getting lost. But mostly it just kept me company. And there were a few words it fitted. The words added to themselves, without much meaning. Then one day it got an end. It finished itself off. I suddenly saw it was all there, so I deliberately thought of words for it. I had made a song. I was only about twenty at the time, or twenty-two. I couldn't make up all the words myself—didn't think of trying anyway. There was an old poem, very old, of which I knew bits. It had always seemed a bit queer to me. It fitted as if made for the tune. I had only to change it a very little, though I had to keep one line of words—the words that had formed in my own head and hadn't very much meaning. There were four verses—not enough for a song—not enough to tell a story. However, there it was, and no more could be done with it. It was finished for me."

He was speaking in his quiet way, without emphasis, and sometimes, you might think, with an arid humour, but that only made his attitude somehow more objective.

Now something like a bleak but friendly humour did touch him. "You see, if we make a song today up here, it must be a comic song, a long rigmarole taking someone off or making a cod of a place. That goes down fine. I enjoy it myself…. The deep things—must be left to the old songs.

"So naturally I kept the song I had made to myself. I wasn't going to have anyone making a cod of me. However, I had a sister. She was in Glasgow. She was older than me and married. She had always been very good to me—always. It was out of her first few earnings that she sent me an old fiddle—the one I still have. Before then, it was the mouth-organ or a chance at the boxie (the melodeon), or a scrape occasionally at hairy Alastair's fiddle. She had a grand ear and the loveliest voice I ever heard. She had always been good to me. A boy has to keep his independence. She knew that, too. In her own way, she could get me to do anything.

"Well, there wasn't much doing here. The herring fishing on the east coast had been bad for two years running. She wrote saying her husband could get me a job in his brewery, where he worked as a foreman on the malting side. I could come and have a trial at it, and if I didn't like it there would be no harm done.

"Her husband was a good chap, and everything went all right. I stayed with them for a time, but after that went into lodgings. You know how things can be. My sister was very Highland and clannish. Nothing could be good enough for me. He was, as I say, quite decent fellow—and is still, for all I know, but he took a sort of pick against me. Nothing that you need notice. But there it was. I suppose sometimes my sister got a little homesick for Arduan and may have moped a bit. But not much, I should say. Anyway, I played her the song, for I would take my fiddle round with me—the little one, her own child, liked it. We would play and sing for long enough. At last I had to sing the song. I never could sing. So I sang it over quietly. I can see her face yet, the air of surprise, and then the eyes—and the tears running down. The little one began to cry next. But it didn't last long. My sister snatched her up and the tears were swept away. She could be extraordinarily happy, my sister. Well, of course, there was no rest for me until she had got that song. She was foolish about it. I told her not to be a fool, and whatever she did, never to tell it was me that made it.

"You'll know the Highland Associations they have in Glasgow, with the grand annual concert, Gaelic songs, speeches and so on. My sister always had to sing at our county one. This song of mine was going to be her great surprise. But one night—some little time before the concert—she couldn't help trying it out on one or two of us. I mean, she sang it. She sang it in her full voice. It had a queer effect on me. I felt—the song—being born. Two nights before the concert, she died."

He sat there, staring into the glow, then slowly leaned forward and pushed a balk of tarry timber into the fire. Ashes and smoke leapt up, tongues of flame and a fierce crackling. Leaning away from a swither of smoke, I saw gleaming points in the back-end of the cave. They vanished instantly. The solid rock trembled under the pounding sea.

"I got another job," Donald went on in the same light, remorseless voice. "It was a job on the docks, heavy lifting work, but I was strong, and there was good money in it. I knew my way about now. Besides, I was thinking of getting married. There was a girl used to come round to see my sister on her night out. She was in domestic service—as my sister had been before her marriage. I got to know her night out. Perhaps, at first, my sister saw to that. This girl came from Melnavreckan. Callum, who wasn't for letting us go home by sea tonight, was her brother—is still, I suppose. Anyway, I have no doubt my sister thought she had got the very girl for me. She had, as it happened. She had been at the try-out of the song in my sister's house. And she was just as mad as my sister on the old music. She hadn't my sister's voice. Her voice was smaller—but it was very sweet. It was also very true, for she had won a gold medal with it at a competition. However, nothing would do now but she must get my song for the next annual concert. I wasn't on for this at all, and as the time drew near we had a few words about it. By now we were engaged to be married. In fact, the date was fixed—for about a fortnight after the concert. But though I stood out—she got round me. And she sang the song at the concert. I was in the audience and she came on, on to the platform. She was there, and she sang the song. They say that she never sang as she did that night. The cheering sort of started—then grew—till it was a storm. She was dressed in white. Two days before the date fixed for our wedding, she died."

He sat for a long time staring into the fire. His face, clean-shaven and full, was expressionless, a natural mask.

I could not move. I had felt the death coming, and when it came it was the sea falling on me. My body thinned to a shiver, rising up. I was becoming physically aware of the intense cold of the cave in my back when I heard him going out.

But I won't pretend to remember his third story. I think I lost bits of it in my own terrible preoccupation. He got a berth on a steamer going out East. He told me where she was going, told me everything about her. He was in no hurry and made each detail clear. There was something appallingly inexorable in this story-telling. He was not doing it in order to draw out the torture, to build up the simple, hellish climax. He was telling it as he had told the other stories, as anyone should tell a story, to make it clear. He had to remember not only carefully, but absolutely. The events were speaking through him—but he controlled them. And behind all that, behind everything this man himself, sitting there, in his unthinkable relationship to Morag and me, and to his song which Morag had sung.

There was a "twist" in this third story, a "surprise". O God! It happened in India. This time it was a man who got the song out of him. I could not begin to tell of the psychological intricacies, the beginnings, of the enmity that grew up between this man and himself. Yet as I write this, I see and understand it all. I actually see the scenery. Donald left his ship. "I felt I needed a change," was the way he put it. And when he added "I struck inland", I knew he was going into the hinterlands of his mind. He was going as far as any road could take him. But not in an obsessive way. He noticed everything, with the extraordinary clarity of a person who stands outside himself. He was *interested* in things about him. He told me of bullocks and ploughing, or rice and poverty. I had read about it all before, no doubt, but now I saw the people moving about. I think they mistook him for a holy man. He could not speak to them, not knowing their tongue, so he just did not speak. He sat in the shade, watching them, interested in what they were doing. He described minutely the face of the first old woman who brought him a bowl of rice. I could see his eyes on her, the quiet detachment of his regard. And detachment is something which the poor in that land understand.

Then again, he already knew about the poor, the poor folk of land and sea, and something of this may have come through, in understanding.

But I am not beginning on that. News of him inevitably got about. There is a man on a horse, the owner or manager of a tea estate. He comes riding along and looks at Donald. He looks him over from the saddle. Sees the beard on the young face. (Donald, remember, was still in his twenties.) Sees the eyes that never waver, and explodes : "What the bloody hell are you doing here?"

This was very interesting to Donald for two reasons: it completely explained the attitude to a white man who "goes native", who "lets down" the horseman of his own race; but the second reason was more interesting—for all his "sahib" accent, the man had a Highland voice.

And then Donald said something of which I am not too sure: "When I did not answer, he did not continue to curse me from the saddle: he dismounted. That made his Highland origin certain."

The man wanted to know if Donald was trying to be a "bloody fakir" or what, but in that early stage the conversation went on between their eyes. It came, however, to words, and when Donald answered quietly that he *would* take a job, the man looked at him long and piercingly—and laughed,

He got the job and was there over a year, Now that I think of it, how extraordinarily revealing would be an absolute account of that period from Donald's standpoint. No political theories, no intellectual assessments. Naked life in its relationships, its beliefs, its labour. Donald did not say he was happy, but I got that feeling, a feeling of his detachment that was yet alive and curious, that learned the language, that caught at the heart of the musical rhythm, that moved about sensibly, strongly, doing its job.

And all the time there was the "White" background. It would not, it could not, leave him alone. Particularly in the shape of "the boss"—a tormented man, whom Donald's detachment drew fatally. Things somewhere in the past had gone wrong with him, and he was having an affaire with a young married woman on a neighbouring estate. He drank at night, and now and then got Donald to drink with him. When he drank too much, instead of getting drunk, he got that awful white sobriety with its craze to penetrate mercilessly. He came at one, feeling for the last fibres of the mind. Perhaps ultimately and in essence he was destructive. Not that Donald said so. To Donald, he was simply like that there, at that time, and something in this was intimately known to him. Towards an end of a bout, there might be a challenging, annihilating intimacy between their minds. One night, goaded to sing "one of these old damned Highland songs", Donald sang his own song.

At such a moment, the man jeered at the Highlands more than at most things. Perhaps jeering at origins, his own origin, ultimately himself. Donald seemed to understand it all. And the song had an effect.

Then a conspiracy started, the sort of intricate business that suited the fellow's perverse mind. The woman was a southern English woman, but her people had had "a place" in the Highlands, had been tenants of a small sporting estate in the wild north-west. To ride forth with Donald and casually meet the woman and her husband was easy. Everyone of the whites within many days' travel had heard of Donald, of course. It was the sort of gossip titbit they could let go on. And the woman made it clear at once to Donald that she "adored" the Highlands.

"You should hear him sing," suggested his boss.

And that was the peg on which he hung his scheme.

There was a big social function in the offing, about a month ahead, complete with field sports, then songs, costume pieces and what not. Originality the keynote.

This woman was due to sing, because of her really fine English voice, and a song in Gaelic just suited her mood down to the ground. Italian or French might have been a bit arty. But in Gaelic—she was entitled to that! And it gave the distinction of her own social origins with its Highland estate, its "place for the season". She could say: "Darling, I have often heard the natives sing these songs." And in truth she had.

Donald rode over to teach her the music and the Gaelic sounds. All perfectly straightforward. Secretly he carried his boss's letters and brought back hers.

Why did he do this, help this rotten intrigue? He admitted he liked the girl—the married woman—and thought her husband a simple, decent fellow, not exciting, but reliably sound.

I don't know. Was he trying to test the song? To rid his own mind? Had he really reached the stage where he didn't care, yet was interested, curious? Or was he moved in some fatal, irrational way, himself against his boss?

As I say, I don't know. Two nights before the show, they were having a final bout. It was then his boss told Donald of the plan that he, Donald, had helped so admirably to mature. Donald was to stay on and run the estate, after his boss had cleared out with the woman. The authority, in writing, was pushed across the table to Donald. Two nights thereafter, Donald would be in sole charge.

Well, the affair came off. First, the field sports. Then the concert party. She did her piece; she sang Donald's song. She was excited a bit, and in her effort at restraint showed too much feeling. The applause was of the restrained kind that made this clear. She hadn't quite achieved the air of being superior to the native piece. The song had "got" her. Perhaps no wonder, because "the boss" hadn't turned up, and by this time she may have burnt a boat or two. Anyway, his absence had made things a bit awkward all round, for he was on the field committee, and there had been subdued curses from some of the men. On a pony he was a star performer.

"I had been watching for him all day," said Donald to me; then, without the slightest change in tone, continued, "and I was still watching for him. There was a little disturbance behind, and some of my own boys came up to me in the hall. They had found him with a broken neck. His horse had come down and thrown him. I had to destroy the beast."

In the silence his eyes broke their stare and moved over the fire. Unhurriedly, he stuck his left leg out, the toe flexing like a footballer's as it caught the, end of a log and persuaded it unerringly into the heart of the fire. I leaned back from the crackling thrust of flame and smoke and saw the gleaming points again—I was going to say in the wall, but it wasn't a wall, it was a blackness, and there was no face.

He must have seen my expression, for he followed my look. The gleaming eyes vanished. Now carried beyond myself and rooted like a stone, I yelled 'Eyes, Eyes' and let go. The stone exploded in the blackness.

Donald's body slowly swayed and held. Then he said: "They're not living eyes." Swaying back, I saw two glittering points. I could not stop my muscles from trembling. I was desperately cold. I drank the whisky like water and was violently sick. Then I really thought I was going to die. I did experience absolutely, for a little time, the death coldness. But death was not meant for me.

I won't tell of his unobtrusive kindness to me, of the rest of the night; but one final question I did ask. He answered that he had never heard the song again.

Neither of us referred to Morag and her singing of the song. Why? It is one of the innumerable questions I ask myself. Donald must have known I would ask myself. Could he not bring himself to talk of it? Had he had a horrible premonition, that time he had walked out? Was he warning me—in order to save Morag?

Morag, of course, had been the little one, his sister's child, in Glasgow. Now, at last, I understood what was between them. I understood it all.

But I could not, in the following days or later, mention it to her. How could I, without going too far into that death region? She had a job as a typist in a big drapery store here in Glasgow. She has, of course, given it up, because in three days we are going to be married.

You will not be so crass, I hope, as to imagine I have not thought all this out, have not penetrated the more appalling implications of superstition to their miserable core. Of course I know that the fatality attending the singing of the song was a matter of sheer coincidence. I even took steps to make certain of it. For example, Donald's own girl, who had died two days before their wedding, had caught a chill through her thin white dress in the shivering ante-room to the concert platform. The chill had "fastened on her lungs".

Coincidence. Chance…. We use the words with an appalling, an idiotic complacency. They drive me at this moment to a cold fury. The gambler gets a hunch, he stakes on this colour or that, this number or the other. The ball stops at his colour, his number. He breaks the bank. Pure chance, of course. Quite! Quite! But it *happens!*

I feel exhausted. This intolerable business of writing has drained me. I had hoped it would. I am going to stretch myself in the guest's bedroom.

Love's Dialectic

She walked up the bank of the river trying to have it out with herself. Would she make a stand and risk everything, or would she continue to slide into a relationship…. It was difficult to think clearly and connectedly because if she took a stand she might lose him, and at the very thought of that her flesh melted inwards blotting the mind out.

Yet every time she rose again and breasted the question it became a little easier to hold on to it, particularly because now at the back of her mind was the large statement she had read in that letter this morning; not that it had been a long statement, but it seemed large now, like a cloud of light behind her mind, and in this light was encouragement, an aristocratic movement, a high sanction.

This business of censoring letters was a very curious one: the private letters of the public, of the ordinary people and the extraordinary. She had never before realised so clearly the existence of two worlds. She had thought that her own inner world, the secretive world of weakness and desires, the place that lay, intimate and lonely, behind all discussion of sex and morals and politics, was somehow peculiar to herself. Her companions and those she met socially would discuss any conceivable topic sensibly, flagrantly, but always with a bright engaging amusement. She enjoyed the fun, and could toss back words like "complex", "repression", and even "dialectical" with the proper dismissive skill. In this pastime, this certainty of knowledge, her own secretive world would be forgotten, and if a word, an inflection, reminded her of it, it hung far inward like a dark round nut. No more than that. An indigestible core Until the time came when, alone, she felt an almost horrible power coming out from it that crept through the muscles of her legs, through her chest, leaving her tremulous and weak and fearful.

The two worlds. The revelation of the censor's office had disclosed the surprising fact that they co-existed everywhere. Like light and darkness. Two planes: the one visible, the other hidden. At first the girls (with ancient ones among them) had great fun over some of the letters. Badly worded, misspelt love epistles of an extremely "juicy" nature; heart-broken appeals of a young swain darkly hinting at self-destruction; urgent implorings of a young female who had been "caught". There was no end to them. A dark turbulent river, an underground river, with peep-hole cracks for the censor girls. Sometimes a letter would be passed under a desk, guaranteed to provide an extra chuckle. Two of the girls got sacked for discussing outside such privately acquired information. Reiteration staled for them somewhat these babblings and idiocies, these dreadful giveaways, these shameless cravings. How girls and fellows could put such stuff in black and white at times quite beat the censor girls. Some of the writers obviously not young at all—probably quite old, over forty—really pretty disgusting. And they stirred their hot forenoon cups.

Light and darkness. Thesis and antithesis. And it did really appear as if you could not apply any dialectical process to them. More light made the darkness deeper. Could you synthesise an object and its shadow? The brighter the sun, the more pronounced the shadow. In matter, in physical fact. Two worlds. Two planes that, however they tilted, kept parallel. She tried to use such engaging ideas in talk, but not very successfully. One had always to be pretty careful of a personal give-away. Eyes would look as much as to say: What's got repressed now? Is this the dodge of staging an argument to cover—something? Eyes looking *from that other plane*, inquisitive, with an expectancy, a greed, mockingly veiled in good nature.

And her trouble was rather desperate. For she loved her young man as shamelessly as any girl in a letter passed under a desk, and when the letter was ungrammatical and misspelt and unpunctuated, when it achieved in this way the very height of the turbulent and grotesque, did it most closely approximate to a correct expression of her own condition. She realised this, in the moment of the reading, with a mixture of understanding and anguish and shame. He had become for her a complete obsession.

Nor was it any good saying to herself that this was sex rampant. For even if it was, that in no way affected the fact as an experience. For the first time she saw that you could not diminish a natural force by putting a label on it. In any case, she knew with complete certainty that this obsessive emotion was something very different from any sex stirrings she had ever had before. She could not even think of him in that direct way. She could only see his face, the slight wave in his brown hair, the movement of his hands, and the expression of his eyes. She felt a craving, a hunger for these features. She wanted to be near them, looking slightly up at them, and the thought of touching them touched the edge of a happiness like a lovely bright delirium.

But he was cool, with the clean coolness that might have come out of the river beside her, out of its clear water; dressed neatly, with a cool blue stripe in his tie, he sauntered on, the glint of the stream in his eyes. His features were never dull or set in repose. They were always alive, with a smile that sometimes paused just before it came to the surface, paused and contemplated with a flick of the eyelid, with a faint humoured irony, then deepened and was set in motion and passed away as he glanced quickly away, or else broke into a pleasant laugh while he said something or other that sometimes she could not quite follow but that always penetrated to the quick.

He was cruel. Often he was deliberately cruel. She knew that. She was so alive to his most trivial expression, physical or verbal, that she could feel the satisfaction he got out of hurting her. But if she tried to act up independently, saying "That was a sly one!" he laughed, and if she went on the only other tack, that of hurt silence, he would turn his amusement into a game, take her arm, chivvy her forward, and ask : "You're not hurt, are you?" and when she answered: "I am!" his apparent astonishment broke into a chuckle of delight.

There were times when he was such a complete enigma that she was frightened to introduce any subject of talk, frightened even to speak, lest she say the wrong thing. This could be extremely distressing because at that moment she lost all faith in herself, even in her instincts, and inwardly went blank, a nonentity. All she could do then was to hang on, passive, until the enigmatic state faded in the quick shift of his mood or interest.

But however she waited, however passive or silent, she never got hold of him, not even when they kissed, for then he was quite silent, void of all endearments, and the cruelty of his nature she felt in the pressure and sting of his teeth.

Yet always she was aware, in terms of the inner woman-awareness that could so surely assess her own obsession, that never at any time was he an enigma to her. Quite simply and certainly she knew that he acted as he did because she did not satisfy him. To say that he had a sadistic streak explained nothing. In her blood she knew that the pleasure he got out of hurting her was a wry thwarted pleasure. There was no final satisfaction in it for him. He was attracted. He couldn't leave off. If he did not find anyone who could assuage him better, he might stick to her. The more she gave in, the more pliant and passive she was, the less she would satisfy him. And her obsession drove her more and more towards this pliancy and passivity, towards anything that kept him near her.

Blind, but she could not help it. She dared not. To stand up for herself—how at this hour could she do so but primally and horribly?—would be to lose him, to stage a last scene, where he would not turn from her, oh no, he would act kindness, laugh her out of her mood, piercing her with his self-protective lightness to the quick, the glint in his eyes growing harder and the core of his mind growing harder, rallying her while he withdrew from her, evading unpleasantness, being unusually pleasant and tender, insincerely tender—for the last time.

She could not. It was no use. She would go where she wasn't wanted. Deeper and deeper she would sink.

Clearly there was no limit to what a woman would do when she was utterly obsessed. No shamelessness went too far. In swift moments of upsurgence, this roused hate. She hated him as the instrument of shame in sudden writhings, in appalling spasms, inducing a tremulous nausea near to vomit, bringing a clammy death-dew to her forehead, yet all the time knowing that she would not break the cool bright stalk of his body, would not obliterate his eyes, even were the power to do so, now, at this intensest moment, put in her hands; but, on the contrary, that, conscious of her power, she would crawl to him.

She was the victim of extraordinary fantasies of this kind, for she did not think her thoughts so much as see them take human shape, her shape and his. After an hour's tossing in her bed, particularly if she awoke to it, say about two or three in the morning, the figures became thick with life, and her own was then sometimes endowed with the magical power of self expression, of getting him to see and understand those deeps in her, that, in daylight meeting, she could never disclose; yet from that culmination of superb illusion, while the golden bridge was still spanning the chasm, she would turn over and sink her teeth in the pillow, crying: "If only! Oh, if only!"

She drew her eyes from the river to her watch. She would be five minutes late. She never risked being more and spent a lot of time before her actual departure calculating the matter. That he was never late, that he was on the contrary always careful to be early, did not deceive her. He was of the kind that would never hurt her in *that* way for worlds. Oh, she knew him. When she rounded the next bend, she would find him leaning over the wall, this side of a clump of wild briar, looking into the stream.

She rounded the bend and there he was, his elbows on the wall, which was breast high, looking into the stream. She knew, by a slight movement of his head, that he had seen her, but he kept on looking into the stream. She was too far away for him to sustain without some discomfort an interest that would grow awkward over too long an approach. She knew it as she knew the flavour of a berry. Her knees weakened. The assurance she had had, the new high assurance which had come upon her this morning out of a letter in so strange, so fantastic a manner, began to sink away.

But she kept her head up on the memory of it, though for that matter she always did keep her head up. And she dressed as neatly as he. That she was bright in movement and manner and had a rather subtle sense of style, he had told her, for he would talk about anything and liked to give the personal—it could be an amusing game—an impersonal edge.

So they met, hailing each other cheerfully.

"You are looking rather bright!"

"Am I?" She nearly laughed. "It is pleasant to get away from that office." She had hardly paused as they met. They were walking on. "Oh, I like this—the grass and the trees, and that great bank of broom. Gorgeous, isn't it?"

"And your spirits. What's happened?" he asked.

"Why? Amn't I usually?"

"Sometimes."

And then the accursed little silence, breaking in upon her. But no fear! She was not losing her gaiety, her high indifference. And all at once she heard her voice, high and laughing. It was beginning to tell him about the letter! Out of sheer nervousness, her voice was betraying her. Appalled, she stopped abruptly, smiling, her face suffused, her eyes brilliant.

"Go on," he said. "What was it?"

She remained silent, glancing at trees and golden bank. "You shouldn't have started, if you're not going on. That's not fair. Out with it!"

"No." She shook her head definitely.

"Oh, come on!" He took her arm and squeezed it, helping her along, companionable, amused.

"I couldn't."

"Why? Feel you shouldn't divulge the public secrets entrusted to your charge?"

"Yes," she answered firmly.

"But," he said, "but—you have told me one or two before." Her face drew taut and stormy-looking, feeling the touch, as if they were probing fingers, of his eyes.

"Sorry," he said, squeezing her arm and letting it go. "That wasn't fair."

The awful paralysing dumbness descended upon her. He remained silent.

"It wasn't much anyway," she said. "There was no secret. It was not that." She was talking at random.

"No?"

"No."

"All right. Don't tell me if you don't want to. I don't mind. Really."

"I didn't mean to be unfair; to start—and break off."

"Please don't worry about it. It's nothing."

"Thank you," she said. "You sometimes make me feel mean."

"Which is not just a generous thing to say, is it?"

"It's not what you say; it's—it's——"

"Yes?"

But she was dumb. Thought got so tremulous that it would not form.

"Do tell me," he pressed her.

Dumb and stupid.

"You always do flatter me," he went on gaily, "by your delicate implications that I should understand your silences. How's that?"

"Very clever," she said.

He laughed.

This gave her heart. She had been looking over the golden bank at the bright sky in the west; at the enlargement of light wherein she had seen aristocratic movement. The memory of it came back with a slight access of assurance, and all at once she said, with a feeling now of daring rather than of self-betrayal: "He was clever, too, the man in the letter, but in a different way."

This seemed to delight him. "How so?"

But that was the very sort of question, short and penetrating, that, when she was moved, blinded her. However, she now had something to tell, a story, and she hung on to it. "It mightn't be good for your morals," she said, "if I told you."

He threw his head up and swayed on his feet, so delighted he was. He was taking no denial now, not on your life. And before she knew what was happening there was her voice, quite loud, inclined to hesitate, to break, laughing, her face flushed.

She did not know who the man was, she began, but he was very educated and full of fun. He was writing to a woman and her husband and said the most atrocious things very cleverly.

You could see his sly smile, hear him laugh. They must have been telling him that his letters were censored, for this had set him off on the censorship. He said that their mutual friend, Captain Somebody-or-other, had been in the other night and was still interested in literature, seriously. He had been reading, in the original, some old French court memoirs, had the Captain. And very disgusted he was over the way these memoirs—written obviously by the most brilliant men of the period—were concerned altogether with the most trivial gossip and intrigue and above all with sex. You wouldn't believe it, said the Captain. You wouldn't credit it. Do you know, asked the Captain, what these women, these society women, would do? They would undress before their butlers—actually undress before their butlers—as if they were articles of furniture. Well, I mean to say!

She choked. He rolled away, head up, laughing. She was excited all over, but intensely dismayed. What had seemed to her before full of the light of freedom, of aristocratic movement, now, in her re-telling, seemed only a blue story.

"Superb!" he cried.

She waited, dumb, slightly sick, smiling, head up, eyes front.

"I had no idea," he said, babbling on, "forgive me, that your wit could be so searching. But as an attitude to the censorship, as a criticism of it, as—as—a putting of it in its proper place, by God it's superb! Articles of furniture!" He staggered away again. "Less than articles of furniture! For at least the butler did not pry. Lord, I say, isn't there something finally vile in the act of censorship! Prying, not upon the body, which can stand it, which is there to be seen—but into the deeps of the secret individual mind. Watching that, waiting for it as for a treacherous snake, ready to hit it. Vile! Oh, vile!"

She began to breathe again.

He was quite excited, extremely alert, his language more free than she had ever known it, accepting her. He was moved by the whole affair, having obviously seen nothing blue in it at all. Then she felt his eyes coming at her sideways, in a subtle new appraisal.

"Do you smell the broom?" he cried, throwing now his glance in front, towards the short-cropped narrow green alleyways, hidden and scent-laden, between the bushes. "Come on, let us sit down!"

She slowly came to a pause, swallowed, and said, "No, I'm sorry. I must go back."

He swung round and stood still as if he had been struck.

"I have to go out tonight," she explained.

He was looking right into her, searching for the meaning, for the meaning of the possible lie.

She looked at her watch. "I must go." Then she looked up for a moment right at his eyes, with the uncertain but pleasant smile that apparently appreciated his surprise.

"You never said you were going out."

"I didn't know last night. I must."

"Must you?"

"I'm afraid I must. In fact," she added, looking at her watch again, "it's high time I was off."

"Oh, really? That's a pity."

"Yes. I must go." She was swaying, smiling. She backed away a pace. Her head tilted and she gave him a brilliant glance. "Please, you needn't come. But—I must go. Good-bye." She swayed round, and was off, but at a few paces half-turned, still going, and gave him a small charming salute, swaying downward as she did so, like a branch of a tree, before her head rose upward and went steadily on.

During all this play, he never moved. He still stood looking after her.

She felt him like a pale outraged statue at the back of her mind; the pallor and the glint. How all her various bits kept together, how her feet kept moving on, she did not know. She had an extreme terror, all through her body, that he would come after her; and when she knew that he was not coming after her, that he was standing still, that he would never come after her, the terror rose up into her head.

By the time she got round the bend her legs were getting out of control, but she managed to reach a wooden seat, conveniently placed for visitors by the riverside. She had hardly been sitting a minute, however, when the pale statue came alive in her mind, striding after her. At any moment it might come round the bend.

From this spectre she got up and fled, and through streets that crossed and wound like the prisoning walls in a maze ultimately got to her lodging, to her bedroom. She threw herself upon her bed, the nightmare flight quivering in her relaxed flesh.

But better that scene than a primal, horrible mess. Better strewn on her bed than strewn on the ground at his feet. She moaned. She would have preferred the mess; preferred the scene, the mess, the end—particularly the end, emptied out, finished, the end. That little bit of silly school-girl acting! She groaned and bit the pillow.

After a time, she came off the bed, feeling more empty than any spectre. She moved slowly; stood at the window. The shades of night are falling, she thought. A smile twisted her pale features as she faced into her room again, seeing it as a strange place, each article of furniture very still, waiting for something to happen. She saw the smooth, hearkening, waiting attitude, characteristic of each piece. She thought: I will look in on Bess's full-moon party. She had said to Bess she was sorry she couldn't go because she had a previous engagement. Bess had looked at her and said: "I am sorry I can't ask you to bring him, seeing it's Ladies."

She took off her jacket and the back of the chair received it. She took off her jumper and laid it across the small reading table. The wooden rail of the bed accepted her skirt like an extended arm. The wardrobe waited her pleasure, creaking a trifle with honourable age and long service as she put forth the necessary effort to open its door. As she took the dress-hanger from its hook and turned towards the tweeds which she had but just removed from her person, she observed the commode. "I regret," she said with calm restraint, in the grand manner, "that I have nothing for you meanwhile."

Whereupon her nostrils closed against a sound that started well down behind them. The sound mounted against great pressure. As it blasted its way through with explosive snort she flung herself face down on the bed.

Hysteria is at first a wild pleasurable madness. It's dark turbulent stream bursts all dams, and as the wreckage is swept forward, bits of it, like arms and legs, rise up and swing over, get fixed for convulsive moments, tremble, and break loose again.

The bed shook under her smothered laughter. Everything was breaking loose. There was no longer any hold anywhere. She couldn't stop. Fear saved itself from the stream by mounting like a monkey into her brain. Pain clung to the banks of her body, its long hands contorting and gripping. Her forehead went bone-cold under a spray of icy spume. After a long time she came into a side eddy, and with the weak fingers of a will that in some miraculous way had not got drowned she held on to herself, floating upon exhaustion; then she let go even so slender a hold and would have fallen asleep had she not hiccupped.

She examined the wreckage of her face in the mirror, lighting two candles to supplement the bulb in the middle of the ceiling. She felt extremely weak and wretched, but the hiccups had not developed, so she was able to bear up before the furniture, and particularly before the two handsome silver-backed brushes which she had inherited along with fifty pounds from her aunt. They were chased, and bore her initials because they were also her aunt's.

Her eyes were the worst, though luckily they never really swole and got red. She murmured with a manner: "Thesis: laughter; antithesis: sobs; synthesis: hysteria." But the slight jest was lost on her aunt. It was lost on herself. Could she face them? Had she the strength to go? Her eyes narrowed. Her face drew taut. She would go, she decided with aristocratic indifference, and refused to haggle. The furniture, impressed, remained suavely silent as she made herself up with languid care. The looking-glass, holding the candles apart, complimented her in bright-eyed silence.

Bess had a real cocktail-shaker and had bought real gin. She welcomed her unexpected guest in a loud cheerful voice.

"What went wrong, Anne?"

"Oh, nothing," said Anne, looking around. "The thought of you shaking that old shaker was too much for me."

"My child!" exclaimed Bess. "Good God, he's not the sort that takes you for a walk?" And she shook vigorously and with concern.

They were simple nice women, offhand and friendly.

After her drink, Anne had some tea and began to revive, feeling at once both very much awake and languid, quite a pleasant state, which left her with assurance and no desire to shine, only a readiness to acknowledge the chance wit of another. This slow motion of her subtle sense of style brought it out rather charmingly, and occasionally a pair of eyes discreetly ran up and down her.

But her turn came when, feeling like a queenly prisoner being led to execution, she told of the French court, the ladies, and the butlers who were furniture.

There was hubbub then. Anne sat silent and saw them seeing themselves in the censor's office as something less than furniture, something prying and low, if not positively evil. They said things then that should have made tingle the ears of the man who undressed his thought before them. But one girl, a regular tomboy, said, "He's quite right. Woman's emancipation—so that she may become a typist to the boss, if nothing less—or more! No, girls; woman's place is the home. Always was and always will be. For why? Because there she rules——'

"Like Britannia—on a penny," interrupted Bess.

They would have grown sick with laughter but for the natural tendency of woman to consider personal matters as still important.

By the time the last girl said cheero, Anne had not far to go. The full moon shone down on the deserted street, on a city in a stony dream. No other light but the light of the moon as she walked the sky, dark-blue mantle thrown off her shoulders, naked, with aristocratic mien, serene and lovely.

At the corner she all but ran into him, but now he was more astonished than she, for, after all, what had he been mooning about her abode for at this unconscionable hour? She felt this and he knew it. So it was no time for excuses that wouldn't deceive a fly.

"So you thought you would treat me as your butler?" he said.

"No," she answered in a voice gentle as the serene moon; "only as a piece of furniture."

"Ha! ha! ha!" he said, but harshly, not at all in his usual manner. Fortunately he tilted up his head or his breath might have blown her over.

Often she had wished that God had endowed her with a modicum of wit. But she was beyond any such desire now, lost in the miracle of her still upright body. "You are like a wolf baying the moon," she said.

From her gentle lips the words came upon him in weird tribute, arresting act and thought.

"Come," he decided masterfully, "let us go for a walk." But she shook her head. "No?"

"I'm tired," she answered simply.

He looked at her face which reflected the moon.

"Is that the only reason?"

She nodded.

"Tomorrow night?"

"Yes."

He gazed at her for so long that she knew at last she was going to fall. In silence he lifted her hand, kissed it like a courtier, turned, and walked away.

The furniture was obviously delighted to see her. Sit here! said the chair. Here! said the bed. "I can talk to him!" she said to herself. "I can talk to him! I shall," she said, as if remembering a marvellous line of poetry, "always be able to talk to him." Pure magic. The bed sighed as she sat on it and stared past the wardrobe which did not intrude. She saw his face as it stooped, and she murmured: "I love him utterly, madly. I adore him." She felt somnambulant, walking in a new world, made out of the union of the old night world and old day world. A new world. "Synthesis!" came a faint ironic breath to seal the cell of honey and keep it from spilling over. Thesis antithesis…dialectic. Toys, male toys, under eyebrows and earnest male faces, earnest and adorable creatures. She dared hardly think about him. She thought about him in a wave and threw herself on the bed and wept, she was so deliriously happy.

Blaeberries

He was thinning turnips when she passed along the sheep-path that ran between the fael dike at the bottom of the field and the edge of the cliffs. Thus from her waist to her uncovered head her desirability was cut like a cameo against the grey floor of the sea, though he did not lift his head to look. By the time the path had taken her out of sight, he had hoed ten yards without stopping his hoe a moment. When she had disappeared altogether he did look up—to find the thin dark veil that her passing had left on the face of the sea. When his head drooped again and he considered the last ten yards of his work, his lips tightened. The mathematical precision of it was beyond all praise.

In the next ten yards, however, his hoe stumbled once. A further twenty yards, and he found his muscles uncertain and jumpy, as though suffering from reaction after strain. By the time he came to the end of the long row, he was fumbling in and out the green line like a beginner. He put in the next half-hour doggedly, and then it was six o'clock.

Down by the cliff-heads at night he sat, looking on the grey floor that rose so steeply to the horizon. A curlew passed under the stars, fluting forlornly. A peewit swung up from the earth with a swift vehemence, its silken wings and two-winged cry roused in persistent protest. The long tremulous calling of the curlew belongs to the impersonal reaches between earth and star, and its forlorn wave dies out into infinite space. The peewit's cry is an insistent, passionate cry, anxious, of the earth.

In his listening to the echoes of the curlew's call, his lips tightened. Something wild, clean, unearthly, in that call. For her image was like the peewit's cry in that it had the same vibrant colour to it and urgency—yet not like it at all in the way of earthly care and anxiety. Her earthliness was provoking and red-lipped and untasted, like wine and honey breathed upon; yet like nothing earthly either because of that veiled light in the eyes with its understandings, its reticences, its inscrutabilities.

For an hour the logical working of his mind was beyond all praise. No image of her could intrude wholly. Below, the grey sea washing the feet of the rocks, washing the eternal grey feet; overhead, the curlew calling to the utmost reach of the night; off the sea, the wind cooling his face, set so stonily to horizons. His body was a cool external shiver—a cool clean sheath. That for the first hour.

In the second hour his mind stumbled once, so that she entered by a simple trick. She became a figure in desert places; she became a night-wrapped figure of lost dim moorland places; loose-haired, slim-swaying, like a nymph or prophetess. The loneliness in him cried out and strove towards her loneliness; strove vehemently; but as he yet caught up with her and stretched out his hand, she turned—and lo! the dimness of mystery about her face was instantly changed to the old light, and her smile, gleaming critically from slanting eyes, stopped him more effectively than would any sword. The trick of it went through him in a hot flush, so that all his strength was turned to water and shamefacedness.… His body stirred there on the cliff head and his heel ground an unconscious oath into the soft turf, while his soul cried upon the night words to which there was no more meaning than to the crying of the curlew.

From the third hour she possessed him wholly, so that curlew and peewit and sea and cliff were but the stage machinery against her playing. She gave him the mystical wine and honey, and she gave him the image of red lips like yielding ripe fruit. And he drank and filled himself, a debauchery of shadows and transparencies and treacheries, till, on a moment, his body cried urgently for substance and his mouth for crushing resistances. His eyes rose flashing—to the nothingness of the grey sea.

His head drooped between his knees, and the cool wind came from the sea, passing round him and over him and swaying gently the tall grasses—a night-expanse of heedless, passionless, immemorial things, in which his doubled-up body might easily pass for a grey boulder.

The turnips swelled to a plump girth, the year waxed mellow and luscious. He came upon her of a sudden on an evening of small rain like a mist. It was the rain that draws out and holds fragrance of flower and fruit and gives to the bloom of a cheek the petal smoothness of a rose. She was eating blaeberries.

Her lips were stained purple, her fingers were stained purple, and there were purple stains here and there on her face besides—a ripe black purple. Tiny raindrops clung to strands of her hair, a wild diffusion of light and colour played on her features, and concentrated light and colour flashed in her eyes.

He stood stuck fast, with no power in him to move any way at all. The skin on his face was drawn taut and pale, and his eyes were on her like the eyes of a trapped animal. The first sign of the breathless intensity of his living was a slight quivering at the nostrils; but by that time she had taken in the knowledge of many things.

Plainly they could not stand like that for ever. She smiles, with an exquisite diffidence, and holds out a hand, in the palm of which lies a little heap of berries. He stumbles foolishly among the blaeberry bushes, and as he comes by the hand, stretches out fingers to partake. Whereupon the incalculable impulse which no woman can command runs swiftly down her arm and jerks her hand upwards above his hand—leaving the berries poised daringly midway between his groping fist and his mouth. His mouth! His heart drums in his ears as his head stoops to the stained fingers and the berries. But it is not for nothing that these same fingers—and lips—are stained, with the small rain a fragrant moistening of the petals; not for nothing that instead of picking and eating single berry by single berry, she gathers a whole handful over against one crushing, ecstatic mouthful. While yet his lips are three inches from her palm and opening in expectancy, a second tremor passes along her arm, a wild, mad impulse this, excited by she knows not what of uncertainties and expectancies; yet knowing, too even to the verge of tiptoe hysteria over man's unbearable slownesses.

And in an instant through the three inches she has smashed hand and berries full against his mouth; and there and then in the blaeberry patch and in the small rain, she is swept off her tiptoes and the unbearable agony of expectancy is crushed like the berries.

The Poster

For a considerable time, Megan had been bored and restless. Not that she found in this any cause for self-pity, for she had the brains to know that most smart-set gaiety was an effort to dodge such a condition. In her case, however, the boredom was sickening into the next horrid stage, a haunting sense of futility. The normal cure is to recognise that life is real, life is earnest, and then to set about "getting an interest" and doing something. But she knew she had no gift for salvation that way. The art world, which has to look at spiritual states with business eyes, refused her any uplifting illusion of the kind. So she entered on the new arid realm with the amused manner of the fatal adventurer. And like all such adventurers who go far enough, she one night got her vision.

It happened in the studio of Oliver Greene (called Orlando, after his Italian mother). The clear light of the revelation had a chill that thrilled her. It was as if all in a moment the sense of futility, reaching its limit, dissolved out the last personal humour in her and left her eyes staring at the secret motives, desires, and vanities of everyone around her. Her detachment became so inhumanly complete that it was clairvoyant and quite drained of emotion. She had never experienced anything of the sort before. For a few seconds she stared so fixedly that her eyes dilated and the upper lids pushed back under their dark arches.

When she became aware of Orlando's teasing by her left shoulder, she turned and looked at him. Before her gaze, he actually flushed—or darkened, for he was very dark. Then her eyes withdrew, conscious now but cool as sea water, her lashes drooped—till she lifted them again with her glass and smiled, rather privately, and drank.

"Superb!" said Orlando.

Her teeth came gleaming from her drink and again she looked across the studio at the little group that had precipitated this state of abnormal insight. Elsa was still attacking Wilson Smith with extravagant vivacity around a large-eyed earnestness. And Wilson Smith was enjoying it in a shy, delighted way. He was a slim, athletic fellow, with fair hair and keen grey eyes; nothing bluff or rude about him, no particular expression of sincerity and integrity, none, in fact, of the usual signs to indicate the coming artist, the new force. Yet clearly as if it were being drawn in charcoal on the pale wall, Megan apprehended the construction of the room about him. In the most delicate ways (as, for example, by the differing manner in which every other artist paid him no particular attention), she perceived exactly the extent of his disturbing power. Elsa's mobile shoulders and arms were at last closing in like fluttering wings about her child-blue eyes, until up went a hand and caught the top button of his jacket and tugged it: "But you avoid the issue. Why? Why? Why?"

Orlando had "officially intimated" the meeting in his studio to discuss "the question of art in industry with special reference to the poster." The terms of the invitation had been a lively joke in themselves. Yet there was this in it, that Orlando had been fortunate enough to land a poster series in connection with Somerset Cream, which had proved very lucrative to the Dairy Combine if not markedly so to Orlando, who had got no more than his few guineas per poster as initially commissioned and agreed. He had, however, got considerable publicity. With continued fortune his price might rise. It was a subject of some importance in view of the normal artist's ignorance of the inner workings of the business world. Yet its real importance lay in the unvoiced problem of the continuance of artistic self-respect, for no man is so sensitive to true caste as the true artist. The party was going splendidly, and Wilson Smith had come down on the side of the poster.

To Megan, Orlando repeated Elsa's "Why?" with the smiling intimacy that implied they both knew the real nature of Elsa's personal art. But Megan promptly and solemnly answered: "Because he doesn't know."

"Doesn't know what?"

"Anything about industry."

"But he doesn't need to. I don't, for example."

She looked at him. "That's different."

His laugh merely focussed the flash of his searching eyes. Her coolness was very fascinating. He suggested as much. She nodded; then drew back apace, and seemed to withdraw a mile.

She knew now that he had got her to come for his own business purposes. And here he was genuinely moved! With a smile, slight enough to be seductive, she turned away and sauntered over to the little group about Wilson Smith.

Smith was not talking ordinary sense. He was rearing a gay artifice on what was to him the obvious foundation of industry's need of art. No call to be solemn about it! In fact, any suggestion of "vital force" in him seemed completely lacking.

There was a subtlety in this that appealed to Megan. For she saw that there was no pose in the inconsequential chatter. He genuinely loved something wanton in the gaiety, and it flickered and flashed in gleams that were like reflections from some hidden polished surface. If there was anything of the real weakling in him, she saw it would, with a terrible secret intensity, merely hold the polished steel until it snapped.

She became aware of his eyes and said: "All the same, you're wrong."

Elsa, feeling the shift in interest, at once turned on Megan, whose unconsciously enigmatic smile she regarded a moment before solemnly announcing the Mona Lisa. There was enough malice in her innocent manner to cause a burst of laughter. But that first moment's secret communion was just sufficient to bring Smith to Megan's side as the party was breaking up. "I think I go your way."

"Then I think you are going a considerable distance."

He laughed, delighted. Orlando, the host, darkened and kept his eyes on her. She thanked him ever so much for so lovely an evening, and withdrew her eyes slowly.

On the pavement she said to Smith: "But I thought your studio was near here."

"So it is," he answered. "Would you like to see it?"

"You didn't know my home was miles away?"

"I suspected it. But there's a telephone box near my door."

"Why did you suspect it?"

"Suspect that you did not belong here? Well, it is obvious."

"Have I the Philistine manner?"

"Yes. Shall we walk along?"

But though they chatted with animation as they went, the real irresponsibility was gone, as if somehow it had been left behind with the lights in Orlando's circus. By the time he produced his key, she was actually reluctant to enter. The old mood of tiredness rose up against her, rose into her throat. That he should be crass enough to offer to explain what "Philistine" meant to him almost hurt her. Her laugh became nervous. But she had to see the inside of his studio, and when the light went on, she looked around her with slow deliberation.

"You have all the Philistine virtues, I see," she said so contemplatively that he laughed abruptly. But she merely nodded thoughtfully to herself. She had clearly found what she had expected. And that was that. She smiled and thanked him.

"Oh, but you can't go! Not you! Not yet!" He pushed a chair towards her.

She looked at him. "You were so sure about art in industry."

"Well?"

"Nothing much, except that you don't know the real factors." She opened her bag.

"What are they?"

She shrugged. "Have you another penny? I must phone." And go she would, though the nervousness had now completely left her and she felt curiously at ease.

Very well, if she must go, she must, he said all at once, and departed to get a taxi. She smiled to herself as she stood alone surrounded by his canvases. He would beg nothing of anyone! Some remote humour in her eyes drew a questioning flash from him as he entered.

"Prepared to bet on your knowledge of art in industry?" she asked.

He eyed her deliberately for a moment, then his expression quickened like a boy's. "If you don't make it more than five bob."

This was friendly, for they all knew he sold little and must live on less. "Done!" she said.

He was more interested now than ever, but she saw that his nice manners would not let him ask her point blank who she was. By the open taxi door she turned and, as if he had spoken his secret thought aloud, answered: "I know you can ask Orlando who I am—but——" and shrugged very slightly. The taxi was some distance away before it occurred to him to laugh.

* * * * * *

The following morning Megan coolly walked past the small army of clerks and typists of Transport Limited, came to the PRIVATE door of Mr James Powell, and without waiting for an answer to her knock, entered. Having closed the door, she stood still, unconsciously watching her father go through his little performance: an effort to register on his mind the last point in the important document before him, the lifted head, the moment's blank stare, and the flow of recognition. He was a tall, heavy man, dark, with a broad face and a strong growth of smoothly-brushed greying hair. He smiled in a friendly, half-patronising way, for he was fond of his daughter. She assured him it was a business call—about the poster.

"Changed your mind about—what's his name?"

"Orlando—Oliver Greene? No," she answered. "Have you written him?"

"Have just dictated a letter, asking him to call. But it's not posted."

"That's all right."

He regarded her cool, pale face, with its dark eyebrows and hair, and blue eyes. The dark and the blue had somehow a witch-like attraction. "Well, what?"

"Nothing. Only—the coming man is a fellow named Wilson Smith."

He leaned back, amused. "In other words, I should write him instead?"

"That wouldn't do very much good, I'm afraid."

"Oh?"

She could only shake her head at sight of his pleasant scepticism. She could not look at him; her eyes would see too much, penetrate too far into him, into his business astuteness, his great city prestige. "Bit of a highbrow, is he?" The quiet self-assurance in his tone was all at once so terrible to her quickened senses that when she did glance at his broad face she saw it corpse-like.

"What about your architecture, this morning?" he asked pleasantly.

"I'm thinking of giving it up."

He looked sharply at her. "Not thinking of going in for house-furnishing? I believe Lord Steen's sister is about to tackle the business on a West End scale."

"I'm sorry I haven't the sticking power."

Brows gathered, he looked out through the window. He despised failure. "I'm sorry, too."

"Everyone has his job if he could find it. I think I have found mine."

"What next?"

"Not quite sure. It's a gift—like being a medium."

"Good God !"

"No, nothing to do with seances. It's merely the awful penetration of genius. Only I see—without sweating blood. The mute inglorious Milton."

"Oh, writing! That!" He breathed freely, then looked at her closely. "Nothing wrong is there, Megan?"

"Oh lord no!"

"Want some extra cash?"

"No, thanks. It's pure business brought me here. In fairness, seeing you were relying on me, I felt I had to tell you about Wilson Smith. That was all."

He considered her thoughtfully. "You're quite sure, by the way, he is the coming man?"

"I rather think so, but I'm not advising you to write him. Orlando would give you a more certain job and would be amenable to suggestion, if the fee was sound. This fellow wouldn't."

"You think not?" He smiled. "What's his address?"

She hesitated. "Seventeen, The Mews. But remember, my professional advice is Orlando Greene."

II

When signing his first batch of letters, Mr Powell withdrew the note of appointment to Oliver Greene and stared at it. Putting it aside, he signed all the others, then took it up again. Megan may have tried to be delicate, but he uncomfortably felt that what she had really wanted to say was that this Wilson Smith was too much of a real artist for Transport Ltd.

Too much of a good thing! suggested his humour. He rang, and while his secretary was coming in, struck out Oliver's name with his own pen. The letter was typed again and directed to Wilson Smith and posted that evening.

The following day at the board meeting, he said: "About our spring and summer advertising campaign, you'll remember we agreed to put the poster proposition to Oliver Greene. As I told you, and as you know, he has done successful work in this line. However, I began to think out the matter still further, and it is my final conviction that we might be better served by a new man. There are various factors. We want something original, arresting, that would stimulate traffic as our first concern, but if in doing that we could also get ourselves spoken of as the employers of the rising genius of the day, then I estimate an extra substantial comeback in publicity. I made it my business to go into the position of the art world at the moment; and the coming man, in my opinion, is a fellow named Wilson Smith. From my special knowledge of his work, I am satisfied we should approach him. We should get him reasonably cheap, and, of course, his completed poster will be submitted to you in the usual way. Have I your permission to approach him?"

There was such an air of restraint, of quiet certainty, about Powell, that he was congratulated on this new move. He undoubtedly went into a thing thoroughly when he was at it! Genius linked up with them! … They smiled. Agreed. You could trust Powell . …

Mr Powell got a slight shock all the same when Wilson Smith was announced. His blank stare held a little longer than usual. Had he expected something dominant, mannered, even farouche?

"Mr Wilson Smith?"

"Yes. Mr Powell?"

"Yes. How do you do? You got my letter?"

"Yes, thank you."

"H'm. Yes." There is a certain sensitive pleasant nature that the strong business mind can hardly help doing something to. "You know, I suppose, our ramifications?"

Wilson Smith's brows ridged questioningly.

"It's a pretty enormous concern, Transport Limited."

"Oh, I know that!" The smile came quickly.

"Pretty enormous. We carry the whole town one way or another. Many aspects of the business. One is, of course telling the public—advertising—so that they may want to travel."

"Even get an itch to travel!"

"We use coal and steel and electricity and roads and engineers to create the reality." Mr Powell looked at him.

"And then you need Art to lure."

"If it can."

"Art has played the scarlet lady pretty successfully in her time." Mr Smith smiled engagingly. He was obviously eager to understand and to assist.

But somehow Mr Powell did not quite care for the last remark. "That's for you," he said, and came at once to the business point of explaining that, to attract people to the country and seaside during the coming season, he wanted a new poster of a certain large size. It would have to be attractive and arresting, and would be exhibited very widely. "I made it my business to consider the work that is being done by men and women in your line. In brief, we have decided to ask you to submit a full-size poster."

"Thank you very much. I should like to have a shot at it. When do you want it?"

"Exactly one week from today."

"One week!"

"Yes."

"But that's impossible! It's not even spring yet——"

"We must have everything ready before the spring."

"Yes, but I mean——" He meant that he hadn't the spring to help him with his poster, but suddenly went silent, looking embarrassed.

"I must put it before my board meeting exactly nine days from now. If you come back here with it at eleven o'clock this day week, then you and I shall still have time to—uh—discuss it and effect any alterations that maybe necessary. This is the world of business, Mr Smith, where everything has got to be exact and done to schedule."

"I understand that. Quite. It's the one week… Sometimes one is lucky, but a big picture can take many weeks, months…. Do you want any special thing, any special feature? I mean, have you——"

"That's your job. We want originality."

"Originality? I see." His expression was already becoming slightly excited, abstracted. "I'd better get started. I'd better go."

Mr Powell's smile was touched with amused pity. "We haven't discussed terms yet."

"Oh, I quite forgot!"

"Fifty pounds—if the work is suitable."

Fifty pounds—one week!

"If I can do it! I must frankly admit to you that I have never attempted a commercial poster. If only you'd given me more than a week. However, thank you very much. I'll have a shot at it."

"I'll confirm the offer by letter." Mr Powell extended his hand, then, his visitor gone, sat down and began to wonder what exactly Megan's game had been. He got hold of her on the phone, and over tea in the afternoon, said:

"I had that artist fellow Smith seeing me this morning, on your suggestion."

"I suggested Orlando Greene."

"You suggested he was the high-and-mighty highbrow sort who would refuse commercial work."

"And he didn't?"

"He accepted with such pathetic eagerness, that I began to wonder just what you meant."

She met her father's eyes for a moment and then laughed.

"Tell me this, at least. You haven't humbugged me? He is actually a good artist?"

"Why should I have humbugged you?" and she regarded him quizzically.

"Are you interested in him?"

"What if I am?"

"So that's it! I—see !"

"Well?" she challenged.

"Well, for one thing, I never allow anyone to fool me in business. Never! You understand! NEVER!" There was all at once the fierce concentration of religious zeal.

She regarded him solemnly, then lowered her lashes and said: "He is the coming artist. You should know I'd never mislead you in a thing like that."

He studied her for a moment.

"You're not really interested in him, anyway, are you?" he asked.

She suddenly smiled. "No, I'm not. That's not what I'm interested in."

"Right. So long as it keeps you amused."

"At the same time, I shouldn't yet take it for granted that he'll do the sort of poster you want."

"True. It may not be in him"

She laughed and thanked him nicely for the tea.

* * * * * *

But she was growing restless and beginning to hate the revelation that had come upon her in Orlando's studio. Her detachment was becoming really inhuman, and occasionally and quite involuntarily she had a view of motive and action almost horrible in its precision. It drove her the following night quite remorselessly towards The Mews and calmly to Wilson Smith's door.

She was turning away when at last the door opened and a haggard, unshaven face looked at her with suspicion, recognised her, and stood aside reluctantly for her to enter.

She went in and, coolly surveying the room, remarked:

"You seem in a state of chassis."

"I haven't tidied up yet," answered Wilson Smith. "You must excuse me." He bowed.

Now that she had entered she did not know what on earth to do except wander out again. There was something malignant in his polite voice.

"Sit down there," she said without any stress. "You're bogged—and need pulling out." Unhurriedly she took off her jacket, put on his filthy painting coat, and set to tidying up the place. She looked rather bored but purposeful, like a younger sister coming in on an expected mess.

"I can't allow you to do this."

"Do you think I like doing it? Don't fuss, please. Sit down."

Then she started in.

"I quite realise this is awfully good of you——"

"If you're trying to imply that I'm so interested as to have fallen for your pleasant manners, you're wrong. I'm just bored, and knowing how you'd be feeling, some poisonous sympathy drew me. And I wish, by the way, you wouldn't try to be so correctly nice. Sort of makes me tired."

He sat down.

"Good." She nodded. "Try to grin and bear it. Put any motive on it you like."

"What do you mean?—'knowing how I'd be feeling.'"

"That was a slip," she acknowledged as she nearly knocked the brush through a canvas. "But I heard you'd been offered commercial work—and I could do with the five bob you bet me."

"Already—it's public. Oh, God!" He lowered his head to his knees.

"Don't writhe."

"Oh, shut up!" he cried. "A week! And two days are already gone. What torture!"

She went calmly on with her work, while he got to his feet and stamped about and declaimed, with bursts of ironic laughter.

"You mean," she said, "you can't get an idea for the poster?"

She was leaning on the brush handle and he swung round. They stared at each other for a considerable time.

"Do you want the five bob now?"

There was something so penetrating, so disintegrating, in his eyes that it started a dull flush within her.

"Not until the week is up," she answered coolly.

He turned away. "I think you'd better get out," he flung at her as if she were some chance lady of the street.

"I think so, too," she agreed. "We're no use to each other."

She leaned the brush against the wall, took off his coat and put on her jacket. At the door she paused, her expression detached, but not unkind. Then she spoke.

"I was attracted, I suppose, by the internal conflict, the inner drama, of the great artist who has travailed for two days and two nights, and produced nothing. The awful horror of slums and back streets and warehouse-warrens; human hordes with backs bent like armies of rats; the whole thing working on his sensitive mind till he becomes obsessed by it as by a frightful nightmare. ... And against that—the country, vivid and lovely, waiting to heal, with tall trees like a song against the sky. Civilisation itself gets caught up in the eternal opposition. It swells to a philosophy. It takes on the passion of a creed, the liberating cry of a gospel. We hear the yelling of the damned who are mute. We will blast the nightmare with bus-loads of dynamite, and build Jerusalem in England's green and pleasant land. So—let's make a commercial poster to help the Transport Company."

He walked up to her, shut the door, and looked squarely at her. "That, as a matter of fact, is pretty near the truth. Seeing you are clairvoyant, could you tell me the next step?"

"Why should I? Five shillings may mean something to me."

"I don't know who you are," he replied, "and you made sure I wouldn't ask."

"That's ungallant. And I always foresaw you going down gallantly, with your smile and your nice manners an' all. Beneath?—I saw the bones of your face as thin, fine steel."

His breath snorted through his smile. "How nice of you!"

"So you don't want any help?"

"No."

"Good-bye." And still with his infernal smile, he closed the door behind her.

As she walked away, she wondered if she had succeeded in her subtle suggestion; doubted it, and felt suddenly tired.

III

On the appointed morning exactly at eleven, Wilson Smith was shown—or rather helped, for the wrapped canvas was very large—into Mr Powell's room. In due course, Mr Powell recognised him and rose. "Ah, so you managed to bring your masterpiece dead on time."

Clean-shaven and neatly clothed, Mr Wilson Smith smiled through his pallor.

"You see, you *had* plenty of time, after all. And you didn't lose much sleep neither, I bet! In the business world, Mr Smith, impossible has got to be treated as Napoleon treated it."

"Though not with the same final result, I bet," replied Mr Smith.

After a moment, Mr Powell caught the idea. Anything concerning Napoleon he was inclined to memorise. He smiled reflectively and waved a hand to the poster. "What about undressing …?"

Wilson Smith methodically removed the wrappings and stood the picture against the wall at the best spot for Mr Powell's observation.

Mr Powell stared at it for a considerable time, saying "H'm!" and then again "H'm!" automatically.

What he saw was something like a charabanc emerging from darkness and heading for a green land with a solitary tree. "Something like a charabanc," because it did not conform to any of the Transport vehicular types, nor did its human cargo correspond to the usual ticket-punched passengers; yet the lines of the vehicle did enclose the strength and speed of an engineer's dream, and the passengers themselves were so charged with the joy of life that their voices half-drunken, could be heard on the wind, it was a successful and indeed spectacular effort at combining the conception of energy and freedom in a shout of triumph. The detail, too, when looked into was interesting. The darkness on the left was smoke and in it could just be discerned the outline of factories and offices, but because this darkness was circumscribed, it also conveyed the suggestion of a caved underground world, where the doomed travelled from tube station to tube station, and out of which the train, by some wild madness all its own, had rushed forth into the sunlight, carrying its human cargo with it. The tree gave tallness to the landscape and to the sky; its green stillness was an aspiration. Beyond the tree, by some subtle trick of perspective, were infinite land and sea. But what immediately held attention was the freedom and triumph of the figures on the bus; and how this was technically accomplished was difficult to make out, for features were not particularly differentiated, and indeed many faces were little more than blobs. The spirit of the whole thing was undoubtedly triumphant.

"H'm!" said Mr Powell finally and cleared his throat. "Yes, I see the idea. It's quite good. But—it's somehow not quite what I expected, or wanted."

Wilson did not turn to him. His face, which had been expressionless, took on a staring hypnotic look.

"I'm not saying it's not good art, you understand," proceeded Mr Powell. "I'm not criticising in that way. But I have to think not only of my fellow directors but of the appeal to the public. That's the reason for getting a poster. It has got to appeal, to lure the masses. Now where really is that appeal, that lure, in it? ... You are beginning to see what I mean?"

The poster was certainly holding the artist's complete attention.

"Actually, it is lacking the fundamental, the principal thing from an advertising point of view." Mr Powell's shrewdness found a knowing smile. "You may not be prepared to agree with me offhand. But then I happen to know my public. In a word, your poster has no sex appeal."

Still Smith kept staring.

"You see it?" said Mr Powell, with the complacency that was certain the artist was now contemplating the most telling way of rectifying his omission.

"H'm!" he resumed presently. "Let me think. Your design makes it very difficult. You know the rather nude bathing figure used for seaside posters? If we could get some of that appeal in it somewhere."

Smith never moved.

Mr Powell looked sideways at him. "Getting an idea? Uh?"

"No," said Smith.

"Well, let me see—if I can help." He thought hard for a minute. "Yes, I begin to see it forming. In the first place you want an obvious bright young girl or two on the bus. Your figures do rather suggest men and women too much, don't they? Then—that tree there—if you removed that, and in its place you had a sort of picnic party?—with a couple wandering off—some pleasant coverts—you know? Some thing like that. Yes, I think that might do the trick." The picture before his mind's eye was beginning to warm him. It recalled something out of a dim past. "Do you begin to see it?" he asked, with some of the creator's enthusiasm in his voice.

"I see it."

"Good. Very good. You must let me congratulate you," said Mr Powell. "I appreciate your strong workmanship. Just these few vital changes, and I think I can guarantee you our acceptance. I'm not an artist exactly, but I can conceive a telling picture from our point of view! Uh? Well anyway, you see now the need for the two extra days. Take it away with you at once—and bring it back by ten o'clock on Thursday morning. Not later than ten. Can I rely on you?"

Wilson Smith turned slowly. "Do you mind if I leave it for a little while? I have—got to go—now."

Mr Powell looked more closely at the face of the artist and found it grey. "Hello, not feeling too fit?"

"It's—all right," said Mr Smith, the voice dragging more obviously. The suspicion of a ghastly smile touched the grey. The eyes, however, were fixed almost glassily, and somehow deterred Mr Powell from taking any step or even uttering a sound, when at last they left his face and focussed on the door.

Not that the eyes really saw Mr Powell, for Wilson Smith had his own acute problem at the moment, the centre of which was the little blind knot of his will. He hung on to that knot so concentratedly that he walked through the outer office without consciously observing anything or anyone, on to the pavement, into a taxi that had been called for Mr Powell—though the unfortunate taximan did not know that—said "Seventeen The Mews", and so after many days won to the exquisite freedom of letting consciousness slip altogether.

* * * * * *

Mr Powell had promised to have lunch that same day with his daughter, who had pleaded that she felt rather responsible to the Company. She was waiting for him in the hotel lounge.

"Ha!" he greeted her. "Late, are we? I've brought Lord Steen along."

"Hope you don't mind?" said that young man, laughing.

"You both seem extraordinarily cheerful."

Her father got hold of a waiter, named his own drink, pointed to the other two, mumbled "Wash," and disappeared.

"Hush!" Lord Steen answered, stooping to her ear. "It's come off—the gold mine deal!" And when the waiter had gone and he was seated beside her, he added: "I say, your father is marvellous. Things developed suddenly—this morning. Cable from mining engineer in Africa. I was hooting with excitement Absolutely outside myself. Then your father did at last turn up and put the whole deal over cool as ice."

"How much did you net?"

"We'll make it a bargain: I'll tell you, if you do the village with me tonight."

"As much as that?"

"I say, do!" he pleaded, gay, fair, and game.

"He's rather promised me a certain long-nosed two-seater. Think he could rise to it now?"

"Phoo! a small fleet of them. I'll throw in one myself—if you come." He gripped her arm, rallied her, begged her to promise. He was still in a splendid state of excitement.

She smiled, turned to take up her drink, and toasted him over the rim.

"It's a go? Hoots!" And he gulped his glass.

The lunch was a cheerful affair. Lord Steen was irrepressible. "So there was I absolutely dithery, dancing—and your father already five minutes late. Do you know why? You'd never guess. Never! A pavement artist had stolen his taxi!" He chortled so loudly that many heads turned round. "Superb! What?"

"Oh, yes," said Mr Powell to his daughter, "I forgot. That artist fellow turned up this morning with his poster." He filled his mouth again.

"Any good?" Megan helped herself to something she didn't want.

"H'mmm!" Mr Powell pursed his lips and then swallowed. "Not much. Not what we wanted really. However, I suggested some radical alterations, and if he puts these through decently, the thing should do."

"Did he agree?"

"Oh, well, yes, naturally." Mr Powell smiled. "Then he left rather hurriedly, looking pretty seedy, or underfed, or something; and stole my taxi."

"Revenge—for your suggestions!" chuckled Lord Steen. "I say, it's not every day a brand new director kills a pig. One last spot of brandy?"

"Thanks, no," said Mr Powell. "I have a few small things to see to this afternoon."

"The supreme artist! I can't say, sir, how much indebted to you I am...." He had just drunk enough to make a small speech from the heart. However, as they were passing out, he cleverly dropped a pace behind with Megan and whispered the time and place.

She shook her head and smiled to him. "Not tonight. Sorry." Then she went on.

IV

The following afternoon, her father rang her up. There was exasperation in his voice. "That artist fellow has never come for the poster. It's still here. And the board meeting is tomorrow. ... Yes, he said he would come back, but he hasn't. It's very annoying; puts me in a damned awkward position.... Very well, I'll wait if you come right now."

And though she came very quickly, he yet had time to work up his annoyance to a considerable pitch. It was pretty cool of the blasted fellow. He could have written or phoned or done something, surely. If there was one thing he would not have in this life it was interference with his business arrangements. "You can rely on Powell." It was said in the smoke-rooms as naturally as "What'll you have?" He had stated that the poster would be before the board to-morrow. ... A thought hit him, and the trick of leaving the poster behind was seen in all its impudent cunning. The fellow had never meant to call back for it! He had banked on there being no other poster available! The door opened and Megan entered. She gazed at her father, whose face, at intervals sufficiently rare to make it striking, could assume an expression of fleshy, petulant brutality. And now it concentrated on her and exploded in a sharp oath.

He proceeded to call it pretty good. He enlarged on the nefarious business.

Megan turned from the poster, and where on her face had been signs of haste and strained anxiety, there was now a faint sweet smile.

"Tell me," she said, as if she had hardly been listening to him; "what alterations did you suggest?"

He glared at her.

"You tell me," he cried, "was this a plant between you?"

She shook her head. "You needn't worry about that. He is probably dying—or dead. You know you saw that in his face."

There could be no doubting the quiet conviction in her manner. He realised in a moment that what she said was true. But he did not take his eyes off her. "You look—pleased," he said suspiciously.

"I am—with the poster. That's why I should like to know how you suggested it could be improved. Do tell me." There was something very appealing about her now; her eyes were so frank and clear that they brought back to him some vague memory of pinafores.

"I don't understand this, Megan. I haven't time to think what you're getting at. I'm a busy man. You know I'll forgive you a lot, but you should not presume on that. I have told you often enough that in business I can't have any personal or family interference. You must understand that once for all. I don't mind helping you—or even any of your friends—but if you are not going to respect my business position—well, we finish."

"You know," she said, "no one realises more than I your business position. You also know that I have always acted honourably in that respect. I am your daughter. You should not compel me to say this."

"Oh, well, that's all right. I admit it. Yes. Uh … what was it?"

I was merely anxious to know what you thought should be altered. I have a certain responsibility in this, and feel it," Looking rather exhausted, she at down.

"As for that, it's pure business. You may know about art, but I know about advertising. That's how I'm here; how I may be able, for example, to give you that car you want. I wasn't really misjudging *you*." He smiled. The filial reference had rather touched him. "The short and long of the thing is that this poster, to be effective, hasn't got one necessary ingredient. To you and me what's missing may sound silly. As silly as it sounds on the film—though you'll notice it's always there. The box-office makes sure of that. This is a business matter, and I treat it accordingly."

"Is it sex appeal?"

"Yes."

"What did he say when you told him that?"

"He appreciated it. I realise now that he probably wasn't well. But he saw the point. And I gave him the new idea."

"And then he went?"

"Yes; saying he would call back."

Her open palms lay on a pencil above a broad white blotting pad. She was looking at the poster.

"It's a great bit of work." Her tone was reflective, remote.

"Oh, that's not the point——"

"Don't get impatient with me again, Dad. It's a great poster. One of the greatest I have ever seen. It's a triumph—as a poster. You know about business. We know about art—the appeal to the mind, to wonder. That's why you employ him. You should trust him when you see that he has original quality. You yourself apologise for the usual poster sex appeal. Call it silly. It's really worse. Makes decent people like you and me a little uncomfortable. And in our emotions, we are just ordinary people. Very ordinary." She spoke almost lazily, and, lifting the pencil, began marking the blotter.

He sat down heavily in his own chair, pulled open a drawer, and selected a cigar. "You are forgetting again that with my experience, I simply know. That's all there's to it. I cannot go against my business knowledge because you have some sort of theory, now, can I?"

"No. But in this matter you have really employed me and should therefore at least listen to my report before coming to your final judgment. Isn't that business? I should have to refuse your payment—of that little car—otherwise!"

He chortled a note or two between his cigar puffs, blew out the match, and looked at his watch.

"Fire ahead!"

"I—I really haven't much to say. It's the power of the thing. It's the feeling of escape from the underground, the underworld—our own people, the workers, the army-fighters, from offices, factories, docks, slums—rushing with a song of triumph into England's green and pleasant land. You know the words from the poet Blake:

> " 'I will not cease from mental fight,
>> Nor shall my sword sleep in my hand,
> Till we have built Jerusalem
>> In England's green and pleasant land.' "

Her mouth dictated the words so slowly to her pencil, that the verse was there on the pad as the last sound ended. There was something very delicate and indirect in the way she did this, and the cadence in her voice was hardly ashamed of its own low, slow loveliness.

Mr Powell was disturbed.

"You see," she said, putting down the pencil thoughtfully "this sex-appeal, bathing-nude affair is used everywhere. There is nothing new in it. You are doing nothing original. No one could say of it: 'This is a Powell idea.' At least," she smiled, "I hope not! … The only other thing that has been done is the bold splash of colour on historic buildings and so on. But here—in this poster—you have English men and women heading for England. The words alone: 'England's green and pleasant land.' There's a cry there. Goes pretty deep. Through the centuries men have heard it and died for it."

Mr Powell was unaware of his own silence as he stared at the smoke he blew. Megan did not even glance at him, remaining absolutely still until he emerged from his business abstraction. Which he did at last with a "H'm!" or two and an official "Well, I must thank you for the way in which you have——" and realised he was speaking to his own daughter.

He got up, brushing away cigar ash importantly.

"As long as it was genuine illness, I don't mind. Do you think he is really dying?"

The thought behind his words shocked her to stillness for a moment, but she showed nothing. "I haven't heard anything of him—since he was here."

"H'mm! I'm dining in town to-night. I must get home first. Coming now?"

"Not— quite yet."

"Not keeping very regular hours, are you?"

"Haven't been to even a supper party for over a week. Most exemplary."

"A bit pale about the gills, I thought."

She smiled and kissed him on the cheek, and had the rather odd experience of feeling like Judas as she walked along the street. Not that she had in anyway acted like Judas. Yet she saw the scene in Gethsemane as she stared into a jeweller's window, and turned sharply away as the grey Face focussed into Wilson Smith's and stared back at her. It was the reference to his dying caused this aberration. As she walked along she heard her father's voice to the board: "This, then, gentlemen is my new conception. As it was finished, the artist was taken ill. I hope he will recover, for I should be sorry to think—however much it would help our publicity—that our poster received universal attention as the last work of a rising genius."

V

The following night she parked her long-nosed two-seater, and with a basket on her arm walked round to The Mews. This dark place that her mind refused to focus must be seen face to face. To pass such another night as last night was beyond the endurance of any wretchedness. Yet she had no clear idea of why all this should be so, of why she was now waiting at this dumb door, and why in particular she should be calm and detached to the point of utter indifference.

She rang and rattled the door and knocked. When she gave up hope she stood so still that she seemed to have gone to sleep on her feet. Stealthily the door opened and she met his face. No greeting passed between them. When she had entered and was putting her basket down, she said calmly: "I called round to pay you your five bob." Then she had to look up at him, he had gone so still.

His eyes were glistening, like those of a man wasting with fever, and difficult to meet. He had certainly been pretty ill, and his body looked shrunken within his clothes. He was obviously weak, for he suddenly sat down. The expression he brought to his face showed the teeth to the gums.

She took her purse from the basket, opened it, and withdrew two half crowns. She laid them on a low dais. "I always pay my money debts." She put her purse back in the basket and sat up again. "You don't look too fit."

"What—does all this mean?"

"Haven't you heard? Your poster has been accepted."

She turned from the questioning, fiery eyes and looked from picture to picture. "I happened to hear it. The board meeting was this morning, as you know. It meant five shillings to me. So I was interested. … It must, by the way, mean considerably more to you." She appeared thoughtfully amused.

There was silence for some time.

"You must excuse my not being able to entertain you." It sounded a long ironic utterance. He went over to his dishevelled camp-bed, which he must have pulled out from behind the screen, lay down, and put the back of his hand over his eyes. She regarded his stretched-out body. It looked deathly.

Removing the covering from her basket, she took out a bottle of port and a bunch of grapes. "I'm just going," she said, "but I want to give you a glass of wine first."

"Please go!" he said intensely.

She saw that she was torturing him, that he was in the exhausted mood to hate bitterly any human intrusion. A visible quivering came to his flesh, a jumpiness. And she couldn't see a corkscrew anywhere. Nor a glass. She went behind the screen and came out with both—to find him on his feet, facing her, and swaying like some boxer half-demented from a long count.

"I know how you hate this assault on your privacy. It's ghastly. Unpardonable." By which time she had got the corkscrew in. The toughness of the pull nearly burst her eardrums, but the cork came away with a great noise. "Your last trump!" she said with wise good-nature. Then she poured out an inch into the tumbler. "Take that."

He turned away. At sight of the action, a quick emotion touched her—the first real twinge in weeks. She followed him until he sat down. "I always knew you were a real fighter. But you have yet to learn to take your medicine. Here it is."

"Oh, God, I wish you would leave me alone!"

"Don't flatter yourself I like doing this. I don't. I need one about as badly as you. So drink it up."

Her calm was inexorable and at last he drank Then she took one out of the same glass. "And now we'll demolish the grapes, like two grubbing beasts." She placed three vine leaves on her knees and the bunch on top. "We'll spit the seeds on the floor and clean up after."

Each berry was big and luscious and burst coolly against a parched palate.

"Pretty good, aren't they?"

"They are," he acknowledged, and continued bursting them with a feverish gluttony.

"An improvement on sex appeal," she mumbled.

He momentarily choked and for the first time looked at her humanly.

She met his look and negligently glanced away. His cheekbones reddened.

"You're a glutton," she said.

"How did you get to know?"

She gave him a swift look. "I happen to know one of the directors of Transport Limited," she replied evenly. "In fact, I lunched with him to-day. He innocently began telling me about a new poster they had approved that morning by a rising young genius. H'm! He was, in his fashion, pretty enthusiastic about it."

"Why should he tell you that?"

"Because normally when a man wants to make an impression on a woman, he tells her what he believes will interest her—in this case the very latest bit of art gossip. It pandered to my taste for exclusive news—and to his own importance in being able to supply it. Accordingly, he was getting away very well. Then I thought I'd come and tell you—hoping to be first with the news. It seems I have been—but so far very little pandering has resulted."

"I'm sorry——"

"There was a certain delicious——"

He looked at her with dark suspicion. "It wasn't that fellow Powell you were with?"

She nodded. "Don't stare like that. It's rude." And then as he turned again to the grapes, she added: 'Why the blasted smile?"

"He's old enough to be your father."

"He is."

"Is what?"

"My father."

She pretended not to see his expression, then faced it levelly. "Well?"

"So that's how I got the commission—and the acceptance—and the five shillings?" He got up; but in a flash she was facing him, the grapes on the floor.

"Well?" Her nostrils quivered with anger.

"Oh, I don't mean—It was all a ghastly mess anyway. But it was very nice of you. Very." He smiled politely, but still being very weak, he went and sat on his bed.

"Why should I work the commission for you—or the acceptance?" she demanded with extraordinary vehemence.

"Forgive me—not caring. I'm a bit muddle-headed, and tired."

"You mean, you happen to be sick with egoism. Well, let me tell you that though I may have mentioned your name to my father, I suggested to him, as my business advice, that he should give the commission to Orlando. That he didn't is his concern—and yours. Not mine. I have obviously had too much to do with you as it is."

"Wait a bit," he said, and got to his feet again. "I should like gravely to ask you this. Why have you had so much to do with me?"

In his eyes she found nothing evasive. "Why do you think?"

He took half a minute, then said solemnly: "Because you have been cursed with a terrible insight, and have no artist's way of working it off. It hunts you on, yet gives you no real feeling, no pain—none of the pain of creation or birth. You see things with a ghastly clearness, yet get no kick out of it. Like the young girl who was God! So you saw how I suffered, and your accursed sympathy drove you round. And I hated you for coming and seeing how sick my ego was. For the hellish struggle got me at a bad time—and I had little left in the way of resources."

She nodded and looked away for a little while. Then she said calmly: "You are wrong in one particular. After the first day or so, this was just the one place I couldn't see, couldn't pry into. I saw the business world. The awful shallowness of it, the almost terrifying haphazard chance and cunning of it. The game by which my father has earned his reputation is quite incredibly simple and childish. He has only a very average poker-face. You would hardly believe that if you saw him in action among his fellows. But it's—so true; if only I could give you a drawing of all the moves and motives that are no more than just below the surface! Take your poster, for example. He wanted the sex appeal for two reasons: one, because of some vague but "safe" idea that the lower orders indulge in it en masse (that's the hunch, or superstition); and secondly—very important this—because he wanted to dominate you. He instructs the genius in art how to do his job; then he tells his board why and how he had instructed him; not blatantly, of course; quietly, precisely, almost casually. And his board are again impressed by his range and power. That's exactly what happened. Let these instances be multiplied, and you have the great magnate, the city Napoleon."

"How then did he come to accept this poster as it stood?"

"When I first went in, he was furious, because he thought you, the art simpleton, had out-tricked him. You see, he inevitably deduced that you had left the poster—because you reckoned there would be no other at the last moment for the meeting. When he was sure that was not the case, I told him what I thought of the poster. Fortunately that was easy for me, because it is a great poster. We talked, and on the blotting pad in front of me I idly wrote out Blake's verse about England's green and pleasant land. In the end, he was secretly moved. Perhaps not so much by your poster or England or the verse, as by the conjunction of these in an advertising assault. He began to see it, poet's words an' all! While contemplating his cigar smoke, he began silently addressing his board. I could almost hear him pointing out his new ideas about departing from the ordinary poster appeal, retailing how he had at last succeeded in getting his ideas represented in what he hoped and believed was a big work, and then moving them with the verse—not as poetry—"I'm not a poet, gentlemen"—but as first-rate advertising material—leaving each Tory breast secretly swelling at thought of England's green and pleasant land.... Anyhow, to-day, when I asked him what had happened, he said, with a shrug, that he had pushed the poster through. Even at the end, he must first impress me! But I got the story out of him."

"Let us sit down," he said. They sat side by side on his narrow bed. "It's a wise child knows its own father."

She nodded. "I know him all right, and honour and respect him—above his peers."

The quiet sincere utterance bred the ghost of a smile between them. The weariness in it freed them from all stress.

"I suppose it was the contrast between that pleasant business world and this infernal underworld drew you here."

"I suppose it was."

"You knew I needed comforting."

She deliberated thoughtfully. "To be honest is difficult, as you know, but I think it really was because I needed comforting myself. I had no feeling towards you."

"Sound, that," he said. "You're not frightened by the truth. I'm beginning to feel a strange sensation of peace. Must be the wine, I suppose. How about you?"

"Yes."

"They do do it on us, don't they, the devils?"

"They do."

"Must one forever have to go through the slough to arrive at the moment of lucid loveliness?" He turned his face to her. "You look rather lovely yourself."

She smiled. "You have two days' growth and blue shadows. It's your own face you should have been after putting in the poster and it rushing towards the green and pleasant land."

"A rather grim idea—but it haunted me. It was your idea."

She nodded. "I have a sports two-seater—round the corner. Or should we go by Powell's bus? To see what's beyond the tree."

She heard him take a deep breath, and on the same impulse they both got to their feet. She met his look and found her body suddenly quivering with an excitement that was painful, as if it were coming back to life after having been long dead. Nor could her brain now put two images together. There was almost a sense of shame mixed with this and a quite intolerable suspense. He said something to her. Perhaps his words weren't very coherent, for this last suggestion of hers described what had been, one night in the more awful throes of imagination, his most tormenting vision. Something of its wild triumphal rush he had carried over into the poster.

But if the words were incoherent, the meaning and intention pierced her, and the last fragments of her detachment fell in star-points about her sight, blinding her a little. Before anything still more dreadful might happen, she gulped: "I'll bring it round," and stumbled for the door.

When she had closed the door, she leaned heavily against it, thus when it suddenly opened she fell backward and in his weak condition he had all he could do to hold her.

Presently she got away again to fetch the two-seater, and on the street she tried to look solemn so that the people mightn't think she was mad. For she wanted to laugh out loud with joy at the green lands of England already rushing on their faces.

The Moor

A few miles back it had looked like a sea-anemone on a vast tidal ledge, but now, at hand, it rose out of the moor's breast like a monstrous nipple. The scarred rock, heather tufted, threw a shadow to his aching feet, and because he was young enough to love enchantment in words, he savoured slowly, "Like the shadow of a great rock in a weary land". With a shudder of longing he passed his tongue between his sticky lips. The wide Sutherland moor under the August sun was silent as a desert.

At a little pool by the rock-base he drank and then dipped his face.

From the top of the rocky outcrop the rest of his tramp unrolled before him like a painted map. The earth fell away to the far sea, with cottages set here and there upon it like toys, and little cultivated strips, green and brown, and serpentine dark hollows.

He kept gazing until the sandwich in his mouth would not get wet enough to swallow. Then his eyes rested on the nearest cottage of all.

The loneliness of that cottage was a thing to catch the heart. Its green croft was snared in the moor's outflung hand. In the green stood a red cow. Creaming in upon his mind stole the seductive thought of milk. Tasting it made a clacking sound in his mouth and he stopped eating.

As he neared the cottage the red cow stared at him, unmoving save for the lifeless switch of her tail. The cottage itself, with its grey curved thatch and pale gable-end, made no move. The moor's last knuckle shut off the world.

The heather had not yet stirred into bloom and, far as the eye could see, lay dark under the white sun. He listened for a sound … and in that moment of suspense it came upon him that the place was bewitched.

A dog barked and every sense leapt. The tawny brute came out at the front door, showing half-laughing teeth, twisting and twining and in no time was at his back. He turned round, but still kept moving towards the door, very careful not to lift his eyes from those eyes, so that he nearly tumbled backwards over the doorstep … and was aware, with the beginnings of apologetic laughter, that he was in the presence of a woman. When he looked up, however, the laugh died.

Her eyes were gypsy dark. Perhaps she was twenty. Sunk in the darkness of her eyes were golden sun motes. His confusion stared speechless. A tingling trepidation beset his skin. A tight-drawn bodice just covered and repressed her breasts. Her beauty held the still, deep mesmerism of places at the back of beyond. She was shy, yet gazed at him.

The dry cup of his flesh filled with wine. Then his eyes flickered, shifted quickly; he veiled them, smiling, as though the rudeness of his bared emotion had gone forth unpardonably and touched her skin.

To his stammered request for milk, she smiled faintly, almost automatically, and disappeared.

Then he heard the beating of his heart. Through the warmth of his tired body swept a distinct heat. Excitement broke in spindrift. He smiled to himself, absorbed.

When he caught himself listening at the door, however, he immediately bespoke the dog, inviting his approach with such a sudden snapping hand that the brute leapt back, surprised into a short growl. He awaited her appearance so alive and happy that he was poised in apprehension.

She brought the milk in a coarse tumbler. He barely looked at her face, for good manners could not trust his instinct; his thanks he concentrated in a glance, a word or two, a smile breaking into a laugh. She had covered somewhat the wide V gleam of her breast, had swept back her hair; but the rents, the burst seam under an arm, the whole covering for her rich young body was ragged as ever, ragged and extraordinarily potent. He said he would drink the milk sitting outside if she didn't mind. She murmured, smiled, withdrew.

He ate his lunch excitedly, nibbling at the sandwiches to make them last, throwing crusts to the dog. His mind moved in its bewilderment as in coloured spindrift, but underneath were eyes avid for the image of her body, only he would not let their stare fix. Not yet. Not now…. Living here at the back of beyond… this secret moor…. Extraordinary! … But underneath he felt her like a pulse and saw her like a flame—a flame going to waste—in the dark of the moor, this hidden moor.

Attraction and denial became a tension of exquisite doubt, of possible cunning, of pain, of desire. His soul wavered like a golden jet.

As the last drop of milk slid over, he heard a sound and turned—and stared.

A withered woman was looking at him, eyes veiled in knowingness. She said, "It's a fine day that's in it."

"Yes, isn't it!" He got to his feet.

She slyly looked away from him to the moor, the better to commune with her subtle thought. A wisp of grey hair fell over an ear. Her neck was sinewy and stretched, her chin tilted level from the stoop of her shoulders. The corners of her eyes returned to him. Just then the girl came to the doorway.

"It's waiting here, mother." Through veiled anxiety, compellingly, she eyed the old woman.

"Are ye telling me?"

"Come on in."

"Oh, I'm coming." She turned to the young man and gave a husky laugh, insanely knowing. The daughter followed her, and he found himself with the thick glass in his hand staring at the empty doorway. A sudden desire to tiptoe away from that place seized him. My God! he thought. The blue of heaven trembled.

But he went to the door and knocked.

"This is the glass——" he began.

She smiled shyly, politely, and, taking the glass from his outstretched hand, withdrew.

His hand fell to his side. He turned away, going quietly.

Down between the cottages, the little cultivated strips green and brown, the serpentine dark hollows, he went jerkily, as though the whole place were indeed not earth but a painted map, and he himself a human toy worked by one spring. Only it was a magic spring that never unwound. Even in the hotel that overlorded the final cluster of cottages, the spring seemed wound up tighter than ever.

For privacy he went up and sat on his bed. "Lord, I cannot get over it!" he cried silently. He got off his bed and walked about the floor. This was the most extraordinary thing that had ever happened to him … without quite happening to him.

Inspiration had hitherto thrilled from within. This was from without, and so vast were its implications that he could not feel them all at once in a single spasm of creation. He got lost in them and wandered back to his bed, whereon he lay full length, gazing so steadily that he sank through his body into a profound sleep.

He awoke to a stillness in his room so intense that he held his breath, listening. His eyes slowly turned to the window where the daylight was not so much fading as changing into a glimmer full of a pale life, invisible and watchful. Upon his taut ear the silence began to vibrate with the sound of a small tuning fork struck at an immense distance.

His staring eyes, aware of a veiled face … focused the face of the girl on the moor. The appeal of her sombre regard was so great that he began to tremble; yet far back in him cunningly he willed body and mind to an absolute suspense so that the moment might remain. Footsteps on the corridor outside smashed it, and all at once he was listening acutely to perfectly normal voices.

"Well, Mr. Morrison—you here? What's up now?"

"Nothing much. The old woman up at Albain—been certified."

"So I heard. Poor old woman. When are you lifting her?"

"Tomorrow."

"There's no doubt, of course, she is . . . ay, ay, very sad."

"Yes. There's the girl, too—her daughter. You'll know her?"

"Well—yes. But she's right enough. I mean there's nothing—there. A bit shy, maybe … like the heather. You know."

"I was wondering what could be done for her."

"Oh, the neighbours will look after her, I'm sure. She'll just have to go into service. We're fixed up for the season here now, or I…"

The footsteps died away, and the light in the bedroom withdrew itself still more, like a woman withdrawing her dress, her eyes, but on a lingering watchfulness more critical than ever, and now faintly ironic.

His body snapped into action and began restlessly pacing the floor, irony flicking over the face. Suddenly he paused … and breathed aloud— "The auld mither!" As it was also an apostrophe for his country, his eyes gleamed in a profound humour.

The exclamation made him walk as it were more carefully, and presently he came to the surface of himself some distance from the hotel and realised where he was going.

But now he cunningly avoided the other cottages and in a roundabout way came in over the knuckle of moor in the deepening dusk. The cow was gone and the cottage seemed more lonely than ever. Indeed, it crouched to the earth with rounded shoulders drawing its grey thatch about its awful secret. Only the pale gable-end gloomed in furtive watchfulness.

Grey-green oasis, dark moor, and huddled cottage were privy to the tragedy of their human children, and, he felt, inimical to any interference from without. Never before had he caught this living secretive intensity of background, although, as a young painter believing in vision, it had been his business to exploit backgrounds of all sorts.

The girl herself walked out from the end of the house, carrying two empty tin pails. On the soft turf her feet made no sound. Unlike her background she was not inimical but detached. And, as her slave, her background spread itself under her feet.

By the time he joined her at the well she had her buckets full, and as he offered to carry them she lifted one in each hand. He pursued his offer, stooping to take them. The little operation brought their bodies into contact and their hands, so that there was a laughing tremble in his voice as he walked beside her, carrying the water. But at the doorway, which was reached in a moment, he set down the buckets and raised his cap.

As he went on into the moor, still smiling warmly as though she were beside him, he kept saying to himself that to have dallied or hesitated would have been unpardonable … yet not quite believing it … yet knowing it to be true.

He sat down on the moor, his heart aflame. The moor lost its hostility and became friendly. Night drew about them her dim purple skin. Silence wavered like the evening smoke of a prehistoric fire. The sense of translation grew in him … until the girl and himself went walking on the moor, on the purple, the rippled skin, their faces set to mountain crests and far dawns.

He tore his vision with a slow humour and, getting to his feet, shivered. As he returned by the cottage he saw her coming out of the byre door and on a blind impulse went up to her and asked:

"Are you not lonely here?"

"No," she answered, with a smile that scarcely touched her still expression.

"Well—it does seem lonely—a bit?"

Her eyes turned to the moor and only by a troubling of their deeps could he see that his words were difficult. She simply did not speak, and for several seconds they stood perfectly silent.

"I can understand," he broke through, "that it's not lonely either." But his awkwardness rose up and clutched him. If the thickening dusk saved his colour, it heightened her beauty in a necromantic way. Mistrust had not touched her, if tragedy had. A watchfulness, a profound instinct young and artless—yet very old.

The front door opened and her mother came peering on to the doorstep. In low quick tones he said:

"I'll come—tomorrow evening."

Her eyes turned upon his with a faint fear, but found a light deeper than sympathy.

By the time he got back to the hotel, his companion, Douglas Cunningham, had arrived, round about, with the motor-cycle combination.

"Sorry I'm so late. The beastly clutch kept slipping. I had the devil's own time of it."

"Had you?"

"Yes. We'll have to get down to it tomorrow…. . What happened?" Douglas looked at Evan shrewdly. "Seems to have lit you up a bit, anyhow."

"Does it?"

Then Evan told him.

Douglas met his look steadily.

"You can't see?" probed Evan, finally. "The moor, the lonely cottage, the mad mother, and the daughter …. My god, what a grouping! Can't you see—that it transcends chance? It has overwhelmed me."

"My dear chap, if you'd been in the ditch with a burst clutch and umpteen miles from nowhere you would have been, by analogy, completely pulverised. You're the pure romantic."

Their friendly arguments frequently gathered a mocking hostility.

"You show me the clutch of your tinny motor bike," thrust Evan. "I show you the clutch of eternal or infernal life. I'm not proving or improving anything: I'm only showing you. But you can't see. Lord, you are blind. Mechanism, clutch, motor bike … these are the planets wheeling about your Cyclops glassy eye. You are the darling of evolution, the hope of your country, the proud son of your race. You are the *thing* we have arrived at! … By the great Cuchulain, is it any wonder that your old mother is being taken to a mad-house?"

"By which I gather that you have found the daughter's mechanism—fool-proof?"

Evan took a slow turn about the floor, then with hands in pockets stood glooming satanically. "I suppose," he said, "we have sunk as low as that."

Douglas eyed him warningly. "Easy, Evan."

Evan nodded. "Whatever I do I must not go in off the deep end!" He suddenly sat down and over his closed fist on the table looked Douglas in the face. "Why shouldn't I go in off the deep end?"

Douglas turned from the drawn lips and kicked off his boots. "You can go in off any damned end you like," he said. "If you can't see things as they really are, I can't help you."

In bed, Evan could not sleep. To the pulse of his excitement parable and symbol danced to a pattern set upon the grey-green oasis of the croft, centring in the cottage ... fertile matrix of the dark moor.

Vision grew and soon wholly obsessed him. He found in it a reality at once intoxicating and finally illuminating. A pagan freedom and loveliness, a rejuvenation, an immense hope ... and, following after, the moods of reflection, of beauty, of race ... to go into the moor not merely to find our souls but to find life itself—and to find it more abundantly.

But the following evening the little cottage presented quite another appearance. He came under its influence at the very first glance from the near moor crest. It had the desolate air of having had its heart torn out, of having been raped. A spiritless shell, its dark-red door pushed back in an imbecile gape. One could hear the wind in its emptiness. A sheer sense of its desolation overcame him. He could not take his eyes off it.

And presently an elderly woman came to the door, followed by the girl herself. They stood on the doorstep for a long time, then began slowly to walk up to the ridge beyond which lay the neighbours' cottages. But before they reached the ridge they stopped and again for a long time stood in talk. At last the elderly woman put out her hand and caught the girl's arm. But the girl would not go with her. She released herself and stepped back a pace, her body bending and swaying sensitively. The elderly woman stood still and straight, making her last appeal. The girl swayed away from that appeal also, turned and retreated. With hooded shawl her elder remained looking after her a moment, then like a woman out of the ages went up over the crest of the moor.

From his lair in the heather, Evan saw the door close, heard, so still the evening was, the clash and rattle of the latch. And with the door closed and the girl inside, the house huddled emptier than ever. His heart listened so intently that it caught the dry sound of her desolate thought ... she was not weeping ... her arms hung so bare that her empty hands kept plucking down her sleeves ...

She came at his knock. The pallor of her face deepened the dark eyes. Their expressionlessness troubled and she stood aside to let him in. Only when they were by the fire in the gloom of the small-windowed kitchen did she realise what had happened.

But Evan did not feel awkward. He knew what he had to do like a man who might have imaginatively prepared himself for the test. He placed her chair at the other side of the fire but did not ask her to sit down. He sat down himself, however, and looking into the fire began to speak.

Sometimes he half turned with a smile, but for the most part kept his eyes on the burning peat, with odd silences that were pauses in his thought. He was not eager nor hurried; yet his gentleness had something fatal in it like the darkness of her mood.

She stood so still on the kitchen floor that in the end he dared not look at her. Nor did his immobility break when he heard her quietly sit down in the opposite chair, though the core of the fire quickened before his gaze.

Without moving, he started talking again. He did not use words that might appeal to a primitive intelligence. He spoke in the highest—the simplest—way he could to himself.

He looked at himself as a painter desiring to paint the moor. Why? He found himself dividing the world into spirit and mechanism. Both might be necessary, but spirit must be supreme. Why? At twenty years of age he knew the answer. Spirit drew to spirit in a communion that was the only known warmth in all the coldness of space. And we needed that particular warmth; at moments we needed it more than anything else. Man's mechanism was a tiny flawed toy in the vast flawless mechanism of the universe. But this warmth of his was a thing unique; it was his own special creation … and in a way—who could say?—perhaps a more significant, more fertile, thing than even the creation of the whole mechanical universe… .

As he thought over this idea, he felt her eyes on his face. The supreme test of spirit would be that while not knowing his words—what did they matter?—it would yet understand him perfectly—*if it was there.*

"I do not know," he said at last, and repeated it monotonously. "Coming in over the moor there I saw you and the woman. Then there was the moor itself. And you in the cottage. The woman could have helped you. Only you didn't want to be helped in her way yet." He paused, then went on slowly: "I can see that. It's when I go beyond that to my sitting here that it becomes difficult. For what I see is you who are the moor, and myself with the moor about me, and in us there is dawn and out of the moor comes more of us. …That sounds strange, but perhaps it is truer than if I said it more directly. For you and I know that we cannot speak to each other yet—face to face."

Then he turned his face and looked at her.

Her dark eyes were alight with tears that trickled in slow beads down her cheeks. *It was there.*

Quietly he got to his feet. "I'll make a cup of tea."

She also arose. "I'll make it."

It had grown quite dark in the kitchen. They stood very still facing the unexpected darkness. Caught by something in the heart of it, they instinctively drew together. He turned her face from it.

In the morning Douglas arrived at the cottage on the heels of the woman with the shawl. The woman had tried the door and found it locked. But her quick consternation lessened when she found the key under the thatch.

Douglas, grown oddly curious, waited for her to come out. She came, with a face as grey as the wall.

"She hasn't slept in her bed at all."

"Oh!" His lips closed.

The woman looked at him.

"Do you know …?"

"Not a thing," said Douglas. "Must have gone over the hills and far away. They've got a fine morning for it." And he turned and left her, his scoffing sanity sticking in his throat like a dry pellet.

The Mirror

It came to the point where he saw Glasgow as streets and workshops and yards, baths of multitude with an upper scum of clever people grown faintly green and cynical. So he left it, deciding to strike out for the countryside, for some remote crofting area, where a cottage would stand on an upland and the people would move like peasants in immemorial landscapes, drawing vital life from the soil. From the soil: that was the idea. Glasgow was a machine; even its hideous social problem was impersonal. Not that it was simply soulless: it was in an ultimate spiritual sense lifeless: an infinitely complicated robot animated by a clanging energy and subsisting on the digestive processes of its iron guts.

In the crofting area of Glendun he found a cottage at the foot of an upland, and the ben room with its iron bed of shining brass knobs was given over to his private use. His portable typewriter in its neat black case, his writing blocks, pencils and typing paper, were disposed on and about an old sideboard with peeling veneer.

This old sideboard, surmounted by its oval cracked mirror, at once repelled and attracted him. Sitting with his back to the little window in the two-foot wall, he could see reflected in the mirror the rising hillside. The reflection, in its frame of dark mahogany, gave the hillside a curious, aloof, quiescent quality; lifted it from the realm of realism to the realm of art. The mirror so admirably symbolised his own attitude … at any rate to a certain extent, for he had "values" to find that were beneath the surface, human values, drawing vital life from the soil. But the crack in the mirror was a problem, providing speculative moments, not without their humour.

For occasionally the head of his landlady appeared there, or the head of one of her two daughters, or of her husband invited ben for an odd smoke of a night;

and afterwards there would appear his own brittle thought running with the flawed glass, particularly if the visitor had been the elder daughter.

She was nineteen, a full-blown woman, clear-eyed, rich-skinned, with a firm busked waist, a quick heavy step, and a ready mirth. In the very colour of her round forearm was red strength. Though he judged that actually he must be as tall as she was, he had the feeling that one of these impulsive jerks of her arm would land him ignominiously on his back.

The first few days he spent looking about him. He was very pleasant to his hosts, very polite, very anxious not to inconvenience them needlessly. Going about in this leisurely way was rather wonderful. No tired home-coming at 2 a.m. with the looming thought of a bolted breakfast and a rush for his police-court copy in the morning. He was in any case due a rest. Moreover, it was essential that he get steeped in the atmosphere of his new environment, which was so much more than merely the place where he was staying. It was going to mean so much more to Scotland, suffering from the incubus of a virulent industrialism, from a complete lapse of any sense of nationhood, from the worshipping of moneyed robots.

As the days went on, however, he began to grow vaguely restless. He found that he could not write. The index finger of a thought did not touch his mind on the quick: it rather sank into it as into a cerebrum of wool.

"You're always at the writing, Mister Craig." His landlady struck him as solidly peasant, with a fat ready smile.

"Ah, but you see, that's my trade."

"You're telling me that?" And the smile paused to look at him, at once credulous and doubtful. "Well, now, isn't that the queer trade!"

"Why?"

'Indeed, then, I don't know," she answered, her smiling wrinkles recovering their humour. "But I never seen anyone who did it before."

Possibly she thought that all books and papers were miraculously conceived! A queer notion enough, worth noting for future use. … His eyes shifted to the mirror and he saw her face slant a curious look at him. As she turned away she caught his eyes in the glass. For an arrested moment, they stared at each other. With a warm confusion invading his mind, he heard her stolidly leave the room.

The woolly consciousness grew. He could stare at his mind as at the hump of a sheep's back. He tentatively tried to convince himself that by some malignant mischance he had selected the wrong spot, where the folk he met were absolutely "ordinary" and the soil earthy, clammy, coldly wet. When his boot sank in the mire and he pulled it out, the sound of the suction was a note of sheer negation. In a quite literal and devastating way there was "nothing in it". When he tried to "reflect" it he succeeded too well, for his brain-pan became the clayey, ooze-filling hole itself.

And this dreadful literalness of the soil was also reflected in the people who worked on it. Which might not have been such a great disappointment if only he himself could have reflected them in the mirror of his art. But he couldn't. He could at the most, and then with effort, merely name the things and persons he saw. He could not rationalise or translate them. They would not permit of such a process. Night after night he deliberately sat down to put them into a short story, but at almost every point he found that he was inventing, or idealising, that he was laboriously importing some mental or spiritual or romantic element into his picture in order to make it "go"; was, in short, "making it up" insincerely, was conscious of his insincerity and ashamed; not exactly ashamed of being insincere, but of being unable to compose his picture out of its native elements, as if his original genius had some fatal flaw in it, like the mirror.

The younger daughter was sixteen and very shy of him. But the blown beauty of nineteen was hearty and vivid. The skin of neck and cheek could flush like dog-rose petals, palpitant and warm. She began to disturb him secretively. He pursued her in his dreams.

But he could not write about her, much less about imaginary pursuits of her. Apart from the thoughts and emotions aroused being quite unprintable, they were too crude, too actual, too fleshly, for art; in fact he would have burned with an impotent shame had they been capable of being whispered at all. Yet they were at least perfectly real, and were completely in the picture. Indeed he had never experienced any other flame quite like it, in the sense that it was so all-enfolding. It could make him gulp, make him tremble, make him feel like an imaginary devil or a real coward. Yet it was not a thing to be written. Supposing he did set down exactly what he emotionally experienced, painting with a free brush in naked colour? … The only printing presses for that sort of thing were in Paris. And even then, how about the "indispensable air of consequence"? Humiliating.

He began to miss a morning's shave; did not put on his collar until the afternoon; refused to have his meals by himself and came into the kitchen for them. Sometimes he gave the crofter a hand about the little steading, or would accompany the elder daughter to the milking of the two cows. The scents of the steading, the byre, the cows, the dung; the life processes of cocks and hens and cattle; the gluttonous gruntings of an only pig quite filled his mind. When he stood in the byre watching her firm pink fists working like pistons into the cow's udder, he could scarcely trust his throat to answer her sound common sense, her cheery sallies.

In the evenings, because as yet he found it impossible to sit with the crofter saying nothing, he always retired to his own room. But he no longer wrote. And being unable to write tortured him almost as acutely as did the flaming roses of Murdina, to whom he was now consciously frightened to disclose himself lest he be repulsed. And to be repulsed by Murdina would certainly be the last word in humiliation … not to speak of the difficulties it would raise in his residence.

Out and about, he learned to meet people in the undemonstrative, offhand way that seemed to constitute good form, deliberately suppressing in himself the impulse to sensitive politenesses. At a dance in the village hall he entered into the robust amusement of the evening in sensible style, but was all the time conscious of being not quite in the swim, of being emptily dissatisfied, positively lonely. Nor could he get his tongue to utter their broad humour. Often he felt so witless that he could not get the crease out of his smile. And his natural attentions of courtesy to Murdina were not overlooked. They were made the occasion of sly winks and nods, so that to free her from possible embarrassment he did not go near her for several dances.

During one of these dances he slipped outside for a quiet smoke, but became so lost in his unfortunate thought that he forgot to smoke. He was roused by footsteps mixing near him in the dark, by the audible strife of soft bodies, the sound of a smothered kiss, followed by the rich suppressed giggle of Murdina's protesting voice. The bodies moved on in their amorous combat.

Back in the hall, he watched for their re-entry. He was a big handsome fellow with a moustache, and, yes, his blue eyes were glittering rather self-consciously. So that knocked on the head any half-formed, feverish scheme for seeing Murdina home in the small dark hours.

Yet he clung to the hope … until it was finally dissipated, for, after what he had seen—or, rather, heard—he could hardly risk a formal offer. He hung about the dark outskirts of the door until he saw her emerge—and taken possession of. Someone called out something which he did not quite catch. It raised a laugh; and intuitively he knew that the laugh was against himself and in favour of the prowess of the blond cavalier.

On the way back to the croft, walking slowly to his shrinking thought, he was overtaken by timid footsteps which would have passed him by, had he not recognised the younger daughter, Elspeth. He spoke to her chaffingly. "What! no one seeing you home, Elspeth? ..."

But she was very shy. And presently he found it difficult to keep the talk going. To most of his queries she gave a simple yes or no, occasionally amplified by a "Yes, it was very nice", or "I don't know", or "I couldn't say". Her timid virgin tautness made him feel not unpleasantly cold. If he laid a finger on her, she would bolt. He did actually catch her arm at an awkward ditch and felt the frightened muscle flex and start away from him. She footed the ditch like a young hind. She was only a child of sixteen to his aged twenty-three. And when he had lit the light in the kitchen—there was no sign of Murdina yet—and turned to bid her good night, she replied in a curious voice without looking at him, without even showing her face.

That husky note in her voice disturbed him immediately he had got into his own room, gripped him so that he stood for a time doing nothing, conscious that by some ineptitude he had missed ... whatever it was ... but that might have been a certain feeling or passion ... towards himself. He grinned at that ... but refrained from breathing, kept listening, excitedly thinking ... paused in the act of taking off his jacket. ... He could go through to the kitchen for ... A sound came from outside. Then silence. Unbroken silence. That would be Murdina and her gallant. ... He saw them at their amorous game and completely forgot Elspeth. "Damn them!" he muttered with weary spite and took off his clothes. Though he did not feel at all sleepy, yet after a few obstinate minutes he sank into a dog sleep of exhaustion.

Daylight and the earth showed him what was happening: his mind was disintegrating, going to bits ... or, more clearly, he saw it lapsing into the vacant soil. Nor could he be disturbed about it. He was satisfied now that the crofter never thought, that he carried on for long hours with his mind hypnotised by nothing. It was easy to do this, and anything but unpleasant. He himself drowsed until the possibility of entertaining an original idea and getting excited about it became so remote that its contemplation was burdensome.

He gave up any pretence of writing. One could write in Glasgow, but not here. There was nothing here but a clayey absorption and persistence. Philosophically it had the immutable sameness of the face of Nirvana or God ... except that it was disturbed by this animal vortex; a warm disturbance, sporadic, whirling downward out of sight, and, when in full career, desperately secretive and cunning. And yet for all its cunning ever ready to egg on the body to its own betrayal. He began to find himself now and then in the barn, on the off chance that Murdina might come in, his heart beating if a footstep came near the door.

Then on the edge of the dark one evening, Elspeth came into the barn. In their surprise, they stared at each other for a naked speechless moment. With the fluttering action of a snake-fascinated bird, Elspeth turned and made her way out. The revelation of their suppressed emotions had been complete.

Shame pierced his mind—as a red lance a quivering core of exultation. He sat down. He would have to think this over. He ran his tongue along his lips.

The debate was fevered and sinful and horribly fascinating. Mind and body got caught up in it. He walked miles in the dark, deciding this, and, in tired moments of reckless devilry, deciding that; but finally coming to no conscious decision … except that by the hot unconscious urge of things there would probably happen … between Elspeth and himself.…

Into the slyness of this interminable debate there swept suddenly a note of sheer weary disgust. He cursed the night and the sodden land. He sat down and bowed his head and cursed himself. And crouched there, at bay, he faced at last the thought that was behind all thought, ultimate and annihilating, and it said to him: *You know what's wrong. … You're not an artist.*

All of life's meaning and beauty withered in its breath and turned to ash. A grey pitiless face.

And when he let himself go and laughed harshly, obliterating the face, he remembered all the littlenesses that were his too. He could not even do a small thing in the royal way, like an artist. Glasgow … he did not simply walk away and leave the damned place. No fear! He had been careful to take his typewriter with him, and writing paper, and all the rest of the paraphernalia. And here tonight now, instead of getting up and walking over the hilltops, no matter what came of it … no fear; he would go back, and pack up, and carefully destroy every scrap of paper that he did not take with him.…

The following afternoon he did leave. And just as he had thrown his last meditative cigarette stump in the fire and was starting from his armchair, he caught the hillside in the cracked mirror, and in its quiescent quality was a curious aloof mockery, watching him. His face rose into the mirror, pale, tight-lipped, bitter, blotting out the landscape.

The crofter accompanied him to the bus, wondering out of curiosity where he might be going to next. But he was not quite sure where he was going. Smiling, he looked about the free world. His mind began to function again; one or two doubtful flashes scintillated from an awakening intellect. As the bus trundled down the glen road, he waved in response to the white hanky at the cottage door. Oh, good-bye, fare ye well! Before the ticket office on the little station platform, he hesitated only a moment, then said, "Third, single, Glasgow."

The Chariot

You think I'm on the mend, Doctor?"

"You just take care of yourself and keep on as you're doing." The doctor nodded agreeably. "Don't get up. Give the old organ a chance. It'll do its best for you."

"I feel a bit easier." The eyes in the spare face had a glassy sheen and looked at the doctor as if they would look through him.

With his characteristic tender gesture, the doctor laid the old man's wrist on the coverlet. "There now!" he said, getting up off the bed. "I'll look in to see you again soon."

The old man removed his eyes. They were inclined to fix in a stare.

As the doctor closed the door behind him, the patient's housekeeper came from the kitchen and asked in a hushed voice, "How is he?"

"He feels a bit easier," said the doctor. "But you mustn't let him get up or exert himself in any way."

"All right, Doctor. He's not so difficult now. He was asking for you last night."

"I'll be out again soon. There's not a great deal I can do for him. He just has to rest."

"When will you be? He'll be asking me."

"Let me see," said the doctor, lifting his eyes from the anxious face, with the wisps of grey hair beneath the openwork dust-cap he always wore in the morning. "Not tomorrow—nor, perhaps, next day—but certainly the day after."

"You couldn't make it the day after tomorrow?"

The doctor thought for a moment. "Very well," he said.

"Thank you, Doctor." She nodded with relief. "I'll tell him that."

As the doctor left the house and walked quickly out to his car, he heard smothered laughter coming from the shop, which stood a few yards up the main road. The village consisted of a loose cluster of about a score of dwellings, but the countryside around was dotted with croft houses and the little fields were clearly defined, the potatoes a mass of flower and the corn just ready to turn. It was a lovely day, and the laughter from the shop was the hidden heart of it.

The doctor smiled to himself as he got under the driving-wheel. It was easy to diagnose the laughter. He took out his cigarette-case; there was only one in it, so he slipped from the car and went up to the shop.

They were all caught red-handed in their mirth—Bobbie, the lovely flashing Johanna with her finger-tips on the counter, the old woman with the basket, a couple of young women and a boy. The laughter was sliced off. But Johanna's eyes held a certain mantling challenge as she waited for the doctor's order.

No one spoke until the doctor had got his cigarettes and was turning away; then the old woman, in a restrained, sober voice, asked, "How is Mr. Macready to-day?"

"Not so bad. It's a fine day."

"Yes, it's a beautiful day, Doctor."

"Thank you," said the doctor, and threw Johanna a glance. She smiled out of a face vivid with life, not exactly a bold smile, but with the unconscious challenge in it which a man feels.

If it is unconscious! thought the doctor, who believed that what Johanna needed was someone a dozen years older than herself.

All at once he felt relieved, almost happy. The truth was he did not like the old man. He had the curious feeling for a doctor of almost having to force himself to call. Accordingly, he made sure that he fulfilled his professional duty. In the past, Donald Macready had made sure that he did no more than that. "I'm feeling much better, Doctor. I don't think you need call again." As direct as that, the old devil! He was not going to pay for an extra visit if it could be avoided. The doctor remembered how angry this had made him the first time.

But things were a bit different now. It seemed to have dawned on Donald at last that the chariot might be drawing near. He looked today as if he had heard it. The sound must have been a pretty bleak one, for visits now were what he wanted.

The doctor's humour took an edge as he reflected what a miser the old man had been. Not that it mattered much in itself, a man's being a miser. If one got fun out of that, why not? It was when this miserliness crushed the fun out of others that the thing became accursed, made you feel bitter against it, and vindictive. He had robbed the countryside, got the poor people in his debt and fleeced them—not dramatically, but in that hellish little by little, that slow grinding that never let up. And it was so easy to do, because they were an improvident lot, leaving tomorrow to take care of itself, hoping for twin lambs, a good fishing, a bumper crop, believing even that the weather would change and be fine at the right time. Yet somehow a people who, in a certain mood, went to your heart.

Anyway, they could laugh—even if they felt guilty with illness so near! The hidden laughter of relief.

And Johanna, Donald's niece and heiress, would fairly make the money spin. Thousands and thousands—some said over fifty thousand. A catch for some bright youth! Though Johanna was all there, and a real good business girl. But how she would do it in style, upright, with her pointed breasts, when she started, when she was challenged! She would all right!

The doctor smiled, for Donald's visit had been the last and he was on his way home. With luck, there would be a round of golf in the evening, so he could let his mind free, even with Johanna!

Though it was interesting to speculate just what Donald must have thought this last year or two as he privately contemplated the passing of the vast horde he had accumulated, with such fisted hardness, over a lifetime, to the flashing Johanna.

The doctor's eyelids crinkled in a measuring humour. But no, there would have been nothing of that dubious warmth in their relationship. On the contrary, he had seen him "short" with the girl. Just as he was with wild flowers that made the grass rank. Weeds. The bluebottle that distracted you by buzzing on the window. The doctor made quite sure of this. He nodded, certain.

What, then? Just the one thing: that Donald so lived—had so lived—that his life of the moment, his money-making life, could not end. Without thinking about it at all, he had felt himself immortal. He had taken the girl to his shop and house because she was of his blood, because he therefore need not pay her a real wage, and because, being of his blood, he could presumably rely on her against the outside world. He would, in fact, have a vague grudge against her. Not because she was not his own child—he had never had time to marry, and in any case would probably have been harsher to her had she been his daughter—but because she was young, not sufficiently absorbed by the business; because she was not—himself.

But it didn't matter. He could tolerate her all right, for at any moment he could send her packing. He had the power, the money, and death was so remote that the thought of it could not touch him.

It was not quite so remote now!

Two days later, as the doctor approached the house, he wondered if he should suggest a heart specialist from Glasgow. After all, the old fellow had the cash and should at least be given the opportunity to use it, for his peace of mind if nothing else. The doctor's lashes flickered in their dry humour as he saw for a clear moment the two planes of his own mind: the professional plane where he would do everything possible to help his patient and that other human plane from which he observed what was happening with an insight so absolute that it was arid. As this insight had been growing in him, he dismissed it. He would suggest that the specialist should charter a plane. It would be expensive, and would take up so much less of the specialist's time that the unnecessary visit could to that degree be given some face. After all, if his patient wanted it …

To keep his eyes from the house he let them rove over the countryside. It was another lovely day, when growing things matured or flowered, with a warmth that ran through the air in a delicate fragrance. Like something long lost from the human condition, this fragrance touched the doctor for a moment.

The eyes were on him from the instant the door opened, but the body was still as a log, as a dead body laid out. The doctor sat cheerily down on the edge of the bed and looked at him, steadily, and the old man waited, not inconvenienced by the inscrutable professional look, but on the contrary seeming to drink it in, with a relief that could almost be seen.

"Just about the same, Doctor." He moved his head, began trying to describe pains he had had, placed his hand on his breast. The doctor nodded, and the old man sighed.

"They're looking after you all right?"

The eyes regarded the doctor, with their thin, glassy light, as if they did not understand. The doctor repeated his question. The eyes turned from the doctor's face to the window. "Yes," he muttered with indifference. "They" were clearly of no interest to him, were already dismissed.

The doctor caught the wrist gently, and while he felt the pulse, the old man lowered his lids and breathed heavily with a mournful sound of ease.

"Yes," said the doctor at last, nodding as he laid down the wrist, and again he looked steadily at the face. "So you're not feeling too grand today?"

"Just about the same."

"It's a slow business. You must reconcile yourself to that."

"Yes. So long as I'll get better?" It was only faintly a question.

"Oh, we'll see to that." The doctor began talking about food and bodily conditions, and had a look at the tongue. Then in the same conversational tone he said, "Perhaps you would like to have another opinion?"

There was a pause as the eyes stared, it seemed uncomprehendingly, at the doctor.

"I mean the opinion of another doctor—a specialist. I could arrange it for you, if you think it might make you feel easier."

"No. Oh no." The words sounded automatic. But the doctor, who was now watching the face acutely from behind his pleasantness, saw something wary in the expression, almost frightened, and decided that the old man was not quite so low as he had thought. The old Adam was still there!

But when the doctor was sent for specially the following morning, he decided that a night's reflection had prepared the old man to slacken the purse strings. And now he almost regretted having mentioned the matter of another opinion. The truth was he disliked all that the old man stood for, and did not give a hang for his money or how he spent it. His own account would not include a halfpenny more than the normal charge, whether the old man were dead or alive. If he had to ring up a Glasgow specialist he would take care to give him his very frank opinion of the case—as well as the old man's circumstances. What then happened could happen, but it was so much extra work, unnecessary, and he was busy enough.

"Well," he said cheerfully as he entered the sick room, "what's all the trouble this morning?"

Something like a smile came to the gaunt features, and as they were not used to smiling, the expression was curiously repellant, particularly as the eyes, in their tendency to stare, took on that glassy light from the window. "I hope I did not take you away, but I was thinking over what you said about another doctor. Would you like me to have one?"

"That's for you to say. If there's anyone you would like, I could arrange it."

"Do you think it necessary?"

"Frankly, no. But that's only my opinion."

He sighed. "That's all right then. I did not wish to trouble you. But if you wanted another doctor, you could have one. I was frightened you might think I didn't want you to have one."

"Don't you want one, then?"

"Not if you don't yourself, Doctor. I'm satisfied."

"You're quite sure?"

The eyes looked at him, and for a moment there was an odd, indescribable tension that the doctor could not fathom but that made him feel uncomfortable.

"Quite sure," said Donald.

"In that case, it's all right," said the doctor, getting off the bed. "We'll look after you as best we can."

It was no good talking to the housekeeper, whose mind had been devilled out of her, so he went up to the shop. Bobbie was opening a wooden box, and Johanna greeted him with her full-open sky-blue eyes. He took some money out of his pocket and she placed his brand of cigarettes on the counter. He glanced at Bobbie, and she said: "Bobbie, you might see about that box in the yard." She was a sensible girl, and the lad went. "How is he this morning?" she asked.

"Pretty much the same—although he seems changed a bit. Anything happened to him?"

"No. Not that I know of."

"Did he mention anything to you, or the housekeeper, about getting another opinion, medical opinion?"

"No." Her fair brows gathered in a small pucker, imperious, concerned for the doctor, as she gazed full into his eyes.

"That's all right, then. To ease his mind, I said to him last night that I could arrange for another opinion if he liked. That's what I thought he wanted me for."

"Was it?"

"No. At least he said he didn't want another opinion if I didn't want one. I couldn't quite make him out."

"I don't think", she said, turning her face to the window with its laden shelves, "that—it would be a question of expense. I—hardly think so."

That was frank and clever of her. She surprised the look of admiration in his eyes, and, with a thoughtful smile at the packet in his hand, he extracted a cigarette and lit it.

"I just wondered," he said easily.

"I think it is because", and she looked away again, "he has faith in you."

"You think so? That's odd, because we haven't been too friendly."

"Perhaps that's why."

He glanced at her quickly.

"How do you mean?"

"Because he saw you were independent."

He considered her face as he did a patient's, but with the smile of tribute lighting up his brown eyes. "Now that *is* clever of you."

She moved at haphazard, trying to keep back the blush, but it deepened steadily. He regarded the window; then, taking out his silver cigarette-case, began to fill it. "All the same, I wonder?" and he looked up sideways with the friendliest smile.

"I know he does," she answered, twisting the end of string that overflowed from its tin canister round a forefinger, head up, annoyed with herself. She dropped the string. "He thinks he can trust you."

"You think that?"

"He thinks it."

He laughed. "You're fairly bright this morning."

"How is he, really?"

"Pretty bad, actually. Anything might happen—fairly soon. I wanted to say as much to you."

"Oh." Her expression sobered and she grew quite still. In the silence they heard footsteps approaching the door.

"I'll keep my eye on him—and let you know."

"I wish you would," she said impulsively, hardly looking at him.

"Don't worry about it," he suggested, calming her. The customer, a woman, entered behind him. "I'll look along tomorrow morning."

"Thank you."

As he drove on to his next patient, he could not help smiling at Johanna's penetration. Acute of her—whether true or not. And for a little while he could not be bothered probing the truth for thinking of Johanna. It was pleasant to smile and feel amused in this careless way. Fresh and new. Another lovely day. The weather would probably break down just when the corn was ready for cutting. There was humour in that, too, the strange, inscrutable humour that hung over the sunlit land.

Perhaps the old man did respect him? One did respect one's enemy if he was firm and of a piece. His vision narrowed, focusing the old man's mind. He began to feel himself inside the old man's skin. Quite suddenly intuition revealed the pattern with all the certainty of a direct sensation. His foot eased on the throttle to let the car go slow. But he could not readily focus thought, so he stopped the car by the roadside and, under the influence of a fine excitement, automatically lit a cigarette.

She was quite right. Money was not the trouble. Very simply what was happening to Donald was this: all his life his relationships had been to things, to cash. But he had now heard the chariot, and the chariot had no relationship to cash—very, very definitely. The doctor's eyes narrowed. Donald now was wanting relationship to life, to another life, instinctively feeling that that would keep away the terror, the lonely terror, of the chariot. In that stark desert loneliness, where the money-hunt had taken him, *money was of no use.*

The doctor nodded and smiled with one corner of his mouth. He's going to use me now! He's terrified! His humour grew so bleak that a withering came to his own face. Suddenly he started up the car and set off at speed.

When, next morning, he sat down on the edge of the patient's bed and pleasantly began asking the usual questions, he was ready to confirm his psychological diagnosis. And from every slightest movement, or intonation, or facial expression, what the previous day had been incalculable was now clear. The old man was not so much greedy for life as greedy for the doctor's life. And the doctor led him on, as though some ultimate subtlety in himself, fine as a knife-edge, had to be satisfied or assuaged. He reverted again to the getting of a second opinion, but this time directly named a consultant in Glasgow. Of course, the chartering of an aeroplane, not to mention a fast car and so on, would be very expensive. But if his patient thought it was worth it …

All this easeful play, wherein the two planes of the doctor's mind got dubiously intermixed, did establish a certain curious nemesis. The old man at last, at the end, could not trust anyone outside. Did not want anyone from outside—if he could put his full trust in the doctor. And for this trust he pleaded, yet not openly, for he had his own character, moulded by past custom.

"Well, I'm pretty busy just now, but I'll look in tomorrow morning."

"*Any* time you're passing, Doctor. I'll be glad to see you."

"Very good." He smiled to his patient and went out.

But there was a taste in his mouth, and when he saw a customer going towards the shop he got into his car and drove off. As he drove off, he thought he ought to have gone to the shop and spoken to Johanna. He wondered if he would stop the car and go back. But the car went on, driving itself with a mechanical persistence that his mind, in its peculiar humour, observed.

The next day, affairs went a stage further. For the first time the old man showed signs of wanting to talk. The doctor decided that this was merely a device to detain him. But presently he saw it was more than that. For in the old man's talk about his affairs there was no genuine interest in how they were getting on.

"You needn't worry," the doctor had said, heading him off. "Johanna is a very capable girl. Things are safe with her."

But he was not worrying about Johanna. He wanted to talk about his business because he wanted to talk about his life. Out of a slightly morbid curiosity the doctor listened for a time. "It's been a hard life, and many folk were against me…" But there was a limit to what he could listen to, so he got off the bed, pleasantly. For he could not hurt the old man, could not mortally offend him.

He wants to make me his confessor next! he thought, as he went outside and glanced towards the shop. He had better see Johanna, if he was to avoid thinking as much about her as he had done last night.

There were customers in, but Johanna must have seen him through the window, for she met him at the door and they walked down the few yards to the car.

"You were quite right," he said, as they stood by the car. "I didn't look in to tell you that yesterday because I saw you had customers. But you were right—about the money."

"I thought I was. He was always wondering when you were coming, and was inclined to blame us when you didn't turn up."

"I suppose he blamed me, too?"

"He did—to begin with. Not now."

"Look here," he said spontaneously, "what about leaving that old shop now and running off with me to town for a cup of coffee?"

She glanced at him, smiling, and looked away. "I should love it."

"Well?"

She dismissed the play. "Perhaps you'll let me know how he is tomorrow?"

"So you won't come? All right. I'll remember that—until tomorrow!" Then as he went into the car he beckoned with his head. She turned away, and because there was a small flush on her face she hurried.

That brightened her up! he thought. All the same, his offer *had* been spontaneous. He had better watch himself! There wasn't a cell in her body that wasn't alive. She was certainly a lovely creature, with something genuinely shy behind that country flash of boldness. Or was he imagining it? He knew he wasn't. She needed her share of self-protection against the country lads, who in their natural improvidence made love naturally. He laughed.

But there was an extraordinary persistence of life in Donald, and the doctor grew to hate the sight of the house. He was finding it more and more difficult to indulge the old man mentally. He would listen, but he was evasive, and after a time headed him off. The reaction of dislike for the old man that this produced hung about his own mouth, his mind, in an inverted distaste for himself. When he felt the patient trying to justify his way of life in an oblique effort to draw understanding, sympathy, his whole body would in an instant quicken with a sort of cold fury that was yet almost passionless, while he smiled and countered with a play of easy optimism. "Time enough to worry—you're not dead yet!" The glassy eyes would look at him.

All this began to have its effect on the doctor, curiously darkening life for spells. Then he decided that it was beginning to have its effect on Johanna. The vivid spontaneous quality, that is the core of life, was netted in its shadow. The doctor could see, in his mind, Johanna moving about in this shadow, her face petulant, dreary with a sort of ill-temper that remained suspended, directionless, in a sordid world.

This, perhaps, was allowing intuition too much rope. But there were ways of testing it, and though Johanna had a degree of loyalty to her uncle which he admired, her reticence and a certain moody, troubled look, however momentary, were all the more expressive on that account. It really was extraordinary how pervasive the old man's mind had become. One could almost imagine it in the cow that, with swollen sides, still kept tearing at the grass in the ditch as she was driven home.

Within ten days the relationship between Johanna and the doctor took a definite change. It entered into a sunless phase, which the bright sun in the lovely ripening weather mocked at with its hidden thought. But though Johanna thus lost her flashing challenge, she somehow came still nearer to the doctor, as two human beings might draw together who had to find their way out of a wood or a wilderness.

It was not that the old man was the ogre in the wood, the invisible devil in the wilderness. But there was enough of that in it to invade the professional plane, to stiffen the doctor against yielding to the potency of the old man's character and influence. And the power of that character he had ample time to think over and to assess, until it assumed, by its terrifying persistence in time, every day, every hour, year after year, a more destroying potency than that of any ogre or invisible devil. It checked here, it checked there, little by little, in this and that, until it baffled and frustrated and subdued. Johanna's flashing challenge had been the rebellion of youth outside the ogre's immediate presence. But now Johanna, having been joined by the doctor, heard the chariot and became aware of the sunless wood.

And Donald would not have been beaten by them had his attention not been divided by the approach of the chariot, which had precisely his own power of persistence.

Ah, more than his own. And as at last he began to realise this, he seemed to withdraw from the doctor and enter on the next terrible phase, the unhuman phase.

The doctor's intuition became extremely acute, and when he thought of that battle—no, not a battle, but a state of endurance cold and tough as stone—between approaching death and the waiting old man, he got out of its filtered loneliness a bitter savour. He went over some of the meaner things Donald had done, and got the impression again of a whole life devoted to money-making, money-hoarding. He couldn't take his money with him now! By God he couldn't! The doctor caught a glimpse of something horribly spiteful and malignant in money, and something of what he saw was caught in his own smile.

His patient's face took on the likeness of stone. He ceased to speak about himself. To the doctor, however, there was in the hollows and bone ridges, in the withdrawn expression, a pathos that affected him, in an unexpected moment of feeling, with a sense of colossal guilt. Not so much his own guilt, as the guilt of all mankind, an incredible and pathetic conspiracy in guilt.

This was carrying the myth too far, he decided, and went up and saw Johanna. Her flame was oddly subdued these days, but, for some reason, he felt its warmth all the more. She looked as if she were trapped and did not know where to turn; or had things to say and could not say them.

And now he found he could not say much to her himself. It certainly had become quite impossible to invite her lightheartedly to the town.

"I don't think it will be very long now," he said, almost casually, as he lit a cigarette.

The skin of her face became transfused with blood, but no longer in a blush, in a strange congestion of feeling rather, that appealed to him profoundly as though, by an act, he could dissipate its moodiness and release the pure light.

To defeat the heavy pulse that began to beat in him, he said, "Don't worry. I'll see that everything is all right."

The suggestion of sympathy in his voice did not help her, and she turned her eyes to the window, stiffening her face against an emotional surge. The eyes were blue wells of living light.

"What about a run into town?" he said lightly, smiling. The sudden words were little more than a perverse hardening against the moment.

She turned from him. He heard Bobbie's footsteps in the back shop and went out.

The smile stayed on his face, as if concerned with something, thoughtfully, ironically, at a distance; but when his lips got a little dry he drew up. Could thought of the old man's death have got her into that state? Partly, of course—but certainly only partly. He looked about the countryside as he automatically felt for his cigarette-case. Odd! he decided, the smiling gleam in his eyes not altogether dry. Very odd! Then, about to tap his cigarette on the silver case, he paused, and stared into the sunlight that lay on the ripe fields. The sunlight smiled back in its evasive, knowing way. It knew all about it all! In an instant his body ran hot, and Johanna came walking, as it were, towards him, out of the potato fields and the ripe corn, along the land under the blue sky.

His hands were a trifle shaky as he, drove on, and he drew the cigarette smoke deep into his lungs, thought shut off.

That evening on a sudden impulse or intuition he went out to see the old man. Johanna and Bobbie were helping to unload a lorry beside the shop. As he got out he saluted them and turned down to the house. He read the housekeeper's face, saw its relief, its sudden resignation, and he knew that that face would have made no mistake.

The old man's eyes slowly turned on him, coldly, distant. The bone ridges and the flesh had caught the final stillness of stone, the everlasting stillness. From the doctor the eyes asked nothing; in their own need they lifted from the face and stared at the ceiling.

Never had the doctor seen such utter bleakness. He sat on the bed and stared at the face. There was nothing to be said.

Then, just before the end, there was an inward movement, a stirring of the mind, an appalling comprehension of the past by the spirit; the doctor felt it in himself with extraordinary power. The loneliness, the bleakness, were intensified a thousandfold; were apprehended now as never before, apprehended finally and beyond all possibility of change. As if the stone face had been struck, the mouth opened in a guttering "Ah-h-h".

The doctor shuddered, got up off the bed, and closed the eyes.

Presently he went out to break the news to Johanna. The lorry was driving off and she came to meet him, her eyes reading his message as she approached. He took her hand and with a smile placed it in the crook of his arm. "Keep your spirit up," he said.

She bit on her lip, but went with him down to the house.

From the kitchen they heard the housekeeper's moaning voice. About the only abandonment left to her was indulgence in sorrow.

"Like to see him?" he asked suddenly, smiling in his light, friendly way. She would have to see him some time, for it was the country custom. She did not know what to do, and not knowing why he did this himself, he opened the door and ushered her into the room where the stone face lay under the ceiling.

She looked at it, and then, as if hit by some primeval terror, turned blindly away, choking.

"It's all right, Johanna," he said, detaining her with an arm. He spoke softly. His arm firmed. He put his other arm round her and she struggled against him as if to walk through him.

But he held her and spoke her name twice softly, his voice searching her out, searching out her face, searching out her face until he found it, and her arms gripped him as the last and only thing in life to which they could hold, gripped blindly and held to him and dwelt in him.

And the mood that had been growing within him these last years, the half-friendly but arid insight, the deadly insight, was dissolved, and life ran in a wild warm tide.

The White Hour

He paused by the water-barrel in a momentary listening, while a little white flame crept in about his eyes; then he took the last step to the back door and lifted the latch.

There were two or three paces of a gloomy passage-way to the kitchen and from the gloom he saw the spectral head of the old woman above her dark clothes. From the stiff wooden chair her body leant a little to the flickering fire, but her face was turned from it to the window. The quiet, early-evening light from the window fell with such a radiance on her face that the young man felt the uncanniness of it.

"Well, Granny!" he cried cheerfully, passing the top end of the boxed-in bed into the kitchen itself. A cold, healthy breeze rustled from him, and as he rubbed his hands before the flickering blaze, he laughed.

"Is it yourself!" she cried, with a start. Her welcoming voice was so quavering thin that its warmth went to his heart. The kindliness of her was a thing beyond analysis. "Take a chair! Take a chair!" Her body swayed as though it would take it in for him.

Before he had right seated himself, she lifted her voice: "Mary! What's keeping ye through there at all?"

"Coming, Granny!"

In the little silence that followed, the old woman saw Mary looking at herself in the glass, with her fingers doing this and that; but the young man could not see anything because of the sound of Mary's voice in his ears.

The chair legs scraped under him.

"Ay, Granny, but you're looking well!" In his mouth the title was one of courtesy.

"Oh, I'm keeping fine! I'm keeping fine!" Thin, bony fingers moved restlessly, caressingly on her lap. "It's not for me to complain." She stirred smilingly.

Then he saw that there was something working on her mind and that he had interrupted it in coming in.

"One feels the cold a little at times, what with the nights drawing in as they are."

"Yes, indeed," she said, stirring even more from the thing on her mind. "And sometimes, maybe, I'll be feeling I'm not just too strong. And then—and then I'll be thinking——"

Because of her years, he saw that she could only throw the thing from her mind by telling it.

"You haven't had another turn since, have you, Granny?"

"No. Not that."

She hesitated, but the way he waited held prompting sympathy.

"It was just at this time yesterday," she said at last. "Mary was out somewhere, and I was sitting here by myself. Just about this time, and it won't go out of my head."

At that he looked at her. Her face, he saw, was worn frail and thin as a sea-shell. Its fragility was incredible. An awful, impersonal fragility. Only the eyes belonged to life as he knew it, and even they burned thinly, transparently. It was in the eyes he had always found the resemblance to her granddaughter, Mary. But these eyes before him had now lost the luminous, welling depth. They had become as thin spirit flames set in the frost-shell of a face.

"It won't go out of my head at all," she went on, drawing strength from him; "and I was thinking about it as you came in. I was thinking about it—and—I was thinking it was coming on me again."

"Was it last night?" he helped gently.

"Ay, it was last night. It was just in the evening about this time. Mary had gone out somewhere, and I was sitting here by myself. The old days had put a spell on me, and I was hearing the patter of little feet running. Then I was a girl myself with the faces of all who are dead and gone laughing and talking, as they would be doing long long ago. They were before me so clearly that there is no telling it. Every one of them by name I had. It was wonderful, so clear it was. … I was remembering, too, that first time behind the ould barn at home. I was feeding a lamb out of a bottle and Maurice came round the end of the barn. It came on us there and then, so that we could not speak. … There was never a better man to a woman."

In his way, the young man understood this, understood her feelings. It was always the same with the very old, as he had noticed. And by the ould barn there and the lamb—he was seeing the way of it with them so that the surge was in his own throat.

But when she spoke again, such a whispering, frightened note crept in her voice as made his mind start in a small shiver.

"And then—and then the feeling came over me on a sudden that there was Something in the kitchen here—watching me! It was such a terrible, quick feeling that my heart nearly choked me with the sudden fright of it. But when I looked up—there was nothing at all, not a living thing. Its trembling I was in a moment, looking for—for the thing. I thought once it was behind me, so that I could not turn round. But I began to feel it—coming.

"Ah, then—then it was the top of the bed I saw, and the edge of it was looking down at me; leaning over a little it was, and—watching me. And then the table, and the chairs. I looked to the door—the edge of it was pointing straight at me. But the most terrible thing of all was the stillness. I had never heard any stillness like it before—except the stillness of the dead. *And it was more than the stillness of the dead.*"

She paused to gather steadiness in a few quick breaths.

"It was an awful thing, the stillness—with my bits of furniture there watching me like strangers, and waiting, and listening. I looked to the window to see someone passing in the street so that I might cry to them. But the light in the window was white, so white it was that it hurt my eyes to be looking at it. And then it came on me what they were waiting for. Ah, I knew in a moment what it was they were listening for and waiting for to come in—to me. … The light from the window was like the light going before a—a Presence."

She just breathed the last word, so that the small shiver went down the young man's spine.

"Old as I am I did not know before that the most terrible of all things to mortal soul is loneliness. There are no words for it. To be left alone, waiting for—that, with not a voice nor a hand, as though you were lost for ever on a great white plain! My heart cried within me for the sound of a neighbour or a child or a beast itself. But it was like as if everything in the world was dead, and me left behind waiting for—that… .

"I got to my feet and made as best I could for the front door. I would see some-one in the village street. But there was no one in the village street, no living soul, no moving living thing. And down at the foot of the gardens not a tree moved, not a leaf. The trees were grown taller, with a white quietness about them, and a listening and a light among their old leaves. And the tops of them were leaning over a little—*watching me*."

She rocked herself gently.

"I am an old woman who should be prepared, but oh, the awful loneliness, with that terrible white light hurting the balls of my eyes and pressing long white fingers against my forehead. Pushing me back, it was, back. … I would not have cared if only some one had been near me. But there was no one, there was no sound. … I came back as fast as I could and covered my head and wept."

Mary came in on a quick, light foot and gave a laughing greeting.

"Granny would be telling you of her weakness," she said cheerfully. She flustered about, poking the fire and lifting the kettle.

She had brought a rustle of air with her and a faint fragrance of violets. The fragrance touched the nostrils of the old woman so that she thought of the little green cake of soap Mary would be using at special times. She felt the nearness of their two young strong bodies and her heart kindled a little at the blaze. From the telling of her story there came relief, and the kindliness that was the whole of her welled up.

"Mary——"

"Ay, Granny—I'm just going to fill the kettle. I'll make a nice strong cup."

"Do ye that, Mary."

When the tea was over and the young man might be thinking of going, Mary was out about the back door, washing the cups perhaps. As he got up he was hoping she would not come in. She might come in easily. He had noticed that when the heart is desperately anxious that a woman do some clear simple thing the chances are she will not do it. Mary, however, did not come in, and an unusual thing happened. The white skeleton fingers came out and caught his passing hand, and held it. A terrible fore-knowledge came from the fingers and trickled through his flesh. She did not speak, but the thin flame of her eyes deepened. He needed no word to understand.

The dread thought of it was made bearable because of a final pressure of both her hands. It was the pressure that finishes a heart's telling and another heart's understanding. "In the world there is no girl like her," was her only saying, and with that her hands dropped. He felt the pressure of words in him, but no word came; one might even force a cheery, reassuring laugh, but no laugh stirred in his throat.

He found Mary by the water-barrel. She did not look at him, busy as she was drying the dish-basin. Finally she wrung out the dish-clout, opened it out, flapped it. Then she spread it over two nails by the door.

Before she might turn round, he quickly lifted his eyes from her to the moor. His feelings tangled themselves to a knot in his throat, making his breathing uneven. Something had to be said, and the only natural thing to be said was about the old woman, and the old woman was dying.

"She's—she's——"

"Ay," said Mary, taking the word from him kindly, and staring out over the moor, too.

Her little word suddenly ran with a strange, dark companionableness on the crest of a wave within him. Surging the wave came. He broke the silence by turning his head from the moor and looking at her.

Her eyes shone luminous and soft and of a depth to drown the soul itself. A small crimson flame crept over cheek and neck. Then the wave broke and engulfed them.

The old woman did not see the crushing of the pliant body nor the smothering of the wild kissing, but the companionableness of it was with her in a great sweetness, so that the glazed white light from the window softened to a shadowy beauty.

Visioning

The old Captain prefixed each of his stories with an account of the weather, the time, and the place. He did it in a simple, nautical way that was merely second nature to him, but to me sheer fascination. Sometimes I would interrupt. "And the flies would be bad, too." So that before he got to the actual story I had the itch of the heat in my skin.

I could never help myself. My imagination worked on the lines of a tormenting realism; not, for love of it, I suspect, but as a sort of instinctive safeguard against the too fatal attraction of glamour. If, for example, the scene were cast under South Pacific skies I not only saw the green fire of the palm-fronds, the shimmering emerald of the lagoon, the dazzling brilliance of the white crushed-coral beach, but I also felt the prickly heat of the sun, the oppressive languor of thc body, the clacking dryness of the mouth, the sweat. No vision, no traveller's description, however magical, however fairylike, could altogether mislead me. My own visioning insisted on flashing to the essentials with a certain unerring sense of direction that not infrequently had in it, it seemed to me, much of the material, even the sordid, but that yet always satisfied me as with a sense of balance.

There was one vision, however, that stood the test. Perhaps I allowed myself to be deceived, though I do not think so. I mention it not because it has had any direct bearing on my life, but because it was a vision that in itself was cool, luring, inexhaustible, and that in its recondite prompting, its subtle influencing, may have fanned the slow-burning fire of desire into a sudden flame, when in the silent tenement street of the grey Scottish port I looked down from my first-floor window on the tinkling hurdy-gurdy.

Somewhere down in the southern lands of Spain there is a country inn. It is evening, and a cool fragrance moves about the little tables white-spread under over-arching foliage of smooth-boled trees. Inside the inn a man in a rich baritone voice is singing a traveller's song to his own accompaniment, sweeping and full, on a mandoline. The music comes floating out through open windows. I do not consciously think of the man, or the quality of his voice, or the theme of the song: I am but dimly aware of it as a background as I sit a little table and look at a maid who is pouring me a glass of red wine from a bottle. The song, the cool fragrance, the restfulness of evening, the delicious languor of my body after walking, all combine to form a vague atmosphere of unfathomable sweetness surrounding the centrally distinct incident of the wine.

That is all the picture—nothing hectic, passionate or dull. If I thought along the line of the singing a moment or two I saw the voyager trolling a song of the road. There is in it a wonderful cadence companionable and known to the heart, there is a courtesy of greeting like the slow weeping of a feathered sombrero, a tale of words simple as the actions of brave men, and throughout it all and informing it a haunting of romance that is neither on land nor sea, but only in the heart of man. Take the wine. One has come over a long road on foot (there is no other way). Tiredness is on the body like a benediction. To eat at such a moment would be a physical debauch. One will eat presently. And meantime there is the wine, but slightly alcoholic, red, glowing red, and in a moment the cool touch of the glass will be on the lips. There is the inn. True, it won't be glistening white and spick-and-span, but even the slight touches of dilapidation here and there—are they not Nature's and wholesome, so that one's nail could test the dry rot in a piece of wood with a mild interest? And it is there so wonderfully set in the calm of the evening, so restful, so lazily inviting. One has but to get up and go in when the shadows have turned to darkness and the mystery of night is impalpable in the soul.

II

To youth vision is incident, and wine the blood thereof—youth itself being colour. How much the history of man owes to wine only the gods know. I knew something about wine at that comparatively early age of nineteen, called it "bottled sunshine," and considered it in my heart symbolical of the splendour and lavish generosity of the great fruitful earth. The thought of purple grapes—clusters of them—being crushed together was in its maddening sweetness almost more than I could bear. For by nature I was not given to excess. Did it not take nineteen years for my imagination to set the stage for my little gesture?

Four of us gathered in that little front room on one special night of the week. I always provided one bottle, and would never permit more than two. The Captain, who was always one of the four, was my landlord—or, more correctly, he was the father of my landlady, who was a widowed woman of about forty. She had accompanied him before she was married on some of his foreign trips, and still had in the kitchen a green and yellow parrot that spoke and whistled with amazing fluency—when so disposed.

All the immediate world of dull business and personal affairs was forgotten. The wine would remind me of something. That would remind the Captain of a story. It would remind the third man of a melody. The fourth of a poem. It was curious how each heart opened, how each listened. Laughter, talk, earnestness, wit, commingling in that little front room. It was as magical as anything on earth, though I did not know it, though probably none of the others knew it, except, perhaps, the Captain, whose great simplicity of mind is more wonderful to me now than it was then.

Very occasionally, too, there were special nights. On these nights discussion never reached the level it did on the recognised nights, probably because of the intrusion of the foreign element. The Captain's nephew was master of a deep-sea trading vessel, and when in port it was his custom to visit the house. He always brought a bottle of something special with him. It was the occasion for a special sitting, a special gaiety. But the advent of the nephew had a certain shrinking effect upon me. The mere way he spoke of Rio de Janeiro (mispronounced according to my school learning), Buenos Ayres, The Plate, shrivelled my physical and mental world into the size of a nut. Nevertheless, we liked each other. I would ask him about the great world, what was doing in this place and that, and how each thing struck him. He was a man lacking in vision, but the possessor of a fine healthy nature, and capable of talking about women with a gay laugh, that because of his very healthiness was forgiven him, even in extreme cases. I suppose I must have mentioned more than once my general desire to see the world, for his greeting invariably was: "Got your kit ready?" and his farewell : "Well, I'll be expecting you to sign on next trip." Jocular remarks on his part (for my salaried job, desk work though it was, was fairly responsible and contained prospects), though on my part the joke seemed as fine as Omar's "A hair perhaps divides the False and True."

It is difficult, even on searching analysis, to tell precisely on what food imagery thrives increasingly, on what mental wine imagination glows supremely. As with the Captain's stories, as with the poem, the song, so with the nephew's stories. My imagination exploited them to such a degree that I not only saw the places, followed the events, but almost grew tired of them in their oppressive, age-long reality—often before the words had had time to grow cold. And once I exploited any place in that way it, as it were, no longer held any romance. I should still like to see it, but it no longer held for me the unknown, the inexhaustible.

For this reason there were places on the map of the world that held little fascination, though the map of the world itself fascinated me endlessly. To present this fascination in its proper perspective would be to make the map of the world the dominant motif of my early life.

It was that—it was that and more, for it not only gave a direction to my visioning, but in itself was an endless source of pleasure. There were names on the map's surface that, in themselves, were poems cadenced and beautiful. To go with forefinger along the coasts of Italy and Spain, to travel inland, or outward to the islands, was a voyage of most magical discovery. A name could hold me in thrall for an hour. The enchantment of Seville! The wonderful glowing riches of the word oranges! In the dull dusk when certain colours are intensified, consider the globes of yellow fruit against their background of green, in the dusk when the world is quiet and the mind full of dreams and philosophy. Even Barcelona. Yes, there was the port with its dirt and its drudgery, but consider the colour, the richness of the vowelled language, the sunset laziness so opposed to that haste which some sage has characterised as "an attribute of devils." Consider coming down on Barcelona from the interior. Consider the word "interior" itself. The interior of Spain! And then down along the lands of Italy, through the slow music of the names, the *i*, the *a*, the *o*, rich as purple-clustered grapes and haunted by memories of passion, of art, of Caesar Borgias. One could stop anywhere and make a vision beautiful and sordid—and then wake up to find one's finger on the Kirghiz Steppes. The Kirghiz Steppes! Such an echoing name: horses' hooves on trackless wastes. And what figure is that coming, head bowed, pack on back? … Whither away? you ask through the gloom, and a voice, Tolstoyan, austere, answers: To the Infinite. What do captains and their nephews know of these places? Beyond the busyness of ports what do they know? Buenos Ayres, The Horn, Cape Town—what magic is there that one may not exploit at will?

The most fascinating places were always inland, because the spirit must be inland. At the seaport towns there could be little or no spirit except the spirit of cosmopolitanism and greed. But that did not mean for me that the spirit inland was a strange, syren, wonderful thing. Had it meant that, I should never have been at a desk until I was nineteen. Benares, Delhi, Agra—wicked and most devilish cunning. Could one live with the spirit that studded idols with pieces of coloured glass so cunningly that they shone a burning mass of living gems? Could one let the straightforward simplicity of one's soul get caught in the serpentine toils of an arabesque? And some of the temples: the work of angels with the contorted souls of devils.

Each place-name had its fascination, held its vision—and sometimes, too, in a curiously double way. For example, Constantinople, with its cloying painted women and its dogs, Constantinople the port, could be repellent; but Stamboul in its inner native recesses—what might there not be there, what piping and sinuous dancing, what veiling of women and heart-devastating secrets? Yet curiously enough, books of travel containing information did not excite me much; indeed, I read but few. Each one seemed to my indifferent fingers a piece of exploitation, like a business catalogue. They took me there and showed me this and that, and never so surely did I exploit a place in all its harsh, material reality as when the writer attempted the poetic.

So I stayed in the silent tenement street of the grey port, month slipping away after month. There was no tangible beckoning to my spirit, nothing decisive, definite, drawing me instantly, magnetically to the strange new places of the earth. In the grey port there were at any rate the certainties of my actual life, however narrow, however one-dimensioned.

III

Then something began to happen that brought my vision up against the realities of life in this undisturbed sameness of the grey port.

On the opposite side of the tenement street, and two doors farther up, there lived a girl of about my own age. One evening I had chanced to see her home from a small social function. Thereupon a certain indefinite intimacy sprang up between us. I would see her at her window and raise my hat. I would meet her on the street, talk, and walk along with her. I had no intention, as it is phrased, other than a purely friendly one as between the sexes, and yet in some mysterious way things began to be taken for granted. Should I chance to be bidding her good night in her doorway I found it embarrassingly difficult just to say good night and go away. There would plainly be something indifferent and insensitive in the action not to be thought of. She was not too good-looking, had no special charm that lured me, and yet I began to feel myself strangely entangled. One night I kissed her in the doorway. Why, I could not be sure, except that she had looked at me in a soft, swimming way. At first there was a mild excitement, then by the mere processes of growth a more loverlike attitude. But as I knew the same might have happened with any other girl I did not place too much importance on it, until one evening my vision—the vision that exploited the earth—began to play on it.

The nephew was in the kitchen talking some business or other with the Captain. I, not wishing to intrude, had casually left them with the excusing remark that I was going to pack my kit. The parrot shouted: "Look out there!" I came into the little front room that looked down on the street.

I stood at the window gazing straight across at the opposite house without seeing it. The nephew was sailing in the morning. It was as well, for in spite of myself he depressed me. All my knowledge, all there was of me mentally and imaginatively, merely seemed, through some process of congestion and restriction, to make me the smaller, more twisted, till by an excess of imagining I became a thin, wizened old man.

And was it going to be ever the same, ever the little round; was there to be no outlet, no adventuring, no tramping into the imaginatively known, the unimagined and unknown? The same futile questions, and more like them, I had disposed of many times before with a sufficiency of logic and robust commonsense, but that evening they got a violent twist by thinking of the girl up the street.

In a series of flashing pictures the measure of life was taken. An accidental meeting, an accidental intimacy, an accidental entangling, a logical—or illogical—marrying, and—an end. With her little pale face there always before me. An end. I would be nailed, like a piece of boarding, to fill a hole in the blind-alley hoarding of life. It was not of my conscious seeking, not of my wishing, yet it was there as inevitable as death—if not with that girl, then with some other like her. Sometime I would be nailed. The blind hole was gaping for me. My youth rebelled with violence. I could face all that later, if need be, in the fateful course of things, but not yet. I was not ready. I was too young. I had not seen. I did not know. …

And crashing through my half-logical, half-emotional outburst of rebellion came the strident notes of the hurdy-gurdy on the street below.

It was a relief. The sudden harsh metallic grinding of its mawkish tune was a devilish sort of contrast, not unlike a harsh laugh. I looked down.

I saw her at once to the exclusion of everything else in the universe. She flooded my mind and my senses with an instantaneousness that had no process of commencement. At once my heart was beating and my brain as clear as a mathematician's. I noticed the carving of her face, the dusky lure of it, the grace of the lithe body, the wild, haughty, imperial beauty of her youth, in an instant, and yet with a consciousness as to detail that was all-comprehensive. She was the living embodied answer to all the visioning, balancing, and questioning of my map-gazing. And I knew it with an almost insupportable certainty in a moment of time.

Outside the direct line of my physical vision I seemed to see a little old man turning a handle and bowing and smiling to me. Then she looked up into my face, and two dark eyes held me for a moment, two perfectly curved lips parted a fraction as though to smile. The head drooped.

Again the smiling and bowing of a monkey-like face. I looked at it. I nearly burst the window trying to lift it against the latch. I threw a piece of silver on the street. Then I closed the window and looked at her again.

But there was now such a pulsing turbulence in my blood that I left the window and began walking up and down the room. …

I do not know whether my imagination played me false then, or whether my memory plays me false now, but I cannot say that I ever saw again such perfect beauty of its kind, so untamed, so sculpturally perfect, so sensitively self-controlled. And she was an answer not to the sensuous in my nature so much as to the unknown. The duskiness of her face, slightly more than Spanish, was a lure, not merely of the feminine, but of the sun and wine and passion and beauty of strange lands. It was the long road, the inn, the maid pouring me the red wine—that and unfathomably more, all inextricably one. It never occurred to me to go down to the street. I suppose I could not have gone, considering the condition I was in, in any case. Whatever the reason the desire never crossed my mind. It may have been, as I now think, that she stood there as a symbol and got lost in the vaster meaning—and that though the warmth of her was in my blood.

I remember I was walking the room when the Captain and the nephew came in.

"Hullo!" said the nephew. "A full head of steam!"

I pulled myself together and came to a standstill. I also tried to smile. I remember how the effort seemed to crinkle my cheeks. But I must have been pale—or perhaps flushed—for I saw the Captain looking at me. I could say nothing, wanted to say nothing. I drifted towards the door.

"Are you off?" asked the nephew. They were both looking at me, slightly uneasy, I thought.

"Yes," I said, quite gravely; "I'm going to pack my kit."

I saw belief spread over the Captain's face in a sudden weak, credulous dismay.

"Good lad!" said the nephew.

"And I shall sail with you in the morning."

Then I saw in the amazed silence of the nephew that he believed me, too.

Such Stuff as Dreams

To the woman who sat by his bedside he was delirious, but to himself he was preternaturally sane. His vision was clear and fine and penetrating, and entirely untroubled by the burning sheath that was his body. Indeed, it was as though the burning sheath had dissolved away the dross of the mind, the clogged pores, the stupid obfuscations of everyday.

Thus he was aware of his illness as of something a little apart, as far apart, say, as the burning sheath from this inner central certainty of the mind, which was his real self, his thinking self, with its inexhaustible power of precise imagery. His illness was an objective thing, like a pack on a man's back. And, as with the pack, he knew it could be got rid of.

But not, of course, exactly as one would drop a pack. It could be dropped certainly, but in its own way. There was a way for dropping it, and he knew the way. Only, no one would believe him if he told them.

He turned over in his bed and muttered, so that the woman in the dim shaded light lifted her weary eyes to his haggard face. From side to side slowly his head rolled on the pillow, then suddenly became still as the eyes opened wide and stared fixedly before them. Involuntarily her hand started out over the coverlet to soothe the demon of delirium. It closed gently on his hand.

A small tremor went over his face, followed by a lessening of tension in the pallor, as a man's face will soften at a vision that touches the heart. The eyelids fell and from between the lips came a long quivering sigh, with a curious break in the end of it, like a wonder-catch of the breath.

She noticed that he seemed to quieten after that, breathing so lightly that the movement of the bedclothes above his chest was scarcely perceptible. If only he would sleep for a little! If only she could give him the tiniest fraction of this great weight of sleep and tiredness that weighed on her eyelids like lead and went through her body every now and then in warm weakening flushes of exhaustion. Resting her elbows on the little table, she could support her forehead with her palms and let her eyelids meet for a little to relieve the weight. He was so quiet now. He must be so weak. Odds and ends of the day's work about the house, about the steading, came back of their own accord, with odds and ends of thought for the morrow. Days and nights, twisting and turning … fitful, terrible… .

But the man was not asleep. He was pondering so deeply that his breathing almost stopped. Hitherto he had merely known how the burden could be dropped, but at the same time had been conscious that the ordinary human forces around him would not allow him to drop it in this way of his. There was also a something somewhere in his own mind warning him to be careful, a secret caution from some far level of his normal life. … But a point had been reached, a point—where he must go. He must! … His head had rolled from side to side in the urgency of his indecision. His eyes had opened wide. He must get there—to that place!

The vision of the place had risen before him clear in every detail. He had felt the cool water of the small loch caress a hand. Ah! … A quivering sigh, and the urgency relaxed, the body sank, while he lay pondering each wild beautiful feature of this place he wanted to go to.

The sheep-track to it was so easy to follow, the peaty track that went twisting on like a black heather snake. It was a sheeptrack so lonely, so lost, that its loneliness induced laughter, a gaiety of companionship; notwithstanding that the black peat and the great breasts of the hills and the austere peaks held a certain sombre quality as an eternal mood. For that sombre brooding was known to him, too, known as intimately as were the hill birds. Let the heather-tops whip the ankles. Here was a freedom that sent the feet lightly; and the austerity, the brooding—one enters at the door with the fearful expectancy of the long-wandered child.

And his was surely a case of the long-wandered child. For this little loch in the hills, whither the sheep-track took him, he had visited only twice in his life, and on both occasions as a grown lad on a fishing ploy. He had caught brown red-spotted trout there; had tucked up his trousers and waded in, had whipped off all his clothes and bathed. Even that first glimmer of it in the distance, with the forenoon sun at his back turning the rippled surface to a molten richness of dark blue—ah, he had never seen such a blue again, it had glowed, a great jewel.

Nearer, the colour had faded into that mysterious darkness of the hill loch. With the afternoon a blessed tiredness had come on his body and he had lain down and felt the place about him and merged in its stillness and secrecy and remoteness, one with it, bemused, drunk with it.

Yes, drunk with it, for what was an experience at the time was clarified and intensified afterwards. The gathering in of the hills, the shape and colour of the loch, the grey faces of the boulders, heather and reeds and hill grass, silence and listening and sound, moor bird and spotted trout, a brooding, a watching—a grouping more choice, more interpretive of the essential Highlander in him, than any chance place he had ever struck, a grouping that lingered like a memory of some magical place known to the heart with an absolute intimacy, with a sense of healing and rejuvenation in its very look.

Healing; that was the word. There the burning body could slip its burden, be purged of its fever. The hill wind would play coolly; he could see it in a dark wave coming round the slope, along the heather tops, into his clothes, through his clothes, and feel its caress on his skin, its clean honey flavour in his mouth. His mind would slip and sink and merge, and out of that mortal sleep would come surely an immortal health.

But he had to get there. He must get there. The forces that kept him back— they didn't understand this imperative need, the absolute certainty of the healing.

And then suddenly all urgency of doubt, of argument, was dissolved like a mist, and in a swift clear light of the mind he knew that he was going. Immediately a thin excitement flickered along his burning flesh, his body tossed restlessly, his eyes opened wide. But no hand came over the coverlet this time, for the head and arms of the woman now pressed down on the little table in the sleep of utter exhaustion.

Yes, he would go; he would go now. It was many hours' walk, but he would manage it, manage it all the more easily because of this lightness of the body that was on him. Yes, he would go, he would go! How the old heart beat at that and caught the breath! Let him swing his legs out… .

He stood on the floor, a gaunt figure in white nightshirt, swaying lightly. The eyes glittered, the cheeks were sunken each to a crease that was a sharp, dark gash, the breath came quickly, audibly, in and out. Without bending the head, without looking, he began to move round the little table with its pool of black hair, between it and the dim-shaded lamp on the mantelpiece, onward to the door. Soft-padding, tall, unbending, he passed out of the room.

The passage-way to the front door was black dark, but that did not inconvenience him; and the dog he did not see at all. The brute had come out from the mirk of the kitchen beyond, uncertain yet expectant, till at last the hair stiffened a little above the neck and a strange whimpering started and choked in its throat. He opened the front door and the greyness in the night smote the eyes that watched him a burning blue-green; but, cowering now, the brute made no familiar rush at the opening, and the man passed out and the door closed behind him.

So much for all that, for the tricks of time between boyhood and this. Now he knew exactly where he was, and already the great black shadow of Ben Fitheich towered yonder, austere, but known with a curious elation to the immemorial in him, to the ineradicable. Human intimacies, human relationships, were well, but there is a last intimacy beyond all others, a last relationship.

It was a long journey, and twice he awoke from a sort of reverie to find himself resting. The second time, that first moon-darkness in which he had started out had given place to daylight, but to a daylight screened by the filmiest veil of shadow, like a twilight of dawn or evening, yet more like evening, because of an imponderable air of dreaming in it, of memories exquisitely saddened, as they might be saddened by the limpid song of a robin as it drips into the hollow of an autumn evening. Only, it wasn't evening, but merely the hill mood playing on the still, yellow daylight.

And all the time a something more than a sense of dreamy peace at his heart, in his vision: a subtle rejuvenescence, a lightness of thistledown to his feet, a freedom exquisite and exhilarating as wine, only rarer, cleaner, less sensuous. Like a dark vein, the sheep-track wound on and on round the great curved breasts of the hills. The heather-sifted wind fanned coolly his face and sent a shiver of cleanliness in among the hair-roots and crinkling along the scalp. Long vistas at once opened out the mountains and closed them in. He was withdrawing from the ever-twisting roots and entanglements of human interdependencies. He was *getting back*.

There was an excitement in it of held laughter and alert eyes. An adventuring back to the lost places, to the ultimate source, with its grey faces of boulders and black clefts of hag, with its watching and waiting and listening, in the loneliness, in the remoteness, where a footfall might well sound like an echo of legend.

Yet in all this there was no inspiration of half-forgotten poetry for him. Of poetry as a bookish lore, a half remembering of forgotten things, he had none.

If the shadow of reflection touched his mood it did certainly no more. He rounded the last curve, and there the little scene lay before him, so that his heart beat and an exaltation pulsed chokingly, till a strange weakening took his body, so that the flesh on his legs trembled and a strong desire came over him to lie down. But no, not yet! He would sit down there by the lochan, he would sink down into fathomless peace, and round about him would lap healingly all this from which the ultimate rhythm of him had been taken.

He stumbled on now hurriedly, details of the scene, altogether forgotten, coming before his eyes as so many little glad surprises: tiny headlands in the lochan, a twisted vein of white quartz in a rock face, a short steep scree on the off side that ended in a mound like an odd flattened cairn ... . How dear these little things! Lord, how splendid the welcoming things! The laughter gurgled in his throat. "I'm coming!" he cried to them. "I'm coming! Hold on!" ...

An hour of the night came when the dog got up from his crouching attitude behind the door. He got up suddenly and began to twist and twine on himself, whining, whining and trying to choke the whine. But the whine, the surge in the throat, became too great for him, overwhelmed him, drowning altogether the careful tricks of training. Throwing his head up, he bayed full-throated.

The mournful howl penetrated the woman's consciousness, and with a sudden jerk her whole body was nervously awake. ...The bed! The bed was empty. She glared at it, the flesh on her face stiffening. Again the dog howled. She cried out at the awful sound, the awful portent, not knowing what she cried, and in another instant was stumbling blindly for the kitchen.

"Allan! Allan!" she called, her purpose gathering; but there was no answer, except the whining of the dog round her skirts.

She got out, rushed wildly round the steading. She woke the three men who slept in the hut. The oldest man had a grey-whiskered, weatherbitten face with steady, kindly eyes. The prime of his manhood had been spent in the mining camps and wastes of Alaska.

"Where's Luath?" he called to her, stretching for his clothes. Then softly, "The lanterns, boys!"

Meanwhile the woman had whirled from the door, and "Luath! Luath!" she called, "Luath! Luath!" But there was no sign of the dog now.

And presently the lanterns moved about the steading, and from a little distance looked like restless, disembodied eyes in a dream more phantasmagoric than any clear visioning of heather and lochan and hill. But they were conscious, these shadows with the lanterns, of no heather or lochan or hill about them; only of the illimitable prairie, the starlit illimitable sky, and a Canadian homestead lost in the vast expanse.

Suddenly a whistle rang out as the old man put his fingers between his lips, and in a little while there were the short excited whimperings of the dog, doubling on himself, yelping, leading them away. The lanterns gathered now, and in a group started out from the steading. Half a mile across the flat they came on the water-hole, which was a drinking-pool no bigger than the floor of a room, and by the edge of it they found the white-sheeted body of the man, stone dead.

Down to the Sea

"Poor Lachie," said the precentor to me, "it 'id hev been better for him, mebbe, if they hed pit him to the poorhouse." We were on the way home from Lachie's funeral, and as the precentor spoke he meditatively rubbed his shoulder-blade, for he was a tall, gaunt, grey-whiskered man, difficult to "pair" when it came to a "change over" at the four handles of the black bier.

But I felt the instinctive humanity in the reservation of that "mebbe"; it struck darkly, dumbly, for it boded forth a levelling sense of fellow-mortality, with a some-thing else of inscrutable, kindly fellow-feeling. Lachie's body had been found just awash on the shingly strip of beach that lies between the off end of the quay-wall of the little harbour and the first precipice of the "braeheads". "Poor ould dodder-ing mannie," he had no doubt, "slippit in." For though nobody had seen the way of it, hardly even the one or two ribald spirits of the fishing village had suggested anything darker. All the same, it was one of the many meanings implicit in Rob the precentor's words that it would have been more respectable, both for himself and the general feelings of the place, if the old man had died decently in his bed, maybe even in a poorhouse bed, God help him... .

At a certain season there moves in the breasts of all migrant things a strong beating urge. Man is not immune, but his season is uncertain, the call at once more ordinary and more mysterious.

In the two-roomed, squat cottage down at the straggling tail-end of the grey fishing village the shadows were gathering. By the peat fire the old man sat as though awaiting quietly his summons. The shadows gathered body all the more quickly because of the piece of "barked" sail-canvas that stretched across most of the window. Only the coming of the darkness did not excite the old man, for its call ran smoothly along the ways of a long-ingrained, powerful habit, a habit that could be indulged without conscious waste of thought or effort, a habit, too, that called minor supporting habits into being.

Thus, presently taking his knife from the cross-pocket of his thick, black-cloth, fisherman's trousers, shrunken round the thin legs and shredded over the "ould bachles o' boots", he started slicing very methodically a twist of bogie-roll tobacco into the palm of his left hand. When he thought he had sliced enough, he rolled the flakes between his palms, occasionally pausing to tease them out with gnarled fingers; then, taking his cutty from a waist-coat pocket, he removed the lid, scraped out the "dottle" beside the new tobacco, blew through the short stem, and, carefully recharging, saw that the old dottle, as good kindling, would be first to meet the light. This done to his satisfaction, and having blown the remnants of dottle dust from his grooved palm, he cast about him for a bit of paper. He found it in the table drawer, which held most of his valuables, from the four or so dented pieces of cutlery to his Old Age Pension book.

As he set light to the black-seasoned bowl his whiskered face and screwed-up eyes glimmered in a sort of wrinkled phantasy. His hair, excepting an occasional silver-white thread, was almost jet-black, and covered head and face generously. His eyes were dark and sharp (though not invariably, for when sitting before the fire in the hour before the darkness, they became lack-lustred, filmed, or, in the local phrase, "far away"—the "far-awayness" of the old, that is, not of the young). His lips made a sucking, smacking sound as they pulled at the cutty, and the blue-grey smoke gathered in his whiskers and round his head in a cloud.

Lifting his old-style fisherman's hat, or cheese-cutter, from the smoke-yellowed cover of the old wooden bed, he gave an instinctive look about him, to make sure that all was ship-shape, then with a slow, doddering gait made for the door, which he did not think of locking behind him as he passed out.

The north-east coast-line of the Moray Firth is wild and forbidding, its grim inhospitality welcome only to gull and peregrine falcon, to cormorant and diver. But wherever a "fault" occurs in its stretch of tall sea-cliff and low tidal-rock there will be found the little fishing village, straw-thatched or slate-roofed, home of a notably hardy breed of seamen. Small, often picturesque creeks and harbours, too often now with a grey silence about them, intensified, perhaps, by the presence of two or three small boats and a salmon cobble or so, that are as the spent backwash of a once virile storm of fishing life.

Along the side-path, with its dockans and grass, round the end of a black shed, once storehouse of herring nets and baskets, and so by a short-cut to the "shore road", went the old man. The stillness of the twilight was in the quiet air and on the grass, a silence that was a listening to one's own thoughts or memories. Yet as he trudged along he was not possessed by memories; his mind lay fallow awaiting the finger of awakening, the thing he would respond to effortlessly, as to some old rhyme to which his marrow was attuned.

It came just as he turned the "look-out" and entered the valley cleft; it came like a crying from the ends of life, a surging and a long-drawn breath—the noise of the sea. Life and death in it, and eternity. He paused a little, and mumbled something that he himself did not hear. But there came a quickening to the eyes, and they looked out on the grey waste with a darkling intelligence; the seaman's eyes, steady, self-reliant, used to far horizons. He took his cutty from his mouth and spat. Was there pride in the eyes—pride of the sea, to which he had been, to which he was, so wedded, body and soul? An uncertain, momentary glimmer of the face, and the cutty went back between his gums.

He moved on now, as it seemed, more easily, much as the pipes give renewed lightness to leaden feet. It is conceivable that one may be proud of the sound of the sea. Never in all his long life had he known it without a murmur, never had its green lips been tired of the rocks. Never. For those who are finished with terror, and whose mistress the sea is, there may be a sharp pride in the thought and a last flicker of human defiance.

Down the grey track to the harbour he plodded on, the evening air about him and the intense glowing of yellow wildflowers. His skin was too insensitive to feel the air's fingers, but his eyes did see one little patch of wild flowers. Lately, indeed, he had been in the habit of pausing in the descent and gazing at that grassy patch, yellow with dandelions and buttercups. Flowers on a grave have a respectable decency, and that women should be interested in them is characteristic and as it should be. But that wild flowers should be growing there, on that little level stretch, was, for a man, a thought full of desolation, more full of desolation than the gaping, roofless curing-shed which sagged stricken beside it. For in the prime of his manhood no grass nor yellow weed had grown there—because of the salt and the herring-brine.

On down the grey track, glancing at the one or two haddieboats motionless in the shadow of the long stone-wall, at the one or two bigger boats "hauled" and rotting at their moorings, past the cooperages, with their boarded windows like blind eyes, past the tall, grey, salmon-net poles, and so towards the pier-head. Usually his walk ended there, with a long, indefinite look out to sea, a slow scanning of sky and cloud, an indistinct mumbling as to weather prospects, and so meditatively back to his solitary cottage. But of late he had got into the habit of climbing on to the top of the quay-wall that faced the sea, and of sitting down to rest himself, feet dangling above the restless water.

Perhaps the spell of warm weather had made the old man feel unusually tired. The morning had been heavy, with thunder threatening; the early afternoon sultry and oppressive; and not until about six o'clock had the change come and the atmosphere lightened. It was his own observation that the weather usually came to "wan thing or anither" round about either noon or six o'clock. He sat down with a pech of relief on the cool stone and let his feet hang in comfort. The heavy weather put one "clean throughither", he muttered, feeling a certain lightness of the head. But the cool stone revived him and the slight lightness of the head was not unpleasant. He had noticed as much before, noticed, in fact, that the lightness gave a sort of incorporeal feel to the body. Fancy gained a little freedom then; could roam backwards more easily; catch faces of boyhood; could certainly tell with far more accuracy and vivid detail what happened sixty years ago than what happened that day, or the day before, or last year, or twenty years ago.

Hunched and motionless on the quay-wall, with the darkness settling about him. No sound but the sea's and the intermittent, cavernous crying of the gulls. Weird the crying of these birds against the deep, reverberant precipices at night-time. Once the old man, troubled, perhaps, by some memory of the Castlebay and Stornoway days, had thought to himself that they might well be the keening souls of drowned bodies. Some such thought came to him now, but affected him hardly at all. In the ultimate quietism nothing is all-important, not death itself. To the hunched figure on the wall the living reality of things shone and glimmered, rather, in the magical days long dead, the enchanted days where not a face that he could now see but was touched by a light that the carnal eyes had, somehow, missed then. Boys together, bare-legged, racing the braes through endlessly sunny days; fishing for "peltags"; grouped round the cooper with his mysterious fire issuing fearfully from barrel mouth to clank, clank of resounding hammer; playing old four-corner games in the wooden gutting stations, where presently, when the boats came in, the cran baskets of herring would be "teemed".... .

Ah, the boats! There they were, with their brown sails, magical sails. Hear the Gaelic chant of the "hired men" as mast left crutch and halyards creaked rhythmically, as mains'l' went aloft. A fleet of them, dozens and scores, making out of this same harbour-basin to court the sea, that passionate, fickle mistress of theirs.

Morning and the boats coming back, racing with feather of foam at the forefoot for a good berth and an early discharge. Then the gutters in their black oilskins, stiff *rustle-rustle*, their gaiety, their wit deft as their incredibly deft fingers should a man dare a sally. ... And suddenly glowing there before him, like a still flame darkening the grey waste behind, blotting it out, a face and eyes, and a light on the face that somehow he had never missed... .

Something stirred, twisting a little and knotting in his breast, as though heart and flesh held a trace of the excitement of youth's red blood. Straightening a little ... he saw only the grey upheave of the sea and the brooding precipices.

Ay, the sea, always the sea, restless, full of infinite variety—yet ever the same, eternally changeless; and the dark, gull-haunted rocks, carven, brooding—yet ever changing, wasting, The old man had no metaphors to shield him from the direct reality of things, no movement of poetic words to bear away the starkness on a bier of flowers.

> *Time writes no wrinkle on thine azure brow—*
> *Such as Creation's dawn beheld, thou rollest now.*

The personal gesture of one standing on the surf edge with raised arm and a godlike, booming intonation. The old man knew nothing of that. Direct the rhythm of the grey water, direct and wordless and quite stark. Stark because of its power, its sheer, destroying power, that a man could respect, and love, too, as one could love, not a god, but a passionate, variable woman. With smell and feel and nearness in the way of it, salty to the lips and stinging, wild laughter and peace, indifference, death....

More mysteriously the night gathered in, and now where waves swirled into one another were born curling eddies of blackness that bobbed on like drowned, black-haired heads. A tidal rock, just awash, assumed the appearance of a monstrous sea-animal that moved about voraciously as the waves covered and uncovered and washed lickingly about it. Movement of hypnotic waves like refluent arms, monotony of ever-varying sound ever the same, green fingers searching the interstices, green lips choking and suffocating, all gathered into one slow elemental spell, aeons old, irresistible. The old man begins to sway a little, his eyes round and fixed, his shoulders ever drooping forward. A last flicker of earth-born anxiety, wherein bits of old visions flash uncertainly—a face like a flame, with wistful, smiling eyes, threading its way mysteriously, like a moon of the soul, through swift, fragmentary passing of brown sails and voices and human gestures and old, old yellow sunlight—and the flicker goes out. Colour dies finally. The hypnotic sea, catching utterly within its rhythm that swaying figure drooping forward, forward.... A suddenly shocked gull sets up a cavernous crying, and the dimline of the quay-wall against the grey sea is unbroken once more.

I was startled a little when the old precentor came to a standstill by the little path that left the road for his own cottage. We had walked the better part of a mile in silence.

"Ay, he wis a bit queer," he said; "in the end he wis a bit queer, mebbe."

For a moment I could not bring myself directly to search his expression, and when curiosity did empower me it was but to find that he had turned his shoulder in leave-taking. Already he was moving off, his face to the heavens. "There's wind in that sky, and it's rain they need," he said. For Rob himself had followed the sea, but he spoke for the crofters.

Henry Drake Goes Home

He's like a man in a story, the country folk said. They also said he had a face like a ripe apple and eyes as blue as the sky. His appearance, at seventy, prompted such figures of speech quite naturally. There was that freshness about him, with his straight shoulders and courteous manner. The children of the Highland village would hang about a shop-door to hear his English tongue. They did not cry words after him, but stood silently and watched him go. When he was out of sight they would sometimes indulge in mimicry by giving a Devonshire twist to their "best English".

All this the Official remembered as he stared through his office window, the letter which he had just read lying on his desk before him. He remembered in particular the first visit to the small thatched cottage fairly high on the side of the glen that went inland and westward from the village. It was rough ground, steep in places, with clumps of broom exhaling a heady fragrance in the calm noonday. There was an occasional rabbit scut and a spilling over of notes from a sleepy warbler. Once he had rested, half in pleasure and half in protest, for with a day's work on hand there is always the urge to get on and get finished. However, the present "case" would not take very long, because on the claim form for "the pension" the applicant had described himself as a trapper, with income "nil".

At last the Official came over the brow, saw the cottage before him, and, at the same moment, a man walking towards the door, a bunch of yellow rabbit snares, with brown cords and small stakes, dangling from one hand. At sight of his visitor, the man turned and waited.

"Uh," said the Official, drawing forth a folded blue form and glancing at it, "uh—you are Mr. Henry Drake?"

"I am, sir—at your service."

"I have come to see you about the pension. I have a form here which you filled up at the post office."

"I hope, sir, that you have found it all correct?"

"Well, I have a few questions to ask, if you don't mind. Perhaps …?"

Mr. Drake nodded, and after courteous invitation, ushered the Official into his living-room.

The Official was used to all kinds of humble interiors, from the polished brightness surrounding an old maid to the last stages of decrepitude and dirt on and around an old bachelor, This was, however, by no means a noisome interior. If it had a dull bareness, at least it had order, and there was nothing smeared over the edge of the table upon which the Official proceeded to lay out his blue and his buff forms.

From long experience the Official could tell at a glance whether a woman lived in a house, not so much from the absence of feminine things, such as clothes or scalloped edges or little curtains, as from the absence of a something quite intangible but admitting of no doubt. Actually, there was many a bachelor kept a house like a new pin, complete with polished grate, scrubbed table, and even a white—not dingy—slip of window curtain, kept it with as much finikin taste as any old maid who had been housekeeper to a banker; yet with a difference, always with a difference, even with a different smell. On the present occasion, the Official had hardly even to glance at the fire, which was a mess of dust and ashes. It was stale and smelt of male death. Yes, there was the distinction: not feminine warmness and living, dirt or no dirt; but male hardness and staleness and furniture like old bones.

To be able to appreciate such a distinction was of some value to the Official. For example, the present applicant had described himself on the form as "married". Had he been a "widower" he would, as instructed, have written the word "widower" on the given line. At least, the post-mistress would have done so, for it was she who had filled up the form, all except the signature, and on such a matter it could be taken as more certain than either life or death that she had assured herself in full "as to the validity" of the descriptive epithet "married".

Accordingly, the Official assumed a pleasant manner. With possible awkward questions in the offing, it is always as well to begin by putting the applicant at his ease. So the Official jocosely asked, as he unscrewed the cap of his fountain-pen: "And what brought you all the way to this far part of the world?"

"Because there is no justice in England," answered Henry Drake.

"I beg your pardon?"

The eyes of the old man never wavered. They indeed filled with a strong light as the mouth repeated the charge against his country.

The Official glanced down at his papers with a smile. Sometimes he had to humour old men who lived alone. They got wasps in their bonnets. "Really!" he murmured.

"Yes," answered Henry Drake. "There is no justice in that land, from which I was persecuted and driven forth."

This sounded bad. The Official squared the folded buff form in front of him and, as he prepared himself to write, said lightly, "Come, now, Mr. Drake, that is surely a bit strong. However, we had better——"

"It's the truth," answered Henry Drake firmly. "There is no justice to be had in England, as I can prove to you." With that, he got up and went to a wooden chest, took a key out of his waistcoat pocket, and presently returned to the table with a mass of manuscript contained by a piece of string.

His features, which had been rosy and gracious, were now stern. The Official saw that he would have to get over this particular foible before he could hope to proceed to business. "I haven't a great deal of time," he suggested.

"It is all there," answered Henry Drake. "All my petitions are there—to the magistrates, to the Lord Chief Justice of England, to the King himself. You can read them for yourself." As he laid the bundle on the table, it shoved the buff form a little to one side.

The Official glanced at the top sheet. It was grimy to the extent of almost obscuring the writing. The writing itself, however, was firm and fluent, with flourishes at capitals. The phraseology was sustained in the legal manner, and charged with such words as "whereas" and "the aforesaid". The Official was trained to pick out from verbiage the words that mattered. "This", he murmured, "seems to refer to your wife?"

"It does," said Henry Drake.

"Is she still alive?" asked the Official, unobtrusively.

"I do not know whether she is alive or dead. She was in league with them. They listened to her, She was a liar. She was a liar born," added Henry Drake, even more firmly, "as this will show." He undid the string of the bundle with fingers that now for the first time shook a little. He exposed a document. "Read that," he commanded, and, with hand open, palm upward, he hit the document with the tips of his nails.

The Official's eye, ignoring the introductory matter, ran over a curious statistical list: 7 eggs, 2 loaves, 3 quarts of milk, 2 rabbits... . It was quite a long list. "Uh——this refers to…"

"That's what she got every week," answered Henry Drake. "Every week. And yet she sued me for maintenance. I laid these facts before the magistrates. They would not believe me. No one would believe me. At that time I still thought there was justice to be had in England. My first appeal, which I carefully drew up …"

And so Henry Drake got going. The Official listened with the remote interest that does not touch sympathy. He knew the woman would have her side of the case. Yet the pattern that formed itself in that remote cottage interior was curiously fantastic. The fight with the woman through months, through years, was gradually transformed into a fight with the forces of justice, until in the end this fight became a complete obsession. When Henry Drake called the woman a liar, he was no longer thinking of a living woman but only of the chief material factor in this fight. As a living woman she had quite died out of his mind.

"And so", concluded Henry Drake, "I saw that there was no justice in all England. I saw it was the one country in the whole world where justice could not be got. It was like living all your days in a bad dream. I could stand it no more. So one day I got up and left it, and took my papers with me."

He was courteous in his manner at all times, but now he had a grave strong dignity. The sky-blue eyes had gone a shade darker. There was a tracery of lines, as if the appley texture of the face, still fresh, was yet slightly wizened. He was a judge before whom his native England stood condemned. He had shaken her dust from off his shoes for evermore.

The Official bowed over his form. All this had taken a long time. There would be the usual small domestic trouble over a cold lunch. Quickly now, yet without the appearance of haste, he found out that all this had happened thirty-five years ago, that the applicant might be regarded as permanently separated from his wife, that there were folk in the neighbourhood who could vouch for his having resided in the district for the last twenty years, together with other necessary details that had to be inserted on the various forms. The question of means presented no difficulty. Although there were some three acres of land attached to the cottage, Henry Drake kept no stock. Neighbours were kind in the matter of milk and potatoes, and there were seasons when he made a few pounds out of rabbit trapping. The Official could see, however, that he was not at all of the begging kind. Quite the contrary. In the end, he entered his total means from all sources as, on an average, eight shillings a week from trapping, and this placed the applicant well within the limit for the full Old Age Pension. There remained only the question of his age. He had no birth certificate, but in due course the Official, who was now genuinely anxious to get him the pension, traced his family in the 1861 Census, where Henry Drake, a son, was shown as three years old.

Each year after that the Official paid Henry Drake a visit, handing him a new book of ten-shilling orders, and getting him to sign a small document to the effect that his living conditions had not changed. As he was himself fond of hill sport and interested in wild life, he would chat for a little while before taking his leave, careful at the same time never to give the old man a chance to introduce his obsession. And in fairness it must be said that, on his part, the old man never again attempted to bring the matter up. With his pension, he seemed to have settled happily and finally into his background, his health good, his cheeks fresh, his step firm, his eyes blue.

Time went on until a certain day in September, when, as the Official sat in his office, there was a knock at his door. "Come in!" he called, and Henry Drake entered, white hair neatly combed and cap in hand.

"Ah, Mr. Drake, come in!" the Official welcomed him, getting up at the same time and offering his visitor a chair.

"Thank you, sir," answered Henry Drake. "I hope I do not intrude?"

"By no means. Take a seat. And how are you keeping?"

"I am very well, thank you, sir, and I hope I see you the same."

These courtesies over, the Official asked: "Well, now, and what can I do for you today?" And then he saw a look come into the blue eyes that he had never seen before. They stared past him in a hazed way.

"I was thinking", said Henry Drake, "of going on a journey, and I was wondering about my pension. I would need my pension."

"Well, I think we could arrange that," answered the Official pleasantly. "Where were you thinking of going?"

"I was thinking," said Henry Drake, in a voice vague and strange as the look in his eyes, "I was thinking of going home."

"Home!" echoed the Official.

"Yes," answered Henry Drake. "I was thinking I would like to go to my own county of Devon."

The Official looked closely at his visitor, then nodded slowly. "I see," he said. "It's a long way, Mr. Drake, and, as you know, war has broken out. You must remember you have been a long time out of Devon. The people you knew there—may not be there now. Let me see—how old are you?"

"I am eighty-two," replied Henry Drake.

It was a great age. Still, something in the demeanour of the old man made the Official hesitate to suggest directly that, for the time being, in any case, it might be wiser for him to stay where he was. "It's a long long journey," he said, "and you would have to get out at many railway stations and change."

"I am going to walk it," said Henry Drake simply. "I walked here on my own feet and I can walk back."

"Walk it!" echoed the Official.

"Yes, sir," said Henry Drake.

And so it finally was arranged. Nothing could move the old man from his decision. It was clear, of course, that he had not enough money to pay for his railway ticket. He had not sufficient shillings to keep him going on the road. Yet he was too independent to accept even the suggestion of help. He would manage all right with his Old Age Pension, he declared, if only an arrangement could be made whereby he could cash an order from time to time. That was why he had come to the Official.

The Official did all he could for him, as if, indeed, the old man were his own father setting out on a perilous but fated journey. As they shook hands, Henry Drake said, "Thank you very much, sir. You have been kind to me. All the people in this land have been just and kind to me. But it has come over me that I must go back to my own country."

"I understand," replied the Official gravely, aware now that the outbreak of war had touched a profound instinct in the old man. "If ever you are in difficulties, you will remember to refer the authorities to me."

That piece of advice, certainly, Henry Drake did not forget. The Official was able to follow the old man's journey by the letters he received from the police.

But in spite of detentions, in spite of what appeared to be temporary illness or exhaustion, Henry Drake went on. Through the Perthshire Highlands, through the Lowlands, he tramped his way. A letter came from Carlisle. He had crossed the Border.

The year was wearing on. Cars and lorries would overtake him, hurtling past along the great south road. But his head would not turn round. To expect a lift would not occur to him. The Official now understood Henry Drake better than ever before. That solitary forsaken figure plodding along the edge of the great road assumed lines of a mythical simplicity. The ways of a wife, injustice among men, were no more than the accidents of life. Henry Drake was going back to something deep in him as life itself. Indeed, the spirit had already gone back. The body was struggling to follow.

When he had got beyond the Lake country, on past Lancaster, the Official began to have hope. He took out his car map, studied the route, and thought that if Henry got through the Manchester area, he might in truth reach his journey's end.

Then came a long silence—broken this very morning by a letter from the local authorities in Manchester, requesting all possible information concerning one Henry Drake, a vagrant, who had died in a poor-law institution. "Deceased", said the letter, "was in possession of a Pension Order Book, No. 1413, issued at your office, of which six orders are due but uncashed."

The Official sat quite still in his chair for some time. Then he got up and removed from the Register of Pensioners the loose-leaf containing the short life-story of the dead man. For a minute he toyed with the idea of adding to his report that the deceased had expressed a strong wish to be buried in Devon. As if that, he thought, with a small ironic smile, would make any difference.

And then, in a moment, he saw that in truth it would make no difference, one way or the other. They could deal with the body as he himself would now deal with this loose-leaf. The spirit eluded all bureaucratic forms. And the spirit of Henry Drake had gone home to Devon.

Hill Fever

At midnight the light goes grey. This grey has the deadness of grey grass; very still and curving with the near breasts of the hills—so near that they are at hand, wherever the eyes rest—and the fingers touch.

At first it is like tracking silence to its lair. Iain Og, to give him his boyhood name again, felt indeed that he had trapped it. Here at last all sound had died and was resumed again into the womb of negation.

At first. Then the silence rose up out of that negation and opened like a flower on a movie screen, silently. The petals were the surrounding peaks set in a whorl, row behind row. Standing on the crest above the high hut was like standing on the sterile centre of the flower of the world's death.

Which was a trifle grandiloquent once the mind, grown cunning, had harried the romantic need for vast contrasts and come deep upon that odd, if final, duality of life and death. Odd, because it stares, or sets the eyes staring—at the near hillside, for example, as it comes down, and slowly up under the fingers. The fingers pierce softly the black peaty earth with its oily ooze and, withdrawing, create their own gentle slimy suck of negation. The suck attracts; absorbs fascination, or horror, into mindlessness.

But opposite, where the breast swells slowly up, the same earth gathers invisible tension. Perhaps it merely cannot be held under the eye like the deathly ooze at the finger-tips. At such a thought the grey air takes on a curious quality, not glimmering so much as watchful or expectant. The silence grows exquisitely thin and taut. The skin grows taut and cold. The roots of the grass and the heath under the brown skin of the slope are invisibly alive. There is a tense twining stress. The mind can sustain in balance no more than a certain weight. The least thing added, even of awareness, makes it topple over like a wave. The hillside opens and out of it in green froth come the fairies. The breast of the earth for the fairies.

Analysis of this kind can have a morbid air. Iain Og himself would have mistrusted the something that crawls in it, like worms in earth, a fortnight ago, when he married his equally young wife (who was a sport and a hill-climber) and brought her here to a just sufficiently commodious fishing hut for the honeymoon. But now he found not the least thing morbid in it. On the contrary, it was all charged with a rare mirth, bridging the gap between black negation under the fingers and that breast opposite.

Indeed it enriched him. He had never felt so full of the very sap of life. It was a health shot through with sunlight. This health could fold over on itself and peer out from the folds like a laughing sprite. Or walk in easy swinging poise, conscious of the toes. All of which, being a trifle undignified, must be suppressed. Hence the mirth, with its glancing, measuring, and even veiled eyes.

Last night, when he had been out in the boat alone and, doubled up over a big trout, had cast his quick smile around, he had seen his wife come ghost-like down to the water's edge. Without straightening himself, he stealthily watched her, until her voice came over the water, calling his name once.

He took the hook out and knocked the head against a wooden edge. The soft slippery body slid from his hand into the shallow bailer. Then he leaned over the boatside. The water was warmer than his hands and his fingers worked in it, each fist cleaning itself.

"John!"

He shook the water from his hands, but did not answer. Not answering was like the holding of a joke in poise. It was detachment from her in a warm assurance. He held the cast of flies against the sky, unravelled it, hooked the tail fly, and reeled in the slack. He liked the sound of the reel at night. He often played with it. Now it was an answer to her. With the point of the rod swaying over the stern, he rowed slowly to her feet.

"Why didn't you answer me?"

He sat smiling up at her quizzically. It had been a hot day. She was in white, and the fold over of the linen left her throat and opening breast shadowy. She looked very cool, even more detached than his admiration.

"Why don't you speak?"

It was idiotic not to speak. Her tone was cool, hardly aggrieved. "I got a beauty," he said, and lifted the wide bailer on to the seat. The spotted pound trout he caressed into show position.

"But we cannot eat any more trout," she said. "Do you know the time?"

"What?"

"It's midnight."

"Midsummer midnight." He looked around. "Edith, do you know, you looked beautiful as a ghost."

There was silence.

"Are you coming or not?"

He stepped ashore, gave a throaty "Heave-ho!" then turned, still smiling. She pushed his face away with her open hand. He kissed its cold palm, used a swift endearing term and watched the effect. Then he laughed out loud. He could have eaten her, and she knew it.

But she was not just in the mood for being eaten. She had hung a whole hour with her pride before going to call him.

At eleven o'clock she had said, I will not go, no matter how long he takes. Then she had thought, I will go to bed. But to go to bed before him would be too absurd. In no time she was working up a resentment. She was being neglected. Oh Lord, that feminine thing—being neglected! She laughed at herself. No, thank goodness, it was not that. But—there was something—the least bit selfish in this queer sort of mindless way of his with the things about him. And it was growing … every day. … There she was again! She blew out the candle, laid aside her novel, and went to call him.

They walked back to the hut. He was silent. She resented this. Out of her resentment rose a sense of tension that became acute. In no time she felt hysterical. This was humiliating and utterly unlike her. It was getting worse. All her body grew stiff. Her head was so high that her feet stumbled. When he caught her she screeched. But he fought against her breakaway, and in the end she sobbed into his neck.

She said brokenly, "I'm very sorry," but she wasn't. She had really no shame at all. She did not care how she behaved. For the moment had given her an awful revelation of the depth of her love. Awful, terrifying. Its light had caught them, the two of them, on a waste. She clung to him.

"I'm very sorry." She felt his hands. His delicacy in lovemaking had day by day got a perfection that made her soul ache.

By the time they got back to the hut her stiffness was broken, her body rich, her eyes and lips wet and glistening in the beauty that rain brings out. She did not look at him much. She was half languid in her movements. But in the tiny kitchen when they hit into each other, a waiting humour in her seemed ready to spill. He set the embers of the peat on edge and blew them to a flame; hung a kettle and blew again until his eyes watered. "Poof!" he said, backing away by the stern. She launched a wallop at the stern and sat on it. For one shattering moment she wondered if her recklessness had blundered. The stern collapsed and she landed beside him on the floor. "Edith!" he said, in that intimate way that made her blind her eyes against his throat.

The kettle sang. They made tea. She had never, never in her life, been so feminine and irrational. She felt the wild glow in her skin, felt its colour and his eyes, and catching his eyes her mouth twisted at them.

He went out. It was bedtime. When he was ready to go in again, he paused and looked slowly about him. Then he went up the slope behind the hut until he reached its crest. He sat down, his mind quite vacant. He did not know why he had come up. Time went on. He could not go down. Edith would be wondering. The vision of Edith in her nightdress was so perfect that he smiled to her in adoration. That she might be puzzled again faintly amused him. He was sure of her as of the sun's rising. The grey was lightening; it was catching at last the inner glimmer. The coming of the sun from the abyss. The air sighed in a chill shiver. The first, the austere breath, of morning. This austerity was love's poise. His mind in its still rapture pierced all this and he saw what it was he had come to this place blindly to seek. Race, as it were, passed under his feet. Love, alone, eats itself to lust and grows rank.

He saw her against the hut. Her calling voice was thin and ragged. He could not answer. She came up slowly. He knew the pain in that uncertain coming, but could not help her. She dragged her feet towards him.

"Edith, come here," he said quietly.

She stood two paces from him. He got up and went to her. She did nothing, could say nothing, she who had hated and could have struck him at the foot of that hill.

His tone was even and friendly out of the grey light. It drained her of all feeling. Her mind emptied. Her body grew cold and stiff.

"Look there," he said, and pointed to a thin light projected upon the sloping crests of a mountain range. "You can see now that the earth is a ball. You can see the light thrown on it out of space. I never saw that planetary light before. Eerie, isn't it?"

She shuddered.

"Are you cold?" He put his arms about her. His voice broke in a laugh by her ear. She looked beaten.

That was last night.

And now this afternoon they lay on the slope by the hut after a long tramp. He had been kind and friendly all day, almost sensitive and shy; she had been cool and normal. One of these long silences, through which the memory of last night was ever threatening to break, held them to a stillness increasingly expectant. When it was pierced by an incredible "Coo-ee!" he swung over on his side as if he had been speared.

He spoke swiftly. "By God, they haven't seen us!" He was on hands and knees. The fierceness of his face amused her. "Come on!" He made sure she was crawling after him and then he moved rapidly.

"I just couldn't stand them!" he said as at last he lay over.

"Why?"

"I don't know. I loathe the thought of people. And Dick is an ass! Oh God, I couldn't stand them! Really, Edith, this is our show. They had no right to come. We should never have told them. Damn them! if we lose this—we cannot lose this. Don't you know what's been happening to us? We'll never—*never*—live like this again. We'll be trapped. Heaven above, listen … !" It came from him in a spate. He bridged the dualities. He lifted her to the grey light and the planetary light. His utmost incoherence had for her an awful clarity. She saw the last level of his mind—spread open to her feet. Her eyes dilated.

When the voice cried from the ridge above she gripped at her breast.

It was Dick. His back to them, he was calling to his companion. They came laughing down together.

True, Iain Og looked a bit surly over the handshakings, but Dick rallied the young dog: "I do believe Jock's embarrassed!"

Mabel chuckled at their embarrassment. "When you waved your hankie, Edith, as you crawled away behind Jock, we nearly died laughing. Follow my leader!"

Iain looked at Edith. So she had waved her hankie to them, after his back was turned. Only a moment their eyes held, then Iain turned away. Edith went pale and sick-looking. Mabel, more amused than ever, prattled on.

The Tax-gatherer

"Blast it," he muttered angrily. "Where is the accursed place?"

He looked at the map again spread before him on the steering-wheel. Yes, it should be just here. There was the cross-roads. He threw a glance round the glass of his small saloon car and saw a man's head bobbing beyond the hedge. At once he got out and walked along the side of the road.

"Excuse me," he cried. The face looked at him over the hedge. "Excuse me, but can you tell me where Mrs Martha Williamson stays?"

"Mrs Who?"

"Mrs Martha Williamson."

"No," said the face slowly, and moved away. He followed it for a few paces to a gap in the hedge. "No," said the man again, and turned to call a spaniel out of the turnips. He had a gun under his arm and was obviously a gamekeeper.

"Well, she lives about here, at Ivy Cottage."

"Ivy Cottage? Do you mean the tinkers?" And the gamekeeper regarded him thoughtfully.

"Yes. I suppose so."

"I see," said the gamekeeper, looking away. "Turn up to your right at the cross-roads there and you'll see it standing back from the road."

He thanked the gamekeeper and set off, walking quickly so that he needn't think too much about his task, for it was new to him.

When he saw the cottage, over amongst some bushes with a rank growth of nettles at one end, he thought it a miserable place, but when he came close to the peeling limewash, the torn-down ivy, the sagging roof, the broken stone doorstep thick with trampled mud, he saw that it was a wretched hovel.

The door stood half-open, stuck. He knocked on it and listened to the acute silence. He knocked again firmly and thought he heard thin whisperings. He did not like the hushed fear in the sounds, and was just about to knock peremptorily when there was a shuffling, and, quietly as an apparition, a woman was there.

She stood twisted, lax, a slim, rather tall figure, with a face the colour of the old limewash. She clung to the edge of the door in a manner unhumanly pathetic, and looked at him out of dark, soft eyes.

"Are you Mrs Williamson?"

After a moment she said, "Yes."

"Well, I've come about that dog. Have you taken out the licence yet?"

"No."

"Well, it's like this," he said, glancing away from her. "We don't want to get you into trouble. But the police reported to us that you had the dog. Now, you can't have a dog without paying a licence. You know that. So, in all the circumstances, the authorities decided that if you paid a compromise fine of seven-and-six, and took out the licence, no more would be said about it. You would not be taken to court." He looked at her again, and saw no less than five small heads poking round her ragged dark skirt. "We don't want you to get into trouble," he said. "But you've got to pay by Friday—or you'll be summonsed. There's no way out."

She did not speak, stood there unmoving, clinging to the door, a feminine creature waiting dumbly for the blow.

"Have you a husband?" he asked.

"Yes," she said, after a moment.

"Where is he?"

"I don't know," she answered, in her soft, hopeless voice. He wanted to ask her if he had left her for good, but could not, and this irritated him, so he said calmly, "Well, that's the position, as you know. I was passing, and, seeing we had got no word of your payment, I thought I'd drop in and warn you. We don't want to take you to court. So my advice to you is to pay up—and at once, or it will be too late."

She did not answer. As he was about to turn away the dregs of his irritation got the better of him. "Why on earth did you want to keep the dog, anyway?"

"We tried to put him away, but he wouldn't go," she said.

His brows gathered. "Oh, well, it's up to you," he replied coldly, and he turned and strode back to his car. Slamming the door after him, he gripped the wheel, but could not, at the last instant, press the self-starter. He swore to himself in a furious rage. Damn it all, what concern was it of his? None at all. As a public official he had to do his job. It was nothing to him. If a person wanted to enjoy the luxury of keeping a dog, he or she had to pay for it. That's all. And he looked for the self-starter, but, with his finger on the button, again could not press it. He twisted in his seat. Fifteen bob! he thought. Go back and slip her fifteen bob? Am I mad? He pressed the self-starter and set the engine off in an unnecessary roar. As he turned at the cross-roads he hesitated before shoving the gear lever into first, then shoved it and set off. If a fellow was to start paying public fines where would it end? Sentimental? Absolutely.

By the following Tuesday it was clear she had not paid. "The case will go on," said his chief in the office.

"It's a hard case," he answered. "She won't be able to pay." His voice was calm and official.

"She'll have to pay—one way or the other," answered his chief, with the usual trace of official satire in his voice.

"She's got a lot of kids," said the young man.

"Has she?" said the chief. "Perhaps she could not help having them—but the dog is another matter." He smiled, and glanced at the young man, who awkwardly smiled back.

There was nothing unkindly in the chief's attitude, merely a complete absence of feeling. He was dealing with "a file", and had no sympathy for anyone who tried to evade the law. He prosecuted with lucid care, and back in his office smiled with satisfaction when he got a conviction. For to fail in getting a conviction was to be inept in his duty. Those above him frowned upon such ineptitude.

All the same, the young man felt miserable. If he hadn't gone to the cottage it would have been all right. But the chief had had no unnecessary desire for a court case—particularly one of those hard cases that might get into the press. Not that that mattered really, for the law had to be carried out. Than false sentiment against the law of the land there could, properly regarded, be nothing more reprehensible—because it was so easy to indulge.

"By the way," said the chief, as he was turning away, "I see the dog has been shot. You didn't mention that?"

"No. I——" He had forgotten to ask the woman if the dog was still with her. "I—as a matter of fact, I didn't think about it, seeing it was a police report, and therefore no evidence from us needed."

"Quite so," said his chief reticently, as he turned to his file.

"Who shot it?" the young man could not help asking.

"A gamekeeper, apparently."

The young man withdrew, bit on his embarrassment at evoking the chief's "reticence", and thought of the gamekeeper who might believe that if the dog was shot nothing more could be done about the case. As if the liability would thereby be wiped out! As if it would make the slightest difference to the case!

In his own room he remembered the gamekeeper and his curious look. Decent of him all the same to have tried to help. If the children's faces had been sallow and hollow from underfeeding, what could the dog have got? Nothing, unless——— The thought dawned: the gamekeeper had probably shot the brute without being asked. Poaching rabbits and game? Perhaps the mainstay of the family? He laughed in his nostrils. When you're down you're right down, down and out. Absolutely. With a final snort of satire, he took some papers from the "pending" cover and tried to concentrate on an old woman's application for a pension. It seemed quite straightforward, though he would have to investigate her circumstances. Then he saw the children's faces again.

He had hardly been conscious of looking at them at the time. In fact, after that first glance of surprise he had very definitely not looked at them. The oldest was a girl of nine or ten, thin and watery, fragile, with her mother's incredible pallor and black eyes. The stare from those considering eyes, blank and dumb, and yet wary. They didn't appeal: trust could not touch them; they waited, just waited, for—the only hope—something less than the worst.

And the little fellow of seven or eight—sandy hair, inflamed eyelids, and that something about the expression, the thick, half-open mouth, suggesting the mental deficient. Obviously from the father's side, physically. The father had deserted them. Was perhaps in quod somewhere else, for they had only recently returned from their travels to the cottage. How did they manage even to live in it without being turned out? But the police would have that in hand as well! There was something too soft about the woman. She would never face up to her husband. When he was drunk, her softness would irritate him; he would clout her one. She was feckless. Her body had slumped into a pliant line, utterly hopeless, against the door. All at once he saw the line as graceful, and this unexpected vision added the last touch to derision.

The young man had observed in his life already that if his mind was keen on some subject he would come across references to it in the oddest places, in books dealing with quite other matters, from the most unlikely people. But this, carefully considered, was not altogether fortuitous. For example, when the old woman who had applied for the Old Age Pension asked him if he would have a cup of tea, he hesitated, not because he particularly wanted to have a cup of tea, but because he vaguely wanted to speak to her about the ways of tinkers, for Ivy Cottage was little more than a mile away.

His hesitation, however, the hesitation of an important official who had arrived in a motor car and upon whom the granting of her pension depended (as she thought), excited her so much that before she quite knew what she was doing she was on her knees before the fire, flapping the dull peat embers with her apron, for she did not like, in front of him, to bend her old grey head and blow the embers to a flame. As he was watching her she suddenly stopped flapping, with an expression of almost ludicrous dismay, and mumbled something about not having meant to do that. At once he was interested, for clearly there was something involved beyond mere politeness. The old folk in this northern land, he had found, were usually very polite, and he liked their ways and curious beliefs. The fact that they had a Gaelic language of their own attracted him, for he was himself a student of French, and, he believed, somewhat of an authority on Balzac.

Fortunately for the old lady, a sprightly tongue of flame ran up the dry peat at that moment, and she swung the kettle over it. "Now it won't be long," she said, carefully backing up the flame with more peat.

She was a quick-witted, bright-eyed old woman, and as she hurried to and fro getting the tea things on the table they chatted pleasantly. Presently, when she seated herself and began to pour the tea, he asked her in the friendliest way why she had stopped flapping her apron.

She glanced at him and then said, "Och, just an old woman's way."

But he would not have that, and rallied her. "Come, now, there was something more to it than that."

And at last she said: "It's just an old story in this part of the world and likely it will not be true. But I will tell it to you, seeing you say you like stories of the kind, but you will have to take it as you get it, for that's the way I got it myself, more years ago now than I can remember. It is a story about our Lord at the time of His crucifixion. You will remember that when our Lord was being crucified they nailed Him to the Cross. But before they could do that they needed the nails, and the nails were not in it. So they tried to get the nails made, but no one would make them. They asked the Roman soldiers to make them, but they would not. Perhaps it was not their business to make the nails. Anyway, they would not make them. So they asked the Jews to make the nails, but they would not make them either. No, they would not make them. No one would make the nails that were needed to crucify our Lord. And when they were stuck now, and did not know what to do, who should they see coming along but a tinker with his little leather apron on him. So they asked him if he would make the nails. And he said yes, he would make them. And to make the nails he needed a fire. So a fire was made, but it would not go very well, so he bent down in front of it and flapped it with his leather apron. In that way the fire went and the nails were made. And so it came about that the tinkers became wanderers, and were never liked by the people of the world anywhere. And that's the story."

When at last he drove away from the old woman's house he came to the cross-roads and, a few yards beyond, drew up. This is the place, he thought, and he felt it about him, gripped the wheel hard, and sat still. Irritation began to get the better of him. Anyone could see he was a fool. He got out and stretched his legs and lit a cigarette. There was no one in the turnip field, no one anywhere. All at once he walked back quickly to the cross-roads, turned right, and again saw the cottage. It was looking at him with a still, lopsided, idiotic expression. His flesh quickened and drew taut in cool anger. He threw the cigarette away, emptied his mind, and came to the door, which was exactly as it had been before, half open and stuck.

When he had knocked once, and no one answered, he felt like retreating, so he knocked very loudly the second time, and the woman materialised. There was no other word for it. There she was, with the graceful twist in her dejected body, attached to the edge of the door. Was she expecting the blow? Was there something not so much antagonistic as withdrawn, prepared to endure, in the pathos of her attitude? She knew how to wait, in any case.

"I see you didn't pay," he said.

She did not answer. She could not have been more than thirty.

"Well, you have got to appear before the court now," he asserted, and added, with a lighthearted brutality, "or the police will come and fetch you. Hadn't you the money to pay?" And he looked at her.

"No," she said, looking back at him.

"So you hadn't the money," he said, glancing away with the smile of official satire. "And what are you going to do now—go to prison?"

156

The children were poking their heads round her skirts again. Their fragility appeared extreme, possibly because they were unwashed. Obviously they were famished.

She did not answer.

"Look here," he said, "this is no business of mine." He took out his pocket-book. His hands shook as he extracted a pound note. "Here's something for you. That'll pay for everything. The only thing I want you *never* to do is to mention that I gave it to you. Do you understand?"

She could not answer for looking at the pound note. If he had been afraid of a rush of gratitude he might have saved himself the worry. She took it stupidly and glanced at him as if there might be a trick in all this somewhere. Then he saw a stirring in her eyes, a woman's divination of character, a slow welling of understanding in the black deeps. It was pathetic.

"That's all right," he said, and turned away as if she had thanked him.

When he got back into his car he felt better. That was all over, anyway. She was just stupid, a weak, stupid woman who had got trodden down. Tough luck on her. But she certainly wouldn't give him away. Perhaps he ought to have emphasised that part of it more? By God, I would never live it down in the office! Never! He began to laugh as he bowled along. He felt he could trust her. She was not the sort to give anything away. Too frightened. Experience had taught her how to hold her tongue before the all-important males of the world—not to mention the all-important females! She knew the old conspiracy all right and then some! His mirth increased. That he had felt he could not afford the pound—a pound is a pound, by heavens!—added now to the fun of the whole affair.

He did not go to court. After all, he might feel embarrassed; and the silly woman might, if she saw him, turn to him or depend on him or something. Moreover, he did not know how these affairs were conducted. So far it had not been his business. Besides, he disliked the whole idea of court proceedings. Time enough for that when he *had* to turn up.

Before lunch the chief came into his room for some papers.

The young man repressed his excitement, for he had been wondering how the case had gone, having, only a few minutes before, remembered the possibility of court expenses. He could not bring himself to ask the result, but the chief, as he was going out, paused and said: "That woman from Ivy Cottage, the dog case, she was convicted."

"Oh. I'm glad you got the case through."

"Yes. A silly woman. The bench was very considerate in the circumstances. Didn't put on any extra fine. No expenses. Take out the licence and pay the seven-and-six compromise fine—or five days. She was asked if she could pay. She said no. So they gave her time to pay."

The young man regarded the point of his pen. "So she's off again," he said, with official humour.

"No. She elected to go to prison. She put the bench rather in a difficulty, but she was obdurate."

"You mean—they've put her in prison?"

"Presumably. There was no other course at the time."

"But the children—what'll happen to them?"

"No doubt the police will give the facts to the Inspector of Poor. It's up to the local authorities now. We wash our hands of it. If people will keep dogs they must know what to expect!" He smiled drily and withdrew.

The young man sat back in his chair and licked his dry lips. She had cheated him. She had … she preferred … let him think. Clearly the pound mattered more than the five days. His money she would have left with the eldest girl, or some of it, with instructions what to buy and how to feed the children. She would have said to the eldest girl, "I'll be away for a few days, but don't worry, I'll be back. And meantime …"

But no, she would tell the eldest everything, by the pressure of instinct, of reality. That would bring the eldest into it; make her feel responsible for the young ones. And food … food … the overriding avid interest in food. Food—it was everything. The picture formed in his mind of the mother taking leave of her children.

It was pretty hellish, really. By God, he thought, we're as hard as nails. He threw his pen down, shoved his chair back, and strolled to the window.

The people passed on the pavement, each for himself or herself, upright, straight as nails, straight as spikes.

He turned from them, looked at his watch, feeling weary and gloomy, and decided he might as well go home for lunch, though it was not yet ten minutes to one. Automatically taking the white towel from its nail on the far side of the cupboard, he went out to wash his hands.

Half-Light

"Where the half-sphered scabious nod in a purple mist." The words were pencilled on a scrap of an old envelope as though jotted down hastily or in semi-darkness, and represented the only writing of any sort found in his clothes. But to me the words represented—what?

I could not answer. They haunted me. Haunted me more uneasily than ever, when, after an absence of some years, I got caught again in the half-light which comes to that grey northern land when the sun has died finally beyond the head-land that crouches like a beast on the sea, shutting out half the western world. There is a quality in this half-light that is at once a closing in and an awareness. Colour intensifies, "runs", so that the ditchside of kingcups at hand becomes a sheet of gold, and the field of "half-sphered scabious" beyond the bank a veritable ravishment of "purple mist". Into the silence creeps a listening stillness. The bleat-ing of a sheep or far barking of a dog dies out in ears that continue to hear the echoing forlornness. Upon the body itself, squatting stiffly, steals that subconscious alertness which, if a sudden hand were to descend on a shoulder, would cause a jump with the heart in the mouth. A bathing, a physical brooding. It is the hour of the earth spirit.

But not alone of the earth spirit. All that has been bred of the human spirit for untold generations is interwoven in this web, so that vision loses focus in a sense of human things forgone, of heroic days leaving ghosts to an unearthly half-light… .

And thereupon, as though waiting its chance, through from the back of the mind comes the thought that possibly he saw it like this, and, having seen, was driven to jotting down "notes" like any conscious, deliberate artist. That was the uncomfortable thing. I *should* have been prepared to accept the tragic circumstances as they were plainly accepted by the village or township. The young headmaster had taken to the practice of bathing down by the rocks in the evening after school hours. Then one night he didn't come back, and later a little heap of clothes was found in Breac Cove.

Deep, green water licks about the black barnacled rocks by the entrance to Breac Cove, the speckled cave, with its astonishing walls of purple and yellows and greens, with its great flattish roof curving to the droop of a gashed upper lip and thick with tiny stalactites, which can draw no answering forms from the multi-coloured pebbles that slither uneasily beneath a foot. Wrack of sea-ware here, too, going inward in parallel lines of high-tidal storm, till all is swallowed up in a threatening gloom. Regarded steadily, this gloom seems pierced sometimes by the beady eyes of monstrous tusked sea-animals lying in wait.

That, and the disturbing scabious "note"—together with my most vivid memories of his attitude to this same grey sea-board when we "digged" together in Edinburgh. His vehemence had startled me. "I tell you I wouldn't go back there—no, not though it meant a fortune; not though it meant——" Wordless, he waved an arm and laughed harshly. "The place is dead, man! It's done! Good God, it's full of ghosts! The little harbours are silting up, the curing sheds are roof-less, the boats are gone. And what else is there? What else was there ever there but life in the heyday of the old mad fishings? What are the few crofts but crouching, squatting brute things—dead, too, by heavens!" He walked up and down, while I continued to stare at him. The face, normally pale, had whitened to a lip-twisted intensity; the eyes, normally lazy, blazed with light. "No, not likely! We've been starved enough! When I get my degree I'm going out East. I'm going to get warm with colour and sun and snakes!" Then he became conscious of himself and sat down; but somehow his throaty laugh died abruptly into a long silence.

That was his first real outbreak. But once he had thus shown his mind, it ap-peared much easier for him thereafter to refer to the matter. Any desolate scene, any description of grey wastes, would draw a sort of commenting undertone. "Just so!" He understood all about it. Not much could be told him. The most fearsome and ungodly places could at best draw a nod. "Quite. I follow. But——" "But what?" "To be the finished article it just lacks that something of decay——" "Look here, Iain, you're getting positively distorted, a bally decadent——" "My dear chap, who's the decadent? Do I go reading all that sort of stuff you do? Do I have anything to do with Celtic Twilights or quattrocentists or any life-at-second-hand business of that sort? You enjoy that; I don't—no more than I do the grey wastes—yonder!" "Well, dammit, why can't you leave the blessed wastes alone?" "I'm going to, I assure you. Don't worry about that!"

I didn't exactly worry about it. Yet like a poison his tormented visioning of our birthland must have got some sort of hold on me, for a chance occurring to spend a protracted period in Italy I jumped at it. Free of his influence, in that land of colour and sun, my memories by degrees so softened that I was guilty once or twice (the stifling heat and the flies of high summer!) of writing verses to that birthland, each line drenched, indeed, in the cool dews of the northern twilights. If only old Iain had been able to look through his eyelashes... Then came chance word that he had accepted the old Oulster school. I was shocked. I should have been infinitely less shocked, I think, if I had heard he had proceeded to the South Sea Islands and gone native.

No one else appeared to be shocked, however. A stray home paper reached me, commenting on how happy the appointment, how fitting indeed that an Honours graduate should return to shed lustre on the places of his boyhood, and (they doubted not) be instrumental in equipping many a bare-legged laddie for future high appointments in Church and State. I laughed. So much for these old proud college-day ideas. How quickly, how smoothly, the world puts them in their place, oftenest without even the sentimental paragraph of the local reporter! In truth, I didn't quite know whether to be sorry or pleased about it; for I am willing to confess that Iain's sensitiveness to seaboard "atmosphere" had not been lost on me. I had always been jealous of justifying the artist, the literary spirit; and how disturbing had been that elusive atmosphere to him then, how real! I had understood intimately—even while I may have wished that the old homeland had not been the subject of it. Still, in this new twentieth century, with its wonderful promise for humanity, its clear vision of progress, the very troubling of Iain's spirit was hopeful and stirring. Yet now here he was apparently, having sloughed this sensitive skin, settling down to the daily round, much in the style of hardfisted business men who have had what they regard as their callow Tennyson or Browning days. And that I didn't like.

However, there was plenty material of assurance for me in Italy, inexhaustible assurance, and it was not until the succeeding autumn that I visited the homeland—to find Oulster hush-voiced in gloom. Breac Cove with that little heap of clothes, the scabious "note", and my Edinburgh memories… . I got up from the ditchside. Could I accept the "accident"? Would there not be some more "notes" somewhere among his papers? … But the northern chill must have crept to my bones, for I shivered again.

2

To come into the presence of Iain's mother is instinctively to perform some act of courtesy. A welcoming, a mysterious something of the spirit, a living hand. Your mind hesitates; words, conventional words of sympathy, wither away in this air of steadfastness, of natural dignity.

"The sea is cruel," she admits. "I've always been frightened of the sea, though we've always belonged to it. We managed to send him away—but he didn't escape it." The eyes moisten, the lips grow tremulous, the worn fingers make a pleat of the black silk dress. "He always had a word for you."

She nods. I turn away.

"He was a good boy to come home—because of me. But I should—I should have left him."

In the end as I prepare to go, it is with the utmost sincerity I manage:

"I thought I might be of some little help. All his books and papers—I could arrange and pack them—anything like that."

My hand receives a quick pressure. It is very kind of me. I mumble something, to find that the tears are in my throat, that they sting my eyes. I turn quickly up the little path from the schoolhouse.

Next day she left the schoolhouse to return to the old fishing cottage, her brave adventure over; back to the old walls, the old memories, to sit through the half-light till the fulfilment of the promise of a final Dawn.

Her going gave me a whole evening, a whole night, alone with his books. I locked the front door, I drew the blinds of his study. My legs trembled with excitement. There was just this about it: I felt that were there anything unusual in the manner of his disappearance, then the information were better in my hands than in those, perhaps, of any other. Whether I could understand better or not was an argument that did not arise: I knew definitely I could so keep the information to myself that his mother, having made her renunciation, should not be aroused by the black iniquity of bowelless gossip.

The first superficial survey of his study astonished me. Yes, he had very decidedly started reading. I skim over the bindings. Fancy gets struck by the prevailing note of green, from the lengthy row of old Bohn's Classical Library to quite a number of books on the sea. Sea-green, I think, and pause to look more closely at obviously new backs. As title follows title I hear the sea's surge, on tropical reef, on grey rock of the Hebrides. The grey note is actually interspersed, too, with an early Yeats and, yes, a grey-covered Fiona Macleod.

Of course! I pluck out the Fiona Macleod… . Ah, I expected it, I knew it! The volume is pencil-annotated into a criss-cross jigsaw puzzle. Here on a double sheet of notepaper are something like the beginnings of a considered essay on the Celtic Twilight! The opening satire is good, if a trifle bitter, sweeping. He finds it difficult to be patient. Then my smile dies. A short paragraph, and our seaboard lives before me. Gathering one or two choice Celtic blooms he tosses them into the seaboard atmosphere, and immediately they shrivel up like flowers in a grey frost. "Here's the Celtic Twilight for you if you like!" he says. I rebel in the first words that come: "Ah, but you forget that you are looking at an old literature with a modern, agnostic eye. That makes a difference!" And suddenly his face is before me, his mouth twisting. "And wasn't Fiona Macleod a modern?" I snap the book shut.

I have got to make a pathway through this jungle of reading and annotating: he has got to put the weapon in my hand. Promiscuous quotation would be like cutting round and round. Let me take a poem of his, both because it hints at the real significance of that scabious "note" and because verse-making does necessitate some thought-refining, a certain quintessential treatment of idea. It is the only completed poem I find—whatever else of verse there is being fragmentary. It is also interesting as carrying on the Edinburgh attitude, so that there is a certain mental continuity—with this addition: that he is now attempting to give concise expression to his physical desire for the seaboard's opposite.

It is headed "The Croft", and the opening verses run:

> *The dark wind up the braes*
> *From the cold sea*
> *Comes whining its barren ways*
> *Through the grey tufts, days on days,*
> *Mercilessly,*

Combing each withered mass
Of wilted hair;
Between the tufts there pass
The lean kine cropping the grass,
Grey-green and bare.

No more colour nor sound
Than that. The stern
Lean years are all around,
Grey boulders that abound
For death's grey cairn.

The poem is called "The Croft" as though instinctively the mind of the writer felt that it is the earth spirit that is the dominant thing—not the dominated human spirit of the old crofter. For from this point it is the old crofter of the poem who speaks.

Here from this sheltered lair
Of blaeberry
And withy stems I stare
At the dead years and dare
My blasphemy.

And so he is off. As the whole runs to very many verses only the trend need be shown. There is, for example, youth's visioning of the "colour and sun and snakes", the seduction of the East:

Days out of mind did the beat
Of my heart rhyme
The pulse of illicit fleet
Passing of sandall'd feet,
Days out of time.

As Chinese lamps come aglow
To a piping flute
Did my secret dream-flowers blow

Into colour and luscious sweet flow
Of forbidden fruit,

Luscious and rich enough, but savage, too, where

Vast scorching noons held sway
Over naked flesh
That trampled down the desert's way... .

The realities are envisaged to the sweat-blinding and the "miraged mesh". Nothing "twilight" about it. On the contrary, a savagery—sometimes more concealed than may appear. For these things have been denied by the grey years that lie about him like inescapable grey boulders. And he misses nothing, as though every forbidden, sensuous thing had to be savoured. Colour cannot be left alone, till in one verse it is positively—or sardonically—cloying:

And colour that ached on the eyes,
From snake-lustred gleam
To scarlet of poisonous lies;
And colour more soft than the sighs
From passion's hareem.

The temptation to quote is strong. I realise, however, that the appeal of the verses to me may be bound up in the personal element, and that to the normal reader they may be quite unexceptional. But the concluding three verses I should like to quote in order that the Edinburgh attitude may be given its due Scots metaphysical twist, and a seal set to his whole thought up to this stage. Here is the croft, here his denial of it, his rebellion against it and its "grey creed"—his "blasphemy", as he calls it. Then:

Sin? And my dried lips twist
On this childish name
For the fire and the knotted fist,
The dream-woven gossamer mist,
The flame upon flame.

Colour and passion and sun,
These three my gods
Over all—and these three were one—
Painting with sundering vision
The very peat sods.

Sin? Till wild laughter shook
When the word it saith:
Till old laughter—stares at the Book
That stares back with Jehovah's look
And His grey breath.

3

In the absence of anything more forceful than "The Croft", I found myself compelled to adjust my premonitions. That the theme should have been a croft and a crofter rather than the sea and a fisherman pointed to one possible interpretation of everything; namely, that he had found in such literary outlet for his feelings some sort of relief; more, that the very "complex" which the seaboard stood for became, through the literary channel, an original unifying theme for essay and verse. I know only too well how scarce original themes are for the modern writer, how he has to hunt for one and quarry in it. Here, on the contrary, was clearly an obsession, instinct with qualities, awaiting a virile development that would be a most realistic counterblast to the Fiona Macleod twilights, from the land of Gaeldom, and using, to begin with anyhow—as will have been seen—the old poetic rhythms that he might one day destroy.

Quite. It explained everything. I became conscious of the loss of a fellow-worker who might have set our seaboard on fire. At that moment I tasted the bitterest sorrow of his passing. Yes, it surely explained everything. The scabious business was just the colour line of some contemplated poem; the bathing no more than a purging of the day's petty toils before the compositions of the night. That he should have been plucked away like that... .

I took a turn up and down the study. The small hours were upon the deserted schoolhouse. A sense of stillness and empty rooms surrounded me. In an involuntary vision I saw some of the doors of these rooms standing agape, others blindly closed. Tenantless; their emptiness crowding round this ghostly brain of a room I walked in. What was I doing here? …

I lifted my mind from this trivial by-play. "Yes, it explains everything," I said. And by the very sound of my words in the silence I suddenly knew it explained nothing. There was a "feel" for life in him, for naked life, that no creative artistry could ever satisfy. Life itself was what mattered, was the blinding thing: not its expression, its "life-at-second-hand business"….

What was I doing here? The question became insistent. The backs of the books regarded me in a certain way. The very swirl in the air I made as I walked was, as it were, populous with the question. I stopped dead.

I had no fear of Iain Mackay. I had no fear even of the appearance of his naked spirit. Whatever of mere curiosity there may have been in the original twist of my thought, there was certainly nothing now but that curiosity actuated by a sense of service. I should like to be the discoverer of knowledge so that his mother might be safe…. Safe from what? For the first time I really faced the question. The books watched, particularly Fiona Macleod, which I hadn't pushed right flush with the others. Safe from—from—I dismissed the halting horror. Iain Mackay, I thought, deliberately, epitomised in himself this particular sea-coast. He knew with an intimacy of the marrow its uttermost essence. He merged again with that essence willingly or unwillingly, but in some way *wittingly*.

I paused, listening, on edge. There was Fiona Macleod. In an instant I had gone up and smashed the book flush. On a level with my face on the top shelf of the bookcase was a tobacco smoker's cabinet, and as the bookcase shook under the impact of my fist the little wooden door of the cabinet swung noiselessly open, revealing to my staring eyes a blue tobacco jar and a black-covered, thick notebook leaning against it.

A notebook! Presently my hand reached out for it; then restraining a desire to look around, I went deliberately to the oak knee-desk and sat down.

4

It was a diary of sorts, at least an irregularly-kept record of evening excursions and midnight thought. It starts with the Edinburgh attitude, toned down, as theory must be toned down, in face of actualities. He notes things, names them, severs the thought from the fact in many a raw local phrase. This impression of coming into contact with things physically is very vivid, the visual sense being curiously abetted by the tactile. You can not only see the grey rock his hands touch, but feel its roughness with his finger-tips; and not only the tactile but the auditory as well, so that when sand is rubbed by his bare soles on a dry ledge of the rock the sound sets your teeth on edge.

And you sense the same old aim in it all. He is at his game of purposely stripping things bare, tearing ruthlessly the films and the fancies, so that the essential starkness may be laid open like a dry fibrous wound. For there is no blood in the body of this land of his, only a greyness and unheeding expanse. There may be a skeleton—of kirkyard bones. He wants to make sure he has no illusions about that, no "Celtic Twilight hallucinations".

And then the change comes.

It comes gradually, almost furtively. A few leaves of the notebook escape under the fingers and it is more pronounced. Little by little he is slipping into the habit of identifying himself with things, at first with the apparent excuse of gaining more graphic force in the phrasing, but then, as it seems, without his always being aware of it. Keats said he could be the sparrow picking about the gravel; but the old woman of Tiree said:

> *"It is the grey rock I am,*
> *And the grey rain on the rock."*

Iain was losing his destroying, logical objectiveness and occasionally identifying himself with the outer forces, the surrounding elemental forces. Not yet at the stage of the old woman of Tiree by any means, but rendered occasionally reflective, subjective, in a new momentarily quiescent way. The process goes on, subtly but persistently, begins to eat into him with a certain secretiveness which he plainly hides even from himself; then less plainly hides; until at last even the human figures he encounters become slightly more significant than spent automata.

Slipping some more pages, I find this entry:

"Went out on the edge of the dark and came on ould Sanny at the Look-out. His grey whiskers were to the sea and he spoke to me without turning round. I wonder what moves in his head? I'll tackle him one of these nights, when I've more time. I know definitely he thinks now and then of the old fishing days, and *sees* them, too. He draws in his breath on that wheezy 'Ay', then spits fully. 'Done!

Done!' he says. 'It's no' what I remember." It's not. God knows it's not. The gaping curing sheds in the darkening, the glooming, pervasive greyness, the lonely calling of the wheeling gulls. As I left ould Sanny I felt like laughing at it all, as it twisted and knotted in me. A husk of a place! A place to be laughed at… .

"I used to laugh, too, at Fiona Macleod and the like, but now—I'm damned if I'm not becoming fanciful myself The tall grey salmon-net poles got me tonight. They stand there in that bunch near enough together, so that you could almost spit from one to the other; yet tonight each seemed lonely and thin and wrapped up in a grey self-communing. 'Apart' is the word. Good Lord—'apart'! Yet there it is. These bits of grey weather-cracked poles! And they got me with a sense of kinship, so that I stood among them till my hearing and sight became abnormally acute and my body stiff. From their little green plateau you look down on the harbour basin. It is empty. Look long enough—it fills. Oh, I know it is imagination, that I am allowing my staring eyes to see things. Obviously there is nothing—nothing material. There is merely this much: the place has its 'influence'. By way of experiment, I have given way to this influence once or twice. I give way again. A certain hypnotic, sinking sensation… . The harbour basin fills. Boat-decks, rigging, masts slanting to rest in their crutches, figures moving about, at first dimly, then more distinctly; a face, faces; sounds: all coming before the staring eyes through stages, as it were, of imperfect focusing, till the picture lives, moves, throbs. A species of 'movies', if you like—for away from the influence one must joke about it to keep balance. But under the influence—my father's stride, a trifle quicker than the others; the face a trifle more alert; the tongue with its ever ready shaft. And there his men from the Lews—the heave-ho! chant of the voices, the *krik! krik!* of the halyards as mast goes slowly aloft. The brown sails—there they go slipping past the quay-wall to breast the sea: out of the smooth harbour-basin to this restless dipping and rising and gliding of the great brown-winged seabirds they are. The smother of life left behind, the ripe richness of the young women gutters' faces, the smiling wrinkles of the old, the incredibly deft fingers, the talk, the laughter, the work.

"An ache comes to the soul, the lips stir to an old savour, salty, brimful of life. Something here of the marrow. Schoolkeeping, shop-keeping, book-clerking, all the pale, anaemic occupations of landsmen and citymen, dear Lord—how ghostly! their passion a hectic spurting, their contentment a grey haze. Teaching children all day long so that they may 'get on', may be successful in attaining the clerical stool or pulpit, or in measuring, at a profit, so many yards of red flannel for a country woman's needs. Eh? And being polite always: it pays. God!

"I am a throw-back, am I? Sort of quintessential heritage? All this centred in me as the living evocation of the dead seaboard? Perhaps my very hate of this place but a sort of wrongheaded, savage worship? What a damned juggling with perhapses!"

Then farther on and one stage farther on, this:

"With what an exquisite shudder the cold green water twists round body and limbs! It ensheaths you. Gracious and savage in a way less obvious than the East. In its coldness what clean passion! You want to throw caution to the winds and write of it in a choice prose, as of a beautiful woman, unattainable, but near, so that her eyes are regarding yours with a measured expressionlessness—that at any moment may break and engulf you.

"I struggle to cast off this twilight phrasing, to regard the sea with clear eyes, knowing the Old Man as he is—veritably 'seagreen and incorruptible'. Yet even that leads me to a choosing of images. And when the caress of the water takes the shuddering body, and an exultation grips overhand at the wavetops … You can keep going on for ever. Turning back is a shattering. On and on, the under knowledge that you are going too far breeding a warning, an excitement. And how vision riots as doubt of the body's safety increases! In such a position is not one justified in dropping the stark logicalities and rioting, has not one earned the right? On and on, arm cleaving, body cleaving …

"Suddenly something pulls you up. You stop, tread water, look back to the shore. Panic forces rush in. You mutter a scattering curse at them—and start back in a long slow stroke. The water grows chilly, gets the back of your neck in a cold grip when you turn over. It is a long way. It is a devilish long way. Limbs begin to drag. A numbing sensation spreads… .

"At last the jagged rocks, the dark weeds, the black entrance to Breac Cove. Feet touch. You drag the body a yard or two and let it lie. The round stones press into it softly, the wet weed is velvety. Your head rolls off your arm on to the cold stones and the sea-water is a gurgling and lapping infinitely far off. You realise with a remote, impersonal unconcern that you could not have gone much farther—and come back … ."

One more quotation, though it is with reluctance I pass over a description of the twilight hour in Breac Cove, not so much because of the wild beauty and lurking ferocity dwelt on, as of the obvious giving way to its "influence".

"The struggle tonight was the hardest yet, for when the pause came and the panic forces rushed the brain, I continued to tread water and did not immediately start for the shore. In going out a saying had come to my mind from *The Little Book of the Great Enchantment*, and prefaced, I think, to *The Dirge of the Four Cities*, by Fiona Macleod. Fiona Macleod! There will ever be a grain of bitterness in my acknowledgement of him, or of Yeats, or of any of the modern Celtic twilighters, an irritable impatience of their pale fancies, their posturing sonorities and follies. Yet on a certain side they are 'getting' me, and sometimes a phrase, a thought, has a positively uncanny, mesmeric power over my very flesh.

"This sort of dream poetry is clearly a drug, an insidious drug. Intellect strives and flashes towards some final illumination—till the effort expends itself like a two-penny rocket attempting the work of a sun. And when failure rushes down in a renewed darkness, swamping all meaning and logic, dream poetry is there, a glimmering half-light, beckoning. Not an interpretation of the ultimates: a refuge from them. The man of action, with his raw grip on the realities, ignores it—till he finds the sphere of his activities dissolved, till (for this is the thought) the routh of life that swarmed the seaboard and clothed the very salmon-poles is left a ghostly greyness and a calling of gulls. Then poetry casts its net, its iridescent net, and the silvery fish of the intellect is meshed in the music of lost days and forgotten beauties. My images get mixed, I think—like my thought, and the bitter-raw becomes the bitter-sweet. Such a lovely vagueness is poetry, if one could but admit it! Perhaps the making of all great poetry has involved this fight—and this admission. Perhaps the men who have written greatly of the half-light have known the stark realities of the light. Let me say as much, even if I don't believe it yet, for, after all, what do I know of the ultimates that I should talk of a refuge from them?—There the fading light on the breast of the sea, there the dim-glowing west facing me as arm and body cleave through: and haunting my brain hypnotically the saying: 'And the symbol of Murias is a hollow that is filled with water and fading light'."

I am conscious of a light, a glimmering light. It is the half-light of the dawn on the window blind.

5

"Come away ben," she invited me, after we had sat in the kitchen for a little time; and I followed her to the parlour. It was bare of the gilt china ornaments of the old days; indeed, it was altogether bare.

"This," she said simply, "is going to be his study."

I knew a moment's insecurity. I suppose I was still young enough to think that tragedy is a thing to be swept into the dark places.

"So we'll put the bookcase there," she went on, gently, indicating a wall, "and the desk there—fornent the window."

I nodded, and, looking away through the window, saw the grey sea.

"My time cannot be so long—and the books and things of his will be company for me." Her voice was quiet and natural. A quietening came on me.

At the doorway I turned.

"He loved being here at home with you," I said. "He was happy with you. And he loved the old harbour and the sea."

"Perhaps, perhaps," she answered, her hands pressing my hand in the heart's quick acknowledgement. "I am so glad you think it. It was sometimes—on my mind. But I think he did love it—in the end; and we've always belonged to the sea."

Hidden Doors

Alan Macdonald came on the announcement in one of those idle moments when an awakening from reveried vacancy sends an arm groping over the wings of the chair. Fingers got entangled in the newspaper on the floor, lifted it, fluttered open the pages.

It was an eight-page weekly of one of the little northern towns, with district news prominently displayed, a column in Gaelic in the form of a letter, trite summaries of political events with a peasant-conservative bias, and odd little paragraphs of a distinctly personal flavour.

It was the heading to one of these paragraphs that caught his eye. "Grave Tragedy." Something of the old human decencies about the adjective. Grave. Not shocking, nor frightful; no catch-word distortion. Vaguely satisfied, he went on to the paragraph:

"Great consternation was caused throughout the island of Gruasaig on Wednesday morning when the body of Michael Turner was found on the lonely stretch of moor between the hotel and Cnoc-an-druidh. Deceased, who had spent many years in the Outer Islands, had latterly made Gruasaig Hotel his home. He was a keen angler and enjoyed the sea-trout sport, so plentiful in these parts. Though not a native, nor, as far as is known, having any family connection whatever with the Western Highlands, he had come to take considerable interest in local affairs, entering into the daily avocations of the people and having more than a passing interest in their traditions and music. Death was the result of exposure, and it is surmised that on Tuesday night, on leaving the hotel for his customary evening walk, he must have missed his way on the moor. From a threatening afternoon the weather had quickly worked up to a night of storm, the wind rising to a gale. He will be much missed. Meantime every endeavour is being made to get in touch with his relatives."

Alan Macdonald's fist had convulsively knotted on the sheet as he had read, and now sheet and fist fell away and eyes stared.

"Great God ! Turner!"

"A night of storm, the wind… ." Significance trickled its dark stream in and out the roots of his being. "Impossible!" he cried, body twisting, recoiling, trying to stem it. But revelation went on trickling, flooding, a weird flickering light playing on it, through it, with a mesmeric irony.

It had to be accepted. Some such dim foreshadowing, some such premonition (duly laughed at) had touched a sudden shivering chord, when Turner that last night had spoken, had hinted, said he had heard. He could see his face now, the dark-brown eyes gone black, glittering, the concentration of expression, the thin almost livid pallor, the curious hypnotic quality that held dominant something of erratic genius… .

Drink can do much in dissolving away the humours of the flesh. And Turner drank, without ever being able to reach the fuddled stage. The more he drank the more self-consciousness and the body seemed to dissolve, till that constant stage was reached of the drawn shell of a face as lantern to the remorseless white light within; yet a light liable to its gusts and flickerings, too.

Flickerings, particularly, for there was a surface, but fantastic humour, an impish, Cockney humour in him, that had a fascination for Macdonald, that touched some agreeable sense of wild, gnomish, but submerged laughter in himself. So that during the ten days of his fishing stay at Gruasaig, the companionship had had an unforgettable attraction.

An attraction, however, with this curiously repellent side. In the evening hours, as the fatal glasses mounted up, Turner could cut his mind open to the last most secret place with an unselfconsciousness, a dark worming morbidity, that got Macdonald on the raw, that made him, with his innate Gaelic secrecy, feel as though he were a forced spectator at a dissection of the unspeakable; which yet need not have called for comment on his part, were it not, as though by some fatal kink in the man, Turner had to search out a parallelism in Highland myth, Highland superstition, had to search it out as in some urgent inner process of self-justification. He would pause, his eye-flash would concentrate on Macdonald. "You have the same sort of thing in a way in that what-d'ye-call-it of yours… ." He certainly never failed to "put it up" to Macdonald.

And if Macdonald squirmed, yet as he made sure of his man, made sure of his guilelessness, he had once or twice the plunging sensation of internally letting go and breasting the dark waters, of diving for frail opalescent shells of thought, of splitting open the shells… .

And even there Turner would get him. In the act of winding up the gramophone, he would twist a sidelong glance at Macdonald: "Don't scientists agree the pearl begins in an irritant? The psychoanalyst also has his irritant, his complex irritant, yet I've never seen him fish out the most miserable seedling of a pearl. Yet gems are necessarily created out of convulsions and travail and a pretty high temperature…. And these pearls of the 'land under the wave' of being, they have to make a string fit for the pale goddess under the ultimate wave of ultimate dream." The thin smile quickened. "You get me all the same. For something which I puzzle out is native to you and you avoid speaking about it with what you feel is the good taste—that bally sort of good taste the Sassenach is conscious of when he avoids discussion on his 'ideals'—or his wife."

At which Macdonald had his laugh:

"I really credited you with more insight! All this talk about our superstitions and fancies—it's merely talk, as you ought to know by this time—mere fools' and poets' talk. What are the crofters out there really interested in? Their business— the price of a stirk, or the potato prospects, or the peat-drying. Simply that, and nothing more. Ask them. Probe them if you like. And then talk sense."

"I grant you," acknowledged Turner, "grub is the prime necessity all the world over, grub and some sort of liquid—heather ale, for instance. Think of a people who could make, who could name, Heather Ale—even at any time in their history! 'Inspiration in essence'—eh ?—'the genius of laughter to all.' But you don't laugh; your laughter is a sort of phosphorescence in darkness. Now the whole island here, as you know, reeks with superstition, as with peat, and as for fancies—no, they ain't the musical dope of the blokes as writes abaht it, I grant you… . You're a deep one Macdonald. You hide it, too—instinctively."

"You have merely got, man, what the French call—"

"An *idée fixe*, isn't it?"

Macdonald nodded. "And believe me, in this business you're merely bolstering up poetic fancies of your own, which you would like to think are real, which you would like to believe have a profound existence, significance, and all the rest of it–for your own sake! You remind me of some tourists I ran into the other day. They were looking for—The Island That Likes To Be Visited."

Turner's face froze in a wild amaze, then it collapsed uncontrollably. Macdonald smiled.

"That's a—ic—good one," Turner hiccoughed presently. He finished up, however, by twisting the tail-end of his laughter at Macdonald searchingly.

"I understand. You have my sympathy. This toy-shop business! How long, O Lord! You have the 'ell of a lot to live down!"

Macdonald looked at him.

"Well, we have, haven't we? And you help—don't you?"

Turner's face straightened, his glance became keen. Eyes held eyes.

"Let's fill up," he said, soberly, "and have this tune on the gramophone."

Without another word, the disc was sent spinning.

In such ways Macdonald had made sure of his man, touched the reticences in him and found them disturbingly kin.

And the nights led up, through the reticences to one last night, that now gripped him as he sat in his chair with a visualisation that was almost too horribly intense.

The gramophone was Turner's, a good instrument; the records, too. Where Turner and his gramophone had come out of Macdonald did not know, could not guess, except that both had the stamp of decent London stock, only his Christian name leaving room for more curious speculation. But he had run into many strange cases of odd men living years and years in out-of-the-way corners of the West to bother speculation over much. Even the crofters didn't bother, though if you got to know them well enough there would at least be a head-shake. For rumour could by relied on for its half-talk of banishment for unsuggested sins—unless your man was drinking altogether too suggestively. Otherwise, live and let courteously live. After all, Macdonald felt that Turner could quite as easily have been sent down as, well, say, Shelley, and lacking Shelley's dynamic purpose, could more easily have stayed down—and out, particularly in a land that plainly called to a mysticism that found Allah and the desert in a peat bog.

To one last night of the gramophone records with drinks in between.

Turner had a not unpleasant habit of officiating at the gramophone. He introduced each record. "Now, here's Kreisler. You listen and you'll see what I mean by Heifetz' 'cello tone. Kreisler is pure violin—all gold. Nothing to touch him in that respect. And as for a shake—listen to the final note. No one else can come near it. They blur it. *Liebesleid*. By gad, I tell you…"

Or "Macleod—Ruaraidh, as they call him—you call him——"

"*We* call him, and be done with it!"

"As we call him. About the only voice I have. Now and then he gets there. Doom in the stuff; sombre, the sea, the calling of the spent seawrack of the soul in it… . Ah, the music. The old things—they can't get spoilt, and they don't give a damn about wanting to be visited. Only, even there you have the puritanical, covenanting innovations of John Knox. The frost of Calvinism is on much of the Outer Isles here like a blight. But thank your stars a lot of the old stuff, the old genuine stuff, has escaped, by the pure mercy and grace of God. And your true seal music, for instance—Mrs Marjory Kennedy Fraser has picked up an echo of, in particular, one unearthly thing, one unearthly thing … but——-"

"Well?"

Turner's expression stilled, then twisted oddly his voice dropping a tone.

"There are things——" He paused, darkly, and Macdonald snapped a sudden insupportable tension by whisking the juice from his pipe-stem.

"No things," he said, levelly; "nothings. Don't become the tourist, Turner. That, too, is all a cult—like the Celtic Twilight of the poets. And, anyway, a man can have too much to drink. Besides, it's getting late. Is that the wind rising? If it petered out in rain it would make a mighty fine difference to the Clach Pool tomorrow."

Whatever Turner may have been on the point of saying, the reference to the rising wind checked it. He half-turned to the window, and stood rigidly, one hand gripping the top bar of the nearest chair.

The wind gust cried in a low searching whine round the gable-end, rattled the window-frame, sent the curtain-folds moving wanly as though animated for a moment by a passing ghostly presence. Far out in the night a curlew called, then another … another … nearer, passing over the house. The night seemed suddenly to come alive.

"They're coming in from the sea." Turner's voice was toneless; then in a moment, with a sudden forced downrightness, "Have another, Macdonald!" He caught the decanter. His hand shook.

Macdonald shielded the top of his glass with a palm.

"We've both—anyway, I've had enough."

"Enough, be blowed! The night is young. The curtain is only being rung up. Come on! What are you frightened of?"

"Frightened?"

"Oh, get away! Come on—unhand there!"

"I've had enough, thanks."

Their eyes met and held, till Turner broke away with a sudden gesture that shook the spirit from the decanter's mouth.

"All a cult, is it—like the Celtic Twilight? By gad, you're right, Macdonald. I loathe these cults. I know the pretty-pretty business to its last sentimental meaningless ineptitude. A man with the second sight—he's the last man on God's earth to open his mouth about it. The man who has *seen*.... Oh, the little gibbering idiots! Come on, man; fill up. In the long night of eternity do a couple of souls meet so often that they should skulk, frightened?"

"Now, now, Turner, we've had enough. Too much of that, you know ..."

A pause; then Turner's voice searchingly:

" 'You know.' What do I know?"

And Macdonald instantly stiffened.

"Well, what the devil do you know?"

"That's better! Now remove your fist, and I'll tell you. No, I've never *seen* anything. It's all right. I'm merely going to tell you one of the prettiest little phantasies that could ever be compressed in a neat little three-act trick. It's a game I play with myself. Say when."

Macdonald allowed him; and when Turner had thereafter filled his own glass, he raised it with a muttered "Slainte!" half-drained it, and dropped into his chair.

"A game I play with myself, and it might be prettily scored under, say, 'Musical Doors'—after 'Musical Chairs,' don't you know! It flashed into mind again at that *Liebesleid*. And Kreisler has a genius for ... But the game is this. An instrument, sometimes a grouping of instruments, acts like a sudden key in a door, an unexpected, hidden door, like a low door in a wall that runs by a weary road or street. And after all, every weary road or street is walled. The everyday round—monotony—easily the most deadly things in walls yet built.

"I mentioned Kreisler. These exquisite trifles of his—there is a strange historic reality in their mere grace. You come on the little door with a suddenness that drowns the miserable questioning habit—or, rather, before you know where you are, you are most magically through the door, and the questioning habit is left behind on the street with the other refuse in the dust bins.

"It is a delightful experience, that first catch of the breath. The lawns, the terraces, the ivied walls, the ivied trees, the trimness, the antique beauty. Yet every promising prospect can be baffled, so that the stepping to a blind turn is a game of breathless expectancy. What could you find, anyway? That airy minuet—traced with the delicacy of lace. Lace ruffles, eh? and finger tips? The rhythm—it creates, embodies. Do you see them? … A little stone Amor, with a smile by a French artist of the old Courts, *désillusionné*—a smile at the shadow on the sundial; complete, sprouting wings an' all… . A peacock, full-spread … pavane, eh? out of Casals' 'cello…. The secrecies …. desire …

"Boyish, all that, in the creation light of dawning things? Yes, but clean, a finished artistry, with the exquisite objectiveness that might be in all mere living.

"But that's not much? Well—what about that door in the off corner? You can go in there, if you like. That *Andante Cantabile* affair of Tchaikovsky, with Elman leading the four strings, will sweetly half-open it. Devil the lawn is there in there at all. Swirls in the air and pale, Russian faces. If you let go, you're in for it! And I warn you you'll come out by the same door where in you went. And it's the hell of an experience with pale beads of sweat on a pale forehead. And oh those swirls of visible air and the deafness of God invisible! I've spent myself there, many a desperate hour—but didn't—go far in, so what's beyond, if there's any place or door at all, I don't know, and maybe they don't either… .

"The brass band doesn't take you through a door at all. You simply cross the street and go along it the wrong way… .

"But the reeds again—ah, that door! There is something without any morality at all in the purity of a reed, and there is a curious forest moon-darkness in its sheer clarity. A dancing, that is a racing with an alertness of the eyes and body and a surging lawlessness of the blood. We don't make music for Pan and his Satyrs, not even for the Nymphs: we make it for our own bodies, cloven-hoofed and healthy, or palpitating and lovely. And when you're played out, you can always go to sleep like a young god, with a bassoon droning like a great humble bee in a clover-field… .

"Innumerable doors. A pretty game, eh? And I'm not forgetting your pipes, the piob mhor, which is to say, the big pipe … Martial music, stirring strains, Jessie's Dream and the Relief of Lucknow! … No, I haven't found that door yet!! … The door leads to night, a sea-inlet, and the slow music coming over. World-loneliness, world-oldness, and a twisting in the heart." He stopped; he reached out an arm, thin unconscious fingers curving claw-like. "You reach out—out—arms out, and watch yourself a ghostly wraith going away from yourself, up and on to the cliff-heads. You find yourself there, head between your knees, and the night wind from the sea passing over... ."

His teeth shut on his suddenly-quickened breathing, so that his nostrils dilated. Then——

"These are the visible doors," he said, "the doors to a house old as the first oaten pipe, and each door with its key. An historical reality, a pretty phantasy—as you like."

But he had to pause again, the words obviously now but a froth, the dark-brown eyes gone quite black, glittering, the face pallor almost livid, hypnotic. And——

"You hear?" he whispered.

The wind had continued to rise. The night held that whining cry in its throat. Out on the darkness of the moor was movement. A crying, a searching, a whirling of shadows, as though something uncanny, alive, rode the heart of it.

Macdonald wanted to shrug, to tear through but could not for the life of him. The face before him was not merely sincere, it was raw. It penetrated the uncanny to the unthinkable.... Oh, what the hell was it staring like that for?

When Turner suddenly spoke, voice low-pitched intense:

"It was a clear moonlight night—when I first heard it—out there!"

Macdonald's jaws ground shut, and he glared back at the man.

"Then I heard it again. Music! Music, Macdonald!"

The livid staring face seemed positively gather a faint darkness like a corpse face.

"Sometime—on a night like this—I shall hear——"

* * * * *

The newspaper was violently rent in a spasmodic movement of Macdonald's fists as memory slipped into vision and he saw Turner on the moor reaching forward, face straining, eyes straining, saw the face stiffening white, remaining white, stiffened, straining forward, clayey white. He leapt from his chair.

"Turner, great God, man!" he cried.

Gentlemen

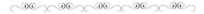

"What strikes me," he said, "is the curious mixture of rawness, presbyterianism, and Scots metaphysic. This little incident of the French girl reformed him, as the phrase goes. Now, I admit it might have reformed anyone, for the passion with which she turned on him was magnificently wholehearted, but, in addition, it held for him something of the elemental, of the bone-marrow, which you find as a searching under-current of the Braid Scots, raw, pervasive, almost worming, like a real worm in a body——"

"Get on with your yarn, man ! By the grace of God, we are not all gentlemen of the Cerebral School—yet!"

He smiled lazily; then proceeded:

"He went out East with a skipper who was a friend of his. A cargo steamer, so that they were some time away—away from all this Europeanism, I mean. Then they came back, and their last port of call before reaching home was Marseilles. I'm sure it was Marseilles.

"Anyway, their last port of call, you understand. The skipper and himself got into their shore togs, the skipper's honest face shining and his eyes glistening in prospect of good company. For in such ports there are little gatherings of masters, of mates; neatly defined little gatherings of an equality. Thus once the 'rounds' are set going they are kept going, each one jealously guarding his point in the circle with a 'Garson! encore!'—as one of them put it, in a way that never failed to produce the utmost hilarity when repeated.

"My friend, who accompanied the skipper, began to get drunk. They were, of course, all deteriorating rapidly. Their gestures were becoming sweeping, their courtesy emphatic, their laughter gargantuan, their tales not a little Rabelaisian. They had things to tell, each other, too; real stuff, of a certainty. And the frankness, the nudity, the colour—required little more than a dig in the nearest ribs to set the glasses on the table jingling and dancing. Not, you will understand, that there was anything in any way ugly. Quite the contrary, I assure you; so that the process of getting drunk was a glowing luxury of the flesh at once insidious and delightful.

"Time goes on. It begins to get a bit late. They are on the street, the skipper and himself. Up to this point, he can remember it all clearly. He can further remember a vast crowd somewhere on the street, a losing hold of the skipper, a desire urging him to get back to the ship, a vague, but yet determined starting out, then—nothing.

"After that he remembers nothing—not a single thing. The whole of the rest of the night is a complete and absolute blank. When finally he comes to himself, it is daylight, and he is lying on his back, his eyes staring up at a ceiling. He is in bed. But how? But where? What the——. His arm gropes—whereupon his elbow instantly comes in contact with a body. Good God! He turns round so quickly that his aching head positively rattles. It is a girl, a woman, slumbering peacefully as a lamb by his side!

"What! He looks down on her. He tries to think. He looks round about him, regarding each strange thing dazedly; tries to remember. No use. The whole blessed thing might be a dream—were it not for the vivid reality of the burning dryness within his mouth, and the awful head, which he suddenly grips. Thick black cheroots and drinks, a riotous evening that had faded off—let him see—into complete forgetfulness—ah, yes, that was it—he lost the skipper—that crowd. Then? … High heaven, what had happened after that? How—who … here?

"She suddenly woke up. Her dark eyes opened on him, smiled. Smiled, with such a gentle, understanding sensibility.

" 'You are feeling better now, aren't you?' She sat up, put her palm against his forehead. Her palm was a caress, but so capable, of such understanding. He might have been an errant schoolboy.

" 'I say—' he began, 'I say—' but could get no further, not at all for lack of French, which, in fact, he spoke fluently. He was bothered; he was embarrassed, and the embarrassment complicated and knotted worse than ever the aching little filaments in his head.

" 'You are all right now,' " she said, soothingly, " 'ah, all right, aren't you?' "

"But, I say——" And immediately there rushed upon him the thought that he hadn't been all right, that, in truth, he had been drunk, very drunk, literally blind drunk. He had never been actually 'blind' before, though more than 'half-seas over' on occasion. For without ever having been exactly vicious, he had not altogether been a youthful saint; and then when finishing off his 'modern languages' in Paris—well, there had been a time, a two or three months, before he pulled himself together—from a standpoint of original puritanism perhaps a trifle questionable that time. So as he stuttered there rushed in on him, as I say, the thought that he hadn't been all right, though exactly what that may have meant—must have meant—for he could never 'carry his liquor'—in quite a literal physiological sense not beyond a certain point … Well, begod there you are. And leaving his head out of it, his stomach was fit enough. Nay, he even saw that big hands had been washed. He stuttered—no wonder.

"But she appeared to understand perfectly, with, as you might say, wifely understanding, with solicitous care for his well-being. Hot water so that he may shave, ah? Wait a moment. She slips out of bed. She slips into a blue dressing-gown wrap affair. And then when Monsieur has had the hot water wherewith to shave—behold the little safety-razor box!—then, by the time he has dressed, will there not be black coffee strong and toast crisp? She smiles pleasantly, reassuringly, down upon him of the knotted temples, and out she goes.

"He lay back and groaned—groaned testily over the state of his head so that he might be saved the worry of thought. But … so unaffected, capable, so understanding—good God, it wasn't decent! wormed an under thread of thought in spite of him. He was not without experience. The little threads of thought multiplied till they became little red-hot wires—teasing, torturing wires. He cursed them—till they writhed. A painful disillusionment, this of the white morning after.

"She returned with the water steaming from a white mug. She was dressed neatly in a simple one-piece frock. Pale face, dark luminous eyes, glorious black hair above the whitest of necks, Good-looking—oh, most assuredly; but of the beguiler, nothing, nothing at all. Except for an indefinable sense of charm, of grace, she might have been—an English hospital nurse? Thereabouts. So capable she was.

"Uhm. She left him to it. He got up. And immediately he found his clothes—he found his clothes neatly folded, most obviously brushed! … No, it wasn't decent! His good Scots conscience, informed by a superimposed artistic sense of the fitness of things, rebelled. Had it all been (metaphorically even), a pig's kitchen—everything in keeping—well, a man sows in his time and his indiscretion—and may walk out of the mucky milieu—to a bath of respectable decency. But this—this ... good heavens! And presently a brick-red, running the gauntlet of exasperation from anger to shame, crept under the skin he tried to lather.

"By the time he dressed, however, he got a little common sense, felt better, got command of himself. He would carry it off all right, Really, to have a grievance because he had been well looked after! ... He turned the door knob and entered to the fragrance of coffee.

"The kitchenette was off the sitting-room to the left. He could not sit down, felt restless, walked about. He could hear her in the kitchenette, and wanted to cut away at once. Then his eyes found themselves drawn to a curtain that hung over a sort of arched doorway or alcove. A movement near one corner at the foot, like the preliminary tremor in a stage curtain; the gathering of a fold or two—and in a moment emerged a very vision of angelic childhood.

"A little girl, plainly barely three, but somehow the completest, most—most striking little thing really. Black hair cut straight across a pale forehead; round black eyes that dwelt on him in that wide-open way, you know; a sort of white cherubic innocence that yet was dark-eyed, if you follow, with all the human heart and its mystery in that same strange glimmering darkness. Begod, he stood like a man knocked stiff, without the vestige of a conscious thought—till she smiled, and then he knew her mother in a moment.

"The smile passed, as she became occupied in immediately toddling towards him—not at all shy, if you can see it, but now with eyes unwinking and grave and full of a sort of measuring wonder,

"What! By heavens, I tell you all the subconscious shades of his covenanting, martyr'd ancestors had a flick at him. Before this grave toddling mite he recoiled one step, two, till his flesh stiffened up in horror, and he stood looking down on her upturned face, on her upturned flower of a face, that was possibly expecting something in the nature of a kiss from the tall gods! ...

"But she sensed him, sirs. A half breath of uncertainty, the slightest stiffening of the little cheeks, a tremor across the eyes—and she recoiled too. And just then the mother came in.

"He had to have an outlet—or burst, so he turned on her. He gave her his mind, the real basic stuff, his good, Protestant, moral mind, the burden of which was that he didn't mind most things, but when it came to introducing little children into this—*this*—by the good God, it was getting a bit too thick, it was getting infamous, (letting himself go) it was vile. And he made a sweeping gesture, and cleared his throat in a squawked exclamation of vileness.

"But he got no further. No, he got no further. She turned on him, like the veritable blood-dripping she-panther, and rent him. Her eyes blazed, black fires of fury. Her fists clenched. The sinews in her neck jerked like whipcords. He was faced. By heavens, he was pitched into! There were no affectations, no insincerities, I can assure you!

"A scene, if you like. The sort of thing that might have been assessed at its emotional value by a Frenchman; certainly the sort of scene that would have made an Englishman deucedly uncomfortable, would have dyed his cheeks. What! Nothing could have been in worse taste, eh?

The sort of thing to back away from—to escape from, before anything went further, don't you know. While you'll always get an anaemic cynic capable of grubbing about the stuff and finding evidence of a sort of affected virtuous exaggeration.

"But the primordial Scot she nailed. Right through the crusts of good taste and emotional values she pierced to where the grey matter crawls along the skull bones. It's rather a lonely little lochan that's tucked in there, with a raw quiver and tremor to the face of it, with a myriad headlands, every one of them a 'sore point.' I tell you she rode it with a veritable skull and cross bones at the mast-head, and when she bore down on the 'sore points'—it was so much the worse for them!

"In short, he saw the naked instincts of a living woman for the first time. Something blood-raw and stark and logical and—and tremendous. They got at him. While yet he winced, they got home. Where one might find emotions, another shocking bad taste (the blind-man's-buff of our labels!) this young fellow, who had Braid Scots in him as an early earthy flavour, found that sort of ultimate reality we label truth. They knew each other—standing there; and when her outburst was spent and her breath came in lessening gasps, they stared fixedly for a terrible moment through the shadows of flesh and bone….

"What had she said? It doesn't matter. In fact, he could not tell, because he could not reconstruct it vitally. But a couple of facts, the sort of emotional facts that linger in the memory, he could tell readily enough. She had used them as scourges of scorn wherewith to whip her pack of instincts at him.

"He had thought, had he, that she was keeping her child always—*in this*? The sort of thought, that, worth at least a burst of demon laughter! No. The time she would keep her child would be very short indeed. When the third birthday had come and gone, and certainly long before the fourth—the child would be sent away. The child would be kept clean, and brought up clean, like a flower of the field, and at long, long intervals, maybe once or twice in a lifetime, she might get a little visit from her mother—perhaps.

"But to do that, money was needed. That, you see, was where Monsieur came in—and his like. Money. One did much for money, one did everything, one did the worst. And there were gentlemen of a conceit solemn as it was profound who believed that she really loved to delight them! Eh? In the name of the Mother of Christ, was it not enough to make one scream, to make one rend? … She went the full length, even to a neat little etching of himself in vitriol point, so to speak, an etching of the night before, stomachic shortcomings an' all.

"He hadn't a word to say. Not a word. But he went and sat down at her table. The little child she lifted up from her skirts and pacified and caressed passionately. Presently there was calm,, and she poured him out coffee and he broke her bread. An instinct worked in him, some dark instinct of amende. He tried for an outlet by passing some egregious thing like pepper to the child so that he might smile and draw a smile But he was not a good actor, though it was possible his awkwardness was not misunderstood. He glimpsed the woman as she caught for a swift instant a trembling lower lip in a row of teeth and he had a sudden intuition that for her the culmination of all this would be a violent passionate storm of tears.

"At the doorway his awkwardness got stiffened by an appalling sense of embarrassment. Then he was given, as it seemed to him, the grace of light. He took out his pocket-book. Quickly he extracted all the notes and rolled them tightly together.

" 'If I may, madame, as a tiny offering-to the little one?'

"She held him with her eyes, lips tight and teeth tight behind them.

" 'For the little one,' she repeated."

"And if he cannot positively say he heard her tears as he went downstairs—well, he believes he has heard them clearly enough since."

The Telegram

"I am now an old woman. The years have been going over me that fast I hardly noticed them—until this came, and now time stands in the houses and on the shore, ay, and on the little field you will be looking at from the door, hearkening."

She spoke like that, not exactly sadly, but with a rhythm in it that evoked a queer feeling, something that seemed familiar far back in time but had got suspended or lost somewhere, and I raised my eyes, too, and stared over the little fields at the sea, a dark-blue sea that went flat to a remote horizon. Had the sea been really flat and my sight good enough, I could have seen the coast of my home State of Maine.

"For five months now we have been waiting," she said, "for five months."

Only the Atlantic lay between the shore I had played on as a boy and this island in the Scottish Hebrides where my mother's grandfather had been born. I began thinking of my mother, about a certain softness in her voice when she used to tell us stories as children.

"Sometimes word would be coming that seamen had been rescued in some distant place of the world," the old voice went on, "and then there was no rest for us until we found out. But always the men were never our men, never our men, and so the waiting would begin over again. Sometimes Shiela down there would be listening on the wireless at certain times to hear if the enemy had any names they would be giving of men they had taken on the sea, but though often enough they have been heard to give the names, they never gave our names, not our names."

From the small green mound on which we sat I could see Shiela's cottage. She was a pleasant, good-looking girl and had been showing me how they work their primitive looms. It's a small loom for one person, operated by the feet, with the hands free to attend to the shuttles, and the cloth it produces is called Harris Tweed. Since coming to Scotland I had learned that there is a considerable export of it to our country, so I had plenty of questions to ask Shiela. I liked her voice very much, liked listening to her, but I find it difficult to describe her smile; it sort of waited, as light waits, and then her eyes flashed on you.

Now a thought struck me and I contrived to ask the old lady if Shiela had a particular interest in anyone aboard the missing vessel.

"She has that," came the answer quite simply. "He was a clever lad—and indeed it's herself that's clever too—and he learned to be a wireless operator, and that's what he was on the ship, on the *Batamor*. Perhaps that's why she keeps on thinking that news will come to her on the air."

"Has she said that?"

"No. She would not say that to anyone. But I know fine she thinks it, for the young have life before them and they cannot believe they will be cheated of it; even though that has been happening…. Nowhere in Great Britain has there been such loss of life as we have had in this land you have come to visit, for here the men were men of the sea and all of them who were able-bodied were in the Naval Reserve. They went at the beginning, the beginning. The sea took them."

I waited, looking upon that sea so quietly blue under the harvest sun.

"But our place was spared. It was spared because the *Batamor* was spared, for no less than eleven men out of this small township were on her. All on her. Eleven of them. And now for five months she has been missing."

The township consisted mostly of straw-thatched cottages with curved roofs scattered here and there, and the small fields were like oddments of coloured squares in a bedquilt. Grey-haired men swung a double-handed scythe and women and children gathered the grain as it fell and bound it with straw bands they twisted deftly.

"The news she was lost came first from Australia. The Navy Minister there said that one of his warships, which was out searching for survivors from a boat that had gone down, came on a lifeboat. It was drifting all by itself on the Indian Ocean. That was the way we first heard the news. We waited and we waited, but no more news came. Then tidings reached us that British seamen had been rescued from an island far in these distant seas, and our hopes went up, for the schoolmaster has all the maps of the world, and he said that it could very well have been the crew of the *Batamor*. But it was not the crew of the *Batamor*. So our hopes now went down lower than before. A long time passed, and then word came that British seamen had been rescued from the coast of Africa. The name of the place, I remember well, was Mogadishu. And they all said that it would suit the circumstances and the time, for they worked it out, them who know such things, and they said it would be a very likely place for a German raider to land any crews she had taken on board, And this time there was truth in the story, for men were rescued from Mogadishu. Yes, they were rescued, but among them was no one from the *Batamor*, no one."

All the oceans came lapping about this remote island, and I realised that here was no primitive spot but a place that extended to the utmost corners of the earth, to all places where seamen wandered and men and women lived. My own coast of Maine and the coasts of Africa; winds over Indian and Eastern seas; empty boats and death, and the strangeness that gathers all into one old woman's voice, with the rhythm in it of the sea itself.

I was caught now in a curious spell, and I know that that is the thing I really cannot communicate. I know, because I have read over what I have written and had to stop at that mention of my mother. If it seems that my mind had gone soft there, just a little sentimental, that's not what happened, for I saw her distantly, I saw her as if I were looking on at what she was doing, at her movements, her pale smooth neck, the expression on the clear skin of her face and the light in her eyes, and I saw the three faces of her listening children, of whom I was the youngest.

Here, again, I was listening to a woman telling a story, and over me there came the old reluctance to speak, to ask any question, as though everything would unfold itself if no voice interfered.

It was the same kind of listening, though my mother was telling a simple story to three small children and this woman was telling the story of all humanity to a man in a soldier's uniform, who had got a short leave and had been moved by an amused or (as it had seemed) absurd curiosity to find out what this little lost spot on the map was like.

One thing more—for I may as well give myself away properly when I'm at it: there was born in me, as I sat on that green mound, a new conception of woman, and I was aware, even as I listened to the old voice with its haunted rhythm, that I should never forget it.

They had had no more news of the lost *Batamor*. But hope was not entirely gone. Not until the war would be over and every port of the seven oceans searched, would hope wander away from these little fields and from the strand where the small fishing boats were hauled up. In the meantime the figure of hope was invisible and somehow dark as it stopped on a threshold or moved silently behind a woman reaping in the bright autumn sunshine.

My time, however, was up, for I had to get to the east side of the island to catch the mailboat which would call that evening on its way to the Scottish mainland. I think everyone in the township shook my hand—and Shiela's hand I won't forget—and as I got to the crest of the slope and turned round, they waved to me, the old and the young, pausing in their harvest work to give a last farewell to the stranger. I was laughing and waving back and indeed was so blindly moved that I all but got run over by a mad boy on a cycle. The small pebbles of the road shot from his wheels as he whizzed by me on his rattling piece of old iron. But I had seen his eyes.

All the others saw him, too, and each stood rooted in the ground. The machine went down that slope like a young tornado. But it must have had some sort of primitive brakes, for when the boy parted from it he was only brought to his knees.

And there was Shiela, not going over to the road to meet him, but waiting by the cottage wall, and she waited until the boy went across to her with the yellow telegram in his hand.

She took it and looked at it, but she did not open it. She had a short talk with the boy first, while the world stood still. Then she opened it.

She started running out into the fields, and her high cry released all those whose feet had been held by the earth.

It was the most extraordinary sight I have ever seen, for of course their feet had been gripped not by the earth but by death, and now they were released and they came running. The old women wore loose wide skirts to the tops of their boots, and they pulled them up a little and, waddling like strange dark birds, converged on Shiela and old Maria, my story teller. The old men were slower, some of them continuing to stand with the scythes in their hands, like figures of time in a story book. Then they dropped their scythes and began to come too, but with a solid purposefulness, as though to a strange rite or to repel enemies. The young went like the arrows their cries shot in the air. The sunlight caught the cries and threw them far and wide over the silent potato flowers and the standing grain. There were glad cries, but also there were high sounds of weeping, but somehow in my bones I knew that the weeping came from some of the women who could hardly bear the knowledge that what they had created was not yet destroyed.

I watched them for some time, terribly curious to know exactly what had happened, yet strangely reluctant to go down. I sat on the roadside and thought I would wait for the boy who had brought the telegram. But only when I was beginning to get anxious about my own time, did he at last appear, driving the cycle up that slope, for they had fed him cream and honey.

I stood right in the middle of the narrow road and he jumped off. I had hardly begun to ask my question when he answered with a shy breathless earnestness: "Yes, they're all saved!"

I shook hands with him and let out a cheer. I asked him who saved them and where they were.

When he told me, the news itself might have acted as a slight damper, for though the eleven men were alive they were actually prisoners in German territory, but it didn't affect me like that at all. For some reason, it was a spur to my spirit. It heightened the fun of being alive, made the thought of action wonderful.

"Do you think", came the boy's voice, "that we will take that territory and set them free soon?"

"Think?" I cried. "I don't have to think—I know."

He walked with me for three miles.

The Tree

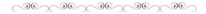

"I've been thinking," said Major Morrison to his gardener, "—been thinking we're a bit too closed in."

"Yes, Major," replied old Cameron slowly, turning his face away and looking vaguely at the trees.

"I think some of them could come down." The humph-humph gruff note was in his voice, his brows were netted a bit, his eyes rather strained.

"Yes," said Cameron. "Were you thinking of any—of any particular tree?"

"Yes," said the Major. "Yes, I was. Uh—I think——" He stopped abruptly. Cameron was still looking away, his expression negative, without any stress. "I think—there's one or two. It's dull. Obstructs the view. I'm going to have them down. Don't you agree?"

"I think it might do no harm."

"Harm? How could it do any harm?" The gruff voice was sarcastically astonished. "I think it would do a damned lot of good. Let in the light a bit. Harm? How do you think it would do any harm? Uh?"

"Oh, it'll do no harm," said Cameron slowly. "Were you thinking of—of any particular——"

"I'll see," said the Major angrily. "I'll go over them and let you know." He walked away.

Cameron heard him mutter to himself. It would be something about "that old fool!" thought Cameron with an ancient humour that touched only his eyes.

"What was he angry about?" asked Cameron's wife, coming over from the end of the gardener's cottage.

"It's that tree again."

"Is he going to cut it, then?"

"I think he had made up his mind to cut it when he started out, but he couldn't just bring himself to it at the last minute."

"Still like that. Poor man."

"He will always argue himself into a temper," said Cameron drily upon the silence.

"Did he say anything to you?"

"It's not me he's saying it to; it's his dead wife." He clicked his long shears and stooped. He was a smallish man with a stone-grey face and warped a bit about the shoulders.

"Couldn't you do something? Couldn't you cut the tree yourself?" suggested his wife, with a rush of vague anxiety. She was a tall, slightly bent, grey-haired woman with a kind face.

"How could I do that?" His lifted look was charged with dry sarcasm.

She turned away, recognising the wisdom in that look, yet knowing, too, that if the tree could be cut down the Major might get some relief.

And yet she wondered if he would. That was the difficulty. She would have egged her husband on and risked their position, if she had been dead sure. In her bones she felt that the tree brought a living warmth to the Major. It brought his wife to him. The tree was like a warm blanket of argument. If it went all of a sudden, his wife might go, and he would have nothing left. After her death he had had things to occupy his mind. But once these things were settled and his newly grown-up family had gone away again, he had been thrown back upon himself—upon his habits and memories. And the centre of his habits and memories was his wife.

It was, in truth, astonishing to so strong a man to discover how empty his world had become, not only in the mental but in the sheer physical sense. It was as if he went out with a long stick and began beating things that somehow were no longer there. The world was a void, without meaning. There was nothing to grip, to order, to push aside. Particularly was there nothing to come up against him, nothing solid, nothing but just damned shadows.

These shadows were the shadows of former arguments, of plans, of disputes about plants and rockeries and trees and paths and the hundred and one things that make up the lively government of a small if ancient estate.

She had been dead about three months and the trees were in heavy leaf. The glory of the rockery was nearly over, but the garden was coming away towards maturity and the forming of fruit. The new strawberry plants had berries of a perfect size and shape. Really wonderful—and the flavour, doubtless, wonderful, too. Only he couldn't quite be sure. The third mouthful had revolted him; the sweetness, too much sugar. Having shoved the sugar from him and taken one neat—he still could not be certain.

A small thing, but it could be very depressing, very maddening, tiresome. Things were without final substance, as if they had lost their reason for existing. She had taken their reason away with her. She had taken the heart out of everything.

Oh, he realised well enough what had happened to him. He had expected to be lonely and find things a trifle pointless. When the danger signal had first been flown, he had in fact got quite a shock. They had still in the normal course of life some twenty active years in front of them, and that death should step in seemed so utterly unreasonable that the idea angered him. As death drew nearer, he began to realise how aimless his life might be without his wife. When death arrived, he wept, his brows ridged darkly, his eyes strained with pain.

But the old lonely world would remain for him to wander in and order. And somehow it hadn't remained.

Here he was actually baffled and groping and unable to make up his mind about cutting a tree!

This tree, a tall birch, slim, yet beautifully proportioned, foliaged in a graceful swaying fashion, was the tree his wife had long wanted to cut down. It blocked up a far view of hills and a middle-distance glimpse of a loch. Her argument had been that they had hundreds of these silver birches, that in fact they had so many trees they were being shut in. She wanted here and there an avenue of escape; a moment of expansiveness for her sight to fly along or perhaps her spirit, though she would not have used a word like spirit to him. She had to be very careful indeed when it came to mention of spiritual or artistic things. Art did not interest him at all, unless it was conventionally unobjectionable, and then only politely. He frowned on her private efforts at painting, not that he really minded—he could even have been vaguely proud of it as an extra sort of irrational feminine grace—but being genuinely fond of his wife, he was jealous of her good name. He would suffer a lot rather than learn the "county" was amused. And none the less because her pedigree was longer than his own, with a few real impoverished titles in it.

For his nature was profoundly conservative. That was why he could not cut down the tree. The trees were his property, many of them twisted and knotted with age. They were rooted, too; rooted. Day after day, generation after generation, they remained in the same place, acknowledging the morning wind or the evening quiet, spring or autumn; green or gold or naked, they were forever permanent.

He genuinely could not understand how his wife could want to cut down this tree. He felt it should be against her very nature, for she professed to love the beauty she found in trees; she painted them. She could exclaim over a tree's perfect proportions. How then could she, without treachery to herself, want to cut down this silver birch? There was a sort of perverse cruelty in it somewhere; either that, or a woman never really did understand—but it was difficult to work out. He was blessed if he could understand it.

Nor could he understand her yet. Though now it was being borne in upon him that there had been far more in her than he had ever quite grasped. For there was nothing clearer than that in going away she had taken the trees with her. And not only the trees, but the garden and the rockery and even the inside of the house, which now had a few hollow sounds with an extra distance between the walls.

And it wasn't much use saying that everything remained exactly as before, for, of course, he knew it did, precisely. Hang it, that was obvious, he was not a fool! Nor was it any use saying that she had taken the spirit out of the trees and plants and things. She hadn't. Oh, God, he knew she hadn't. Why? Because she wouldn't. The realisation of it now came out of him like a shout. She would have done everything for him she could, quietly, her head bent over the rockery, turning round a tree-trunk here, over a shrub there, everywhere, her calm, pleasant face with its concentration, its occasional humour, its sheer sense, and her hair with a touch of that pale gold seen in the birch leaves when they first begin to turn. She would have left everything for him, in healthy fitness, not with any expression of emotion or love, not out of duty, but with an unobtrusive, perfect naturalness. He knew that—as he had never known it before. The trees had not been taken; they had gone with her.

His love for her, thus vague and chaotic, began to gather shape and to grow. At sudden moments of discovery, he would quicken with pride of her. His simple, frank nature was gratified by any words of praise which another might utter: "She was really marvellous—such quiet insight, and—nothing personal. The simplest folk—extraordinary." He felt like thanking the speaker very much. He generally did: "Very nice of you to say so."

Really he might as well cut that tree down. Of course, nonsense and all that to say it would help his dead wife. Still—it would let in some light. She had been right enough in a way there. Though, after all, how she could actually want to cut down.... Still, dammit, there were probably one or two oozing firs that could be well enough out of the way. And, anyhow, he could not go to Cameron and ask for this one only. Would look too much like—Cameron knew all about their arguments.

It was exasperating.

He would not mind cutting the tree for his wife. He was prepared to. Even secretly now might want to. But—the weeks went on. Besides, in any case, to hurry such a thing, as if acting on impulse, emotion... .

He so rarely acted on anything else, that exasperation grew. Once he entertained the mad idea of sending Cameron and his wife on a holiday. It rather shook him.

So by the time the trees had attained their heaviest summer foliage, he was completely shut in—and for the first time since the death of his wife he felt stir in him a certain vague satisfaction, a measure of fullness, like the fullness of the foliage.

The trees began to gather about them a new, dark, heavy life. This was something his wife had never known. Or was it life—or death—or what?

He did not speculate. He was covered over. His wife was beyond this, as she had been beyond his near male strength that had always to reach out to take her or to shove her aside.

When the August invitation to the shoot came, he did not reply at once. Of course, he had to go. That was as inevitable as that grouse should be shot. He delayed until he had to wire his arrival. And, surprisingly, he stayed a long time, far longer than he had ever done before. His hosts understood, naturally, that he was postponing the inevitable return to his loneliness and made his stay as pleasant as possible.

But at last the exodus to London compelled his return, and all at once, during preparations for the journey, he became eager and excited to the point of ill-temper. A longish stay at a little wayside station infuriated him. The desire to see his woods was consuming him.

There came the last rise of the road, the dip down and turn round, and there they were.

And then all in a moment he realised that his wife had come back.

Here and there a hanging spray of birch leaves had turned yellow. An odd bracken frond, too. Everywhere could be caught a glimpse of the colour of her hair, and between the trees and down the paths was an openness frank as her face. It was exactly as if from every place he gazed at her presence had just been removed, leaving behind the light of that presence.

It was at once exhilarating and extraordinarily intimate, and was made almost unbearably exciting by throwing into contrast quite involuntarily in his mind the darkness of the closing-in trees before he had gone away. That darkness had been for death. A man shuts himself in, lets the dark trees grow up and over him like the walls of a mausoleum.

Now she was alive again, all through the woods, letting in colour and light. She was doing it herself, as she always had done things, here and there, with bent head or uplifted face.

For the first time in all his mortal career, there came to the Major some conception of the word Resurrection. He had never definitely thought of his wife as lying dead in the earth. To picture her body as rotting away in its black hole was a morbid indecency that could not even involuntarily occur to him. Yet the unadmitted shadow of that picture was now consciously released and dismissed.

And this Resurrection had no religious or church significance at all. It was something entirely personal and unexpected, and so glimmering with light that he did not really entertain it in his thought. It was outside, everywhere, as she herself had usually been. Nothing actually new. Something from *before*, that—well, there it was. As inexplicable as the way in which confidence or delight or belief ever does come to a man.

"Hullo, Cameron!" he shouted.

Cameron emerged from the trees with his scythe. "Welcome back, sir."

"How are things?"

"Fine. I hope you had good sport."

"Yes. Very good. We'll have to get busy tidying up, I see. A whole lot to do, uh? A bit too shut in about that house. We'll be getting lazy if we're not careful!" When he smiled or laughed his expression became very pleasant, almost seemed to flush with colour in a boyish fashion.

Cameron smiled, too. Obviously going out among his fellows, shooting and moor-tramping and that, had worked its healthy wonder on the Major. He was very glad to see it. The Major would become bossy for a bit and then things would settle back comfortably.

"Had you your nephew with you?"

"Yes, Major."

"Enjoy himself?"

"He did, indeed."

"I hope he kept out of mischief!" The Major laughed, for the previous year the young rascal had burst the dam of the duckpond and nearly drowned himself. He had the notion of creating a secondary pond for breeding trout. The Major's wife had had a weakness for the lad, who could work all day quietly by himself in an absorbed fashion. The Major thought he was rather like an eel.

It was really very pleasant to be back. The elderly housekeeper and the two maids were plainly charged with excitement and welcome, as if this were a state occasion and he justified their existence. Very nice of them. Even the younger girl who was given by nature to a warm, stout disorder was all fresh and tidy, with a shine on her face. The tea was refreshing, the linen very white, the blackcurrant jam pretty good. He would have a look around before dark just to see the lie of things. There was a fair amount to think out. Light. Colour. (He could not get these out of his head.) That tree was coming down. And one or two others. Nothing could get at a man unless he opened himself out. Quite suddenly he was overcome with a profound longing for his wife. Tears started to his eyes. He went to his room. He sobbed her name to himself. She was everywhere—and so he realised she was nowhere. And yet she was so near, and he had so much to give her—the trees, the garden, the light, the rockery—everything given over to her with his hands, bearing the weight of them from against his chest—there, Grisil, there! Where are you?

Oh, damn, this was nonsense! A profound stroke of self-pity made him weep again, but quietly, sitting down. Then he wiped his eyes and blinked strongly. Curse it all! He smiled wryly. The weight had been taken from against his chest, however. The light—the light had leaked in.

That tree was coming down.

All along in a sense it had been pigheadedness that had been wrong with him. Had merely felt he didn't want to lose a tree and so had grown obstinate and domineering—in the usual way!

The tree would be a sacrifice.

Nor was there religious significance about the idea of sacrifice any more than there had been about the notion of resurrection; less, if comparison were possible, because he recognised in the tree-cutting a certain giving way to emotion. It was suddenly as if he laughed, knowing she was behind him. They had often had culminating moments of sheer fun—and not infrequently after vociferous language on his part. For with her steady sort of autumn face she had a way of ignoring or mocking him that was a mad temptation. How furious she had made him sometimes, absolutely furious! Calm and wise, she would go on with her job, not giving in at all, rather short with him if need be, and then her look, smiling, penetrating—Grisil, curse you! the itch for her, the laugh!

He would go out. All at once he was in a hurry, impatient. And though he nursed his impatience by deliberately pausing to examine this or that, it took him a very short time to reach the fatal birch, with not another soul in sight—for he had grown sensitive about being seen gazing at that tree. And it was really a rather fine tree. The sky had grown dull, stormy-looking, full of tailed windclouds; and the trees were not so much swaying as flattening under hand-claps from the sky; flattening and even cowering a little, with a swish and a surge like the sound of sea water—all except this birch, whose every new movement had interest and grace, as if it couldn't help itself, after the fashion of a woman graciously endowed. However the blow came, the resilience and sway-back were unhurried. And the leaves trailed through the wind like fingers through water. Upon the green were two drooping sprays, yellow as if they had been painted. Very charming—and strong, the stem persistent, full of life.

When a man is going to sacrifice, let him be handsome about it. There is little satisfaction in sacrificing the unimportant. The Major became charged at last with something approaching exaltation, and his eye, clarified thereby, observed minute physical things as it had never done before; not merely the shape of the tree as a whole, but individual branches, even individual leaves, the leaf, the branch, the stem. And the clothing of the stem, the silvered bark, the rough excrescences, right down to the disappearance of the main roots into the earth, the earth itself. It was a seeing eye, and such an insignificant matter as a recent surface abrasion not so big as the heel of a boot attracted it in almost startled curiosity. Extraordinary how alert his senses had become! He stooped; a small pad of moss came away in his fingers, revealing a root, as thick as his wrist, neatly and recently cut through!

The shock of this, followed by the pounding of his heart, weakened him physically. He sat down and called upon the Deity in guttural surprise. Then he took His name in vain and went cursing and rooting about that tree like a mad boar.

That only the one root had been severed did not allay his fury; it merely complicated and whipped it, as only a quite senseless thing can.

There came a pause, the slow birth of a black suspicion, followed by a demoniac possession that heaved him to his feet and sent him striding vastly towards the gardener's cottage.

What in the name of the four-headed dogs of hell did this mean?

Cameron's face was the grey boulder in a thunderstorm.

"Speak, curse you! Did you do it?"

"No," spoke Cameron quietly. "I didn't do it."

"What! Who did it then? Who did it?"

The grey stone remained unexpressive; but the Major's eye had not lost its sight. "You know!" he cried. "Out with it! Out with it at once, or———" and he swore by unwritten things that Cameron would be sacked now, on the spot, instantly and for ever.

"It was my nephew," said Cameron.

"Lord!" roared the Major; "that pasty-faced eel!"

Then their eyes met.

"Who," said the Major, voice low-pitched, terribly intense, "who told him—to cut—that?"

"No one living that I know," said Cameron stonily. There was a long pause. Cameron looked away.

Then his black unreasoning fury got complete control of the Major. Cameron faced him.

"You can sack me if you like———"

"Sack you? I'll murder you!" The large body of the man was trembling convulsively. Cameron saw that he was going to be attacked. He gripped the scythe strongly. His face furrowed. The spirit of the evil wild came glinting out of his eyes. The naked antagonism made murder possible and even desirable. But Cameron's wife threw them back on themselves; shackled them again agonisingly.

Presently the Major could hear her words in his drumming ears. But he did not listen, his hatred was so fierce.

And Cameron had become truculent. He was shouting. "Take your damned scythe! I'm through with you!" His flesh was jumpy. He stamped the earth. He threw the scythe from him and walked away, muttering defiantly and harshly.

"Ah, excuse him, sir; excuse him, Major. He was so sorry, so vexed, when he discovered the boy cutting—cutting——He was——!

"Shut up!" roared the Major.

"He did not know——"

"If he did not know, who told him?"

Before this cryptic yell, the woman bowed her head.

"You knew I would never cut down that tree for all the powers in heaven or hell. Never! And yet you would drive the boy to cut the roots—the roots! Oh, God, to cut the roots! Such blasted treachery!"

"We didn't——"

"How did he know, then?"

"We don't know——"

"You're lying!" cried the Major.

"Unless he overheard someone——"

"Overheard! Ha, so you were talking!"

"We asked him. He would not tell us. We don't know." She looked at the Major. She was not frightened of him, nor apparently was she afraid of the sack. But there was pain in her face. He saw this pain. It came out to him—with an intolerable understanding. Her eyes were tear-washed. Choking with rage, he turned away.

They would go at once, lock, stock and barrel!

He walked a long way, stumbling over roots, down banks, all round his property, until, in the darkness, he stood before his tree again.

The wind had risen. The branches were threshing, tossing and threshing, in maenad fashion.

He could never cut the tree down now. Never!

The intrusion on his privacy had been unbearable. The eel-faced boy had listened to his aunt and uncle talking. The most secretive and terrible thing in his life was their common talk! Oh, God, it was intolerable! He felt betrayed—betrayed even by his dead wife. She had liked that boy, had called him imaginative and clever. Perhaps, sneaking about the trees, the boy had even overheard himself and his wife having a few words on their favourite topic! And now the eel, in his "imaginative and clever" way, was helping fate—perhaps he had actually thought he was helping him, the Major!

It was too humiliating. Too utterly humiliating. In his travail, his groans mixed with the creakings and flailings of the trees under the dark and ominous sky.

As exhaustion came upon him, carrying tiredness beyond spite, he realised that in some way again he had messed things up. Life happened to him like that. Before his wife died, all his energies somehow had had a direction. Now, damn, everything was empty and meaningless. This afternoon, coming home had been like a reunion; the cutting down of the tree was to let in light. He had felt his life being given a direction once more.

Now his wife was farther away than ever. Dead again in her grave.

He could never cut down the tree. To cut it would have no meaning, would make him out a fool; a giving-in he would never be able to recall without squirming.

It was too late.

All light was lost in the darkness of the sky. And would be lost for ever. In the darkness of trees, shutting in, like walls, like tombs.

He felt lonely and lost, and the ancient instinct rose in him to blame his wife, to accuse her. "Grisil!" he cried, but his voice caught the broken sound of one crying in agony.

He blinked his wet eyes angrily and went stumbling down to his home. He forced the food down his throat. He drank. The rising storm accentuated the quietness of the sitting-room as the hours passed. Once when the window suddenly rattled he got to his feet, and the whisky warmth ebbed from his skin, leaving it icy cold. The idea of someone's being outside the window began to torment him. There were curious noises, whimpering, whining sounds. The whisky was having less than no effect; it was positively sobering him to an uncanny apprehension.

Then he faced it: he was afraid to go to the window.

He went, pulled back the shutters, glared out, and saw a pale face peering from the shrubbery. The face of the boy! The face of the dark eel body, storm-pale, unearthly. It took a few seconds before he recognised a mirrored reflection, outside, of the opaque electric globe in the room.

He banged the shutters violently and went up to bed, full of the relief of blasphemy. But the pale face followed him, and in his dream it wore no opaque mask of any kind.

It was almost as luminous as the ghostly globe of light as it flitted about the roots of the birch tree, burning with an elvish excitement, jerking backward now and then as the grubbing hands tugged. And the tree itself—its swaying branches touched him—the leaves were silk. Rough silk that whisked away from him, ballooned and moulded and draped. And up above—her long hair like yellow feathers. She was the tree—and yet not the tree. And then he understood what was happening. She was taking the shape of the tree, entering into it and bending it over, trying to break it.

The conspiracy between her and the pale face at the roots was perfect. There existed indeed so intense a glee that it became painful. He saw the strain in the high countenance, in the tree-arms, in the mad heave-up and thresh forward to that point of stress that would not break.

The stress entered into himself, but he was imprisoned and could raise neither hand nor cry. Shut into the black wood, entombed in the mausoleum. She was trying to break down the door, to get him out. Her features, forming human size, flashed full of an agony of endeavour, every muscle taut. "Duncan!" Then the upthrusting tree swept her back, and his name fled down the wind.

His cry to her stuck in his throat. His body was powerless as though wrapped in its winding-sheet, yet he knew he was standing on his feet in the dark wood, and in the knowledge was an unclean, shameful impotence. His chest was bursting with an upsurging power. If he could not release it he would swoon and sink into the earth, into death.

Release me! Release me! The silent shout rose in him, surged out of him under terrific pressure, surged with his wife against the tree, surged and sustained the stress—yet!—yet! *Crash!*

With that crash he probably swooned in his sleep, for when he awoke it was daylight.

The storm had been very violent. As he went downstairs he met the housekeeper who said she had hardly slept from the sound of it. She looked hushed and a trifle scared, as if she had heard unearthly voices in the night.

He smiled, his mind curiously at ease. Before eating, he would have a look round, he said. Green leaves and bits of broken branches were scattered about the lawn. Some of the trees were quite noticeably stripped. The air was fresh, with clouds here and there against the pure field of the sky. The scent of the woods, tinged with earth, was exquisite in the nostrils.

He was in no hurry. But only when he came to the birch tree and found it uprooted did he realise the tension in his breast—by the grateful way it eased. He smiled. It was a lovely morning.

The slightest crisp touch of the exhilaration of autumn. And the scent—invigorating. Lifting his eyes, he beheld far hills, finely outlined in the clear light, and in the middle distance a loch wrinkled its glittering skin. And there, coming up the new avenue, was Cameron, solemn as an old owl! He saw the tree was down. The Major choked back his laugh.

"Well, what is it?"

"It will take us to Saturday to get all our things out of the house," said Cameron quietly.

"Four days! Why so long as that?"

"Because it will take that long," said Cameron.

"Will it? Not if I can help it! And in the first place, anyway, aren't you damned well ashamed of yourself?"

"No," said Cameron.

"You won't apologise?"

"No," said Cameron. "You——"

"Yes?"

"You were as much to blame as I was."

"Oh, was I? Very well, then. I'm prepared to apologise." For the first time Cameron's stony calm lost its certainty.

"No," he muttered. "I don't want——"

"What!" roared the Major. "Do you think I was going to apologise to you?" He laughed. "You fool!"

"I'm not a fool," said Cameron doggedly.

"Aren't you? Really? I think you behaved like a blasted idiot, if you ask me." Then Cameron looked at him.

"Quite so," nodded the Major. "Two blasted fools, and we'll now have to go and apologise to Mrs. Cameron. Don't you understand how badly you have behaved? Lord, you were nearly as bad as myself. Come on!"

They had often had rows. After them they had liked each other none the less. The Major was in extremely handsome form this morning; full of plans, as they walked along.

He expressed his regrets to Mrs. Cameron. "Your husband is as big a fool as myself. If you forgive us this time, we'll try to do better." There was sincerity behind his smiling fun.

And she accepted his fun graciously and thanked him.

Dammit, he liked the woman, had always liked her. She had a sense of manners. Never overdid such a moment. "That tree", he said, quite involuntarily, "got blown down last night."

She looked at him for an instant and looked away. It was suddenly an intense moment, as if his heart had bared itself. He was just about to laugh, to crash through it, when she said pleasantly to her husband, "Won't that make the tree you wanted for the new rambler? It's long and won't need cutting."

"Yes," said the Major. "Yes," and turned away abruptly. "See you after breakfast," he shouted.

Obviously he was moved from the way he walked. His wife had planted the rambler. He strode at a great pace.

"He would hardly have liked maybe to cut it for firewood," she said quietly.

A smooth peace had come back to Cameron's face. He disliked these quarrels. They made him feel very awkward inside, and because of that roused in him sometimes a devil tough and gnarled as an old root. Peace was what he liked and quietness about the garden and among the trees. He took out his pipe. It was a nice morning. A smile glimmered in his eyes. He turned to his wife and saw slow tears on her quiet, absorbed face.

"What are you crying for?" he asked.

"I don't know," she answered, with profound sadness, and went into the house.

Snow in March

She went out to have a last look at her plants. The grass bank in front of the old farm house had been rank with timothy, dandelions, bishopweed, and one or two stunted unflowering shrubs, before she had cleaned it up and turned it into something like a rock garden. Her brother had got one or two of the farm hands to help in the navvy work; and, for the rest, it was a bit of a joke to him. That had been in the off-season, before last harvest. At the first threshing of the harvest he had been standing by the new machine, when the slim top cover, not properly put on by the second ploughman, had been shot by the whirling mechanism to the roof, whence it rebounded, hit him with a sharp corner fair in the temple and killed him.

The blues were predominant: grape hyacinth, scillas, and glory of the snow, with the aubretia coming along, it was always a marvel to her how fragile these early flowers were. The yellow crocus was like a tuning fork out of some tropical clime. The snowdrops, delicate in their green veining, chaste in their bowed heads, nun-like in their pallor, would surely shrivel at a harsh breath. Marvellous to think that the mature, lusty growths of summer would shrivel in weather that gave to crocus and snowdrop a lovelier grace, a more glowing colour.

Ah, and here at last some flakes of white—on the wild cherry tree! Her heart gave a bound. She had lived through the long winter for this. She had said to herself she would see one round of the farm year before she sold the old place and went back to her school in the city. And now, with the bright, cold air of March, behold the cherry blossom!

As she gazed at the blown petals, two or three more petals came blowing past them. Snow petals. Snow! She looked into the depth of the air and saw the flurry of myriads of snowflakes, not falling, but swirling darkly in the air, like swarming bees. Then they began to shoot past in front of her, all white; to settle on the flowers, her hands, everywhere. A ewe bleated beyond the garden wall in the home field; day-old lambs answered in their thin shivering trebles.

She woke sometime in the dark of the night and heard the young voices crying out in the field. They sounded forlorn and lost. The snow had been an inch deep before she had gone to bed. How much deeper now? The sheep were Leicesters and the grieve had told her they were soft because they were so well bred. Though actually an arable farm, it had always been famous for its sheep. The men folk had taken a pride in breeding them. This had been the tradition, and her brother had kept it up, making money even in the worst of the slump by buying sheep in small parcels from near and far and sending them south, for he knew all about sheep markets.

In the darkness the bleating of the lambs was very affecting. And there came one thin, persistent plaint that she knew instinctively to be the crying of a new-born lamb. She thought of the heavy ewes, square market-bred ewes, soft, having their lambs out there in the snow. She wished she could do something for them.

She became restless and wide awake. *Waulkrife* was the Scots word. How deep went the native word, down through the muscles and round the bones to the roots, the last thin roots that went about the heart and gripped it, so that if you pulled them up you could hear the sound of everything tearing out—leaving an emptiness, a blank, that might be peace and sleep. A flurry of snow against the window, blind fingers against the glass, before the eddy of wind bore them away. Bore them away in a small, whining, anxious sound into space. Nothing conveyed the idea of space so well as the wind at night.

And all the time the lambs kept bleating, bleating, and the wind carried away their emergent bleating into the gulfs of space in a way the heart could hardly bear.

To ease this burden, her mind presented her with a clear picture. She was out in the field, going from ewe to ewe, gathering the lambs, carrying in her arms those that could hardly yet stand, and taking them all into the kitchen, where there was a good fire in the range and warmth and comfort.

Her whole being craved to do this, and suddenly in the thought of doing it was a profound mothering joy. Involuntarily her arms crossed and hugged her own breast.

That made her think, for she had developed the disease of thought, the analytical mental effort that affects instinctive action like a poison. For all that was troubling her now was the mother instinct, or in her case presumably the mother complex, for the instinct had been denied, and as she was now forty she realised that it was probably permanently denied.

That's all it is, she told herself, and felt the roots of her virgin body thin and sinewy about a contracting heart. And recognising this in a bitter way, a hopeless agony, she had her own sorrow, and in a sudden spasm cried soundlessly except for a small, whining sound behind her nostrils.

Whereby she recognised, more certainly than ever, what was wrong with her, and for a time in a release of irony, used all the psycho-analytic words that expressed her case. She had been German mistress in a Lowland academy until last June, when her mother had died, and, after the funeral, she had decided to stay on to keep house for her brother (her father being no more than a childhood memory). The decision had been the easier because of the headmaster, whom she had disliked for his thoughtless, bullying ways. But also she had had an urge to get near the soil and the ways of the soil, the manner of life that had been her forefathers', not for any specific reason, but simply out of a vague longing, which she joyously refused to analyse because of its air of adventure. With her qualifications and experience, she could get a job again when she wanted one, for she had a reputation in educational circles. She was quite an authority on German literature, particularly modern German literature, and kept in personal touch with the continent. She could discuss the devious ways of Viennese psychiatry with some knowledge, even to the extent of quoting apt case-histories.

And here was the joyous adventure: listening to the ewes and the lambs, out in the snow, and being reminded of motherhood and defeat!

What about all her theories now, her precise knowledge, her apt case-histories?

This self-questioning was crude; she knew it was crude; yet the crudeness had an appalling reality, like the lambs with their red birthmarks in the driving snow, the mother licking them in the whirling snow, each lick making them stagger.

Or the cherry blossom.

The bleating would presently be too much for her. Emotion would rise up and up until it got hold of her head and drove her forth.

For her little intervals of ease, of half-mocking amusement at herself, were getting less frequent, less assured.

Quite suddenly, in a lull of feeling, there came upon her a deep compulsion to have it out with herself; as if she had dodged the real life issue until this moment, but now could no longer do so. It stared at her, and she stared back, her mind stripped, her eyes with pain in them, wanting to glance to left and right, but held by the lonely naked figure of herself on the lonely earth.

In the town, in her work, in her travelling and reading and social contacts, her societies and committees, she had seen the truth all right; nay, she had learned the truth, for was not that what education or book-study was for? For learning. A fine, wise word, against a background of good manners. And a lovely word, too!

But she could not slip away on the vague emotion induced by a word. The ruthless mind behind her mind was not going to be taken in any more by an easy trick. It had been tricked long enough by words, by labels, by analysis, and above all by the continuous movement, the brisk contacts, the fun and importance of social-life amongst the more or less intelligent. In these days the intelligentsia suppressed nothing—in talk, at least. Compared with former generations, they were liberated, freed from inhibitions.

A harsh sound came through her nostrils, an irony that heard all their talk as the chattering of monkeys. For in this talk they were hiding themselves, without knowing it. Hiding themselves more than ever, because they were imagining they were evacuating their emotions. As indeed in a sense they were! They were continuously dosing their emotions and instincts with medicinal words. Trying to abolish their secrecy, to wash them clean. And feeling a sort of hectic ease as the process appeared to work.

But you could not go on purging and washing the instincts and emotions and expect them to fructify. You had to bury your seeds and put a roller over the earth above them, and keep them down, out of sight, certainly out of sight of the rookery, if you wanted them to fructify and sprout and become the stuff and the staff of life!

Her intuitions became so extraordinarily acute that a whole argument was apprehended in a flash of pain, as all motherhood was contained in the anxious cry of the ewe, and birth in the pitiful bleating of the lamb.

And when she grew exhausted, the crying from outside continued to play on her mind like an irritant, exquisite, clamant, ever more urgent. The night assumed fantastic proportions, extended into vast moorlands, endless wildernesses, immense gulfs of space, wherein the snow whirled like infinite manifestations of the physicist's dead atoms. And always spiring into this, the lamb's cry; the frail, blind, brittle cry, the first cry, the beginning of life—at last clutching at her heart, washed clean of words.

Driven out of bed, she pulled the curtain aside. The snow shower had passed and the sloping lands lay spectral white under the stars. Something in the whiteness of utter purity, of chill, virgin austerity, of light, touched her to a half-frightened wonder.

She dressed quickly, and in the kitchen went quietly lest she wake the servant girl. Into her long gumboots, her heavy mackintosh, tightening the belt about her waist; then to the back door, which she opened carefully.

The snow was surprisingly full of light and this suited her secret purpose, for she could not have taken a lantern. She did not want to be seen. She wanted to slip through the dark of night, unobserved, from ewe to ewe, intimately, from lamb to lamb, seeing that all was well. The universal mother, the mother of night! The sublimation of motherhood!

The labels were a secret joke now and she smiled to herself as she got over the fence, for the air had a biting nip. Yet not a bleak coldness. Life was in it, left over from recent good days, something of promise, of spring. Glory of the snow.

She was suddenly full of a bounding, secret invigoration, and when some of the beasts, with lifted faces white against their grey fleeces, looked at her coming and, instead of showing fear, cried to her, taking even a step or two towards her, she was moved to cry back to them softly: "It's all right. I'm coming. Don't worry."

As the bleating increased all across the field, she got into quite a stir of excitement, and kept speaking softly all the time, so that she might be at home with them and her mind not distracted or invaded.

As her dark figure went about the field, it began to snow, and soon she was wrapped about in the whirling flakes and completely blinded, so that she could not see a yard in front of her, and when the wind got into her open mouth it roared there and choked her. She stood quite still, her back to the wind, leaning against it. The complete irrationality of her position, its futility, was a joy. For it was not quite so irrational as all that, she cunningly told herself. Not quite! And she got blown along a bit and kicked into a ewe giving birth to a lamb.

On her knees she could half see what was happening. Something deep in her sensitive nature had told her long ago that such a business would make her squeamish, would urge her away from it, as from something too intimate, as all blood is intimate, and coloured by primordial fear or terror.

But now, to her amazement, she was not repelled at all, she was not even overcome by her own inexperience and helplessness. On the contrary, she was charged by a confidence full of the utmost tenderness and optimism. She spoke to the beast, sheltered her, encouraged her, caressed her with a tender hand, wisely, helping her, used terms of endearment in a practical voice. And, as though some of her vitality and encouragement were indeed of practical assistance, the ewe had a short and easy delivery.

"You're feeling it a bit cold now!" she said to the lamb; and then turned on the ewe: "Don't get excited, you old fool!" She would shelter them until the shower passed. She looked half over her shoulder, but the laugh died in her throat, for coming upon her was a smother of yellow light, swinging, growing—at hand. She rose up.

At that the light stopped and there was a harsh exclamation. Her slender-coated figure, rising snow-white like a ghost above the crying of a newly-born lamb, in the whirling ebb of the shower, might have startled a less sensitive mind than a shepherd's. In a moment she knew what was happening and cried to him by name. "It's all right, Tom." She kept crying to him to give him time. Took a step or two towards him. "It was foolish of me to have come out without a light."

"I wondered what you were," he said at last with a touch of grim humour, wondering actually why she had come out at all. Could she not trust him to do his job? Was that it?

And she could hardly explain! But his natural suspicion did not down her good spirits, though it made her a bit shy. So she talked in an easy, friendly way, evolving the half-lie that she had thought a ewe was in difficulties, the cries had wakened her, and she had come out to see if he could help.

She soon had him thawed completely. There was a dourness in him, but once you got him out of that he could be friendly, even show a certain charm. He was probably about thirty-five and came from the north of Sutherland. Amongst her folk of the Moray country she had already noticed him. For she knew his type quite well; had even suffered a little herself in an innocent affair of student days with a youth from the glens. Whether this type became a student or a shepherd was largely a matter of economic luck. But the type had a natural friendliness at such a moment as this, because the atmosphere, the difficulties, the world around, suited the old nomadic spirit. His quiet voice conveyed a complete confidence, a sheltering reassurance. The environment revealed him.

"There's a ewe over there I'm worried about," he said presently, when he had got to the top corner of the field. She was now all glowing with warmth.

The shower gone, what had been half-frightening in the still, white landscape was no longer so.

"We have been lucky," he said. "But we cannot expect it to hold. They are pretty soft."

So that when they came to the ewe that he had been worried about, she was prepared for death. He did everything he could with a strange concentration. When he spoke to the woman, he was speaking to himself. She sensed his deep, instinctive skill. The lamb was born, but the ewe died under his hands. On his knees, widespread in the snow, he looked at the humped body, his hands hanging.

He got up and said quietly: "I'll take the lamb to the bothy. We may have a mother for it soon enough."

"Come into the kitchen," she said." I'll make you a cup of tea." The kitchen, with its hot water, was often of service in the ailments of beasts and regularly for the washing of milk pails and pans.

"Don't you bother, ma'm," he said. "I have the fire on and could get the milk for the lamb in no time."

"Come," she said calmly. "I would like to give you a cup of tea." And she moved on.

She did not want to lose him now, did not want to lose his company, did not want to lose sight of the lamb. And she did not even smile at herself. What she wanted she wanted.

He began tugging at the stiff latch of a cross-barred gate with one hand. "Give me the lamb," she said, and took it from under his ann, holding it as he had held it. He opened the gate and let her through.

As they came by the deep shadows of the house she paused and looked back. "Do you think it is going to be much?" she asked.

"No," he said. "There is life still in the air."

"The wireless forecasted snow-showers and outlook unchanged."

"Did it?" he said politely, cleaning his hands with snow.

"Come in."

He scraped his boots clean. "I'll make such a mess of your floor."

The bleating of the lamb sounded startlingly loud inside. He struck a match and cupped it under his face. She saw the glow of the light in his brown skin and the glitter of it in his dark, attractive eyes. He needed a haircut. His eyebrows were gathered together in concern. Then his face cleared and opened as he tilted it up, and she said: "Here's the lamp," softly, as if she might awaken the house.

He took matches out of his pocket and lit it while she stood beside him. "Now," she whispered, "if you go out to the shed next the dairy you'll find some boxes there and straw."

She stood on the middle of the floor listening to his footsteps and making soothing noises to the lamb. "Hsh-sh!" she crooned, and cupped her hand under its head, her fingertips at its mouth. The fragile body butted, the little bones slithering under the thin skin. The head waggled again. "Hsh-sh!" And she saw the discoloured skin and her own hands and wrists. But, again, instead of repelling her, the streaks of colour gave her a curious thick comfort. He cane in with the box and put it on the floor by the kitchen range. "Now," she said to the lamb, and placed it in the straw.

"It's a feed he wants."

"I know." She nodded. "I'll wash my hands and then put on the fire," She was no longer excited by the crying of the lamb. The eager anxiety had passed into a calm of efficiency and knowledge. Life was a healthy glow. She liked the way he took the sticks Jean had drying over the oven and set about putting the fire on. There were red embers still under the ashes. He put a wisp of straw over the red embers, the dry sticks carefully on top, and blow, up came the flame and he built a few coals around it. She poured some milk into a pan.

"You haven't a feeding-bottle?"

"No," she answered slowly, trying desperately to conjure a bottle.

"I'll be back in a minute with one," he said, and went out at once.

She smiled at that idiotic momentary dismay. As if she had been about to lose something! And holding the pan over the briskly-crackling sticks, she put a little finger into the milk, moved it around, and then transferred the milk-dripping little finger to the lamb's mouth.

She laughed softly to herself at the lamb's antics. And by the time he had returned she had the kettle over the flame, with no more water in it than would make tea for two, so that it would boil quickly.

They still kept talking in undertones, and thus was spread about them an amusing and warm air of conspiracy. Here was natural life, and he was adept at all things concerning it. It went back to beginnings in time far beyond rationalisings and labels. The knowledge gave her a sense of freedom, lifted her utterly beyond complexes and other strange modern diseases, gave physical well-being a lovely ease.

She put a tea-cloth over the corner of the large white-scrubbed table and set two cups on it and biscuits, and added a friendly, bright air with knives and butter and plates.

"Leave him now and wash your hands," she said.

Artificial restraint, after the first few minutes in the field, had passed quite away from him, and now in their friendly work his manners were easy and good. One small trick he had of looking sideways with a smile had recalled to her, almost startlingly, her old student affair.

She was lifting the teapot to fill his cup when a noise arrested her. The noise came nearer. She knew it was Jean, but could not say a word, could not move the hand with the lifted teapot. They both stared at the door. It opened—and, her face half-petulant and flushed from sleep, there stood Jean, the maid. Her eyes widened as she gazed at Tom, and then right down her neck, as she turned her face away, went a deep blush. Dark, well-made, with a clear skin, she was inclined to moods occasionally, but was a capital worker. At this moment, in her twenty-fifth year, she looked extremely attractive.

"Come in, Jean," said her mistress quietly. She glanced at Tom. He was looking at his plate.

The emotion between them, whether it had ever been declared or not, was so obvious to their mistress that her hand shook with the knowledge of it as at last she poured out Tom's tea.

"You're up very early," she said to Jean.

"I heard the lamb and I wondered," said Jean, her back to them, attending to the fire.

"Put some more water in the kettle, because there's hardly enough tea here for you."

She began telling Jean about their experiences in the snow, disjointedly, while she drank her tea, so that the whole affair of their being thus together became normal and without strain, if still with an undercurrent of excitement, not in her own mind now, but self-consciously between these two.

"Well I think I'll have an hour or two in bed. What's the time? Five. No need for you to hurry, Tom."

She left them and went up to her room.

She was feeling very tired now, but when she had undressed and stretched between the cold sheets she experienced a pleasant sensation of ease, almost as if she had become disembodied. A crush of snow, softer than the lamb's mouth, smothered itself against the window. And all at once she thought of the ewe—that she had quite forgotten—with the head thrown out and back, the neck stretched to an invisible knife. The snow would be drifting about the body, covering it up.

She began to cry soundlessly, effortlessly. The tears ceased and she fell into a deep sleep.

In Lewis

That first morning stroll to the pier and the meeting with two or three fish-curers, old friends, is as pleasant as the light that sparkles on the waters past Goat Island and out to the Point.

"How's the fishing?"

"Bad. Very bad."

The drifters are lying alongside, nets neatly piled, and no stir of life. Every night they go out, and every morning come back with the same story. "You wonder sometimes how they can have the heart to do it. Expenses piling up. Calm and cheerful. They are triers, and no mistake."

We walk up and down and I get all the news. This absence of a fishing has a certain gloom. These curers do not complain of their own lack of business. Their sympathies are with the seamen, who work hard to catch nothing (except debt), and who can weather the financial loss less easily. In the evening—for the most likely grounds, as it happens, are not far away—to watch them, boat after boat, setting out, is to have the emotion of sympathy touch the heart. For I hardly know of a more gallant sight than a drifter heading out of a spacious harbour at full speed for the open sea, all shipshape, nets ready, men standing about the deck, with a rush of foam at the forefoot. The gamble of the deep. Night after night after night they have drawn a blank. But perhaps this night? Not so long ago one of these boats shot her nets somewhere off Skye, hauled over sixty crans, made for Mallaig, and realized in cash just over £250. Such a stroke of luck does not come too often. But it can come.

So the gloom is irradiated with hope, as the sea with light. And what work they can pack into twenty-four hours when the herring do come on the ground! No ca'-canny, no eight-hour day then. The main problem is to defeat sleep. It is an adventure for ever creating new stories, and in the saloon bar of the Caley we hear a few, from the Highlands, from Donegal, from Lowestoft, or Norway, or Grimsby.

Here is one from Ireland, told that morning by a quiet-mannered curer with a Scots tongue, a dry humour, and a belief that he is practically teetotal.

Anyway, he was very illuminating about conditions on a certain part of the west of Ireland while he was opening up curing there many years ago. "I got on well with the Irish," he said. "They are all right, if you know how to take them. I always took them that same way. If it's a new bit of ground you're wanting for a curing station, the crofter will ask enough to buy half Ireland. He thinks you're made of money. But after a while, the priest comes in and it's settled at once. No trouble. Sensible fellows, these priests, free and easy. Oh, I got on fine with them. One day when I was over at B—— a fellow I'd done a good turn for asked me if I ever put anything on a horse. 'No,' I replied truthfully, 'I never bet.' 'Sure, that's the great pity,' he said, 'for I have a dead snip.' Well, he named the horse in a whisper, and it must have stuck in my mind, for when I went back I told a friend of mine, a local chap, and within half an hour that whole village had it, and to a man they put their shirts on it. The horse came in first."

"And you didn't put anything on yourself?"

"Ay, I made thirty-four pounds. But if you'd seen that village! For over two whole days not a stroke of work was done by anybody. All the champagne from near and far was drunk off first, and then they settled down to it. After breakfast the following morning they were still there. When I came out from my lunch, some were gone, but there were a few new faces, and only one or two old ones. By the following forenoon, I think I was the only old face left among the lot. I was stopping at the inn, you understand, and thirty-odd pounds could go a long way then. So I thought it might be as well to get a breath of fresh air. There was an open sort of charabanc belonging to the place, and we got the fellow who could drive it, and he managed to start it after a while, and we set off. We had a nice ride, and the charabanc stopped at a few places. Then we came to a wayside inn and found it shut. Perhaps it was getting a bit late by this time, though I don't think so, because it was now daylight again. Anyway, a window over the door went up and a man's face hung out, looking down on us. I nodded to him, for I remembered he had stuck it until yesterday afternoon, and he was a hearty fellow, who would take drink for drink with you and would see that you took it, too. But he wasn't in a good way at that moment. As he gaped at me, you could see his grey face open in astonishment. Then he gasped: 'B' jasus, is it still you?'"

Not that there is much drinking done in Stornoway, or no more than in any other town of the size. There are whole drifter crews that do not touch liquor, but if you go out for a night with one of them and take a bottle with you for luck and good fellowship, the skipper may disarm your surprise in the pleasantest way by accepting the gift for the medicine-chest. The sea breeds a great tolerance.

Many of the crews, too, are quietly religious men. Yet these extraordinary religious revivals that were now taking place in Lewis are for the most part confined to the purely crofting townships. Revivals among fishing communities, from Lerwick to Cornwall, have not been uncommon in the past, and explanation has been sought amongst the emotions that the sea, with life and death in its arms, can so readily and vividly evoke. Crofters are for the most part more immune from spiritual upheaval, being rooted in the earth with its slow-moving seasons.

Out here, however, sea and land come close together and as news reached us of one place after another "going down" with "the revival", I could not help wondering. Much sensible talk there was of adverse economic conditions and especially of the demoralizing effects of "the dole" on a community for which it was never designed. But I was not quite satisfied with the most searching explanations, even when they became knowledgeably psychoanalytic. I knew the high unemployment rate on the Island. I had myself investigated and advised upon claims for the dole. On the practical or economic side I had not a great deal to learn, and I could make fairly precise comparisons with other places in Scotland where unemployment also ran high. After nights of talk, I merely knew that here was something I did not really understand.

I do not profess to understand it yet, for that first effort of mine to attend a religious revival meeting seems in retrospect even more strange than what we set out to discover. That I may not here name the little township or people concerned is of no importance. That it is difficult to convey weird psychic effects, that seemed at once so illusive, and yet so momentarily real, is obvious. Again, these meetings for the most part took place in private houses, and, naturally, one cannot intrude into a private house out of a spirit of mere curiosity. Some newspaper correspondents had done this, and those concerned were naturally angry about the reports that appeared in the public press, whereby what was to them a matter of profound religious emotion was made matter for cheap sensationalism. I sympathized deeply with this attitude. Any manifestation of spiritual life, in whatever form it may take, even the extreme form of apparent hysteria, may have come to be regarded too readily by us with scepticism, if not with discomfort and some contempt.

These meetings do not begin until late in the evening and frequently go on until four or five in the morning. As we drove through the township at midsummer midnight a single light was on in each house, but in one house all four windows were lit up. "That's the place," whispered my friend, who had the wheel.

We found ourselves talking in low voices, and when we reached the home of the local man who was to conduct us to the meeting, we were in a properly receptive mood. Our intelligent host had been anticipating our arrival with a certain misgiving, and I at once tried to put him at his ease by saying that I realized the delicacy of the situation and would, after all, rather not go. This induced the state of indecision which can last for hours and is in so many ways typical of the West. It is often a very wonderful state, full of subtle undercurrents of thought and intuition. You do everything except reach a definite conclusion. But in process of time the pattern of decision forms itself. We travelled from the East, from Buddha and Pantanjali; we touched upon the shamanistic studies of anthropologists and the mysticism of the medieval church; we sat amid the visions of St. Columba on a Hebridean island.

"You have no idea," said our host, his eyes shining in the soft paraffin light, "of how the very atmosphere is charged with this religious feeling. You cannot get away from it. It is palpable. It hits you. It is nothing—and yet it is everything. You could never believe it—until you lived amongst it. They go into trances. They cry out. They moan. They stretch their hands. But it's not merely that; it's—I don't know what. It's easy to be critical, to analyse, but—there is a core, a something, and it's that *something* that is the mysterious force, that *something*—whatever it is!" and he spread his fingers with a Gallic gesture.

Presumably I had shown some understanding and made it clear that I would never dream of going to the meeting, for he suddenly decided that it was time we set out. It was now two o'clock in the morning. We went out into a dark-grey world to fmd the close-packed rain descending in vertical lines. We approached the township, where all the lights were as before. But the meeting was just over and folk were standing about in the rain, which they heeded not.

Our host was disappointed. The meeting should now have been at the height of its power. We discreetly drove past the house and drew up. In a startling way, two figures materialized by our side windows. A voice said we had fulfilled a prophecy, for though it was known we were coming, yet hope had been given up by all except by the voice—which belonged to a young man who now entered and took the fourth seat in our car. His words of greeting were, "The arm of the Lord was made manifest tonight in a wonderful manner. Not often have we so powerfully felt among us the presence of our Redeemer, Jesus Christ …" A young voice, with an urge in it to be pleasant and happy. I was disappointed that it was not a Lewis voice, not even a Highland voice. But "Quite!" said our host, with his perfect manners. The voice went on. At the first moment our host interposed again, agreeably. A third and a fourth time, at lengthening intervals, he nodded: "Quite so."

But the stream of the young man's oratory was too constant, too strong, and I have a memory of our three heads bowed at last, silent, like boulders in a river, throughout a long period of time. Actually it was not much more than an hour—about an hour and ten minutes as far as we could calculate afterwards.

But it seemed a new kind of time, and I once awoke from a reverie, induced by a quotation from Micah, that was like a waking from sleep. I looked at the other two heads, bowed still. And the river flowed on under the drumming rain, with the queer grey light outside, a lamp in a window, and a solitary figure passing like a wraith.

At last I did my best to move, perhaps in some vague effort to emulate my host's politeness, perhaps in some dim but still genuine curiosity, and asked this religious young leader what happened exactly in the mind of the person who all at once became greatly conscious of "the spirit of God moving in him". In particular, I have a feeling that we all wanted "to *see* the light". But I fear that we were still involuntary thralls to the merely analytical, for the car remained dark. Everything was put down quite naturally to the presence of God, to the spirit of Christ Jesus, who redeems us from our sins. In a subsequent effort at discussion we found ourselves considering the state of the world, wars and rumours of wars, and, of course, politics. Yes, he had been a Trade Unionist, a Socialist. Did he still believe in Socialism? "When you have seen the greed and the graft and the jealousies and the strife"—I will not try even to indicate his amazing resource in biblical quotation—"you despair of the materialistic doctrines of any worldly creed. I am no longer for or against any political party. The Lord welcomes everyone, whatever his political or economic beliefs. All I am sure of is that the present state of the world is a result of godlessness, a falling away from God's grace, and that no material beliefs can ever put it right. As St. Paul said, writing to …" And he was off once more.

It remained a youthful voice, anxious to have gladness in it, and having gladness in it; a young man prepared for personal rebuffs, who had received personal rebuffs, but was hanging on to some revelation inside him that induced a state of humility. How deeply in his nature this humility was founded might be a matter for thought, were it not that to look for the perfect humility would be foolish, even had we still been capable of looking. There was, above and over all, the note of serenity, that tone of gladness, like something memoried or legendary. It might be destroyed as swiftly as it had come; it might be the efflux either of a sanguine or of a potentially hysteric nature; it may have been induced by a life of continuous economic uncertainty and hardship, for he knew many kinds of occupations, some of them invariably accompanied by small but harrowing personal humiliations (a Paisley woman had notably rebuffed him for trying to sell her a vacuum cleaner), just as he knew unemployment and the dole; from all that, he had escaped—to find himself of some importance in the high communion of the spiritual life"; a leader in his small way; a man listened to and followed. Here was compensation and to spare, and here the acceptance of rebuff or humiliation might be as unction to the soul.

Such analysis was easy, yet it did not satisfy, not altogether. It did not help with the "*something*—whatever it is", which remains, when all is said, at the basis of this revivalism, however characterized it may be occasionally by wild physical manifestation and an undeniable hysteria. The subject is hardly so easy as the cynic or materialist may pretend. Indeed, the attitude of the cynic or wholesale sceptic may here be highly suspect. For the cynic is too often a man who has already taken care to "escape" from responsibility before opening his mouth.

At last he shook hands with us and, after putting his head inside again for a final few words, he hoped, a smile in his voice that was propitiatory but not ingratiating, that we would come to his next meeting and enter with him into the fellowship of Christ.

"When did you say you were going away?" our host asked him, polite to the last.

"I was going on Monday—but it may be revealed to me not to go."

Our host understood.

The lights were gone at last; and the gable-ends of the cottages, down from the road, were like grey striding men. All at once I felt the force of the atmosphere that our host had spoken of, and realized what he had meant when he said, "It is palpable. It hits you." Here was illusion all right! For the whole place seemed to have gone psychic; the pale faces, the stationary-striding gable-ends of the cottages, the curve of the earth, the green corn, the ditches, the motionless cattle; the sensation of invisible movement unaffected by the steady windless rain; the incredible living stillness, emanating from sleep, from houses whose lights had withdrawn before the grey morning. The mind suddenly thought, *This is the place.* And the place was stranger than any place of desert and sphinx, or valley of ruined temples, or palaces of Kubla Khan, for it was ancient but it was alive, and its history was happening in it while its bodies slept. We pushed through this atmosphere and came to our host's house where we were adequately refreshed. It was now after four in the morning and high time that we set off for sea to haul nets that had been set. But we delayed. The rain came down incessantly. The sea was grey and wet. We would go home and leave the nets to a later hour. And home we went, after a final lengthy leave-taking, including a long, involved, agreeable discussion in the rain, but not before stopping once on the road to get out, and listen to an invisible sea-bird calling from the surf along the western shore, and light a cigarette, in that weird hour of mist and morning, under a sky whose sluices were open. For it is the hour when the thought of bed departs and one wonders—whither now? It is a long way home. But home like slaves we must go and to bed, for all that Pantanjali or St. Columba may be walking over the mist-veiled moors. It is the moment, none the less, when one may adventure in the clear thought that is like vision and that is emptied of fear.

The Gentle Rain from Heaven

I fancy I can hear the ground drinking in the rain, drinking it in with a myriad dry upturned mouths like the mouths of lambs. The morning is completely windless, and through the mist in the glen I can dimly see the outline of the ridge on the other side, with here and there a vaguely shrouded solitary tree. All is still and thundery warm, and the rain is coming straight down, not pelting but steady and even, in a monotony that is like a consummated ecstasy. The long leaves of the cherry tree hang like hard feathers, and now one, now another, moves on its stem as it is hit by a raindrop. So a hen settles down to abide the rain, its head sunk, with now and then a faint meditative croak and a blinking of its round bright eye.

I can feel the rain doing good, can see the thin pale delicate roots of the ear of grain, of the grass, of the potato and lettuce and strawberry, of everything that grows absorbing this drink from heaven, after the long drought that has baked the clay to rock, with a slow swelling enrichment. The waiting fruits will stir now within themselves, will get busy, prepare for enlargement.

The grieve will be pleased. I met him last night when I went out to have a turn round after the midnight news. He was keeping his eye on a couple of mares about to foal. The fields were looking richly green in the evening light, but "Oh, we could be doing with a drop of rain!" I told him of a farm I had visited some days before in the West. One whole hayfield had been literally burnt brown. There would be no crop on it. We looked at the sky. Indications of rain had been there for two or three days but none had come, as if the sky through long abstinence had lost the natural art of raining. As I turned away a thrush started singing, or perhaps a blackbird, for the notes were rich and mellow rather than urgent. It was exactly half an hour after midnight, new time. I tapped the glass. It was still steady. But the bird may have had some premonition more subtle than the atmospheric influence which affects a weather glass.

From my trip to the West, I had brought back some books of modern poetry from a man who finds in poetry a natural enrichment of life. Sometimes I must confess I read this "modern" poetry with the same sort of reluctance with which I approach a crossword puzzle. Once I get going it's not so bad. There is some intellectual excitement, and one spots the economic leftish influences, the travail of the mind in subtle European embroilments of ideologies and what not, the clever learned allusions, the personal fun that remains obscure because you do not know the poet's friends or clique, the momentary but thick self-complacencies, and that ever-present air of disillusion, dry and arid but offhand. It never has a very enlivening effect, unless you happen to be interested in "new technique" for its own sake. And even if you are, new technique will not carry you all the way. Under the brazen sky, however splendid or terrifying to look upon, the delicate white roots, the hidden roots in the dark soil, slowly wither and die.

But among those I had brought back was one slender volume of poems by the Austrian, Rainer Maria Rilke, translated from the German by J. B. Leishman. This, I thought, will out-modern the modern young London men, for Rilke is admitted to be a prime influence upon most of them. This would be a very Torquemada among crossword puzzles. So I made an effort to get my mind to step out of its laziness, to gear up the intellectual apparatus, to prepare it for a maximum if short (for this can be tiring work) penetrative effort, to leap the untranslatable foreign words (after the manner of Ezra Pound) as nimbly as might be and still not leave go of some slender thread that I fancied I had got a hold of—in a word, to prepare myself for a battle which I was bound to lose.

And then Rilke's poetry fell like rain from heaven upon the arid place beneath. No intellectual strain searching for intellectual values, no vast effort in the head. A close absorbed attention, an utter receptiveness, and down the rain falls, gently over the body and seeping deep into the blood. This is poetry and the magic of poetry, and it has been known of all time, for it is neither modern nor ancient but timeless. Time may give it its form and the spirit of the age its turn of phrase, perhaps, but the communication itself is timeless, and coming out of a last refinement of all experience it is not arrogant but gentle, gentle as the rain that falls on the dry ground.

When faith is restored in poetry, it is restored in humanity. Though "humanity" is little more than a lumpish word in the head, when it is not an ideal for which groups of men are prepared to commit the most fiendish atrocities. We all believe in humanity, especially the modern young poets. But this humanity is so often humanity in the head. Not you or me, and the people we know, and the myriad individuals we don't know but who in all profound respects are like ourselves. The true poet's communication is individual, to one at a time. And one by one we become conscious of the gathering of ourselves in common understanding, in brotherhood. We know what it is to have understanding and sympathy. We go beyohd ourselves, to a mouse, to a daisy. The most ordinary of us suddenly has his vision of the pale roots drinking in the rain, and he rejoices, and the work of the land is touched with wonder and mystery and happiness.

Not that I meant to mention these poets at all, for I have seen our North and West at their summer best. I have been to some remote parts of the West Coast, too, where this "time" business has become very confused. There are, in simple fact, three times, and we found all of them in use among different townships on Loch Torridon. When the appointed hour for the arrival of our ferry-boat had passed, we began wondering whether we had made it clear that it was the hour of the "new time" we had meant. The "new time" or steamer's time is two hours in advance of the Creator's time; the "old time" is one hour in advance; and of course there is basically and eternally the "Creator's time". In our simple way, we at last made up our minds that a mistake had been made, and that, with luck, we would have to wait only for the "old time". We were wrong, for there is a fourth time, the time that is outside all time and is "just a little late".

I have to report that the West is still yonder, with the green sea-water over its white sandy bays, as it has always been. On the rocks and skerries below the cliffs, the tide as usual had left pools of every shape and size and of every colour. From a plunge in a pool, the naked body squatted on a ledge and dried in a soft wind. A timid merganser drake and his less timid consort. Two gulls that swooped like dive-bombers to within a couple of feet of our heads. The three dark-mottled eggs of an oystercatcher. Tufts of seapink in blossom. Caves, with a rich glory of marsh-marigolds upon the damp that oozes and drips.

I am trying to assure those whom it may concern that the lovelier parts of our Protected Area have not changed. They abide all our transitory issues. They knew human tragedies in the past, intense bitter holocausts local to themselves. Before

I left I had a letter from a distinguished writer who has helped to free the tragic spirit in poetic drama. The war bears hardly on him (writes Gordon Bottomley) in preventing his getting to the North and West, and the Isles. "I am Antaeus to Scotland, and if it were to go on long I should fall into a real fright that my feet's lack of contact with that fertilizing earth would dry me up."

Antaeus, it will be remembered, the giant son of Gaea, the Earth, lost his power when his feet were parted from his mother, but whenever contact was renewed his strength returned.

We can't tell the Greeks much.

According to the gardener, however, one of the most delightful parts of a holiday, even a short one, is the coming back. Not but that it is full of concern and anxiety. Click goes the gate and out comes an exclamation at the serried ranks of daisies on the lawn. The mower will never do it! And the rockery—what a riot! And, oh lord, the goat has been in again. The two new wall roses—even the buds are eaten off, the brute! I am informed that it is too bad. Look at this! Look at that! But I go and look at my onions. I never grew them before. The leeks are tall and lanky. There is a flower on the new potatoes. A cry—the old cat has vanished and her kitten. I refrain from suggesting that the goat cannot be blamed for that. But I would require many pages to deal with the hungry beasts that gather around and my necessarily wary attitude towards them. Some sort of balance in nature has to be kept. I'm the dread keeper.

By midnight, I have attended to a few things and in a last look around am led to an outhouse where the old cat is purring over her offspring once more. We can close the door of our home now until the morning.

Sources

The Black Woollen Gloves, Dundee: *The Scots Magazine*, January 1928, Vol. 8, No. 4, pp. 261–268

Paper Boats, Dundee: *The Scots Magazine*, April 1931, Vol. 15, No. 1, pp. 29–33

Dance of The Atoms, Dundee: *The Scots Magazine*, August 1939, Vol. 31, No. 5, pp. 347–35

Whistle for Bridge, as 'Bridge', London: *Spectator*, 26th May 1933, Vol. 150, No. 5474, pp. 755–756

Pure Chance, Dundee: *The Scots Magazine*, March 1945, Vol. 42, No. 6, pp. 452–468

Love's Dialect, Dundee: *The Scots Magazine*, May 1941, Vol. 35, No. 2, pp. 133–143

Blaeberries, Dundee: *The Scots Magazine*, February 1928, Vol. 8, No. 5, pp. 325–327

The Poster, Dundee: *The Scots Magazine*, August 1936, Vol. 25, No. 5, pp. 346–348

The Moor, Dundee: *The Scots Magazine*, April 1929, Vol. 11, No. 1, pp. 10–18

The Mirror, Dundee: *The Scots Magazine*, June 1929, Vol. 11, No. 3, pp. 180–186

The Chariot, Dundee: *The Scots Magazine*, December 1943, Vol. 40, No. 3, pp. 13–24

The White Hour, Dublin: *The Dublin Magazine*, March 1924, Vol. 1, No. 8, pp. 741–744

Visioning, Montrose: *The Scottish Nation*, 24th July 1923, Vol. 1, No. 12, pp. 4–5

Such Stuff as Dreams, Dundee: *The Scots Magazine*, February 1925, Vol. 3, No. 1, pp. 489–493

Down to the Sea, Montrose: *The Scottish Nation*, 4th September 1923, Vol. 1, No. 18, pp. 14–15

Henry Drake goes Home, Edinburgh: *Chambers's Journal*, March 1941, 8th Series Vol. 10, No. 569, pp. 129–132

Hill Fever, Dundee: *The Scots Magazine*, January 1934, Vol. 20, No. 4, pp. 264–268

Tax-Gatherer, Dundee: *The Scots Magazine*, August 1943, Vol. 39, No. 5, pp. 175–181

Half-Light, London: *The Cornhill*, November 1925, Vol. 59, New Series No. 353, (No. 791), pp. 607–620

Hidden Doors, as 'Musical Doors', London: *The Cornhill*, Vol. 62, March 1927, New Series No. 369, (No. 807), pp. 351–358

Gentlemen, in *Hidden Doors*, Edinburgh: The Porpoise Press, 1929, pp. 142–152

The Telegram, in *The White Hour*, London: Faber, 1950, pp. 251–256

The Tree, Dundee: *The Scots Magazine*, February 1936, Vol. 24, No. 5, pp. 352–364

Snow in March, Dundee: *The Scots Magazine*, June 1938, Vol. 29, No. 3, pp. 191–199

In Lewis, in *Highland Pack*, London: Faber, 1949, pp. 234–242

The Gentle Rain from Heaven, in *Highland Pack*, London: Faber, 1949, pp. 162–166